The Brazen Serpent Chronicles

The Caduceus

By

R. Dennis Baird

Bloomington, IN Milton Keynes, UK

authorHOUSE

AuthorHouse™
1663 Liberty Drive, Suite 200
Bloomington, IN 47403
www.authorhouse.com
Phone: 1-800-839-8640

AuthorHouse™ UK Ltd.
500 Avebury Boulevard
Central Milton Keynes, MK9 2BE
www.authorhouse.co.uk
Phone: 08001974150

This book is a work of fiction. People, places, events, and situations are the product of the author's imagination. Any resemblance to actual persons, living or dead, or historical events, is purely coincidental.

First published by AuthorHouse   06/15/2011

ISBN: 978-1-4259-3988-5 (sc)
ISBN: 978-1-4259-3989-2 (hc)
ISBN: 978-1-4520-6500-7 (ebk)

Library of Congress Control Number: 2006904751

Printed in the United States of America
Bloomington, Indiana

This book is printed on acid-free paper.

Dedicated to
my children
and grandchildren.

With gratitude to Dani who believed in me and Elizabeth who gives me
hope and Christopher who supports my efforts.

Cover art by Nicole Pederson.

Table of Contents

Maps ix

Chapter 1. A Promise to Keep 1

Chapter 2. River Crossing 19

Chapter 3. The Dark Hand 37

Chapter 4. One Choice-Two Paths 55

Chapter 5. Black Eddy 75

Chapter 6. Annel's Lament 93

Chapter 7. Arena 111

Chapter 8. Foundation of Evil 129

Chapter 9. Empty Shoe 147

Chapter 10. Serpent on a Pole 163

Chapter 11. Riptide 183

Chapter 12. Gulth's Tribulation 203

Chapter 13. Silver Lining... 223

Chapter 14. Knife's Edge 243

Chapter 15. One Faithful Child................................. 259

About the Author... 271

The Brazen Serpent Chronicles

Aelandra

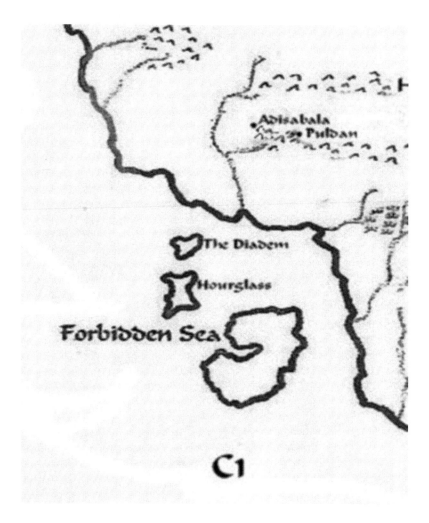

Sea

Grabad Peninsula

ire

Ismus

Rawn a

Bilbrg

Sourstrom

Deathsport

South Sea

C3

*Under the direction of Shelda, the queen mother,
King Fyan began a rule beset with uneasy alliances
and troubled city states to the south and west of the
newly organized Confederation of Standel. The
Representative Councils instituted by Fyan did
much to further the young king's dreams of equality
throughout the realm, but they also engendered fear in
the noble families that provided so much support for
him. Veramag, the great dragon of light, disappeared
from the casual conversations of the realm, but at
night around the fires in many homes, parents told
marvelous tales to young children about her deeds
and the wonders of hidden Dragada. Widseth
vanished from northern tales of the war. Occasionally
travelers seeking the New Aelfene Kingdom would
walk the streets of Standel, inquiring about the road
to Dragada or teaching simple truths they had been
taught by a master teacher in the wilderness. No one
knew of Widseth's travels to the southern countries
until much later.*

*Early Years of the New Order by Winna—
Master Historian of the court of Standel*

Chapter 1. A Promise to Keep

R in touched the bloody hair covering his father's forehead with
the tip of his finger. Tears stung his eyes, and the lump in his
throat blocked his breath. Looking up, he glared at the overseer.

"Ya kilt m' Da. I'll kill ya," he said.

He flung himself at the man on the horse, but he could reach
only the top of the high leather boots just below the big man's
knee. From the saddle, the overseer leaned toward the boy and
backhanded him with his gauntleted hand. Rin fell hard beside
his father. Struggling to breathe, he sucked air through his teeth in

jagged gasps through pain and tears. Several other workers rushed to restrain him.

"Take him to the stocks. He'll spend a few days in shackles," the overseer said. He spat on the boy.

The servants pulled Rin to his feet and helped him toward the manor house.

"Be still, or he'll kill ya too," an old woman whispered in Rin's ear, as she walked beside him.

"He kilt Da."

"I know," she said. "I saw, but there's nothin' ya can do. You're only eleven, and a skinny piece o' bone at that. I don't wanna see yer head wi' its curly red locks layin' in a basket next ta the headman's block. The overseer's been livin' the life of a lord since Count Fendry left. He's strong and he's got the horse and the whip and men who'll back 'im. Maybe he'll be the new count."

"Get outta here woman," a man said. An armed guard shoved her to the ground and cuffed Rin along side the head. Blood oozed from above his ear where the metal gauntlet cut his scalp. Three men thrust the servants aside and hauled Rin from the field, dragging him toward the stocks outside the gates of the manor at the edge of the road.

A wave of nausea filled Rin. The old woman's words faded in his memory. Barely conscious, he realized muscular men shackled his legs at the ankles and put his neck and wrists into the depressions of the wooden stocks. The locking bar pressed down across the back of his neck, and he heard the snap of the lock.

"He's so scrawny, he could pull his hands through the holes," a man said.

"Not now," another replied.

Rin recognized the voice. The captain of the overseer's guard tied ropes around his wrists. Rin had seen this before. He knew the other end of the rope would be tied to rings in the platform. He winced as the bonds cut into the boney flesh just above his hands. The men tore his shirt off. He wanted to scream, but he kept his eyes closed and swallowed anger. They left him to his ordeal, and after a couple of hours, the intense heat of the summer sun blistered his back.

As the sun slid toward the western horizon, the shadows of the trees across the road lengthened, and the afternoon heat gave way to a gentle evening breeze. People who passed on the road ridiculed and spat on him or threw things. A rock had hit him on his bowed head. He could smell the rotted fruit and vegetables that had splattered on the wooden platform. With his tongue swollen, he longed for water, and as he passed in and out of consciousness, piercing pain in his legs and back amplified his senses. When he relaxed his legs, the hole in the stock for his head pressed against his throat restricting air. Hallucinations plagued him as he envisioned a hooded man with a huge axe forcing his neck across a wooden block.

Another couple of hours passed. The people on the road were home now, safe and comfortable. Rin opened his eyes and looked at the sun just above the horizon. A hooded figure stood in the road, holding a staff in his right hand. He walked toward the stocks and stood before Rin.

"I can help you," he said.

The setting sun backlit the hooded man. Through stinging sweat and tears in his eyes, Rin could distinguish only the shape. He tried to talk, but his tongue stuck to the roof of his mouth, and he could not swallow. The man approached until he stood in front of the stocks and then studied the boy. Rin could see a dragon entwined about the top of the staff. The brass serpent was delicate and beautiful.

"What do you want more than anything?" the man asked. He reached the staff toward Rin and touched the tip of it to the boy's throat. The hooded man kept his left hand tucked within his robe.

Rin coughed, but the touch of the staff soothed his tortured throat, allowing him to speak. "I wanna kill the overseer," Rin said.

"Do you want that more than water? More than protection from the sun? More than freedom?"

"Yes," Rin answered.

"Very well. I will come for you, and I will help you fulfill your dreams. Will you consent to serve me if I help you do this thing?"

"Yes, master. I'll serve ya with all m' heart," Rin said with no hesitation.

"Remember your words Master Rin. I shall hold you to them." He leaned on the staff, peering at Rin. After a few minutes he turned and walked away.

Rin ground his teeth. *He would show the overseer. How did the hooded man know his name?* As the sun slipped below the horizon, Rin ignored his pain and closed his eyes again. If he turned his head, he could rest his neck without restricting his breathing. He dozed off and on for several hours as the day faded to night, and nocturnal noises and smells filled the air.

Each time Rin awoke he broke into chills because the cool night air sucked heat from his blistered back. *No matter, he had a friend who would help him kill the overseer. Was it a dream? Was his new friend real?*

About an hour before sunrise Rin woke with a start. He had been dreaming of a time when he and his father had been boating on the river, fishing. He caught one, but then he was at a small stream, and he wanted to taste clear cold stream water more than anything. Tears formed when he thought of the experience with his father, and he wondered if his father was now with his mother, maybe fishing somewhere. Rin's mother died giving birth to him, and he wondered if she liked fish.

He looked up. A man stood in the road, and in the dark twilight of early morning Rin was not sure if he saw with his eyes or if he dreamed again. The man wore a golden tunic that shimmered as if it radiated light of its own, and his skin was of a golden hue. Rin realized that behind the golden man two other figures stood, holding the reins to three horses. One of the individuals was a woman. The other was a man with his left hand tucked inside a dark robe. The golden man walked toward him.

"We are here to help you," he said. His simple statement filled Rin with wonder as the man touched his head and chest. The pain vanished. The woman picked the lock on the stocks, and soon Rin heard a click and felt the weight of the upper bar lifted from his neck. The other man stood behind watching, and then he made a motion with his right hand and began a low chant. The beauty of the song filled Rin's mind. He felt the scorching pain of his back evaporate. The man in the gold tunic untied the ropes, and the woman released him from the leg shackles.

Freed from the stocks, Rin collapsed into their arms.

"Put him here on the grass. I sense darkness in his mind," the other man said.

"M'lord Widseth," the golden man said, "shall I give him some water?"

"Yes, Gulth, give him water, and Annel inspect for any other wounds he might have. I'll check the road," Widseth said. He walked back to the middle of the road and studied the ground.

When the man named Gulth lifted a water flask to his lips, Rin tasted the cold water of his dream. The water filled him to the point that he thought he would never thirst again. He thought he saw his father holding the hand of a woman standing behind the golden man.

"Ya've come back to help me kill Aljezra. He's the overseer. I'll serve ya good sir," Rin mumbled.

He couldn't keep dream from reality. The woman caressed his brow. The golden man hoisted him into the saddle in front of the woman after she mounted. He felt safe as he slipped into peaceful sleep.

* * *

The magistrate scowled at his assistant.

"I want no appointments this morning. I've lunch with Lord Calbra, and there's no time for interruptions with all the paperwork that needs completion. Besides I want to go to the arena this afternoon."

The magistrate was a finicky dumpling of a man. His immaculate desk reflected his general outlook on life. He straightened some papers before signing the top one with a trimmed quill pen. Morning light illuminated the large room, filled with bookshelves punctuated by beautiful mahogany paneling. Stunning area rugs covered the granite floor stones.

"But sir, the man insists on seeing you. I've told him you are a busy man, and that he should make an appointment for next week."

The magistrate looked up. "And?"

"He said there were some matters of Count Fendry Baran's property that he needs to settle. I thought … ."

"Fendry Baran?"

As the magistrate looked up, he dripped sealing wax on the top of the desk, missing the document. His hand trembled.

"Fendry Baran," he repeated. "Didn't Fendry's old servant Micah come back over a year ago? He said that Fendry went mad, searching for the lost treasure of Taina. But didn't Micah die a few months back? I seem to remember Aljezra, the overseer of Fendry's estate, brought some documents to that effect so he wouldn't be taxed on a dead slave."

"No, Lord Xeran, Micah lives. I saw him in the market last week. It must have been another."

"I was sure … ."

The magistrate bit his lip, and his assistant stood awkwardly shifting his weight from one foot to the other.

"My lord magistrate, I don't like this talk of Count Fendry. Most are quite comfortable that Fendry Baran is gone." He looked around to make sure no one heard his words. "And the man outside is a foreigner. I'd say from up north somewhere by his accent. He has a kind look about him, but that doesn't mean he couldn't hide a cruel nature."

The magistrate straightened his papers again and clasped his hands trying to squeeze the moisture from them. He looked at the royal seal on his desk. He was the emperor's voice here. What did he have to fear? Besides, it wasn't Fendry himself.

The magistrate composed himself and straightened his papers one more time. "Show the man in, but insist he leave his weapons with the door keep."

"Yes, my lord, but I saw no weapons."

"Well, just have him come in." He waved his arm with an exaggerated flourish.

The assistant backed through the door and, after a few minutes, returned followed by a young man wearing a lightweight burgundy cloak covering a blue tunic. He looked as if he had traveled some distance. Although his hazel eyes made the magistrate feel a little uncomfortable, the man did not look particularly threatening. His left hand was misshapen with a scar on his left forearm and wrist.

The assistant gestured with his hand and said, "I present you to Magistrate Xeran, Recorder for the High Emperor Padwalar the Third."

The young man bowed before the magistrate. "Hello. My name is Widseth." The pitch of his voice lifted Xeran's anxious mood. His muscles relaxed, and he felt no anger or fear.

"I am Magistrate Xeran. You look to be a stranger in our land. The High Emperor rules from the borders of the Hegemony of Teradar in the north to all the islands of the South Sea and the Grabad Peninsula."

"Good. I'm in the right place," Widseth said. "I don't mind telling you that I'm uncomfortable in cities. I much prefer the open country."

"Yes, the country is nice. My assistant said something about uh … the Baran properties. Count Fendry Baran has been out of the area for some four years. If you're looking to purchase some of his land holdings or business enterprises, I am afraid I can't help. Is there any other way I can be of assistance?" The magistrate stared at the papers on his desk, avoiding Widseth's gaze.

"No, I'm not looking to purchase properties, but I believe you have to record transfers in ownership when I pay the appropriate taxes. Is that correct? Please look at these documents to make sure everything is in order."

Widseth pulled a packet of rolled scrolls out of a worn leather pack from under his cloak. The magistrate's eyes widened as the rolls of parchment were stretched out on his desk. He immediately recognized Fendry's strong hand and the affixed seals at the bottom of each document.

"How did you come by these? Count Fendry would never willingly give up his estates or free his slaves." Xeran's eyes flashed, and anger increased his agitation. He wanted nothing to do with freeing slaves. The unsettled political climate caused by the defeat of the fleet by Marhome's navy demanded stability, not the unpredictable current that could be caused by releasing slaves. Not in this place. Not now.

"Magistrate, these are Fendry's documents written by his own hand."

"I know the hand, and I know the man. He would never do … ." Xeran's voice trailed off. Widseth leaned forward to unroll another scroll, and Xeran noticed the symbol of the white tree on his tunic when his cloak fell open. "Aelfene … . You're Aelfene. Are you an emissary to the Emperor? Fendry sought the Aelfene kingdom. Did he find it?"

"Fendry found his treasure. He won't return here," Widseth said. "He bade me look after his estates. Can we continue and complete recording the deeds?"

"Yes, Master Aelfe, yes, of course. By all means."

"Please. I'm simply Widseth."

"Yes, but you're of the Aelfen … perhaps from Taina, or Meliandra."

"Dragada. And I'm simply Widseth."

"Oh, Dragada." The magistrate paused. He swallowed hard, and looked down at Fendry's papers. He sorted them into a neat pile and began leafing through them. "They will be ready in the morning for you if you will return just before lunch."

Widseth stood. He pulled another roll of papers from his pack.

"Count Fendry made two copies of each document. I trust that if I leave a set with you, that nothing will happen to it," Widseth said. He emptied a small pouch filled with gold and gems on the desk. "I believe this will cover the taxes."

"Of course, my Lord Widseth. Everything will be safe here. I'm the Emperor's man," Xeran replied.

He rose and extended his hand toward Widseth. Widseth grasped the magistrate's hand with his right hand, cupped his misshapen left hand around the back of Xeran's hand, and bowed. He turned and left the office. The magistrate motioned to his assistant to make no sound. He waved him over to the desk.

"Don't speak," he whispered. "The Aelfen can hear so well that some say they can perceive your thoughts."

This is not good. An Aelfe here. No more Fendry Baran. No more house of Baran. What will Fendry's overseer think? Freed slaves ... . Then Xeran tried to block his thoughts. He bade his mind to be still just in case the Aelfe might be listening, but thoughts erupted all afternoon and evening.

***

Rin kept his eyes closed and listened to the conversation at the other side of the room. The voices were indistinct. He opened his eyes only enough to see a woman and a golden skinned man sitting at a small table. The bed was soft. His back and legs were stiff, but the pain was gone. *How could that be? The fair skin on his back and arms should have blistered in the sun. They must have brought him here. Could it be that he was in one of the rooms at the Turtledove Inn? A bed like this could be found only there. What would the overseer say?* Rin didn't care. He wanted the overseer dead.

The golden man rose from the table. He said something to the woman and walked toward Rin. Rin closed his eyes tighter so he could no longer see, but he knew the golden man stood near his bed. Long delicate fingers touched the top of his head where the rock had hit him, and then he felt tender pressure on his brow and under his jaw along his neck as the man's fingers massaged the tissue to alleviate any tension.

"I think he is no worse for his experience," the man said.

"Physically I'm sure you're right, Gulth, but Widseth sensed some deeper pain in this boy," the woman said. "The boy said something about us coming back to help him kill the man who killed his father. I'm sure Widseth won't consent to that."

"But he has to," Rin said. "He promised. M' Da did nothin' 'cept spill grain for the overseer's horse."

Rin sat up in the bed. Gulth backed away, but Annel approached the bed, leaned toward the boy, and studied him.

"I didn't think you were sleeping," she said.

"You're liars. The man w' the hurt hand promised t' help me kill the man who kilt me Da, an' I said I'd serve him, if he'd help me."

Gulth and Annel exchanged a quick glance.

"Yes, boy. We'll help you, but probably not in a way you expect. We can discuss it later. I'm Annel, Widseth's wife. He's in town on business. This is our companion, Gulth." She gestured toward the golden man.

"And your name?" she asked.

"I'm Rin, son of Ronald. I'm a servant at the Baran estate. I'm the fourth son of a son t' serve there, but I'll kill the overseer and I'll lose m' head, and I'll be the last son of a son t' have t' be a slave."

Annel smiled at Rin's bravado.

"What? A fine lady think it's funny that poor Rin'll lose his head? I'll show ya," he said.

Rin jumped from the bed and snatched Annel's dagger from the sheath at her side. In a quick move he slipped behind her and pressed the tip against her back. Gulth started to move, but stopped.

"Put the dagger in the sheath," she said.

"Ya can't order me," Rin said.

Annel moved faster than Rin had ever seen and disarmed him. Almost before he knew the dagger disappeared from his hand, he saw it in the sheath at her side.

"How'd ya do that?" he demanded.

"I wasn't always such a fine lady. Some of my playmates would've slit your throat and stolen your belt while you were in the stocks. Besides, I wasn't laughing at you, Rin. I promise that you'll be the last slave in your family line, and you won't have to lose your head. You'll see."

Gulth cleared his throat.

"My lady Annel, I need to check the horses and scout the area, if you will excuse me," Gulth said. "Will you be all right with this ruffian?"

Annel smiled. "I think we'll be fine now."

Rin watched the golden man leave the room.

"Where'd he come from?" Rin asked. "He's kind of a stiff board isn't he?"

Annel barely contained her laughter.

"Yes, he has a lot to learn about our world," she said.

Rin frowned, puzzled. "What other world is there?"

"Gulth is from the world of light. He's a dragon."

"Ain't such a thing. M' Da told me they all just live in stories. Dragon! You're a funny lady. Tryin' t' scare me? Huh?"

"No, Rin. I've no reason to scare you," Annel said. "Gulth never brings fear to good people, but there are things worthy of fear."

Annel smiled, but her serious tone unsettled him because he knew some of those things.

***

Almost two weeks had elapsed before the magistrate completed the final paperwork and official transfer of title. Widseth sat at a table in the manor house with the magistrate, Xeran, and the overseer, Aljezra. The overseer looked like a grey cat with a paw caught in a trap. His dirty black beard with grey streaks covered thick jowls. His eyes looked like arrow slits in a castle tower turned sideways. He scowled at the paperwork that the magistrate showed him.

"As you can see, Aljezra, the paperwork is all in order. Master Widseth is now the Lord of the Baran estates with the title of Count. Count Fendry signed everything into Widseth's name," Xeran said. "Everything is recorded and in order for the records of the Empire. The taxes have been paid. In time the Emperor will no doubt request your presence at court." He looked at Widseth.

"And what if I don't accept these papers? Lord Fendry left me in charge, and I take my orders from him, not some snot nose from the north," Aljezra said. He looked at Widseth as he spit the words out.

"Nevertheless, Widseth rules here now. I can do nothing if you choose to leave his service. It is not my affair," the magistrate said. He looked around and scanned the darkened corners of the room. Two armed men by the door with imperial signets on their armor gave the magistrate some confidence.

"Peace, Magistrate Xeran. All will be well here. I sense your fears. You are safe here," Widseth said.

"And who's gonna keep him safe, boy? You? Me and my men are leavin' for now. But we'll be back to feed your carcass to the hogs." Aljezra stood. His left hand grasped the hilt of his sword at his side. His right hand stroked his beard as he glared at the magistrate. Hatred spilled from his eyes like darkened darts.

Widseth stood and faced Aljezra.

"There will be no violence here today, Master Aljezra," Widseth said. He held his hand up palm forward. Imperceptible at first, a soft pallid light filled the room. Aljezra lifted his gaze from the magistrate and peered into Widseth's hazel eyes. Widseth met the stare with warmth and kindness. Aljezra hesitated as Widseth countered his anger with a slight smile.

"None o'this … playin' tricks w' m' thoughts … miserable conjurer. I'll cut yer honey tongue out," Aljezra said to Widseth. "I … uh … ."

Aljezra blinked his eyes as words abandoned his mind. Widseth's enchantment filtered the anger and calmed the big man. Aljezra's hand slipped from the hilt of his sword.

"I'll be goin' now," Aljezra said, as he motioned to his men. As they departed, he looked back at Widseth. "To the hogs," he said, "to the hogs." No other words escaped his mouth, and he seemed confused as to why he had said anything.

Widseth stood for a few minutes, and looked around the room. He put his hand on the magistrate's shoulder. He could feel fear in Xeran as he tried to calm the uncontrollable quivering in the man's shoulders and arms.

"You'll be safe if you leave now with your assistant and the emperor's guard. I expect we'll have trouble with Aljezra, but we'll take care of it," Widseth said.

"Yes, I best go now. How did you …?" Xeran asked.

"When you face fear, you have two choices … succumb or overcome. I overcame," Widseth answered.

"I saw that. I just wondered … well, never mind. Just a couple of things … there may be a few minor things your slaves have to do when they receive their freedom—papers and such to sign. We'll have to arrange to have the brands on their arms cancelled … you know rebranded with a freeman mark over the slave brand. We can do that next week. Uh … well, there is one other thing."

Widseth sat down, leaned back, and rubbed his eyes. He rolled his head back and forth stretching the muscles in his neck.

"How can I help you?" Widseth asked.

"It's kind of a personal thing. I've been thinking a lot. The other day you said you were from Dragada. That intrigued me. It's my hobby to study the ancient records. I just wonder if there might be a time you could tell me more about Dragada?"

Widseth laughed. "Of course, I'll tell you all you want to know."

"Good. Good. I would like that. I worried when you first came to my office, but I think maybe freeing Fendry's slaves might not be such a bad thing."

Xeran nodded his head up and down several times and straightened the papers in front of him, rolling them neatly and putting them into his travel pack. He stood and motioned to his assistant, who hurried over to the table and took the pack from him.

"Good day, Widseth." In a lower tone Xeran added, "Take care. Aljezra is no one to be trifled with. He's a dangerous man."

Widseth covered his damaged left hand with his cloak. He smiled and said, "So am I."

The magistrate and his assistant hurried from the room.

***

"Well, Rin, you've been free for four hours now. How does it feel?" Annel asked.

She and Rin walked along a slow moving stream that fed the orchard irrigation system. Rin wanted Annel to see some of the tasks he performed as a slave. On irrigation days he had to keep the water channels clear and free moving. He had spent many hours digging and clearing channels for the life-giving water during what the workers called the water run days.

"I dunno know, m'lady. Two weeks ago m' Da died. This mornin' I'm free. What's it s'pose ta feel like?" Rin asked. He took a long stick and cleared one of the runways in the water channel.

"To me freedom is more precious than the water you are directing to the trees. Did you know I was once a slave?"

"Go on. Not you, m'lady," Rin said. "I mean you're nice and all, but I don't see no scars or even a slave's tattoo. You musta been a house slave in a pretty nice house w' a nice master or mistress."

Annel put her hand on his boney shoulder, and gently turned him to face her. She started to say something, but the words caught in her throat. Rin tried to read the message in her countenance, but he saw a confusing pattern of sorrow mixed with joy. Bright sunlight glistened off tears streaming down her cheeks. She tried to smile at him but her quivering lips were a poor mask for her feelings.

"Lady Annel, I'm sorry if I said something … ."

"It is all right," she choked out. She composed herself. "Sometimes scars aren't visible on the outside, and some pain can be healed only by time and a master healer."

Rin looked up into the branches of the trees. He wanted to fly away like a bird. Something about this lady unsettled him. She could look right through him. It was like she knew his feelings before he did, but when he looked at her he wished she were his mother. It would be all right if his mother looked at him that way.

They walked in silence for a few minutes. He wanted to change the subject. "Sometimes leaves and dirt makes little dams and the water backs up. I clear it so the trees get their water," he said. "We gotta keep the path from the head gate clear."

"What happens if a tree gets a disease like the one over there?" Annel asked.

She pointed to a fruit tree with withered leaves. The bark had begun to split, and the fruit had fallen to the ground blemished and rotting.

"That's bad … I gotta tell the orchard master. Gotta burn it … gotta burn it … cause the other trees'll get it. That sickness I saw b'fore. No help on that one."

Annel walked over to the tree, and placed her hands on the bark. She closed her eyes, and began a soft chant.

"Don't touch it m'lady. You'll spread it," Rin said.

But her melodic voice made the hairs on his arm stand on end, and he marveled as beams of sunlight entered her hands and flowed into the tree. Rin stood back and shielded his eyes from the insistent light. To his sight, Annel became translucent. She was as a vessel filled with light that flowed like water into every part of the tree. He could see light filling the ground around the tree, eradicating dark shadows. *How could he see underground?* The light affected every leaf and twig, and the hanging fruit on the tree was healed. Rin sank to his knees. The leaves began to uncurl as the blight fled Annel's touch. All at once the light subsided.

Annel stood in front of the tree. She lowered her hands.

"That should do it," she said. "Come here, Rin. Let me show you something."

He hardly dared raise his eyes to meet her gaze. What kind of person was she that she could heal trees? And Widseth ... he was sort of like a noble, but like the older brother everyone loved because he protected them. Rin wished his father knew Widseth. What was the golden man? Was he a dragon like Annel said?

"Rin ..." Annel said in a voice just above a whisper.

She reached down, took his hand, and lifted him to his feet. He kept his head bowed refusing to meet her eyes.

"M'lady, how'd ya do that? Never seen nothin' like that." His hand trembled even though she held it.

"I learned it from the Master Gardener of Meliandra. Meliandra is the hidden city of the north. After Widseth freed me from my life on the dark streets of Eventop, I went to Meliandra and learned to use my freedom. Do you want to learn what I can teach you?" Annel asked. Her tone soothed him.

"M'lady, I'm no good at this learnin' stuff," Rin said. "And this freedom's like walkin' on a rope 'cross a high place like the circus players at holiday in Tabul. It scares me."

Annel led Rin to the tree she had healed, and they sat down with their backs against the tree.

"I was afraid, too. Sometimes, I still fear things," Annel replied. "But I learned fear is simply our response to something we don't understand, or something we can't see. Were you afraid when I healed the tree?"

"Yeah, it scared me good, seein' light like that goin' into ya an' then goin' into the tree. M' bones was shakin' ta be sure," Rin said.

"What I did with the light is no different than what you do with the water channels. I cleaned out light channels so it could flow into every part of the tree and heal it," Annel said. "Widseth did that for me when I first met him."

Annel paused and looked upward. Her eyes were closed as if she remembered something important. Rin looked up to try to see what she saw.

"Ya love Widseth a lot don't ya? I think m' Da loved m' Mum like that."

"Tell me about her." She looked back at Rin.

"I never knew her. She died when I was born."

"I'm sorry. I'm sure she was a special woman."

Rin looked away. "I saw Da an' her standin' in the air behind the golden man the night ya came and got me from the stocks. Least I'm thinkin' it musta been her. Da was holdin' her hand. Course ya see lotsa things that might not really be there after a hot day in the stocks."

Rin broke off a long blade of grass and chewed on it. Annel looked down at the grass and then met his gaze.

"Yes, I love Widseth. When I met him he took away all my fear and freed me from my slavery."

"How'd he do that?" Rin asked. "Did he buy ya and set ya free like he did us?"

Annel smiled. "No ... not exactly like that. He gave me hope, and I found courage to make a choice that led to freedom. In a way, we both found freedom together after that."

"Are ya gonna have kids?"

A troubled look crossed Annel's face. Rin detected deep sadness, as she looked away.

"Remember when I said there are some scars that a slave has that aren't seen?" she asked. "Well, I can't ever have children because of what was done to me when I was younger. Widseth and I want children more than the air we breathe, but it can never be."

"Sorry ... Maybe Widseth can heal ya like ya fixed the tree. Ya said he healed ya before."

Annel nodded her head up and down. "I thought that once, but now I understand it's one of the burdens we'll suffer together. All of us have things we can't change. Widseth even refuses to heal his arm, although he could. He keeps it as a reminder of a mistake he made. I keep the scar of childlessness to remind me that I'm to be a mother to all who need me."

Rin and Annel sat silent for a while. From their seats with backs against the healed tree they watched the water flow in the channels and listened to the wind in the trees and the insects in the grass. Rin broke the silence.

"Maybe ya can be m' Mum after Widseth kills the man who kilt m' Da. I promised ta serve him."

Annel wiped tears from her eyes.

"Widseth never promised to do that. He would never do such a thing," she said.

"But he promised that night at the stocks. It was 'im in his cloak with his hurt arm and a staff w' a dragon on top." The agitation in his voice grew, and he angrily stabbed at the ground with his stick. "He promised me, and I promised ta serve 'im."

Annel stood up. She appeared alarmed. "I think we better get back to the manor. We can talk with Widseth about it."

"I'll be there in a while. I gotta check the other channels." He walked in another direction. He was afraid he would not get revenge, and anger replaced the kind feelings he felt with Annel. He stabbed the stick he used to clear the water channels into the ground wishing it was the chest of Aljezra.

"Rin ... please ... ."

He ignored her.

After the flood washed the bridge away, the farmer tried to ford the river near the bridge. The current carried him more than a mile downstream. When he told his tale to the fisherman, the fisherman replied, "It's hard to gauge the strength of the current where the surface appears calm, but why do you think they built the bridge there?"

From the Country Tales of the Farmer, the Fisherman, and the Blacksmith

Chapter 2. River Crossing

From the steps leading to the door of the Baran manor house, Widseth looked over the contours of the orchard. The road to the manor cut through the fruit trees for half a mile until it passed through the gate in the high rock fence that surrounded the immediate property of the manor house. The stocks, headsman's block, and gallows were just outside the gates on the edge of the main road to Tabul. The sun rested just above the horizon. The full moon would rise just after sunset.

"M'lord Widseth, do you think they will try something tonight?" Gulth asked.

"I'm not sure, but I feel that Aljezra won't wait long to try to reclaim his position by force. He had at least ten men but not more than fifteen according to the house steward. The steward told me they're well armed," Widseth answered.

"What would you have me do?" Gulth asked.

"Assume your true form, and wait in the orchard near the gate. No bloodshed unless unavoidable. Keep yourself hidden unless Aljezra and his men appear. Annel will stay in the manor house. I'll watch the back orchards."

"As you say m'lord." Gulth's neck began to stretch and his arms and legs lengthened. He shook his head, and reflections of the sunlight scattered like wheat sown from the hand of a farmer. The dragon's scales caught the dying rays of light and mirrored them into

19

the manor house yard. Black edging on the golden scales formed diamond patterns along his back and wings, but his underbelly glistened like pure gold illuminated by flame. He looked down at Widseth as if from a second story window with his body stretched some fifteen to twenty paces behind him.

"Take care Gulth. If problems arise, I'll know, and I'll be there. I think your presence will fill them with fear that will avoid bloodshed."

Gulth beat his wings. Widseth shielded his eyes against the dust stirred up by the dragon. The giant creature flew low over the trees, hovered for a moment, and descended into the orchard.

"I don't think I'll ever tire of seeing them. They're so majestic," Annel said. She walked down the stairs to join her husband. Widseth turned and took her hand.

"You should've seen Rin's face when I told him Gulth's a dragon," she said.

"Do you think it was wise to tell him? Rin hides a lot of pain," Widseth said.

"But there's joy too. When you gave him his freedom this morning, I thought he'd burst," Annel said. "He's a lot like me when I was young. I hid a lot of pain from my younger life. You can do for him what the Aelfen did for me. We talked this afternoon in the orchard while he showed me some of his duties. He said some things that worry me … something about you coming to him and promising to kill the man who killed his father."

"You know that I didn't do that."

"I know, but he believes it, and who did come to him?" she asked.

"Maybe it was just a hallucination from a day in the stocks under the hot sun." But Widseth knew better. He had felt the disturbance in Rin's mind and had seen the signs in the road, but he kept silent, longing for more concrete evidence.

Widseth smiled. He wanted to talk with Annel longer, but he knew that tonight might be a difficult trial.

"Keep the servants who chose to remain as employees in the house tonight," he said. "Warn them there might be trouble. Gulth will be in the orchard. I'll be in the back."

He kissed her and squeezed her hand with his good hand. He put his left hand under his cloak and pressed it against his body to remind him of Annel's courage when she saved him from the ancient Dragon Master. Annel walked up the steps and entered the manor house. Widseth inhaled, filling his lungs with the early evening fragrances. A lone cricket began to chirp, and Widseth walked around the corner of the manor toward the back orchard.

***

In the twilight Rin slipped from behind one tree to another. He cautiously approached the huge golden serpent, concealed in the trees near the gate in the rock wall. The beast remained motionless.

"You *are* a dragon," Rin said when he drew near the creature's head.

Gulth blinked a large golden eye with a black pupil.

"You need to return to the manor house, young one," Gulth said. "It may not be safe here tonight."

Rin could not tell if the words that he heard entered his ears or his mind.

"I know. Widseth an' you're gonna kill Aljezra. Aren't ya? I gotta see. He promised t' help me. I'll serve 'm forever." Rin said.

"Widseth would never promise such a thing," Gulth said. "We will do all we can to avoid bloodshed, but if need arises, we will protect the manor."

Rin cocked his head. "Horses," he said, as he moved behind a tree. Gulth shifted slightly and focused his attention on the road outside the rock wall. Two riders rode into view and entered the estates through the opening. They dismounted and tied their horses to posts inside the gate.

"Aljezra said to meet here. I wonder where he is," one said.

"Patience. He'll be here," the other replied.

"Are we doin' the right thing? I mean the people said the new Count freed all the slaves and offered t' pay any who'd stay and work. He can't be such a bad sort."

"Aljezra'd put yer head on a pole if he heard ya."

"But ..."

"Quiet. I hear somethin'."

Rin strained to hear what the men heard until he made out the distinct sound of hooves growing louder. The overseer and eight or nine men rode through the gate. Rin looked toward Gulth. The dragon remained motionless, hidden among the trees, as the men dismounted and tethered their horses. Aljezra drew his sword.

"We'll have the blood of this northern scum and his companions tonight. Nobody takes from us what we've earned," he said.

Rin was close enough to sense sudden tension in the dragon, and he looked in the direction the dragon gazed. In the deepening twilight a cloaked figure walked from the direction of the manor house, and in his right hand he held a staff, but his left arm was tucked under the cloak. A hood shadowed his face. He pointed the staff in the general direction of Gulth and Rin. Rin smiled because he saw the staff with the dragon entwined around the top, and he knew that the man who killed his father would die. He nearly stepped from behind the tree, but some force from the staff held him prisoner.

Aljezra and three men started toward the man with swords drawn. Rin shouted, but no sound emerged. Curious tingling pricked in a thousand places on his skin like tiny webs holding him in place. The cloaked man faded from sight. Rin strained to see him, but nothing prepared him for what he saw.

Rin watched as one by one, Aljezra's men fell to the ground writhing in pain. He could not see clearly, but sound returned. Men screamed. Deep gashes through armor and bone felled them like trees at the hands of an unseen woodsman.

Aljezra stood alone. He whirled looking for an adversary he could not see. None of his men remained standing.

"Show yourself, coward," he bellowed.

The magical bonds released Rin, and he stepped from behind the tree. He looked at Gulth, but the dragon continued motionless. *Could the dragon be doing this?* Men were in the road, lying in contorted positions. As Rin approached one of the bodies, he touched the wet sticky substance oozing from a gash on the man's back. Steam rose from the wound and the pasty liquid was burning hot, and in the twilight it appeared almost black, caked on the dust of the man's armor and in the road. The wounds reeked of a damp rotted smell like the air in a storage room where food had spoiled.

"You ... How'd you get out of the stocks?" Aljezra demanded. "What are you doin' here?"

"I'm here t' see ya die," Rin said. "M' friend's gonna kill ya. I'm a free man, ya know."

"I don't see a friend. I'll spit ya on my sword." He started toward Rin, but a form materialized between the two.

Aljezra stepped back, but the cloaked figure dropped the staff with the serpent on the ground and grabbed the overseer's throat with his right hand. Blood dripped down the overseer's neck and his sword fell to the ground.

"I promised the boy I would kill you. He promised to serve me. Is that still the bargain, boy?" the figure asked, turning his head slightly. Aljezra's body sagged.

"Yes, sir," Rin replied. His nose flared, and his breath came in jagged inhalations.

The body dropped to the ground. Aljezra's arm twitched momentarily before the muscles contracted into their final position. Rin picked up the staff, but nothing magical happened. The figure turned, and extended his right hand, and Rin handed him the staff.

"Master Widseth, I knew you'd help me," Rin said.

"I call you to my service, and in due time I will serve you if you are willing to learn what I can teach," the figure replied. "Do you accept?"

"O'course ... said I'd serve ya and I will."

"I am not Widseth, but I can give you more power than you can imagine. Gold ... servants ... you need never to fear the whip or other people again. Your name will become a terror to all who oppose you. You are bound to me now, Rin, son of Ronald."

The figure pulled the cowl back from his face. A man-sized dragon stood in the twilight. He appeared similar to Gulth, but much smaller and his scales were a midnight black color. The creature stood holding the staff in his right claws. His left limb was a stump cut at the joint where the clawed hand should have been.

In the dusk Rin could not be sure what he saw. His mind numbed.

"Come, boy. Follow me."

Rin struggled, but a power pushed against his will, and he followed the creature as if chained to it.

***

Annel surveyed the scene. In the torchlight she examined the bloodied bodies of Aljezra's men. One man struggled to breathe, but his muscles contracted with spasmodic rhythm. Poison. She touched the man's forehead and transferred healing light from her inner resources into him to counteract the poison, but to no avail. Blood flowed from many wounds. Annel ground her teeth because she realized that the damage from the bleeding was minimal compared to the toxin. She touched the tip of her finger to one of the wounds on a man's neck. The blood was not just warm, but hot as if it had been boiled. The tip of her finger burned until she counteracted the poison with a mild healing command. Her healing power did not help the man. He gasped for air, closed his eyes, and died.

Annel looked around. Her torchlight reflected Gulth's glassy stare, as he lay flattened on the ground with his length entwined around two trees. She discerned no animation in his eyes.

"Gulth … Can you hear me?" She placed her hand on the dragon's head. Light emanated from her finger tips.

"My Lady Annel … what …? Where is the boy?" Gulth blinked his eyes to clear unseen shadows. He began to rise and shake his head.

"Easy. Stay here with me. What boy was here? Who killed these men?"

"I remember the boy. You know, the one from the stocks, Rin. He was here. But then … ."

"Then what? Did you kill these men?"

The dragon's raspy voice trembled. "No … never … I told the boy to go to the manor. Then horses and men … then darkness … a spell immobilized me. I heard screams. Then silent dark … I have never been … never been … uh … ."

24

Annel's hand on his head calmed him. Her light entered his mind and unlocked the reservoirs of peace darkened by his experience.

"Be still, Gulth, and let the light of the eternal worlds calm you. I'll try to see the memories your eyes recorded if you'll allow it."

"Yes, m'lady." Annel felt his demeanor calm as the glow of her light searched his memories. After several minutes, she hesitated.

"Could you see anything, m'lady?"

"No, nothing but shadows." Her voice trailed into the gloom of the scene. She stood immobile trying to remember something just beyond the reach of her thoughts. The sounds of insects filled the trees, and the moon rose just above the manor wall. Annel inhaled, but instead of the rich fragrance of summer night air, she smelled the dank odor of a dark alcove. Her mind snapped to attention.

"Gulth, find Widseth. I'm going to the manor to get help. Hurry."

***

Annel stood at the foot of stairs leading to the front door of the manor. Several men and women stood around her. A few held torches. The flickering light caused shadows to dance with the breeze as Annel told of the men slaughtered at the gate. The warm feeling of the morning's freedom fled before the chill of dark shadows.

"M'lady Annel, this will have to be reported to the magistrate," Micah said.

"I know. After we've attended to the bodies ... no, we can't wait. Micah, if you'd go now, I'd be grateful. Tell the magistrate that we're at his disposal, if he wishes to meet tomorrow," Annel said.

"I'll go now." Micah handed the torch he held to another man and mounted a horse. He nodded in Annel's direction and flicked the riding whip on the horse's flank. The animal jumped into motion carrying him on the road through the orchard toward the gate in the outer wall.

The other servants waited quietly for instructions. They were afraid. Their first night of freedom would be remembered caring for the bodies of men who had abused and whipped them. In the torchlight men and women looked from one to another, not daring to meet Annel's gaze. Their eyes held the high expectations of freedom mixed with the fear of retribution.

"Come with me. Bring some carts from the stables," she said. "These men thought to bring us harm, but we need to treat them with respect and return their bodies to their families if they have any."

No one moved. Annel scanned their faces.

"Where's Widseth?" a man asked.

"He's in the back orchard. Gulth …"

"Well, he's kilt us. Kilt us all. We're free … free t' die."

"Calm y'self Harrin," an old woman said. "I says w' alright wi' Master Widseth. He would'na free us an' leave us t' die."

Annel looked at the old woman, grateful for her support.

"Get the carts," Annel said with authority. "If you'll help, I need it now. If not, you're free men and women. You can go your way."

Harrin and two others walked away, but five men and two women bowed to Annel and hurried toward the barn to get the carts.

Annel wiped her brow with the back of her hand. Her hair, damp with sweat, clung to her temples like the webs of a garden spider. *Where was Widseth? Gulth should've found him by now.* As she stared into the night sky, evil memories invaded her thoughts. She tried to clear her mind, but dark shadows filled her with ugly images. She smelled the rank odors of corpses rotting in darkened chambers within her psyche. Corpses of evil memories … corpses of evil people … corpses of evil places.

Then she saw the stars, the pinpricks of eternity, and one star in particular drew her attention. Its light increased in intensity until the luminosity generated a simple melody within her. She knew that song. Widseth had sung it to her after ruffians had beaten her on the streets of Eventop. She stretched her arm upward and slowly closed her fingers as if to gather in the light, and then she perceived the source of the light. The image of a metallic dragon affixed to a stone column outside the gates of Dragada appeared in the center of the glow. Comfort flowed from the dragon's sapphire eyes as the dark shadows fled, and the corpses of rotting thoughts dissolved into fine dust, dissipating like the morning mist on a warm day. She smelled the fresh night air.

Annel straightened her posture and turned toward the three carts pulled by donkeys, led by the servants of the manor. Widseth and Gulth would catch up.

"Come this way with me. The bodies are at the gate of the outer wall at the end of the orchard," she said. She walked with the first cart. Her hand strayed to the dagger at her right side, and she clutched the hilt firmly. She wanted to wait for Widseth, but the need to do something useful urged her to attend to the dead men at the gate.

***

From the air, Gulth circled the back orchard. The fruit trees covered twenty acres with service roads and trails that followed irrigation ditches and canals. At the far extent of the orchard the rock wall surrounding the manor property stretched like a thick rope. The Fendry estates stretched for miles, but the rock wall defined the manor house.

From the night sky he peered through the foliage searching for Widseth, scanning every band of spectral light until he found a black abyss in the trees that should not have existed. Gulth wheeled around the vortex of the void for several minutes gradually decreasing altitude until the rush of air created by his wings ruffled the tops of the fruit trees. The unnatural darkness radiated from a central point like the web of a great spider. Gulth landed at the outside edge of the darkness on one of the service roads. He gazed through the tree trunks into shadow that deepened into a blanket of darkness that dampened all sight and sound.

"Gulth, enter with care."

Startled, Gulth looked behind him to find the source of the voice. The shimmering image of a dragon filled the service road. With light visible only to Gulth's eyes the dragon illuminated the road brighter than noon day.

"Father," Gulth said. "Why …?"

"My son, the Dragon Master Widseth is in danger," the huge dragon said. "His call reached me, but I cannot respond in time. I could appear only through the medium of light to help you. Only you can help him. Be a beacon to guide him back from the shadows."

"Father, I … ."

Energy filled the area. Leaves on the trees stood on end away from their stems like hair charged with static. The image of the ancient dragon cast a spell that bolted from his right claw forming a bridge of light through the dark webs.

"Gulth, hold to the light. Do not waver."

"Father, stay with me. I am not ready."

But the image of the ancient dragon faded into the night air. Gulth remained. Alone. A straight path with a rail of light plunged through the webs of gloom in the trees toward the hub of darkness. The shadows shifted and swirled around the light like an eddy in a river. Gulth moved toward the light and began creeping into the gloom keeping his footsteps on the path illuminated by his father.

Shafts of darkness launched themselves in churning currents at Gulth. Pinpricks of black darts stabbed at his eyes to blind him, and shadow waves assaulted him to confuse and knock him off the path. He stopped, and almost panicked, as the feelings of the slaughter at the gate earlier in the evening returned, blinding his mind. Looking down, he focused on the light and began to crawl forward again.

"Be a beacon." He heard his father's voice.

"Nonsense. Come with me," another voice said.

Gulth stopped. He clung to the path, but he looked in the direction of the second voice.

"Who would call me from my task to assist the Dragon Master?" Gulth asked.

"Join us. A new Dragon Master will rise. A Dragon Master of our choosing … ." Voices rose in a discordant harmony.

Horror filled Gulth. The voices were dragons of light, fallen into darkness. He knew some of their names. He knew their history, and their power. The spinning current of darkness began to suck him from the path. The power of their magic stabbed at him from every direction.

"Hold to the light," a voice said. "Be a beacon."

Gulth dug his claws into the soil on the path of light and pulled his hind quarters out of the maw of darkness. Looking ahead, he saw Widseth on the ground, propped against a tree. Blood stained his cloak, and a staff with a metal dragon entwined around the top rested on his knees. His eyes resembled the dull stare of the dead.

Gulth inhaled. The peaceful reservoirs in his mind, touched by Annel earlier, reopened, and the light of the eternal worlds flooded his awareness. Dark shadows fled from him as the flickering flame grew to a fireball. He exhaled. Night sounds returned. Widseth blinked his eyes.

"What evil has happened?" Widseth asked.

"Master Widseth, come. Flee this wickedness." Gulth lifted Widseth and cradled him.

As he looked back to the light path, little shadows carried away the light like ants with spilled sugar. The distortion of the light led in several directions until it was lost in the gloom. Shards of darkness stabbed at Gulth, slicing like razors. Only gravity told him where the heavens should be, and looking skyward, he glimpsed one star amid the murky vortex. Gulth wasted no time as he leaped upward. He beat his wings with all his might, but the dampening darkness clung to him like weights on a fishing line pulling him to the bottom of the current.

"Focus on the star," Widseth gasped. "Have courage. No doubts."

Widseth stretched his right hand forward. Light from the star flowed into his body where he amplified it into a magnificent torch. Brilliant beams flooded from his eyes extinguishing all the unnatural darkness, punching holes in the canopy of shadows. Moonlight and starlight replaced the dark abyss. Gulth landed between the trees.

He helped Widseth to stand.

"What was that?" Gulth asked.

Words tumbled from Widseth in an uneven cadence. "I think it was a demonstration for my benefit." He stood with head bowed.

"M'Lord?"

"The powers of darkness are real," he gasped. "They're not only revealed in flesh and blood enemies. They're derived from the depths of evil principalities."

"But M'Lord Widseth ... you are the Dragon Master. When I passed through the dark void on the path of light, I heard and saw dragons. I knew the names of some of them. They called to me."

"I know," Widseth said. "I know."

"But you are the Dragon Master. You could control them."

"Yes and no. I could control the dragons of darkness only if I chose to enter the darkness and employ the evil they've embraced," Widseth said. Strength and resolve appeared to return to him. He straightened and looked Gulth in the eye. "I prefer to control no one—not you nor any of the other dragons of light. You serve me, and I serve you because we select that course, and in doing so we choose to serve the powers of light."

Gulth craned his neck looking around the trees in the orchard. No artificial darkness remained, and the smells and sounds of night had returned to the woods. Widseth's demeanor appeared calm, but Gulth felt tension building. Widseth examined the staff with the brass dragon entwined around the top and the blood on his cloak. The young Dragon Master scrutinized the stains on the material, and Gulth sensed that he explored the cloth on levels unseen by natural light.

"Twelve men ..." The words entered Gulth's mind although there was no audible expression from Widseth. "Twelve men died. Poison ... I know that poison. And Rin's hand was here on the staff ... and another's hand was there ... the other wore this cloak. He is one of the dragon's you heard calling to you from the darkness."

"We need to go to Annel," Gulth said. "Terrible things have happened."

"I know," Widseth said aloud. The finality in the young dragon master's voice unsettled Gulth more than the unnatural darkness he had endured.

***

Annel and the servants had just placed the last of Aljezra's slain men in the carts when Gulth landed with Widseth on his back. The startled servants cowered in fear. They fell to their knees begging for mercy.

Annel rushed forward and helped a man to stand.

"Please ... . It's Widseth and Gulth. You needn't fear." Turning to Widseth, she said, "They're terrified. The slaughter tonight has taken a terrible toll. Seeing a dragon for the first time may break them."

Widseth dismounted, and Gulth immediately transformed into the golden hued man the servants knew. Widseth walked toward the nearest cart. A woman knelt by the wheel with her head down.

"Safer facin' the whip, than bein' free," she said.

Widseth knelt beside her. He took one of her hands in his and squeezed gently.

"If its keeper tends to its needs, a bird in a cage fears no enemies or lack of food. A bird in the wild faces the prospect of death every day from predators or lack of food," Widseth said. "But the caged bird will never see the ground from the top of a tree or feel the rush of wind on its feathers. It will never know the value of choice."

As the other servants edged closer to hear his words, Widseth stood and helped the woman to her feet. She clung to his hand as a young child in a crowd clutches a parent. The flickering torches cast shadows into the trees around the carts in the road.

"We've had little time to teach you," Widseth said. "I'm sorry this shock has come so soon. Gulth is a dragon from the world of light. Annel and I are from Dragada where the dragons of light have reestablished a kingdom of peace. If you choose, I'll provide an escort to Dragada where you can find freedom and the peace it can buy."

"Kind words, master Widseth, but doin's like this ... well, they be beyond our know." The man shifted his weight from foot to foot and avoided looking directly at Widseth.

Annel approached Widseth and stood beside him with a torch in her left hand. She reached and took Widseth's crippled left hand in her right hand. The other woman still gripped his good hand.

"It's time they know who you are," Annel said, looking at Widseth. She addressed the servants with a quiet voice. "Widseth is the Dragon Master. He is the shepherd who can lead his sheep to safety, and he can help you tune your lives so you can hear the music of eternity."

As Annel spoke, Widseth released the hands of both women and examined each cart. Tears welled in his eyes as he examined the rent flesh and the effects of the poison. Holding his hand palm forward, he scanned each body with a soft white light emanating from his palm.

After a few minutes he said, "Some were not evil men." He motioned to a couple of the servants, and pointed to three of the crumpled bodies. "Please, place their bodies here on the grass."

Gulth stepped forward and helped the servants move the armor laden men. Annel held a torch in each hand. In the flickering light the scene resembled a macabre gathering of sinister intent until Widseth knelt beside the bodies and one by one touched each of them on the bridge of the nose with the tip of his index finger. Torrents of white light shot from his finger into each of their faces. The light illuminated the area until the torches paled in the brilliant luminescence. Torn pieces of flesh knit together. One of the men sucked in air. Another's eyes fluttered, and the third moaned.

The servants cowered and backed away from Widseth. As he stood, the light receded, and two servants fell to their knees.

"No, please stand up." Widseth said.

He reached over to help them stand, but they shrank from his touch. He pointed to the men on the ground.

"They'll need care and rest. Let's get them to the manor house. Bring the carts. We'll arrange for the burial of the others tomorrow."

***

"I'm tellin' ya he put his hand on 'em and called 'em back from the dead."

"Don't talk the crazy man talk. Listen t' yer self. Naught but moonlight … terrible slaughter … can't say Aljezra deserved a better death, but I think ya've had a wee too much o' the potato squeezin's tonight."

The man drained the mug in front of him. The inn common room was quiet. Most of the patrons had long since departed. Two men in light colored robes with dark cowls sat in the corner closest to the fireplace. The blaze of early evening had consumed itself leaving fiery coals with occasional flickers of flame. Oil lanterns on each wall illuminated the room with a murky glow.

The first man raised his voice.

"I may be drunk, but if ya'd a seen it, ya'd be yammerin' to the world about it. It weren't 'naught but moonlight'. I'm tellin' ya that when he touched 'em, he was brighter than sun at noon day. He's a mage I'm tellin' ya. Powerful magic of the worst sort … dead bringin' magic. He had a bloody staff too—just like them what came two months ago chantin' and singin' their new religion. Upset the Emperors priests, that bunch did. Do ya remember? Dragon on top of the staff and all."

"Your tales are nothin' to me," the second man said. "I wouldn't give a rotten pomegranate to hear any more. Besides, the Emperor's priests'll have a bit t' say 'bout somebody comin' an' raisin' the dead. They're a nasty lot to run against f'sure. I'm goin' home." He slid off the stool and staggered toward the door.

The men in light colored robes followed him out.

"Hey, this mornin' they made me a free man, but I dunno what that means," the first man called after his friend. "Powerful magic … I guess … maybe magic of the worst sort." He stared into his mug.

***

The old servant, Micah, reined his horse to a stop outside the barn and dismounted. Annel and Widseth stood beside the three carts. Near the barn entrance nine bodies covered with sheets had been placed on the grass.

"Micah, were you able to speak with the magistrate?" Annel asked.

"He finally consented to hear me after I woke him near midnight," Micah said. "He'll come in the morning, which by the light in the east is not far away. I'm sorry to return so late, but I had to sleep for a couple of hours."

Widseth smiled at Fendry's old servant. Micah had served Count Fendry and Fendry's father before him. He had seen the evil years, and the change when the powers of light touched Fendry. In torchlight the old servant appeared gaunt. Widseth reached and grasped Micah's hand.

"Come friend, I know you're tired, but there are things we need to finish before morning," Widseth said.

"Where's your golden friend?" Micah asked.

"He's above." Widseth looked up. "Watching ... ."

A creature circled above, barely illuminated until it passed in front of the full moon revealing large wings and a long sinuous neck and tail.

"I knew he was a dragon. It would've taken a dragon to kill these men," Micah said.

"Gulth didn't kill them, nor did I," Widseth responded. "They were killed by a dragon, but not Gulth. Micah, the servants respect you, and I need your help to get all who'll leave to make a new start somewhere else."

"Leave? To go where?" Micah asked. "This is our home. You freed us to flee? I'm old. Many of them are old."

"Nevertheless, if they stay, many will die. You know this. I think the magistrate's a good man, but his hands will be bound when the Emperor's men take control. And I assure you they will, because an old enemy has been setting snares for me, and he'll kill any who stand with me."

"How do you know these things? And where would we go?" Micah asked.

"There are powers in the world that have arisen that challenge the darkness of the past age," Annel said. "Once again the light of the universe fills Dragada. It's a long journey, but there are homes and land and freedom there for people who'll pay the price to enter the land."

Widseth added, "You'll be killed if you remain here, or at best returned to slavery. I'll send Annel and Gulth with you to protect you in your journey."

"I'll not leave you," Annel interjected. "And I'll not leave the boy, Rin."

Widseth lowered his head. A tear unseen by anyone dropped from his eye and exploded on the ground. Annel loved Rin as the child she would never have. She endured the pain of knowing she could never give birth because of things done to her when she was young. *Why would his powers not let him see the path before his wife?* He looked up. Torchlight glistened off his moist cheeks.

"Gulth will accompany you, if you'll lead the servants," Widseth said.

"Well, my wife died years ago, and my son died in the arena. There's really nothing here for me. Dragada huh …? It might be an interesting adventure at that. I've heard tales. None good, mind you." He paused. "Well, I'd rather die a free man in the wilderness than a slave in a palace."

Widseth nodded. "Good. May the powers of light be your guide. Gather your things. It's been a short night, but you need to leave at first light before the magistrate and Emperor's men arrive. Gulth knows the way. Rely on him. There'll be others to help you. Allow any to join you who have a good heart."

"I hope to see you in Dragada," Micah said.

A society steeped in slavery rarely produces individuals who can rise above mundane attempts at art, government, or social interaction. Usually the common slave is content with security afforded by the system. The malcontents often strive for something more, but they have not been trained in the talents of freedom that allow them to exercise choices that will produce change. On the other hand, in a free society some individuals make dreadful choices in the name of freedom. Good and bad choices often create disparity in the general populace that tends to cause instability and inequality in the culture.

  From the Teachings of Leanna, Master Mentor, of the Abbey de Testrey—found in the Library of Vindry

Chapter 3. The Dark Hand

Unable to sleep, Widseth sat in a comfortable chair in the manor library with Annel curled up next to him, her head on his shoulder. The candles in the wall sconces and on the table burned low, and the flickering flames cast dancing shadows on the bookshelves. Through the east window, Widseth could see the horizon beginning to blush early morning pastels before the sun crested the distant hills. When he was a boy, he loved the early morning when the air was fresh and alive. He remembered rising early to feed the animals at the mill, where he and his mother lived before so much changed in his life. On days like today, he longed for those simpler times. He nudged Annel.

"Annel, wake up." Sorrow tinged his voice. He wanted to let her sleep. "It's been a short night, but we've a long day ahead."

Annel stretched and yawned. "I had dream."

"A good one I hope."

She rubbed her face and coughed to clear her throat. "We adopted Rin, and he tried to show me how to fish, but we were in two separate boats. The current carried him away, and I couldn't catch him. You were on the shore trying to tell me something, but I couldn't hear you. I … I was afraid because I knew the falls were near, and I couldn't catch Rin, and I couldn't hear you. Then you woke me."

Widseth began to say something and stopped. Annel stood and walked to the window. She looked out at the orchard in the morning light.

"I know what you're going to ask," she said. "Why I'm so drawn to Rin? Isn't that what you want to know? I see so much of myself in him that he could be my son. He is the mirror of me when I was that age—bold, angry, scared, and lonely. He's so much a little boy in need of a mother and father, and I've wanted to help him since the night we released him from the stocks."

Widseth walked toward Annel and stood behind her at the window for a minute. He enfolded her and rubbed her bare arms.

"We've much to do this morning. We'll talk of this later." He forced a smile and took her hand.

***

Although the early morning air was warm, Rin shivered like a wet dog crawling out of an icy river. His night dreams continued into the daylight hours, and then he realized that his nightmare was reality. The dragon creature turned its head and stared at him.

It uttered a guttural whisper. "Rashanarth nuanthaa."

A weight lifted, and Rin's numbed mind snapped to attention. The binding spell fled in the morning light, and he could feel his arms and legs again. His fingertips burned, and an intense acrid scent overpowered the morning fragrances of the orchard.

"I released you, boy. It will take a moment for the spell to fade, but I have no reason to fear you might flee because you have promised to serve me. Am I correct?" The honey toned voice belied the creature's appearance. The silken vocal quality grated against the usual morning sounds of the orchard, like the ropes that had chaffed Rin's wrists in the stocks.

Rin nodded his head. *How could he have mistaken this creature for Widseth?* His stomach tumbled like a log rolling down a hill, and it took all his strength to contain his nausea.

As the dragon looked away from him, Rin studied the beast that seemed to be made of smoke and reflections. He wanted to touch the dragon to see if anything about it was real, or if it was just a mass of uneven shadows in the shape of terror. Just as he began to feel unchained from the spell, the dragon shifted again, and Rin observed cruel claws on the right hand, and a mouth filled with daggers for teeth. The left hand ended in a stump.

The beast looked back at him.

"Yes, the dried substance on my claws is the blood of your overseer. When I crushed his spirit and bled his throat, I felt his fear melt into my palm. Just as you wanted, more than water, more than protection from the sun, more than freedom. I allowed you to watch. Did his death bring all you desired?"

Rin tried to steady his voice, but he trembled.

"Not exactly, m'lord dragon."

The sound that erupted from the dragon's throat startled Rin until he recognized it as a hideous laugh. The birds did not cease their morning songs in the tree tops. A sound like that should have startled all the wildlife into silence, but the peripheral noises continued. *Could it be that no other creature heard this beast?* Rin peered through the trees. He could barely see the gate in the wall where the slaughter had taken place, but there was activity there. He wished he could join the other servants gathering there. Widseth and Annel were there with the golden man. He knew if he called out they would not hear him because of the dark dragon's power. No one knew they were there, watching his friends preparing to depart.

"You need not call me lord dragon. I am Deorc, first among the dragon kind, and I shall instruct you that *you* may control the dragons of the universe. There need be no fear between the pupil and the tutor."

"But ya forced me to follow ya w' a spell. Don't ya trust me?"

Deorc's eyes narrowed as he considered his response.

"You are a clever boy, maybe thinking to lull me to a sense of trust. Let this be your first lesson, Rin, son of Ronald. Trust is a fragile word, manipulated by the weak to control the strong, and if the strong trust the weak, who then wields the power?"

Deorc extended the stump of his left limb as if to make a point.

"Who cut yer hand off?"

The abrupt question surprised Deorc.

"Not for you to know at this moment, young one."

Agitated, Deorc paced between two trees as if attached to both. His eyes flashed every time he shifted his gaze from Rin to the party of servants gathered around Widseth. The dragon's anger culminated when he looked upward and loosed a keening wail that shocked Rin, causing him to recoil in fear. Looking around, Rin realized he was the only one who could hear the sound. Deorc stopped himself, but damage was done.

Rin dared not smile, and he stared through the trees toward the gate to avoid the dragon's gaze. A small but invaluable piece of information lodged in his thought. *Who had power now?*

***

Gulth, the golden dragon in his man form, and forty-four men, women, and children, including the three men called from death by Widseth, gathered at the gate where the massacre of Aljezra and his men had taken place. Widseth augmented their meager possessions with stores from the manor pantries and provided a couple of mules and carts. As a dragon, Gulth could provide all the food they needed, but Widseth cautioned him to conceal himself in man form as much as possible to avoid drawing attention to the company. Widseth motioned for Micah to step forward, and he gave him several gems and a small bag of gold coins.

Holding Annel's hand, Widseth watched the party of former slaves prepare to travel north on the coast road. Fatigue from the short night was obvious, but their spirits were higher than Widseth expected. As he approached them to wish them well, most bowed or kissed his crippled hand.

The three who had been given new life approached him and knelt.

"M'lord ..." one of them began.

Widseth cut him off. "Rise. No one kneels to me."

"But, m'lord ..."

"There's nothing to be said. Have you gathered your families?"

"Yes, they're here with us."

"You're trained men at arms," Widseth said. "If you assist Gulth and Micah, your experience will make the trip easier for the others, and you can repay me by serving them."

"Master Widseth, it may go hard for ya today. Mayhap we should stay t' vouch for ya."

"More the reason for you to leave now. May the light of the universe guide your steps in safety." Widseth bowed to the men, turned, and walked with Annel back toward the manor house. They stopped and turned to watch the company.

The small company loaded the last of the supplies into the carts, and the group started their trek. Someone began a walking song. A warm breeze and the morning sounds of the birds in the orchard accented the departure. Widseth and Annel stood alone in the road as the group moved out of sight, turning back to the manor house when the last cart disappeared from view.

"I wish Rin had gone with them," Annel said.

Widseth remained silent. In the dark web of the previous night he had seen the path Rin walked. He knew the darkness the boy had entered, and he sensed darkness growing in his wife's heart created by sorrow, but she would have to face that darkness alone.

"How many servants are still at the manor?" he asked.

"Not many. Maybe eight or ten at most."

"Give them some gold or silver and encourage them to go into Tabul for the day."

"What do you fear? We can explain to the magistrate when he arrives."

"Xeran may look kindly on what happened," Widseth replied. "He had no love for Aljezra, but Aljezra had friends and relatives, and they'll take his death to the courts of the empire. If I'm taken ... ."

"No ... no ... not possible."

"Annel, listen to me. First things first. The bodies must be returned to their families. Rin's whereabouts have been hidden from me. Last night some power blinded and made me captive, but I recognized some of the patterns."

Annel stopped walking and turned to face Widseth. "I've felt the patterns before, too. They're of the dragon Deorc. I recognized traces of his presence when I first reached the bodies. He's the dragon of darkness that served Ruga. Once, as your great grandmother, Meliandra, and I ministered to your mother, Deorc surprised us. We traveled the paths of light, masked from the normal world to supplement your mother's light with our own, but the last time we entered the alcove, he was there waiting. It was an evil meeting, but your grandmother thrust me back through a conduit of light to a protected area, and she faced him alone. She wouldn't tell me about him, but even your grandmother was anxious about his power. He blocked us from ever entering the chamber again to help your mother."

"I knew you and grandmother cared for my mother, but you never told me that a dragon of darkness confronted you."

"I thought maybe when Ruga returned to the grave that his dragons of darkness followed," she replied.

Widseth looked up at a wisp of cloud in the sky. A tickle of fear crept up his neck and initiated prickly sensations on the back of his scalp.

"Deorc was one of the first dragons of light to come to the mortal world, but evil seduced him long before he entered Ruga's service. I wounded him at the gates of Dragada where I severed his left forelimb, and his evil designs are fueled by his hatred for me. He has Rin, and I suspect that he proposes to fashion him into a Dragon Master like Ruga. The depth of Deorc's darkness can confound even my sight if I don't focus, but I've had a feeling of being watched. He must have observed us for some time. I think he knows you love the boy, and knowing that he'll try to cripple me by destroying you."

Annel stooped and picked up a small stone. She held it in the palm of her hand, and then rolled it like a small ball of dough.

She licked her lips. "The last few days, I spent a lot of time with Rin. All I wanted was to spare him some of the pain of growing up."

Widseth nodded. "I know, but misfortune often strengthens individuals in unmeasured ways. You're who you are, in spite of your past and because of it. You can't protect a seedling from storms and expect deep roots that will weather tempests when the tree is mature. I've watched Rin too, and already he's a strong tree with deep roots for survival. I suspect Deorc has miscalculated Rin's inner strength."

"But you're saying I should have gone with Micah and Gulth so I won't be a liability."

"You'd never be a burden to me. With you I could face anything, except what I'll face when the Emperor's men arrive."

Shocked, Annel stared at Widseth. "What is it you've seen?"

Avoiding her gaze and staring into the trees, he ran his fingers through his hair.

"Annel, I don't know if I can face separation from you. For the crimes committed last night, I'll be imprisoned, maybe … I … ."

"But you did nothing. It was Deorc. You know that."

"I know it. You know it, but there are dark forces here, manipulating the surface powers."

"Why didn't we flee with the servants?"

"They would've tracked all of us down. At least a few will make it to Dragada if they're faithful. Deorc won't concern himself with them if I'm here."

Widseth took Annel by the hand, and led her to an apple tree, and plucked a low hanging apple. After handing the fruit to her, he ran his fingers over the bark on the trunk.

"Sometimes the bark is rough and scarred, but unless wounded through the depths of all its layers, it can heal itself and protect the whole tree."

"Widseth, I don't want to hear this. Call the dragons. Use your power. You're unjustly accused."

"And how will that save Rin? He made a covenant with darkness. The dark current sweeps him under and holds him down until someone standing on the shore reaches to help him. All the dragons of light assembled could not save him from the promise he made, if he won't reach his hand toward the light. Only Rin can obtain release by finding true freedom. I see my path, and it leads away from Rin."

Annel bit her lower lip.

"Still, you could call the dragons and deliver yourself from judgment here. They've no right. You're their judge and they don't know it. You're their shepherd. You're the Dragon Master now. And I won't give up on Rin. I won't abandon him … no … he'll not be like I was in Eventop." She choked back tears.

"I said nothing about abandoning Rin. I said my path leads away from him. My greatest fear … ." He paused and touched her cheek, his finger lingering with the weight of a feather. "My fear is your path because I can't see it."

Annel dropped the apple and the small stone she held in her hands. Widseth put his arms around her and pulled her close to him. Closing his eyes, he held her tight, trying to steady the trembling he felt in her. After a short time, he took her hand, and they walked to the manor in the morning light, but darkness plagued their footsteps.

***

Widseth and Annel sat on the top step of the stairs leading up to the manor house's double doors. They looked out over the front orchard.

"Deorc's here," Widseth said.

"I know. I can feel him, but I can't see him yet," Annel responded.

"He's there among the trees, but don't give it more than a glance. His shadow spell displaces the light, but the shimmer in the spectrum reveals his presence. He's unaware that we sense him, and he won't reveal himself yet, but I know what he seeks." He gripped the pouch attached to his belt.

Dust rose among the trees from around the bend in the road. A company of horsemen rode into view, and the banner of Emperor Padwalar the Third streamed above the horsemen.

"Look at me," Widseth said. He touched her forehead with his right index finger. White light flared, and the radiance they exchanged carried them to an unfamiliar room where a tree glowed with dim light. As memories of sacrifice and love filled them, they knelt beneath the tree. Physically they remained on the manor house steps, but space expanded and time stopped as their essence of light traveled to a tree of life.

Widseth opened his belt pack and withdrew a blackened severed hand. The black scales on the appendage reflected no light. Dried poison encrusted the cruel talons at the tips of the digits. *How many had died stricken by this poison and raked by these claws?*

"I choose to hide this here. Deorc seeks what I cut from him with the Talon of Light. His powers, although formidable, are diminished somewhat because of his loss. I place it here beneath the tree because he can never come within reach of this place."

"Why tell me this?" Annel asked.

"You can approach the tree without fear, and, if the currents of darkness become too strong, you have a bargaining chip."

Annel swallowed hard. Widseth brushed the hair back from her cheek. The rhythm and tenor of the light vibrated at the touch. Though the light imparted sensations of intense joy, sorrow surfaced because he wanted more than anything to protect Annel, but he realized the shadowy path shown him in his dark dreams of the previous night led toward light. He must follow that light, and he saw only his footsteps on that path; her path wound in a different direction. The music of the eternal world of light imbued them with confidence, and Annel took Widseth's crippled left hand in hers and squeezed it. She dispensed healing light into his hand and arm, causing full strength and form to return to his forearm and hand. He looked at her quizzically.

"I don't think …" he said.

Annel held her hand palm forward and placed it on his lips. "Just as Deorc's powers are lessened with his wound, your power is lessened because you think you need this infirmity as a reminder.

You're whole because I choose to fill you, as you fill me. You don't need an outward symbol to remind you of your inner commitment any longer."

Widseth nodded.

She continued, "If we're to walk different paths for a time, I need to know you've full use of your abilities. Otherwise I can't face the path ahead."

"I understand." In the physical world he heard horses. "It's time."

Like dew in the warmth of the sun, the affection and tenderness faded as the ethereal light dissipated. He took his index finger from her brow. They sat on the steps in the midmorning sun watching the approaching horsemen. Together they rose to their feet.

***

"Master Widseth, there are some matters to discuss," Xeran said as he and his assistant dismounted. Xeran looked at the covered bodies laid out on the grass near the barn. He squeezed his hands together as if wringing moisture from a towel. His lower lip quivered, and he kept glancing back at the entourage behind him. Widseth and Annel stood on the steps of the manor facing the royal retinue. Six men at arms remained on horseback, one of which carried the Emperor's standard, but three other men dismounted. These men wore ornate yellow robes with purple cowls. Two of the men were of large stature, and one was a slender reed of a man.

Widseth started up the stairs. "Please, will you join me in the sitting room?"

"No, we are not here for tea or conversation," the largest of the men said. His unfamiliar accent clipped his words, and he spoke them as if they were objects spat from his mouth. The other men stood beside him like doorposts.

Widseth remained on the higher step. From this vantage he could see the entire party as well as into the orchard where the shimmer in the natural light marked Deorc's hiding place. A light breeze lessened the early heat of the morning sun, but it would be a hot day. Widseth noted the embroidered symbols on the robes of the men in yellow and purple. The threads emitted complex trails of magical energy. He recognized the patterns characteristic of an ancient order of low magic. In Meliandra he had studied the basic orders of magic. All these orders were offshoots or counterfeits of the higher powers of the world of light, and some of them had become terrifyingly powerful in the eyes of men. These representatives swaggered in their confidence as if they had never been challenged.

Xeran spoke. "Lord Widseth, these men are Inquisitors for the Emperor." His voice trembled. Widseth knew that Xeran had probably never seen three of them together at one time.

"They are here to question you," he continued. "Their names ... ."

One of the inquisitors stepped to the forefront. "Silence! We've no need of introduction from you." Xeran backed away with his assistant toward their horses.

The inquisitor and his two companions stood motionless except for the hypnotic movement of their robes in the morning breeze. Widseth studied the man. The rich brocade of his robes and cowl matched his precise movements. Unseen to any other than Widseth, the man moved the tips of his fingers on his right hand to continue a spell. The patterns in the energy engendered awe and fear.

Widseth pitched his voice to open a path to a vibration that would negate the spell. "Well, since there is no need for introduction, I can assume we are friends here."

The timbre of his voice shredded the spell of the man in yellow. Xeran relaxed, and the atmosphere of hostility faded with the breeze. The men in yellow and purple appeared confused for a moment, but, regaining their attitude, they stared at Widseth.

Widseth continued, "I assume you come from the Emperor with regard to the transfer of Count Fendry's property, and now to judge the unfortunate incidents of last evening. Am I correct?"

"We have no interest in property rights or even murder. We are here to curb your heresy," the man said. "When your disciples arrived six months ago and began to spread your pious dogma among the people we were amused, but we cannot allow the revival of the Order of the Brazen Serpent."

Widseth narrowed his eyes. The staff with the serpent ... the bloody cloak ... he reviewed the events of the previous evening. *This was not about Fendry's property. Not even about Aljezra's death ... what disciples?* The foundation to these accusations had been fabricated with meticulous care.

The man continued, "Last night concerns us because twelve were killed, but only nine bodies are here for burial. Where are the other three?" The man glared at Widseth.

Widseth paused, bit his lower lip, and stared into the orchard before replying. "They're not dead. They're on their way to Dragada under the protection of a dragon of light, a choice they made."

Widseth pitched the tenor of his voice so the bold pronouncement reverberated in the morning air. He spoke with the intention that Deorc hear his words, serving notice that dragons of light had returned to the world.

"You and your woman will come with us," the man said. "Your blasphemy will be examined under the High Bishar's court of Tabul. Your lands here are forfeit to the Emperor Padwalar the Third including all chattel, bond servants, and slaves. Put them in chains."

Five men dismounted and two of them pulled shackles from their saddle packs. As they approached, Widseth held up his hand, palm forward.

"My wife has nothing to do with this. She must be allowed to return to her home in the north." He turned to Annel.

"No, I'll not leave ..." she began.

One of the guards clamped his hand on Widseth shoulder, but Widseth raised his other hand with fist closed, and opened his palm toward Annel. Brilliant white light exploded from his palm and engulfed her. Her form dissipated with the light. The energy surge ejected the guard and sent him tumbling down the steps, bowling over two of the robed inquisitors. Two of the horses bolted, and the emperor's men stepped back as fear neutralized their bravado.

Widseth scanned the orchard and directed a flash of light at the shimmering camouflage hiding Deorc. The man sized dragon phased into focus for only a second, and Widseth knew that the temporary confusion would cover the path of light he had created for

Annel. Deorc could not follow. Widseth stood on the steps above the men, composing his thoughts. One of the men in purple and yellow stood and brushed the dirt from his robes. Xeran stood next to his horse with his assistant. Widseth nodded to him and smiled.

"I'll go with you," he said. "There's no need for the chains unless they make you feel more comfortable. I'll give you no trouble."

The guards rushed up the stairs and pummeled him until he lost consciousness.

***

Deorc turned his head from the flash of light. "Curse the Aelfene scum."

The orchard noises ceased, as if in an instant every living thing knew some beast stalked them. Rin studied Deorc, as the dragon paced between trees. The creature's form shifted from tangible physical substance to smoke-like shadows that swirled in reckless patterns. At times the form began to dissipate into the afternoon air, and then it coalesced into a dark physical form again with the head, limbs, torso, and tail, appearing and fading in random order.

A dank odor assaulted Rin's senses, triggering memories of the time he found old Nib's body in the storage cellar, three days dead. He gagged. The stench of the old man's maggoty flesh haunted his dreams for a year.

Above the stink and amid the confusing and shifting patterns, the hairs on Rin's arms and neck rose. His sight began to falter. The outside world grew dim, and he struggled to stay focused, as a brooding sense invaded his thoughts. He watched Deorc, noticing barren sensations replace his familiar world, and he felt himself ebbing like rainwater into the sewage drains in the streets of Tabul. Nothing he knew mattered any more because there was no familiar world left to him.

"I want my father back." His simple vocal statement shattered the darkness between the trees. He remembered how Annel healed the tree. He could smell the fragrance of the trees in the orchard. The emperor's men passed nearby on the road with Widseth in custody.

Deorc shifted into physical form. "Come with me."

***

Standing to the right of the judgment table at the front of the great hall in the Emperor's palace in Tabul, Xeran gazed over the gathering crowd. The Emperor's High Inquisitor dressed in satin purple robes sat at the high table flanked by the three who had taken Widseth into custody. The judges conferred in low tones.

The elderly Duchess Tabrona sat on the ivory inlaid throne of the High Bishar, above and behind the judgment table. As the widowed aunt of the Emperor she convened the court under her authority as Duchess of Tabul, but Xeran knew others manipulated her age stricken mental abilities. Counselors stood on either side of the throne.

Nobles and members of the merchant class filed through the double doors at the opposite end of the chamber and squeezed between the carved sandstone columns. A few select noble families took their seats near the front of the hall. Rich brocade tapestries, depicting the history of Tabul, hung just below the high windows along the east and west walls.

The Aelfen were legends of the past. People lined the hall and conversed in hushed voices. To see an Aelfe would be like reading a page from a book from their childhood about the myths of Aelandra. The columns flanked the wide aisle from the double doors to a circular dais two steps above the floor of the hall with the judgment table. Four steps higher another dais rose with the throne of Tabul overlooking the court.

The Emperor had been advised that an Aelfe had fomented the rebirth of the Order of the Brazen Serpent cult, long thought dead in the region, but he deigned not to leave the high palace in the capital of Dol Ismus and make the fifteen day trip to Tabul. Xeran assumed the Emperor, preferring to remain above religious squabbles, had sent his Inquisitors to deal with the heresy under the controlled direction of his aunt.

All heads turned as a side door opened, and six of the Emperor's elite personal guard marched in a haggard man. As Widseth stumbled into the room, the unending circulation of rumor and legend paused. Xeran hardly recognized Widseth's face. It was bruised with bloodstains and welts. He still wore his blue tunic with the white tree on the breast, but whips had bloodied and shredded the back. A bar behind his back held his arms immobile at an angle where it passed in front of the elbow joints. Manacles on his wrists held his hands tight to his body so he could not slip the bar. Chains, attached to a metal collar that his guards held, pulled him in four directions. The guards hauled him forward or yanked him to a stop at their will. They halted ten paces in front of the high table.

"He looks to be a beggar rather than a noble of any sort," a man near Xeran said to a woman.

"He's a fraud," she replied. "If there ever were people like the Aelfen in the legends, they're long dead."

Xeran stared at Widseth's left hand. There was no sign of deformity. Although bound it was whole and healthy. As Widseth stood to face the table, afternoon sunlight, flooding the hall from the west windows, bathed him. Xeran glanced from face to face in the throng of aristocrats lining the walls and sitting at the table. Excited whispers filtered through the throng as the light appeared to be drawn to the Aelfene captive. Open lacerations closed, and swelling in his face diminished.

A woman stepped forward and knelt, raising her hands above her head. "He *is* sent from another world. The light obeys his will." Two guards grabbed her and dragged her toward the exit.

A nobleman rushed toward Widseth and spat on him. "You have your reward for freeing slaves. You are spittle and shall die wallowing in your own dung." Friends restrained him and pulled him back by a column.

The High Inquisitor rose to his feet. "Silence! Bring the prisoner forward to stand before the court of the High Bishar of Tabul. Close the curtains." Servants hastened to obey. With the light subdued, he continued. "You are found guilty of heresy and practicing a magic forbidden and outlawed for two hundred years.

You shall be sent to the gem mines of Bilbra on the Grabad Peninsula to serve a life sentence."

Widseth's calm voice reverberated through the hall. "Is there to be no trial ... only a decree for punishment?" The judge's hand halted as he tried to pick up a quill pen. Widseth's voice unmasked all the pretenses of aristocracy, rank, and fashion.

Xeran could not believe it. The Inquisitor's hand shook like a leaf in the wind, and he glanced to his right and left like a rabbit cornered by a fox. Instead of gawking at Widseth, the nobility edged away from him. Like thin, almost transparent gauze, their aristocratic trappings veiled their alarm created by Widseth's voice. The panic that lurked just below the surface of the assembled nobles moved along currents of whispers. Xeran had felt Widseth's power on the steps at the manor. *Why had he made his wife disappear, and what was he doing now? He could snap his fingers and burst his fetters.* Xeran knew he could. *Maybe he could call a dragon like the old tales.* Xeran looked around again. Majesty in chains standing in the sunlight filled his mind. The only person in the hall without fear was Widseth.

Widseth bowed his head and said, "I will abide your judgment. I shall give you no trouble." The pitch of Widseth's voice ended the tension.

Xeran shook his head. It was as if the Aelfe wanted to go to his death as a slave in the mines. He shuddered. So many tales about the mines haunted his memory. As a teen, he had met an old guard who served in the gem mines of Bilbra. The stories the old man told him had given him nightmares ever since. Widseth did not understand the horrors waiting for him. Xeran was sure of it.

The High Inquisitor regained his demeanor. "Get him out of here. Guards, put this scum on the first ship to Sourstrom. If you have luck, master Aelfe, the sea will end your life before you get to the mines."

Widseth bowed before the council of judges. "May the powers of light ever grace your lives."

The guards behind him jerked the chains, and Widseth fell backward. He struggled to get to his feet as the other guards pushed him and beat him with a short club.

"Take him away," the Inquisitor shouted. The venom in his voice filled the room with anger and despair.

Xeran struggled to look at the high table. The High Inquisitor had cast a spell to cower the assembled nobility, but Xeran did not remember the fear or intimidation of the spell. He remembered only light and the peace in Widseth's voice.

***

At the sound of voices outside his cell, Widseth roused himself from a meditative state.

"Only a moment ... not a second more."

"That should buy more than a moment."

He heard the sound of coins jangling.

"Open the door."

"Not on yer life. He ships out come mornin'. An' m' neck'd be stretched by noon, if they found I let ya be here. Talk through the bars."

Rising to his feet, Widseth walked to the door of his dark cell. Flickering torchlight from the outer hall provided little illumination through the small barred opening in the heavy wooden door, and when a head filled the opening in front of the torchlight the cell darkened even further.

"Widseth ... Widseth."

"I'm right here, Xeran." Widseth uttered a soft word, and a delicate blue flame ignited in his hand and illuminated the cell.

Xeran blinked and motioned Widseth to the opening in the door. "I spent every thing I could spare in bribes to talk with you. You can't go to Bilbra."

Widseth smiled. "Well, the judge said that's where I'm going."

"But nobody survives Bilbra. Men sentenced to five years know they will never return. No one ever returns. I talked to a guard once. Most times even the guards don't survive. If the guards don't kill you, the mines will. Men go mad from the dark. They die from disease and lack of food and water. And there are the mine creatures."

"Mine creatures? Now I think you're remembering the stories of your Granny."

"No. There are creatures. But that's not the point. I've read about the Aelfen. You have powers and could escape. Why are you doing this?"

"I have to go to Bilbra."

"But why? No one returns."

Widseth moved closer to the opening in the door. He whispered. "At least one returned—my mother. She was in the mines for over thirty years."

Xeran paused. There had been one who survived the mines; the old guard had brought her to compete in the arena.

"Your mother was Vandria, the witch of Standel?" His words were not so much a question as a statement. "I was young, maybe thirteen, when I saw her escape the arena. That's why Fendry left. He wanted to track her down and kill her."

"I've never heard my mother called the witch of Standel, but yes, Fendry found us. He found remnants of the Aelfen, and he found peace."

Xeran shook his head. "Widseth, use your power. You could do much to free our city from … ."

"Time's up. Get movin'," the guard said.

Xeran turned away from the opening. "I'll be there … just finishing now." He turned back to Widseth. "Master Widseth, consider my advice … please."

Widseth shook his head. "I'm sorry, Xeran. I can't give Tabul freedom. Freedom comes from within and is exercised with discipline. Go now, or you'll endanger yourself."

He reached into the flame in his open hand and pulled out a scrap of parchment. Xeran stared in wonder as Widseth handed the scrap to him through the bars.

"A friend of mine will meet you on your road home," Widseth said. "Please give him this. Thank you for your concern."

Closing his hand, Widseth extinguished the blue flame.

A man cannot walk on two roads at the same time. If his purpose is divided, he will become unstable and surely fall into the abyss between the roads, but if patient he will find the occasional bridge that will give intersection to the paths for a brief moment. If he chooses to act rather than linger, he can endure the transition between the roads. Joy and sorrow are two such roads.

> *From the Manual of Discipline found in the library of Vindry—author unknown, but this particular passage was signed by Yael—no other reference given*

Chapter 4. One Choice-Two Paths

Annel stumbled over a tree root and fell to the ground. She struggled to her feet and tried to conjure a path back to Widseth, but anger clouded her emotions and prevented her from configuring any of the abilities she had learned with the Aelfen in Meliandra. She could travel the light channels with her spiritual essence, but lacked the skill Widseth used to teleport her physical body through a conduit of luminosity. She drew her dagger from its sheath, slashing at the air until her knees buckled, and she knelt down sobbing. She stabbed the dagger into the ground repeatedly until she let it fall from her hand.

Sorrow and loneliness, her old foes, were her companions again, as her mind slipped into a world she hated. She was eleven again, and her mother was not two months in the grave. *Why did she have to relive this?* She heard her uncle's voice, ringing in her ears. His foul breath assaulted her nose, and she felt the lash rip through the back of her shirt and into her skin.

"Two coppers won't pay your keep, girl. If you can't steal it, find a way to earn it, or I'll beat you 'til you join your mother," he said.

Every day for thirteen years she ended her waking hours with tears until the most beautiful night, when Widseth rescued her from a beating, and sang one of the eternal melodies. She could hear the music now, and she could feel the touch of his hand on her cheek and the warmth of his breath on her neck.

She fell forward, embracing the moss on the forest floor. Her angry sorrow leeched into the moss carpet beneath her, and she lost track of her loneliness. Curious combinations of aromas of rich loamy soil and fresh raspberries filled her nose, and a sense of timeless wonder invaded her mind. The only sounds were a dull roar in the distance through the trees and the thin piping of a bird above the soft rustle of leaves in the breeze. *Where had Widseth sent her?* She sensed safety in the surroundings, despite her loneliness and anger. *How could she find her way back? What would they do to him? Rather, what would he allow them to do to him?* Her thoughts became a measured response to her respiration, and soon she could not tell reality from a dream, as she slipped into peaceful sleep under the morning sun.

A sticky sensation, like honey being separated from its comb, preceded the feeling of air being expelled from her lungs. Her essence of light pulled away from her material body, and she could see herself below, reposed on the mossy floor. The separation of spirit and body was not an uncomfortable feeling, as much as it was odd to be able to see the environment and yet have little power to affect it. The experience was unlike any Annel had undergone in her training. She had been taught to travel the paths of light and to see the full spectrum and glory of the world unseen by natural eyes. She could see the minuscule rifts in the elements of unhealthy plants and animals, and she could even effect changes to heal things, but this was different. *Was she dying?* She could see roots entangling her wrists and ankles binding her physical body to the earth.

Radiance gathered into the outline of a doorway near a large oak tree. Through the glowing mist of light in the doorway Annel began to see the outline of a large object. Through curtains of light the object moved, weaving a hypnotic pattern that opened a path toward the door. The door expanded a bit, allowing a head to emerge, but the size of the opening blocked the body of the creature;

even so, the head attached to a long scaled neck snaked toward her physical body. It paused. Misty vapors wafted from the nostrils, and Annel watched as the dragon exhaled air and in a whispered breath wove unseen patterns over her material body. Light emanated from the vegetation, and Annel heard the familiar melodies of the eternal world pulsing from every living thing. The dragon bent low, kissing her brow. In language she could not understand, the creature chanted a melody with deep guttural tones, sounding as if they emerged from the depths of a well. The roots entangling her limbs fell away like chaff in the wind.

Annel's conscious light essence strained to hear the words. *Why wasn't she permitted to hear the instructions? A dragon of light ministered to her and she couldn't understand. Who was this dragon? Why had it come to her?*

Satisfied, the dragon raised its head and surveyed the forest. It retreated back into the doorway, stopping every few feet to sniff the air. Annel sensed the awe the dragon felt as it enjoyed the material world. The last vestige of the dragon slipped into the glowing curtain in the door, and a man walked through. He immediately looked up at Annel's essence and beckoned her to return to her body. He looked familiar. She recognized him although she had seen him only twice before in Meliandra. *He had ferried Widseth to Dragada before Widseth became the Dragon Master. Widseth called him the boatman. Yes, he was the boatman. He had ferried her, too. Why was he here?*

"Annel," he said in a soft, but piercing voice. "Return now to your body. There is much for you to accomplish yet."

He knelt and touched her brow where the dragon had kissed her. His fingers traced a line from the center of her forehead to her temples. Appearing pleased, he stood and walked back through the doorway which collapsed on itself until the last residue of eternal light winked from sight. Annel felt like a whirlpool of energy snared her as her physical body pulled her from above and integrated her conscious light force within the fabric of its structure.

***

Rin struggled to follow the black man-sized dragon out of the orchard. His vision still suffered impairment after the brilliant flash directed at them by Widseth. He grabbed Deorc's cloak with one hand and fended off lower hanging branches and undergrowth with the other. A tingly burst of energy shot through his hand, holding Deorc's cloak. The exhilaration tickled, and at the same time terrified him because of the empty void that he knew Deorc represented.

Rin gasped. "Stop. Please stop. I can't see."

"There is no stopping now. He knew I was here and blocked me. He is more skilled than I imagined."

They walked for another ten minutes before Deorc slowed his pace and stopped near the tree line of the back orchard and looked skyward.

Rin thought about the light from Widseth's hand that caused Annel to disappear. "Where'd Annel go? She was kind t' me."

"The woman is of no consequence." Deorc bit off the words. His tone implied that she was an unknown who mattered little. He raised his head and unleashed a throaty, animalistic bellow.

Though it hurt his eyes to look into the sunlight, Rin looked skyward. His heart raced as a small black smudge emerged from a cloud, and he watched it grow in size until he perceived a huge dragon descending. He did not experience the feeling of wonder he felt when he first saw the golden man stretched around a tree in his dragon form. Rin's hands trembled, and the ground seemed unsteady. He wanted to run, but he knew a greater terror than the dragon above stood beside him, because he sensed that Deorc controlled the creature descending from above. Rooted to the ground, Rin felt tears welling in his eyes. He choked back a lump in his throat and wiped his nose with his sleeve.

"Do you want to run, boy?"

"Yeah, but I wanna live. An' I know ya'd kill me."

Deorc laughed the same throaty growl. When Deorc had approached Rin in the stocks in the dark of night, he had seemed so noble. Even when he killed Aljezra, he appeared as highborn nobility in a rich cloak wielding a staff of power. Now unmasked in daylight, Deorc represented only a dark blight … a miserable mistake.

"Boy, there is no need for fear. I will teach you to control the dragons. I will give you all you can imagine and more. But if you run now … yes … either I … or he will eat you."

The dragon landed not twenty paces away. Rin raised his arm to shield his eyes from the gust of wind created by the dragon's wings. A musty, metallic stench masked the pleasant summer smells of the orchard, and sulfurous air with a slight tang stung Rin's lungs. A bitter taste filled his mouth. He choked and fell toward the ground, but Deorc clutched his shoulder and pulled him to his feet.

"Come, boy. We will use this lesser creature to give you your first lesson."

"Lesson? I would rather … ." Rin wheezed, but his voice fell silent as Deorc pulled him toward the dragon. Rin could see a saddle just in front of the wings. Deorc lifted him into the saddle and strapped him in with leather bands. His legs and feet slipped into leather chaps attached to the saddle, and held him tight against the body of the dragon. Even without the leather bands, it would be difficult to fall out of the saddle. There were no reins, but the handles at the front of the saddle had narrow extensions that reached either side of the creature's neck. Rin assumed that by using the handles he would be able to direct the dragon, but he had no idea how they worked.

Rin sat above in the saddle, and Deorc stood below croaking to the dragon. Rin inhaled when he felt the wings behind him begin to pump. He looked back. The dragon lurched and with a jerk lifted into the air. Rin screamed. The trees fell away. Tears formed, and he fought the lump in his throat. He wished he could close his eyes and wake up to a pleasant morning as a slave again, but the fear from every nightmare he had ever dreamt faded in the reality of riding this immense creature. His entire body shook as he looked down gripping the handles. He tried to fix his eyes on a single tree, even as it grew smaller, but it soon melded into a green carpet. The rush of cold wind enlivened his senses.

Peering over the side of the dragon, he could see Deorc flying just below. *How was he flying? No wings. Maybe they were invisible. Deorc could be invisible whenever he wanted, and sometimes there was something that was a part of the dragon, and then it was gone like it never existed.* The cold air stung Rin's face and eyes. Tears ran down his cheeks, but they were not from the cold air. *How could he survive this? Is this power ... to fly like this?* He clung to the dragon like an animal clutching a floating log. The air rushing over his body cut through his rough clothing, yet internal heat from the dragon warmed him.

The grassland stretched forever, but after a couple of hours, Rin noticed a snake winding through the land. He guessed it was a river, but from this height it was little more than a bluish creek laid out on a greenish brown blanket of grass. He had been able to make out faint roads, but they had ended some time ago, and the patchwork of farmland had been left behind an hour before. Only occasional hills and gullies along with the river broke the monotony of the grassland.

Time passed and Rin felt a little bravado return. The rhythmic motion of the wings and the sinuous undulation of the dragon lulled Rin into confidence. Nothing had hurt him. He loosened his grip on the saddle and reached for the handles with the extensions. He moved them ever so slightly, at first, until the right extension touched the dragon's neck. Without hesitation the dragon drifted to the left. When he tapped the rod more firmly, the dragon reacted immediately and veered sharply to the left again. Using the left rod, Rin corrected the course. If he hit the back of the neck, the dragon descended, and if he touched both rods at the same time to the sides of the neck, the dragon ascended. Rin grinned. *A dragon carried him across the land. He was master of a great beast that could kill a hundred men. Maybe this wouldn't be so bad. He was more powerful than the emperor. He had powerful new friends, and he was free.*

***

Annel struggled to her feet. Looking around, she examined the forest. The dull roar that she heard when she first arrived filtered through the trees, and the terrain sloped downward. The trees thinned as she walked toward the sound until she came to a sandy beach with waves crashing on the shore. The ocean. She had seen the ocean only once before when she and Widseth were in Standel. *That was so long ago, or was it? Yesterday ... what was yesterday? What happened before today, before this place? How could she get to Widseth?*

The dry sand soon became compact and wet. Water splashed around her feet, and for a minute she wished she could play a game with the water as it chased back and forth across the sand as waves spent their energy in an unending procession to blanket the shore. The wind and salty tang in the air invigorated her.

She looked back at the dense foliage, and detected a game trail that led upward into the deeper woods away from the shoreline. She could see the crest of the hill, and although it would not be a difficult walk, she paused, undecided. A wave of depression washed over her like the water on the sand, sinking deep into her awareness. She was alone. Even in the loneliness of her youth there had been people around. She remembered the conduit of light Widseth used to send her here, but he had masked the path to prevent Deorc from following her, and she could not remember any significant markers that would help her ascertain where he had sent her.

The game trail beckoned, and setting her mind to reach the top of the small hill, she walked away from the beach back into the forest. The dull thunder of the waves subsided until she hardly noticed it. After a steady walk for nearly half an hour, she stopped short. At the crest, in a small clearing, she spied a cabin. The deserted area displayed no signs of recent habitation, but the cabin door was open. Annel drew her dagger and crept from tree to tree until she could see into the open door.

There was no movement. In stark contrast to the beach, not a breath of wind stirred the limbs of the trees. Gripping her dagger, Annel stepped from behind a tree and walked toward the open door. Nothing happened, but she sensed that someone studied every movement she made. She strained all her abilities to see the full spectrum of light, but there were no clues other than the normal light patterns for her to follow. She remembered the doorway of light, the dragon, and the boatman; she could not understand the significance.

Hesitating at the door and looking into the structure, she saw a table with two chairs in the center of a single room. A pitcher and a basin were on the table with a small wheel of cheese, a round of bread, and a quill pen and ink with paper. Someone had laid out garments on a bed against the far wall. A small object glittered on the mantle above the fireplace, and a mirror hung on the opposite wall. The dust on the floor had not been disturbed for some time.

Annel stepped into the room. As she entered, four candles in sconces on the walls burst into flame, and logs crackled in the fireplace, as tongues of a hungry blaze sprang to life. She whirled around, inspecting all the shadows of the room for any sign of movement. Though the cabin appeared empty, she approached the mantle with caution. A crystal globe rested in a metal stand. Lifting it from the stand, she held it in her palm; at her touch, light sprang from within illuminating a white tree in a stone planter. A dark clawed hand was at the base of the tree. Darkness oozed from the hand, and veins of darkness slithered around and up the trunk of the tree and over the edges of the planter.

***

Wide-eyed, Rin clung to the saddle as the dragon angled its wings back and sliced the air like a huge hunting bird, following Deorc toward a clump of rolling hills sculpted on the grassland. The two dragons plummeted toward a dark mass located in a small valley between the hills. Rin knew the harness and leg chaps would keep him from falling, but his stomach did not enjoy similar security. His screams melded into the racing wind.

In a matter seconds the dark mass gathered definition. In the evening light Rin distinguished an outer wall with a gate to the plains. A massive door led into a cliff at the base of the hillside. He spotted another dragon on the top of a nearby hill outside the compound. Men carrying weapons walked on the parapets and ramparts, and a small company rode on horseback through the gates toward the open plains. The compound within the wall contained few surface buildings, but most of the traffic centered on the gate leading into the hill.

As Deorc and Rin's dragon landed, a group of armored men led by a man in a brown robe approached. The man held a staff like the one Deorc carried the night he killed Aljezra. As Rin struggled with the straps on the saddle, he caught snatches of conversation. He slowed his efforts and observed, as the men bowed before Deorc.

Holding the staff before him, the man in the brown robe approached and bowed. "M'lord, it is good to see you again. Did you find the man you sought?"

Rin slid from the back of his dragon and moved toward Deorc, trying to stay out of the line of sight. Listening to Deorc, the armed men behind the man with the staff looked like evil statues. Lean faces accented hardened exteriors, and all stood with expressionless features that they wore like masks. None of them acknowledged Rin or seemed to take note of his presence until the man with the staff looked at him.

"What have we here? Is this the new one, m'lord?" he asked Deorc.

"Yes. This is Rin son of Ronald. When we are ready, his name will run through the land like wildfire," Deorc answered.

Rin studied Deorc when he said that. He wondered what it meant that his name would 'run as wildfire through the land'. When the man with the staff spoke, Rin turned his attention to him.

"Rin is a good name, boy. I'm Brulon, Master Prelate of the Order of the Brazen Serpent." The robed man leaned close to Rin's face.

Rin noted the pocked marked skin partially covered by a scraggly beard. The man's breath smelled as if he had a rotten tooth. Rin stepped back and met his gaze. If what Deorc said was true about controlling dragons, maybe he would rule men like this too. The man reminded Rin of Aljezra. He sensed this man knew how to use a whip.

"Ah, he knows he's the rooster of the yard. His eyes tell the story," Brulon said. "You chose well, Master Deorc."

Deorc gazed at the wall and then to the gigantic gate in the cliff into the underground. "What of the work in the city?"

"There's plenty of living area cleared, but some of the tunnels to lower regions are collapsed. We can hear the underground river, and any day we should break through to it," Brulon said. "The dragon maps you gave us are accurate, and the mine bosses have had little trouble reconstructing the original plans."

"Good. And what of the new *converts*?" Deorc asked. He turned to look at Rin, but Rin avoided the dragon's stare and studied a company of armed men exiting the broad gate into the hillside. They marched in formation toward the outer compound wall.

"Yes, the converts. Groups of five to twenty arrive daily from all areas where we've sent your followers. The acolytes are doing well. A week ago a company of men arrived from the north. Their leader said he fought for the Dragonda in the northern wars. He indicated that other companies were following."

Deorc looked around and sniffed the air. "Good. Come, Rin. This is your new home."

Rin noticed the dragon's nostrils as they flared, and he sensed taut emotion in the beast's words. Rin remembered two years before when he saw a desert cat, a feared predator, slip into the orchard. When Deorc said *'new home'*, Rin felt the same heightened fear and awe when he looked at the massive door into the underground, as he felt when he helped the other slaves track and kill the cat.

He hurried to keep up with the dragon, as they headed toward the underground. If this was his home, he wanted to know every inch. A new concept took shape in his mind. If he controlled all these men and dragons, he would be free. He could do anything, and nobody could stop him. That was better than what Widseth had given him. No more water ditches for him, as a slave or a hired man. He was his own man. And Aljezra was dead. Deorc had given him revenge and it tasted good.

***

For three days Annel searched the forest, finding no one. Every morning when she awoke, she thought she would find Widseth lying beside her, but nothing changed in the cabin from the night before except a new wheel of cheese and round of bread with a pitcher of clean water replaced whatever was left from the day before. On the fourth morning she decided to return to the sea and walk the coastline until she found someone. Before leaving the cabin, she sat at the table eating some of the bread and cheese, putting the left over food into her pouch for later. The quill pen and paper drew her attention. *She might as well leave a note in case Widseth came looking for her.*

> **I waited three days. I will walk the coast to find a town.**
> **Annel**

Startled, she stared at the paper. Words appeared below her message.

> **Don the garments that were on the bed when you arrived. Walk to the ocean and travel north until you see a calm inlet. It will take the better part of a day. Sleep away from the beach with no fire. Take the blanket from the bed. In the morning you will be met.**

"I could have done this three days ago," she muttered.

She smiled, grateful for assistance even from a piece of paper and ink, but she knew the smile masked how close she had approached the edge of her control. She felt one more thing might push her into an abyss that she might not be able to endure. She longed for Widseth's warm touch and quiet confidence.

She walked to the bed and held up the garments that she had carefully placed on the foot board the first night. The unattractive clothing seemed to be old and well worn, but it looked to be about the right size. The fabric of the stockings stretched, but appeared almost metallic in composition. She tried to pierce it with her dagger, but to no avail. The hosiery fit like a second skin, and the leather breeches reached to mid-calf and tucked into the supple boots that she found at the foot of the bed. The white blouse, edged with antique lace, buttoned up the front over a single piece undergarment similar to the hosiery. Over the blouse she put on a jerkin of the same leather material as the breeches. She strapped her short knife to her right leg and the long dagger on her left hip.

Though the morning was warm, she pulled the old blanket from the bed. To her surprise she found a plain metal clasp on the edge. With a mock flourish she wrapped the blanket around her and fastened the clasp at her neck. Although functional and well made, the pants, jerkin, and blouse were mismatched both in size and color, and the blanket had been patched several times with various colors and fabrics.

She looked at the clothing. "I must look like the empress of a patchwork kingdom."

She twirled around, holding the edge of the blanket, stopping in front of the mirror. She stood motionless for a moment before stretching her trembling hand toward it. As she stared at her reflection, the clothing tightened and loosened until, like living skin, it fit as if she had been born to wear it. The jerkin and pants transformed to a deep golden hue, and her blonde hair, tied back in a braid, graced a deep maroon cloak with a white oak leaf embroidered on the left shoulder. In the morning light, streaming through the window, the blouse shimmered with silver radiance. The clasp on the blanket had transformed into a silver brooch inlaid with mother of pearl. She fixed her gaze on the beautiful brooch holding the cloak, and a similar emblem embroidered on the right front of the blouse—opposing dragons wrapped around a shaft.

She turned to the table and took the quill in her hand, dipped it in ink, and wrote again.

Who are you, and how do you know me?

Writing appeared.

Don the garments that were on the bed when you arrived. Walk to the ocean and travel north until you see a calm inlet. It will take the better part of a day. Sleep away from the beach with no fire. Take the blanket from the bed. In the morning you will be met.

"So ... just a repeat of what you told me before. Well, this is better than no answer at all." Annel strapped her belt pouch around her waist and made ready to leave the cabin. She stopped short, staring at the paper. Writing appeared. A cold chill crawled up her back, and she had the uncomfortable feeling someone or something watched every movement.

> *No, not a repeat, but a conduit to lead you to where our paths can converge.*

She quickly turned and walked through the doorway.

***

Xeran paused and looked back at the prison's entrance. A sense of satisfaction swept him that he had found the courage to enter, and that now he walked out. He inhaled, filling his lungs with clean night air, hoping to expel the odious dank aroma of the dungeon complex. The prison stable master brought his horse, but for a few streets Xeran held the halter and walked beside the horse on the dark streets, until he came to a tavern with two torches flanking the doorway. He stopped and pulled out the scrap of parchment that Widseth had given him. By torchlight he read the message.

> *King Fyan,*
> *My wife, Annel, requires any help you can send. I think she can be found in Adisabala. A small band, perhaps twelve or fifteen of the best you can spare, should suffice. My messenger will provide more information. Widseth*

Xeran stared at the parchment before rolling it and putting it into an inner pocket. He mounted his horse and directed it through the streets toward his home near the Ministry building on the outskirts of the inner business district. To avoid attention he had dressed in his worst clothes, but he still imagined that bystanders watched his every move. He took a roundabout route to his house to avoid any possible suspicion that he had visited Widseth.

After an hour, he approached his home. The street was empty, but his assistant paced in front of his house holding a torch. When he saw Xeran, he hurried to meet him.

Out of breath he said, "Master, it's so good to see you safe. Where have you been? A man has been inquiring about you. He came to the Ministry just before sunset. I was leaving, but he was so insistent."

"Your tongue is running on like a wild brook. Stable my horse for me," Xeran said.

"We need to go to the Ministry building, now. He's wouldn't leave, and he's not the sort to be kept waiting."

Another voice resonated from the darkened street. "Master Xeran, you have a message for me." The deep grizzled sound reverberated like it came from a deep cavern.

One of the largest men Xeran had ever seen stepped out of the shadows into the torchlight. He was a head taller than any man in Tabul, and dressed in full battle armor. The armor was of ancient design, and although aged, it appeared exceptionally well fabricated. The burnished brass breastplate gleamed in the torchlight, revealing the head of a dragon, engraved in the metal. Xeran took the torch from his assistant and handed him the horse's reins.

He approached the towering man. "Yes, I have a message, but can you share a moment with me. There are some things ... things, I need to know."

"I have little time for questions. Make them brief."

Xeran tried to steady his hand holding the torch. With his other hand he wiped his brow. He looked into the shadows on either side of the street to make sure he would not be overheard.

"Who is Widseth?"

The man laughed. The sound resounded in the night air. "Who indeed ...? He is the Dragon Master, one of the Lords of Light who serves the One we do not name. He is high king of the Aelfen in the material world."

Xeran bit his lip. *What would the Emperor or his Inquisitors do if they knew this?* "And who are you, and how can I be sure you're the one I should give Widseth's message?"

The man removed his helm and shook his head. His wild hair and beard looked like a mass of tangled nets until he shook his head again, and Xeran deciphered the shape of a dragon's head outlined in the tangle of the man's shaggy mane and beard.

He replaced his helm. "I am Anfelt, the anvil, the sturdy, the studious, protector of the plains of Misdara, the marshes of Marshkata, and all the land south of the Puldan Desert. My deeds and titles mean nothing to you, but you will give me Widseth's message because you know I speak truth." Anfelt extended his hand toward Xeran.

Xeran withdrew the small piece of rolled parchment from his pocket and dropped it into Anfelt's huge palm.

"One last question," Xeran said. "Why is Widseth doing this? I've read in the old books about the ancient Dragon Masters. They used dragons to serve them. Why couldn't he call the dragons to aid him?"

"That was two questions." Anfelt's laughter echoed into the evening. "The second first—dragons assist him all the time. The first second—everything Widseth does is born of obedience. His tests refine not only himself, but everyone whose life he touches."

"Tests? What do you mean tests?" Xeran asked.

"His tests define character, but they are not frivolous trials to waste time. They reveal true nature and eternal potential."

Anfelt held out his fist and dropped the piece of parchment to the ground. "Do you think if he contacted me and told me to meet you here, that he needed this scrap to give me the message you carried?"

Xeran knelt down and picked up the fragment of parchment. He put it in an inner pocket near his breast. It was a token, a treasure. He had proven himself worthy of trust to ancient powers. He looked at one of Anfelt's forearms. In the torchlight the skin that covered the sinewy muscles looked more like some sort of hardened leather armor until Xeran realized the skin was actually composed of scales.

"You're a dragon," he whispered.

The tall man bent close to him. In a soft voice he said, "I already know the message for King Fyan. I will deliver it. *You* need to leave Tabul tonight."

"Tonight?"

"You passed the test, but others have not. Leave alone, without delay."

"But where shall I go?"

Anfelt stood up straight, nodded his head to Xeran, and walked into the dark street.

Xeran looked for his assistant, but he was gone. Xeran hurried to follow Anfelt into the darkness.

***

Just before nightfall, Annel located a defensive position on a high mound at the base of a small cliff where she sat in a dry crevice in the rock face to wait for morning. She wrapped herself in the cloak and surveyed the peaceful scene. Almost no ripples disturbed the bay except where a small freshwater stream emptied into the inlet about two hundred paces from her location. The land which flanked the bay looked like two sandy arms embracing a beautiful azure jewel, sheltered from turbulent waves crashing on a protective reef perhaps a mile in the distance.

She watched sand crabs scuttling along the beach, seeking salty morsels that the water might deposit. Sea birds floated on warm air currents above the water searching for an evening meal. Their cries resonated like musical instruments across the bay, but as the sun began to dip into the west sea, night noises from the forest above and behind her increased, and the sea birds disappeared.

As she sat in the sand just inside the fissure in the rock, she wrapped her arms around her legs and pulled the cloak about her. The cool onshore breeze increased with the twilight air, and the fresh smell of the sea air pleased her, but she longed for Widseth to share this moment of peace and beauty. She wanted his arm around her. She wanted to put her head on his shoulder and feel the back of his hand caress her cheek. Using her dagger, she wrote his name in the sand just in front of her feet. It was just an empty motion, but the name served as a talisman in her mind to protect her. She wrapped the cloak even tighter and leaned back against the rock.

She closed her eyes and drifted into uneasy sleep sprinkled with murky dreams and sudden awakenings. In the dark night visions, homes were burned. Armies clashed. Men, women, and children died. Instead of magnificent dragons of light guiding her, menacing horrors in dragon shape pursued her through gloomy valleys and dank caverns. A figure in black armor, wearing a plumed helm rode a great dark dragon, destroying everything in his path. She was alone, holding Deorc's severed hand, and she gasped for breath as the evil crushed her spirit. As the rider and the dragon cornered her, she jerked awake. The first thing she saw was Widseth's name in the sand.

A beam of morning sunlight touched the sand in front of her feet, and she stood, staring in amazement at the sun, rising from the same point it set the night before. *How could this be?* The sunbeams banished the night terrors to memory, and, what had seemed so real, faded in the brilliant glow of morning.

A white horse drank at the stream that emptied into the bay. It looked up, and stared at her. Annel gathered her things and walked down the hill toward the horse. As she approached, the mare tossed its head, reared on its hind legs, and trotted directly toward her. The sunlight, catching its white coat, scattered myriads of prismatic reflections.

"Who are you, and why have you come to The Diadem?" The sound drifted lazily through the air from the direction of the horse.

Annel froze. *Had this beast spoken to her?* She gripped her dagger, but she felt awe more than fear. From childhood, she remembered an old seaman spinning fantastic tales in the tavern about a forbidden island called The Diadem, where his ship had dashed to pieces on a reef. He had been the only survivor, and had marked thirty days on a tree on the island. He said that a porpoise saved his life and carried him to the mainland, but upon arriving home, he found that he had been lost for two and a half years. Everyone said he had swallowed too much sea water, and it had pickled his mind.

Annel studied the dark eyes of the horse. The flat black surfaces reflected no light. "I'm Annel. My husband sent me here on the paths of light to protect me."

"Annel is a name. Who are *you*?"

The emphasis on "*you*" pierced all the facades and fences that protected her inner self. She was uncomfortable because she feared the creature before her could see everything about her hidden hopes and dreams and her repressed failures and fear.

"I'm not sure what you mean," she said.

"Did you watch the sun set last night? Did it set in front of you or behind you?"

Somewhat puzzled she stared at the horizon. "Into the sea in front of me."

"And the sunrise this morning … did the light come from your back, or did it greet you as you faced it?"

"The sunlight in my face this morning surprised me. It didn't make sense, but it rose from where I saw it set," she answered.

"Ah … and what color am I?"

Annel looked around the bay. The sea birds noisily began the morning, merging sound and movement with the peaceful lapping water on the shore. In the distance she could hear the roar of waves breaking on the reef.

"You're all colors. You appear white, but when the light hits your mane, the light is split and showered in all directions. And you're no horse," Annel said.

"How very perceptive you are, but this shape will suffice. You approach me wearing the clothing of the Aelfen, but magic could have counterfeited that."

"Why this conversation?" Anger edged Annel's voice. "If this is The Diadem, I want no part of it. I need to get back to the mainland."

The horse continued as if it had not heard her. "You are a daughter of light. The light lingers to touch your face at night and eagerly rises to warm you in the morning. And yet you do not know who you are. Curious."

Frustration grew in Annel. "It makes no difference who you say I am. If I can't get back to my husband, I'm nothing."

"Nothing?" The horse shook its mane and snorted. "A daughter of light, a receptacle of life and healing, is not 'nothing'. I perceive that your husband sent you here to learn that. You have your wish. You may not return here until you know who you truly are. Can you manipulate the pathways of light?"

"No, or I would leave this cursed island."

"You're of no value to me, so you shall have your wish."

A flash engulfed Annel. When the light subsided, she stood on dry grassland outside a walled city. She wrapped her cloak tighter, as a chill wind swept down from a mountain flanking the right of the city. A merchant caravan that had bivouacked outside the walls for the night began to filter through the gates. She approached a man and woman leading a donkey with a cart, filled with potatoes.

"Good, sir, I am sorry to bother you, but can you tell me what city this is?" Annel asked.

"Are ya daft, woman? Have ya never been to the gates of Adisabala? 'Tis the center of the world. We're takin' the last of the harvest to the market before the winter storms. The lowlands can be cold this time o' year."

Annel looked up at the mountains. The first snows had already fallen. *But it had been summer in Tabul, and she had been on The Diadem only three days—at most four. How much time had passed ... months ... years?* She clenched her fists. The physical action did not quell the empty terror that began to build. She tried to swallow her fear for Widseth. Wiping her eyes, she started for the gate.

*In swift flowing rivers, eddies pull objects out of the
main current into deep holes. In the river of life the
strongest ships can be sucked into the backwater, if
they pay little attention to the currents. Pride, laziness,
and failure to heed experienced river travelers are
most often the loose rudders that lead to a life of an
endless vortex around nothing of worth.*

*From the Manual of Discipline found in the
library of Vindry—author unknown*

Chapter 5. Black Eddy

For over three years Widseth had worked in the gem mines of
Bilbra. His fingers were raw from working the sluice screens.
The milky wash water originated from the bowels of the volcanic
mass that towered above the valley. Gem mines honeycombed the
southern spur of the range of mountains that ringed the Grabad
Desert. The wash water stream eventually joined countless rivulets
and waterfalls from the volcanic range to become the Sourstrom
River, a navigable waterway from the city of Bilbra to Sourstrom, a
major trade port five hundred miles away on the coast.

For hundreds of years slaves, called diggers, had cut passages
deep into the mountains and diverted underground rivers through
the tunnels to wash pockets of gems into the alluvial lowlands where
workers sifted and washed the soil to find gems for the cutters in
Sourstrom, Tabul, and Dol Ismus. Sometimes the diggers cut into
long lava tubes and found pockets of gems scattered throughout the
lava tunnel almost as easy to pick from the walls as apples from a
tree.

The washers who worked the sluices for extended periods lost
feeling in their fingers and hands, and eventually their skin peeled
and cankered. Leprous sores, that would not heal, covered their
hands, arms, and legs as they stood in knee deep water, scooping
the water, mud, and rock into clay pots. The workers agitated
and rotated the pots and then dumped the aggregate on the sorting

screens. Usually the heavier gem material settled in the bottom of the pots and appeared near the top of the pile when the washer dumped them.

"Widseth, m' boy, help me w' this pot. It's a heavy one," Efran said.

Widseth looked at the old man. All the pots were too heavy for his old body. He doubted Efran would survive another week. After three years, Widseth had become adept at gauging the life span of fellow workers. There was no escape for these men, and none ever outlasted their prison term. Harsh mountains and the Grabad Desert hedged the north and east, and to the south and west inhospitable plains, inhabited by predators of every description, spread for hundreds of miles.

"I'm coming." Widseth waded through the caustic water, the odorous mud sucking at his leather sandals, but he was not quick enough.

A guard noticed the old man waiting for help and raised his whip.

"Get t' work, ya mud sucker," the guard bellowed.

As the tip of the whip painted Ephran's back with a long bloody welt, the man stumbled into the knee deep wash water of the trench. Widseth pulled the man's head from under the water.

"Lemme go. Can't do no more," the Ephran said, as he choked on the foul water. He closed his eyes.

"Find peace, brother. May the dragons of light guide your path," Widseth whispered. Holding the man's head, Widseth wiped strands of thin hair away from closed eyes, as he caressed the slave's muddy brow. He lifted the body onto the ledge of the sluice trench.

"He's dead," Widseth said.

"I'll call f' the body wagon. Get back t' work." The guard cracked the whip just above Widseth's head.

Widseth grasped the old man's pot, lifted it to the screens, and dumped the contents. Four large rough sapphires surfaced in the mix. In the hands of a skilled cutter they would adorn a nobleman's cup or dagger. Widseth rinsed them in the muddy water. Before placing them in the gem bag at the end of the screens, he turned them in his hand and examined each. They contained no life, and yet they would be valued more than the one who gave his life to find them. Widseth looked one last time at the old man as other slaves lifted him into the body wagon.

The whistle sounded, signaling time for the evening meal. As he climbed out of the trench, Widseth's skin tingled from the acidic wash water. He felt filthy. He fell in step with the others moving toward the compounds in the caves.

"Was that ol' Efran they put on the body wagon?" a man asked.

Widseth bit his lip. Past the lump in his throat he said, "Yeah. It was old Efran."

***

Wind whistled through the narrow streets of Adisabala, and Annel blew on her hands to warm them as she stood outside the inn called The Magician's Hat. The inn was only one lane off the heavily traveled market district streets. She had spent all day familiarizing herself with the layout of the city and felt confident that The Magician's Hat would provide economical and safe lodging. A helpful farmer had told her that merchants from Teradar, Puldan, and even Dimron frequented The Hat, as the locals called the inn.

As she began to push the door open, she heard a voice filled with incredulity. "Lady Annel? Is it you?"

Annel whirled around searching for the speaker. Across the street a man stood staring at her with golden eyes. The rich hues of his skin intensified until he appeared as if he were a metal statue in the refining fires of a sculptor. Annel ran to him and threw her arms around his neck.

"Gulth! I am so pleased to see you." Tears streamed down her face

"M'lady, we expected you some time ago, but Widseth instructed us to wait here for you no matter how long," the golden man replied.

Annel's heart jumped. "Where is he? I must see him."

"He is not here." Gulth looked down and shook his head. "He is stubborn, and we hate to see his condition, but he will not allow us to assist him. Occasionally he ... ."

"Condition? Where is he?" Annel demanded. "I'll go to him."

"M'lady."

"Now. Take me to him now."

For the first time Gulth refused her.

"No." He looked around the street. "I have a room for you at another inn. The Magician's Hat has too much traffic. Others have inquired about you." He turned and started down the street.

Annel bit her tongue and followed him in silence. After a few minutes, a smaller inn further from the market district came into view. A man, wrapped in a heavy cloak, stood outside. When he turned to greet Gulth, Annel noticed the flash of metal armor under the cloak, and insignias of Standel. She recognized him. He bowed to her as she approached.

"Will Willowman, why are you here?" she asked. "How?"

Looking up he smiled. "M'lady, please come inside and warm yourself."

After the Aelfen from Meliandra had departed the physical world for the world of light, a few returned to assist Widseth and Annel at Dragada to build a new Aelfene kingdom. Annel knew Will had developed a strong bond with King Fyan of Standel during the Great War that ended the terror in the north, so it did not surprise her when he returned. After Fyan's coronation, to Will's delight, Widseth had named him the ambassador for Dragada at the court of Standel.

Gulth held the door as Annel entered the warm common room. A fire blazed on the oversized hearth, and soft wizard's light illuminated the rest of the room. Several men sat at tables, eating stew. As Annel looked at each group, they hesitated and nodded in her direction. The courtesy puzzled her. It was as if they knew her and paid homage.

"Please, Lady Annel, have a seat here." Will motioned to the innkeeper. "The supper isn't a feast, but it'll warm you."

Will hung his cloak on a peg near the door, and removed his baldric with sword and hung it on a weapon's rack.

Annel looked around as she sat down. She tried to sort things out in her mind. It made no sense that Gulth and Will were here.

"Gulth, I thought Widseth told you to accompany Micah and the servants to Dragada," she said.

"Two died on the journey because we had unfavorable weather for about a month. But the others are safe in Dragada," Gulth answered.

Her hand trembled. The innkeeper placed the bowl of stew with some bread and a cup of warm milk in front of her. She grasped the spoon to steady her hand and tried to cover her discomfort by taking a bite of the hard black bread after dipping it in the soup. She fought the uncertainty in her mind. *Could this be a dream from the island? Or was the island a dream?*

"How long since you left the manor with the servants?" she asked Gulth.

"Winter begins after the third summer," he replied.

"M'lady ... ." Will began.

Annel held her hand up. She held her forehead in her other hand covering her eyes. Anger mixed with sorrow boiled to the surface, and her thoughts swam in a chaotic vortex. In some manner three years had passed while she spent a few days on the island. She wanted to flee the fear of losing three years.

She looked up with a piercing gaze at Gulth, "Three years?" she asked. "What of Widseth? Where is he?"

Gulth stared at the table with his head bowed, and said nothing.

"M'lady Annel, please," Will said. "If I may, I will speak for Gulth. I believe the purposes of the children of light are being fulfilled, but guilt has tormented Gulth these past three years. He feels he failed the Dragon Master and has brought ruin to the cause of rebuilding the Aelfene kingdom."

Annel shifted in her seat. She reached across the table and put her hand on Gulth's arm. Tears streaked the golden face.

Will continued, "These men from Standel wanted to leave a year ago, but you know how persuasive dragons can be. Gulth would hear none of it."

Annel forced a smile. "Yes, they can be persuasive. Please continue," she said.

"Three years ago the dragon, Anfelt, and a magistrate from Tabul, named Xeran, arrived at the court of Standel. They brought a message from Widseth to King Fyan, begging the king to send some of his best men to Adisabala to assist you in your quest."

"My quest? What quest?" Annel asked.

"Your quest is your business," Will said, "but I assume it has something to do with the clothing you wear." Will answered Annel's puzzled look. "You wear the maroon and gold raiment with the crest of the ancient Aelfen of Misdara."

Annel studied the apparel that she had been instructed to wear in the cabin on The Diadem. As Will spoke, she felt energy emitted by the clothing melding with her light essence. In the hidden city of Meliandra she had been trained to feel and use the channels of light.

She scanned the room again and squeezed Gulth's arm. Confidence replaced doubt as the shreds of uncertainty fled her mind.

"There's no fault, Gulth. You fulfilled Widseth's desire by taking the servants safely to Dragada," she said. "I don't know Widseth's strategy, but I have faith he follows a higher design. Where is he?"

Will spoke. "He is in the gem mines of Bilbra on the Grabad Peninsula. Dragons have ministered to him and brought messages from him to Gulth and Fyan. He follows his path, and he begs you to follow yours to completion."

"I have no idea where my path is," Annel said.

"There is trouble on the plains, and darkness is beginning to find root," Gulth said. "M'lord Widseth said you would appear here in Adisabala, but he could not be certain of the time."

"He sent me to The Diadem to protect me from Deorc and the emperor's men at the manor," Annel said.

Will's eyes widened. "The Diadem," he said. Men from other tables looked at Annel when they heard Will's incredulous tone. Will almost laughed. "It makes sense. Legends of the Diadem are as old as the world. It's the ancient ... no, more than ancient. It's a realm without time, a meeting place of the High and Low magics. Some conjecture it's the birthing bed of the powers of light and darkness. No one can ..." Will stopped speaking.

"No one can what?" Annel asked.

"I am sorry m'lady, but legend has it that no one can set foot on The Diadem without protection of the highest powers of eternity, and even so there is great peril. Deorc would never risk that price to follow you, even if he knew the path."

Will's words triggered a memory. A dragon had spoken words of protection over her, and a man had called her back to life. Her adrenalin surged.

"To me it was three days. Here it was more than three years. What's happened in those three years?" she asked.

***

In the late afternoon of a chilly winter day, eight mounted men remained at the bottom of the hill that Annel and one of the rangers of Standel climbed on foot. Dark smoke rose above the crest of the ridge, and the smell of burning timbers permeated the air.

"M'lady, I'll wager a boat o' fish that it's another farm," the man said.

"You're right, Kreigar. It's the fourth in two days," she replied. As she approached the crest, she dropped to her knees and crawled to the ridgeline. She peered over the edge, confirming her fears. A farmhouse smoldered. She inched back down the hill and buried her face in her hands, as she sat cross-legged on the cold ground near her horse. In two months she had witnessed the creeping darkness of fear spread over the winter plains.

Soon after arriving in Adisabala, Annel and the small band from Standel began to investigate the rumor of a skulking horror on the plains. After two months and several close encounters, Annel realized the darkness had risen again. In dragon form, Gulth had scoured the plains from great heights. He reported weekly that men in small numbers and supplies moved from the east and north into the central prairie toward a small grouping of hills. On one of his flights he tried to approach the hills, but four dragons rose to meet him, and he avoided the encounter.

The plains of Misdara were part of the Southlands Empire ruled by the Emperor Padwalar the Third, but the ruling seat in Dol Ismus stretched weak fingers of control over the plains. No large cities graced the grassland, only castle guarded fiefdoms, ruled by petty nobles with titles greater than the men and women who wore them. The great city of Adisabala considered itself a free trade city, but it paid tribute to The Hegemony of Teradar, and did not heed any troubles on the plains.

The man named Kreigar touched Annel on the shoulder. "M'lady, Gulth reports the storm's past and the farm's as empty as sails with no wind. I suggest that we … ."

"I know," she replied. She rose to her feet and blew into her cold hands. "Let's go see what we can find." In her heart she knew there would be no survivors. Kreigar started up the hill. In the short time she had known him, she had come to love him as a father. After the first reports of dragons, she sent Will Willowman back to Standel to report to King Fyan. The men of Standel followed Kreigar without hesitation. He had been a mariner from the northern island of Frostella all his life until he swore fealty to King Fyan during the Great War. Annel smiled as she followed him. His hair and beard flew in every direction battling the cold wind as he staggered up the hill, lurching like a man on the deck of a ship driven by the wind as it cut through an ocean tempest. Kreigar laughed at the cold and wind of the grassland. He came from an island locked in ice and pummeled by storms most of the year. Annel followed him as the others brought the horses into the farmyard.

The men scattered in practiced style to investigate and secure a perimeter. A body charred beyond recognition rested behind the smoking ruins of an out building. The rangers from Standel found two more bodies in the ruins of the collapsed farmhouse, a mother with a child in her arms. The first time that Annel saw a similar scene two months ago, the experience unsettled her, but now she calmly inspected the ground for clues. Kneeling in front of the farmhouse, she used a finger to trace around the outline of the huge impression left by a dragon frozen in the mud.

"M'lady. Over here," a man shouted.

She looked up from the track. "I'll be right there. I want … ."

"Hurry. We found one alive."

She leaped to her feet and ran to the smoking rubble of the out building where two men stood over an open root cellar door. About three feet down in a cavity half filled with straw and potato, carrots, and onions, a child huddled. The clothing was charred and a broad expanse of back, shoulder, and head were terribly burned, but the child still labored to breathe. Annel jumped into the pit picked him up and held him in her arms.

"Get ointment and a blanket from the saddle packs. We camp here tonight. Start a fire!" she shouted.

"M'lady, this place may not be safe," one of the men, named Karga, said.

"Move. Now." Her voice betrayed tense emotion that erupted from her controlled demeanor. The men obeyed without hesitation.

She held the child close, cradling it in the crook of her left arm. As she began to sing one of the peace songs she had learned in Meliandra, she held her right hand palm forward and circled it about six inches from the chest of the small body. Soft white light gathered in her palm and began to flow into the child. Almost immediately his breathing stabilized.

Kreigar approached the pit and knelt near the edge. At the same time Karga returned with the ointment and blankets. Little sunlight remained, and a cold wind began to kick up.

Annel stopped her canticle. "Kreigar, tell Gulth to circle above and warn us of any movement. I know this isn't the best location, but we'll need cover and a fire to heat water," she said.

"It'll be done." He turned to the other men. "Hop to it lads; ya heard Lady Annel. We need shelter an' fire. Two on at a time fer two hour watches 'til the morn breaks."

Already exhausted from a long day, Annel leaned back and rested her head against the dirt wall of the pit, humming the melody of the song, all the while continuing to minister with the soft light from her hand. She paused.

"As soon as the water is heated, I'll need it to clean the wounds. The ointment will help lessen the scarring. Make sure the men take some warm food tonight," she said.

"The men'll take care o' themselves. Will ya be alright, m'lady? Ya seem troubled more 'n usual," Kreigar said.

She felt her mouth go dry, and she blinked back tears. "I don't know what I'm doing here. For two months we've done nothing but bury remains of farmers. Farmers … what did they do to merit this kind of death?"

Kreigar met her gaze. "M' mother used ta tell me that when the storm on the sea gets rough, and clouds cover the stars, and the compass is spinnin'; ya have ta hang on 'til morn and look for yer path by the sun. I'm thinkin' that the morn may bring the direction ya need, but tonight ya need to save the life o' that child in yer arms."

Karga approached with a small pot of steaming water and some dressing cloth.

"Thank ya, Karga. I'll help the Lady Annel. Cover the bodies we found ta give 'em respect. We'll bury 'em in the morn. Get the men and horses bedded down," Kreigar said.

***

Widseth stretched out on his straw sleeping mat in the dark community cell. About forty men slept in each cell, and he could already hear the snores and night coughs of men whose bodies begged for rest. Efran's death lingered in Widseth's mind, spurring thoughts that would not let him sleep.

After about an hour, he rose from his mat and scanned the cell. The only light came from a small opening in the iron door where torchlight from the outer corridor spilled into the dark chamber, but Widseth scanned the entire spectrum with eyes accustomed to deciphering all light produced by any material object in the physical world. He could see the orange body heat from the other men and the olive hue from the straw mats and even the various shades of cobalt produced by the rock in the wall.

Without a sound he moved about and studied each man in the cell; if he found a malady, subdued white light issued from his palm and began the healing process. He knew two of the men would be dead by morning. He drew their spirits out of their bodies and comforted them. Speaking no audible words, he gave them hope and direction for the experience when the body would no longer support their life forces.

After two hours of ministering to each man, he returned to his mat. For a moment he bowed his head and thanked the powers of light. Then he reclined and meditated until he conjured a conduit of light, masked from the physical world. To his spiritual eyes it was a clear tunnel of surging light, lit by brilliant beacons, but the guards or any awakening prisoner would see nothing but a dark room. Widseth's physical body lay on the mat, but his spirit stepped into the channel and melded with the racing river of luminosity. The tunnel ended in a farmyard.

When he stepped out of the channel, he inspected the remains of the charred family covered by blankets, and then he knelt in the root cellar next to Annel, who held a young boy about seven years old. The burned child clung to her as she slept, overwhelmed by fatigue. Widseth noted other sleeping figures in the farmyard. Two men walked a perimeter around the small farm. He stretched his hand forward and stroked Annel's golden hair, but the strands did not move as they slipped through his light force. He had touched her cheek and kissed her brow so many times without her knowledge since he sent her to The Diadem for protection, but tonight he needed to give her more than that.

He used the cold light of the moon to conjure a sphere of silence and invisibility to avoid any interruption. Anyone looking at the root cellar would at most detect a faint shimmer skipping around the edge of the hole. He began to sing a beautiful peace song. The resonance caused light to flow into Annel and the boy.

Widseth ended the melody. "Sweet wife," he said. "Your skills are considerable, but let me help you heal this child. His infirmity is more than physical burns."

Only Annel's soft breathing answered.

He touched the child's brow with his finger and traced a pattern on his forehead. The boy's eyes fluttered open. He still clung to Annel, but he turned his head toward Widseth, and they locked gazes.

"What's your name?" Widseth asked.

"Sir, I'm Marcus," the boy answered.

"I'm Widseth. The woman who holds you is Annel. In the morning you'll remember me like a dream."

"I saw a dragon eat m' Da. An' then burned m' Ma and sis. M' big brother got away, and I hid here," Marcus said.

"Your brother died also," Widseth informed the boy. He hesitated and then said, "They are all here with me."

A man, a fifteen year old boy, and a woman holding a young girl in her arms appeared, standing on the edge of the root cellar.

Marcus reached up. "Da ... Ma ... Cristobal ... sis Elena ..." Annel stirred, but remained asleep.

"Marcus," the man said. "We enter the world o' light now. In time ya'll be with us, but not yet. Do as this man, Widseth, tells ya." A conduit of light formed, engulfing the four figures. The light closed around them, and they winked from sight.

Widseth cupped the small boy's cheek in his hand.

"They're protected," Widseth said. "Nothing can ever harm them again."

Marcus sniffled and snuggled next to Annel, hiding his face.

"In the morning, tell Annel that she needs to rouse the noble houses. The darkness has risen again," Widseth said. "An army must be raised to defend the land. Then she must take the battle to Misdara, but no army can enter there. Only a trusted few. Tell her that if all goes well, we shall then be reunited."

"Yes, master. I'll tell 'er."

"One last thing. Remind her to always trust the light."

Marcus nodded. Widseth moved his hand in a circular motion a few inches from the boy's face. His eyes closed and he slipped into sleep.

A quiet voice broke the moment of silence. Gulth, in dragon form, approached the root cellar.

"Master Widseth, you were most kind to comfort that boy."

"Hello, Gulth," Widseth said absently. Thoughts of Annel occupied his mind.

"Is there any progress at the mine?" Gulth asked.

"I've not yet found any trace of the crystal that I seek. The ancients called it the Eye of Light, and it's said that a dragon hid it in Bilbra after the fall of Misdara."

"To restore that legendary gem would do much to redeem the disgrace felt by the dragon-kind, but can you tell Annel nothing? She wrestles with despair," Gulth said.

Widseth bit his lip. He felt conflicted. "I know, but this is her time, and I have to obey to the will of the Unnamed One, or she will never learn who she is." He looked down, fearing that Gulth would guess the empty sorrow he felt by leaving Annel alone.

Widseth stood and stepped out of the root cellar. He put his hand on Gulth's large head and stroked the dragon. He made a motion through the air with his other hand, and the natural night noise returned to the farm.

"I have to go now," he whispered. "Thank you, dear friend, for the sacrifice you are making, safekeeping my precious wife. Guard her well." He stepped into the conduit of light.

"As always, Master Widseth."

***

Rin strutted along the parapet behind the stone battlement of the outer wall, followed by Brulon and two acolytes. Below him, outside the wall, men labored, digging wide trenches and filling them with jagged debris from the underground city that would slow any advancing army. In the cold morning sunlight Rin's breastplate gleamed. The armor had never needed adjustment, since Deorc fabricated it from a black metallic substance found in dark recesses near the underground river. For three years it had served as a second skin for Rin, adapting to his growth as a lean and lanky physique replaced his boyish frame. With the exception of the helm, he never removed the armor, even for sleep. Of late he slept less and less. He held the black helm, adorned with a miniature dragon and wings outstretched, under his arm. His red hair provided sharp contrast to the dark armor and black cloak. A dragon's head, embossed in silver, adorned the upper right quadrant of the breastplate.

To compliment his powerful physical image, Brulon and other selected teachers had instructed Rin on economic, social, and military skills. Always in the background, Deorc directed Rin's education, as he learned the Lower Magic proficiency that controlled dragons.

"I'm tired of killing farmers," Rin said. "When can we show our power and destroy one of the noble families who won't join us?"

"Patience, Lord Rin. Deorc will know the time," Brulon answered.

"I'll wait no longer. When Deorc returns, tell him I've taken three dragons and one of the companies of horsemen."

"Lord Rin, this is not ... ."

"Brulon, you forget yourself. My word is not to be questioned. I'll start with the Baron in that miserable caer near the farm we destroyed two days ago."

Rin knew his teacher seethed, but he took delight in putting the old man in his place. Rin turned and stared at Brulon. The metallic substance that composed his armor creaked like dry leather as it conformed to his movements.

"Go now and assemble twenty men with light armor on horse. I want them ready to depart within half an hour," Rin said.

The older man turned away. "As you command, Lord Rin."

The acolytes followed Brulon to the stairs. Rin watched as they descended to the courtyard below. Smug and satisfied, he turned to look out over the plain. He took a deep breath, tilted his head back, and began a guttural chant that carried from the wall to the plains below. Men stopped working and held their hands over their ears, fearing the enchantment of the raucous noise.

Within minutes five dragons rose into the air from small hillocks and depressions in the landscape. As Rin changed the pitch and cadence of the mantra, two dragons settled back into the countryside. Two sailed lazily high above, and the other one landed on a huge perch near Rin on the wall.

With expert hands Rin adjusted the harness on the creature and mounted. He donned his helmet and closed the visor. Grasping the control rods, he touched both sides of the dragon's neck, and the beast ascended. He knew it would take at least ten days with the horsemen to reach the noble's stronghold, but he did not want to destroy it. The dragons could do that. He wanted to take control and raise his standard. The three dragons circled until a company of men with a black standard flying in the breeze emerged from the gate and cantered across the causeway over the rubble filled trenches. Workers in the trenches looked up when they heard the hooves, but returned to work as whips began to snap in the morning air.

Rin looked down. *Better freedom as master than being a slave.* Deorc had said it was the way of life, and the name, Rin, would flood the world. *No reason to wait. No reason to fight freedom.* Rin embraced the freedom of his power. He signaled one of the dragons to fly ahead to scout the land.

***

Annel awoke with a start. She realized the child was gone and jumped to her feet.

"Easy, m'lady. The boy is over w' the men havin' a bite o' breakfast. We thought ta let ya sleep fer a bit." Kreigar reached his hand out and helped Annel step out of the root cellar.

She rubbed her eyes and yawned. All the gear had been packed on the horses, and only the barest essentials were left to stow. The men and a young boy sat at a small fire eating potatoes from the root cellar for breakfast.

The men stood as Annel approached, but the boy kneeled and kissed the hem of her cloak. Embarrassed, she reached down and helped him to stand.

"M'lady, he is a most gracious host," one of the men said. "We tried to give him some of our grain mush, but he would have none of that. He said he would give us the finest potatoes in the region. And I believe he has. Nothing has tasted so good in the last three years to me and the men."

He winked at Annel and nodded toward the boy. The boy stared at the ground until Annel reached down, lifted his chin, and looked into his brown eyes. Dark hair framed his pale complexion.

"On behalf of the men here, I thank you for a fine breakfast. What's your name?" Annel asked. The boy's spirit amazed her. He should have still exhibited the effects of his injuries and severe burns.

"I'm Marcus."

"Well, Marcus, let me have a quick look at the burns on your back." She lifted a shirt that one of the men had cut off and given him to wear, tied like a tunic at the waist with a scrap of material. Marcus stood patiently while she removed the dressing bandages. Perplexed, she stroked the smooth undamaged skin on his back.

"Kreigar," she said.

"I know. I inspected 'im this morn when he woke. Yer a mighty fine healer, ya are," he said.

"I don't understand. There should be some scarring." Annel forced a smile at Marcus. "You've no need of bandages. Put your shirt on." The healed burns puzzled her. It should have taken longer.

Marcus pulled on the oversized shirt and tied it at his waist.

"Come … eat a potata. They're the best in the Baron's realm," Marcus said.

Marcus motioned for her to sit on a log where he had piled some straw from the root cellar. It bothered her that the boy seemed unaware that his parents were dead. He must have seen terrible things. She delayed until everyone finished eating.

"Marcus, bad things happened yesterday. I'm sorry but we have to bury your family."

"Yeah, I know," he said. Tears stained his face. "I was jus' pretenin' that Da, Ma, Cristobal, and Elena were at the market sellin' the best potatas. An' I was here entertainin' fine folk. But I know the dragon ate m' Da and killed Ma and Elena and Cristobal." He stopped and buried his face in his hands.

Annel knelt in front of him. She wondered what the men would think, but when she looked around, they were all on their knees. Gulth knelt near the root cellar in human form. He had placed the family members carefully in the depression, and had begun to sing a powerful melody that invoked not only the sorrow of loss, but also the hope a new day. His voice resonated through the morning air warming and comforting everyone.

When he stopped, he placed a stone in the hollow and began to cover the bodies. The men rose and gathered stones and burned timbers to cover the grave. Marcus and Annel remained kneeling near the fire with heads bowed.

"We're finished, m'lady. There's no' a king in th' wide world that's had so fine a restin' place," Kreigar said.

Annel looked up. "Thank you, Kreigar. Have the men ready the horses."

"Yes, m'lady." Kreigar turned and shouted instructions to the men.

"Marcus, your family is safe now," she said.

"I know," he replied. "They came t' me last night in a dream. They tol' me they was safe, an' ta listen ta the man."

Annel almost stopped breathing. She closed her eyes. She felt her heart beating, as the world stopped around her. She clenched her hands until she knew without looking that her knuckles were white. She could only hope.

Opening her eyes, she asked, "What man?"

"I can't remember his name, but he tol' me ta tell ya some things. He said to wake the nobles 'cause they need armies ta fight th' darkness," Marcus said. "Then he said about Misdara or someplace, but I can't remember. It was somethin' about no armies can go there. Maybe I'll remember better later."

"Who's the lord over this land? Who's the baron who has the best potatoes in the land?" she asked.

"Da used to pay potatas fer tax to Baron Aelan O'Dai. I been ta the Baron's caer only twice. It's a mighty stronghold wi' maybe twenty warriors."

"How far to the Baron's keep?"

"Wi' the potata cart an' ox it took four days, but ya got horses, so maybe only two days on the north trail."

Annel called the men to gather around. When they assembled, she bowed before them.

When she rose, she said, "You have faithfully discharged your duty from the obligation placed upon you by King Fyan. You've assisted me to find my quest. I release you to return to your families with a charge that you advise King Fyan that the darkness has risen again here on the plains. May the light speed your paths, and may the dragons of light guard your footsteps. Thank you for the service rendered to me."

None of the men moved.

"I will scout ahead," Gulth said. He nodded to the men as he walked toward the north trail out of the farmyard.

Kreigar stepped forward. "We're all one ship m'lady. Ya can't tell the starboard half to bid farewell ta the port half without sinkin' the ship. Some o' these men lost family in the wars in the north jus' like young Marcus here. We'll not be turnin' tail, tryin' ta flee the storm. No, m'lady, we're turnin' the rudder ta keep us into the wind. And that be that."

Annel examined each of the men. Resolute faces repeated 'that be that' with no words exchanged.

"Thank you for your support. Kreigar, I need you to rendezvous with the other scout parties at the prearranged spot toward the marshes. Meet us in Caer O'Dai. Karga, take one man with you and find the best route to Standel. King Fyan must be made aware of events here. The rest of you will come with me to the stronghold of this baron. We'll seek help there or at least find family for Marcus."

The men stirred to swift motion with cold military precision. They were legendary northern rangers. These men had served with Fyan through the horrors at Falcon Ridge. They were common men from Beltor, Vindry, and Marhome, who had cultivated uncommon courage and honor. They had faced overwhelming odds and survived dragons.

Conflict produces sorrow. Sometimes wars involve bitter skirmishes and battles where both sides lose several times before the final outcome. The victorious army, most often, is willing to endure sorrow one more time than the vanquished. Remember nations and individuals are not dissimilar. Conflict within a person produces casualties, and victory for the individual depends how well he or she copes with sorrow. It is seldom injurious to remember what is lost, but it can be devastating to dwell upon it.

> *From the Teachings of Leanna, Master Mentor, of the Abbey de Testrey—found in the Library of Vindry*

Chapter 6. Annel's Lament

"Hold. What's yer business in Caer O'Dai?" the guard inquired.

His apprehensive mannerisms alerted Annel that something was amiss. The sentry's hand had moved too quickly to his sword hilt when he saw Annel and the six rangers as they approached the gate into the castle complex. The guard relaxed his stance when he saw the child, Marcus, in front of Annel on the horse.

The old stronghold had been built on a hillock on the northern plains, overlooking the river, a few day's travel south of the marshes. The caer stood in the center of an increasing concentration of farms that had eventually evolved into a town surrounding the fortified walls. Annel studied the ancient design and workmanship of the gate and portcullis housing. It reminded her of the massive gates at Dragada.

"We seek audience with the Baron Aelan O'Dai. We've important news," Annel replied.

The guard scanned each individual. At length he motioned for them to remain outside the gate, and he retreated inside the compound. In a few minutes he returned accompanied by a tall man with blonde hair. The clothing he wore announced station and class.

"I am Perigreen, the Baron's regent. You look to be honest folk, but what could common travelers have to say that would interest the Baron?" he asked.

Undaunted, Annel replied, "Of necessity we travel your lands to find the roots of a growing evil. I prefer to say no more, but these men are northern rangers of Standel. The least of them is held in high renown. They held faith in the worst of circumstances in the Great War."

"Worthy of a tale at the feast tonight, but who are you m'lady? And why do you grace the halls of O'Dai? And how is it you speak for men who seem to hold you in respect?"

Annel lifted Marcus to the ground and dismounted. She bowed before Perigreen. "Lord Perigreen, I must speak with the Baron. I can say nothing more."

"The Baron returned late from hunting boar in the north near the marshes. He yet sleeps today, but I extend our welcome and invite you to stay the night. Tonight we mark the turn of seasons from winter to spring. We welcome you to share our table and the songs and tales that will be sung. Perhaps one of you can share a tale of wonder of the northland. I cannot promise he will speak with you, but I can extend the simple hospitality of Caer O'Dai."

Perigreen turned and walked through the gate, motioning them to follow. Stewards met them and stabled the horses in a barn by the blacksmith shed just inside the walls of the castle. Annel held Marcus' hand and followed Perigreen toward an inner compound.

She scanned the outer wall defenses, and concluded it would be a mere formality to an invading force. The general deterioration of the ramparts disappointed her. Most of the old barracks' compound had been converted to a produce and livestock market, and merchants were beginning to stream through the gate to set up stalls to sell their wares. In the huge open area between the outer wall and the inner compound, men toiled to set up large pavilion tents around a complex of fire pits. She guessed that half the town might attend the celebration to observe the arrival of spring. Even in the cool winter morning, the merchants appeared festive and ready for a good day.

"How old is your child?" Perigreen asked.

The question startled Annel. "Oh, he isn't my child. We found him at one of the farms to the south. His family was ... ."

She stopped herself, but Perigreen pursued the answer. "His family was what?"

"They were loyal subjects to the Baron and paid taxes with potatoes," Annel answered.

"Potatoes? What's this about potatoes?" Perigreen asked.

"I come to pay m' tax, m'lord." Marcus dug into a pocket and held out a potato in his hand. "Ya can have it now, if you'll help us."

The tall man looked at the slender boy, and then he bent down, almost kneeling, until his eyes were level with Marcus'. Discomfort settled in Annel. She knew the man would get the information he desired.

"And how is it that the Baron can help you?"

"It was a dragon. A dragon killed m' family. Ya gotta stop it, or it'll kill lots more," Marcus said.

"Dragons," he said. Perigreen looked up at Annel. "And this is what you want to see the Baron about?"

Annel felt like a child no older than Marcus who had been caught stealing sweets from a street vendor. She nodded her head, but had no idea how Perigreen might react.

Perigreen took the potato from Marcus' hand. "Well, you've paid your tax. Now you've a right to the Baron's protection. Tonight before the celebration, I'll arrange an audience."

Annel smiled as relief flooded her.

"Thank you, Lord Perigreen," she said.

"Please follow me into the inner complex. There are rooms where you may rest."

***

In the open field, wood in the fire pits had burned down to hot coals, and the smell of roasting boar and beef permeated the late afternoon air. All afternoon revelers from the surrounding area had begun to fill the compound between the outer wall and the inner castle. Musicians, jugglers, and acrobats punctuated the festive atmosphere as the populace bid farewell to winter and welcomed spring. Actors and puppeteers had entertained children and adults alike with love stories, quests, and ribald nonsense.

Annel had taken Marcus to some of the festivities to divert his mind and entertain him, but now she stood with her hands on his shoulders, flanked by the rangers of Standel, in front of an outdoor throne under a pavilion. Baron Aelan O'Dai sat on the throne. Although balding, he appeared to be a young man in good condition, as if used to pursuing physical activities. He seemed annoyed that an audience had been scheduled before the official commencement of the feast. At first Annel thought he was an incompetent fool, until she noticed his astute green eyes studying each of them in turn under the guise of complaining to Perigreen about the audience.

"Perigreen tells me you've come a distance to tell me something. So tell me." The Baron's attitude established no standard for civility.

By his tone of voice, Annel knew this impromptu meeting irritated him, but she calmed her inner uncertainty and decided to stick to the plan she discussed with the men on the trip from Marcus' farm.

"My Lord Baron Aelan O'Dai, regent for the Emperor Padwalar the Third of Dol Ismus, I bring greetings from King Fyan of Standel and the High King and Queen of the Aelfen in Dragada," she announced. She noticed Aelan's eyes narrowed when she mentioned Dragada.

"Those are a lot of words that mean little here on the plains. The emperor is nigh a thousand miles away," he said. "And I've no need of greetings from any king of Standel or Dragada. Dragada and the Aelfen are myths to tell children around the fire at night. Maybe you can tell us a tale tonight at the feast, or perhaps I should put you in the dungeon because you trespass on my lands without my leave."

He looked around at Perigreen and laughed as if he had made a joke.

Annel continued, "We seek only to serve you, m'lord. Our purpose is to thwart dark attempts to gain a foothold by evil that was not destroyed in the northern wars and has surfaced here on the grasslands of the south."

The Baron held his hand up. "You can entertain us with tales of war and evil later tonight when the bards sing. It's been a hard winter, but I see no evil. You bring a boy who claims dragons killed his family. Perigreen told me. For this I'm sorry, but more like, it was one of the giant marsh lizards that strayed onto the prairie."

"And do giant marsh lizards fly and use fire?" Annel asked. "These men beside me can track field mice. A dragon landed and burned the farm. We're lucky Marcus survived."

Aelan broke off eye contact and looked out of the pavilion at the crowds gathering near the fire pits.

"I have duties to perform. You are welcome to join us for the four day feast," he said. "We will talk later."

Annel swallowed her disappointment. "Yes m'lord."

The Baron stood, nodded to Annel, and walked into the crowd, greeting commoner, merchant, and landowner alike. As Annel watched him, she realized that even though he had treated her with little regard, he loved his people, and more important, they loved him.

***

Three days of games and feasting had helped lift Marcus' spirits, but Annel found no joy in the celebrations. Quiet sorrow depressed her. She sat staring at a cup of sage tea at the guest table just to the right of the Baron's high feast table where the best entertainers and bards would provide the night's amusement. Throughout the compound, groups of people gathered to hear minstrels sing and act out tales of wonder and comedy around at least fifty campfires. Unseasonably warm weather had graced the holiday, but Annel's mood did not fit with the festive spirit. She had tried to provide a happy diversion for Marcus with all the activities, but her inability to talk with the Baron frustrated her. He avoided her. Every time she approached, he excused himself to assist with one of the common people.

"Your furrowed brow could be read many ways."

Annel looked up. She recognized the man who had spoken to her. He had sung and played for the Baron's guests each night of the celebration. He was Angus the royal bard. His bright eyes matched his smile. Annel noted his long slender fingers that had commanded the stringed instrument he used in his musical presentations. The songs he had sung betrayed knowledge of history and events in the world beyond the prairie.

"May I join you?" he asked.

She nodded assent.

"M'lady, if I may say it, you look as though you grieve at a funeral instead of three days of feasting."

She tried to smile, but the corners of her mouth wavered. "Maybe it is a funeral," she replied.

"How so m'lady? We welcome spring, the season of promise and hope. It's been a hard winter, and there have been unusual happenings that can't be explained, but look at the people. They know their lives will continue, and they abandon melancholy better than you, a noble woman leading six rangers from the north."

The rangers sat, conversing in low tones at a nearby table.

"We've heard of them, you know," Angus said. "A man from Dimron visited the hearth last year and sang the praises of these rangers. Why does a woman lead them?"

Annel looked away and avoided the question. Dusk began to encroach, and the servants began to light the tall torches that surrounded the compound. Campfires and oil lanterns throughout the complex provided ample light for the evening activities. The almost full moon, pasted against a backdrop of stars, adorned a perfect night. Temperatures had risen in the last few days and signs of spring flourished. From the past two nights she knew the celebration would linger long into the night.

"Tell me master bard ... the tale you sang last night about the fall of Misdara ... can you tell me more?" she asked.

"Not much. It is an old song handed from father to son for two maybe two and a half thousand years. When Misdara ruled, it was the Age of Beauty." He fell silent for a moment, reflecting on something. "No written records reach back to that time, but it is said three Aelfene kingdoms existed—Taina, the crystal pyramid, Dragada, the crystal palace, and Misdara, the caverns of crystal wonder. Taina passed from the knowledge of men, Dragada fell into darkness, and Misdara, the greatest of all, is an empty ruin filled with evil shades that wander the caverns."

He stopped and waited for Annel to respond, but she remained silent.

"I've talked with your men hoping to get scraps of stories to construct a tale to be sung honoring your visit, but they are a silent lot. It took the better part of a day for one of them, Ferron I believe, to finally answer my questions about their unusual armor. He said it was fabricated from the scales of dragons killed in a battle. That is quite a tale. I am not sure I can give much credence to that one. I think the armor is a sculpted and dyed hide from a cow."

Annel looked at the men who had become her constant companions.

She smiled. "I've found that most men who dare great things are reluctant to speak about them, and they do not lie about them. You see the two at the end of the table, Ferron and Hector. They are cousins from Vindry near Standel."

"Is there really a library there with records back to the last age?"

Annel nodded. "Ferron's father is a caretaker in the library. And the man in the blue cloak is Lambert. He is from Marhome. The other three, Pelton, Wallace, and Carston are knights of Beltor. All serve King Fyan."

Angus shook his head, and Annel read the amazement on his face.

"You name places that I have dreamt of visiting so I could sing their tales at the campfires of our people," he said.

Annel sat in silence. She remembered her youth in Eventop when she heard names of foreign places in the market place and at the inns. The travelers had always appeared strange with their customs and clothing that seemed so exotic. She had never supposed she would leave Eventop, let alone travel to other cities and lands with mysterious sounding names.

"You announced to the Baron that you brought greeting from the High King and Queen of the Aelfen in Dragada," Angus said. "What did you mean by that? If the Aelfen ever existed they are long in their graves. I think they are mostly legend and story, sung around the campfires at night. Brave men seeking treasure have traveled to Misdara, but there is nothing left but ruins of a gate into a hill and an impassible tunnel filled with rubble. Someone may have started to change legend to reality and make a city there, but their efforts ended about twenty feet into the hillside."

Flickering torch and lantern light caused shadows to dance around the campfires. Annel spotted the Baron and his retinue weaving through the fire pits in the middle of the compound toward the high feast table. His amiable manner with his subjects impressed her.

"Dragons of Light have returned to Dragada. The Aelfen are gathering there." Annel's eyes shown in the firelight as she spoke. As her thoughts turned to her husband, Widseth, she licked her lips and blinked away a tear. Angus appeared not to notice.

"No living man has seen a dragon, despite what you or that ranger, Ferron, says. They are in all the tales to be sure, but alive, in the world today? No, m'lady, I cannot accept that."

Annel was about to answer, but she hesitated.

"Master Angus, is there something beyond the south wall that would cause that glow in the sky?" Annel pointed to a reddish hue rising above the compound wall.

Angus looked where she pointed.

"I have never seen anything ... ." He started to reply, but she cut him off and stood up, gazing at the crowd and the skyline. She spotted a man running toward her through the crowd. She scanned the throng for Marcus. As Gulth approached in human form, the rangers rose as one and scrutinized the sky. The ruddy glow rose higher above outer wall. Gulth reached Annel's table and bowed to her.

"M'lady, they are here—at least twenty on horse and three dragons. They have fired the town at the southern edge, outside the wall near the river," Gulth said.

Annel continued to search the multitude of people gathered around the campfires.

"M'lady, who is this man?" Angus asked.

Those words snapped her to reality.

"Master Angus, this is the first dragon you have ever seen. Gulth, get into the air. No mercy—take the dragons out. Ferron, get the men on horse," she shouted. "You have to stop the mounted men outside the outer gate. Go."

"M'lady, we'll not leave you."

"I command it. There is no force here, except you that can stop them outside the gate. Go now."

The ranger saluted and motioned for the others to follow him. Following Gulth, they ran through the crowd toward the barn.

"Angus, we need to avoid panic if possible, but tell the Baron to get archers on the wall and footmen at the gate. The darkness is at your door."

Angus looked stunned.

"M'lady, what is happening?"

She pointed in the direction she had seen the Baron earlier. "I saw him over there earlier. Just find him."

"But your clothes ..."

Annel looked down. Flames from the torches reflected off the golden tunic and pants. The blouse shimmered as if it emitted moonlight, and the rich maroon cloak transmitted some sort of energy that caused goose bumps to rise on her arms. The fabric appeared to generate and emit light.

"Find him," she said.

As she ran into the multitude, calling for Marcus, a man ran through the main gate shouting that there was a fire in the town. People began running in every direction. Some tried to get groups organized to find buckets so they could bring water from the river, but for the most part, the mass of people became a random wave pushing and shoving against the confines of the outer wall. As people spurted through the gate most of them ran in the direction of their own home rather than in groups to fight the fire. Annel could see Gulth and the men of Standel caught in the confused throng. She lost sight of them when they finally slipped through the gatehouse, but she heard the wild call to arms as the knights of Beltor sounded their battle horns.

Men at arms within the compound mulled about, uncertain as to their course of action. A few mounted the walls to view the spectacle. All around men shouted contradictory orders. Annel heard panicked screams that began outside the south wall. A bellow resounding through the night air, warning her of what approached, and in the same moment she spied Marcus. The Baron carried a child in his arms and six or seven other children ran with him. She could see him guiding them toward the gate of the inner castle, but Marcus stood rooted to the ground. As he pointed to the south wall, she followed his line of sight, and then she broke into a run.

A huge creature that looked like the ugly combination of a serpent and a monstrous hunting hawk perched on the wall. Large leathery yellow scales with green edges glistened in the firelight. A horrendous bellow shook the night as the creature extended its wings and expelled fire and smoke from its gaping jaws into the crowd below, not one hundred paces from Marcus. The beast began to climb down into the complex, crushing and burning anything in its path.

***

As soon as the rangers and Gulth escaped the crush at the gatehouse, they slipped between the houses and down a small lane that ran parallel to the main approach to the gate. Gulth transformed into the beautiful golden dragon and rose into the air. Ferron took command.

"Hector, take Lambert and Wallace. Get on the other side of the street in the shadows. Pelton, Carston, you're with me. Take as many out with the bows as possible. Shoot and move. Use your shields. There may be dragon fire. To it men. No quarter tonight. These people have no defense but us. Let's give them a song to sing at their next holiday."

Three men on horseback slipped across the main avenue and into the shadows between the small buildings on the other side. Men, women, and children ran in every direction from the castle, but, after a time, some began running back toward the gatehouse. Screams pierced the night, and Ferron heard hooves on the graveled road. The smell of smoke filled his lungs. Fear hung heavy in the air. Riders in dark livery rounded a corner and advanced toward the gate of the outer wall.

Arrows flew as one, and four of the advancing men fell from their horses. Another quick flight of arrows and three more died. The other men dismounted and used their horses for shields. A few slipped into the back alleys, but the main group formed a shield wall and moved into the shadows on the left side of the street. One more man died from an arrow, but shields blocked the other shots.

To draw them back into the light, Ferron stepped out of the shadows. He raised his sword in challenge, but the air stirred into a foul gust from a dragon beating its wings. Sand and debris swirled, and trails of smoke obscured the moon. Ferron choked when he breathed the acrid vapor, but reflexes born of experience took over. He raised his shield above his head in time to deflect the fiery blast from the descending dragon, but he could not parry the beast's sharp talons that ripped into his shoulder and pulled him off his feet.

The creature landed in the middle of the road and played with Ferron like a cat with a mouse, pulling him closer to its jaws. Although groggy, Ferron saw two arrows strike the dragon in the underbelly and neck. He recognized Hector standing over him slashing at the beast. Amid the smoke and ruin, he thought he saw the others in hand to hand fighting with the invaders. A battle horn sounded above the grunts and bellows of the dragon. Ferron tasted the dust of the ground, as darkness overran his mind, and his blood mixed with the gravel in the roadway.

***

Perigreen and ten armed men pushed through the crowd at the gate and ran toward the blazes raging in the south section. The town was not large, and from his vantage he could see most of the fires were at the edge near the old market by the river docks. He and the men raced along the road at the base of the wall until they turned on the south road toward the docks. As others saw Lord Perigreen running toward the fires, they began to join until a sizable number followed after him. Along the way they scoured yards and broke into homes grabbing buckets, basins, pans—anything that would hold water.

When they arrived at the square, Perigreen organized a line from the river to the fires. The people rallied behind him and gradually they were able to stop the advance of the flames toward the docks, but he noticed a dark shadow cross the moon, and then an immense creature with a raucous croak plummeted toward the square. Fear seized him. He knew all these people would die and there was nothing to be done but wait. The water lines began to break as people noticed the dragon and ran into the shadows.

As the creature descended, Perigreen observed a man in black armor in a leather harness just in front of the wings. The dark figure controlled the beast. *Caer O'Dai after hundreds of years of existence would be destroyed. It would become another ruin on the plains.*

A blinding flash filled the night sky and a low pitched musical tone filled the air. Perigreen shrank back, when he turned and saw another dragon careening toward the first beast. The light from the fires reflected off brilliant golden scales, as the second dragon intercepted the first and blasted it with magical energy. A fireball exploded in the night sky, and Perigreen's hair stood on end as energy filled the air.

Watching from below, he witnessed a delicate aerial ballet of strike and counter. Repeated blasts of fire and energy illuminated the sky, and amazement filled him as the dragons swooped at one another like huge kites on a windy day. Without any doubt the golden dragon held the advantage, but abruptly it hesitated and dove toward the main road to the gate. The other dragon with the rider wheeled and sped into the darkness of the southern sky away from the caer.

Perigreen made a quick decision. He left a man to organize the water line again, and took all the armed men with him toward the main road to the gate.

***

"Run, Marcus, run," Annel shouted as she sprinted toward him.

But Marcus stood like an immovable statue cemented in place. By the time she reached him, the dragon had approached within fifty feet. She scooped the boy up and ran after the Baron who had just entered the inner gates with the other children. The Baron shouted something, but it was lost in the din.

As she looked over her shoulder, she glimpsed the dragon closing, and then she felt the concussive blast of heat, as flames engulfed her and Marcus, but her cloak shielded and diverted the fire. She stumbled and fell to the ground. When she arose, she pulled Marcus to his feet and stood with her back to the dragon between him and the beast.

"I remember the dream. His name was Widseth, and he said to use the light," Marcus screamed.

"Run to the Baron. You've helped more than you know. Run." Annel stood and slowly turned to meet the gaze of the dragon. Marcus dashed toward the inner gate.

In a clear voice she began to sing a peace song. The melody rippled across the open compound, and the dragon appeared bound by the calm atmosphere for a short time, but after a few minutes, it snorted and bellowed. It shook its massive head as if trying to get rid of an irritant. Annel knew her attempt to control the dragon had failed. She had not mastered Widseth's skill, but she assumed the beast would try to kill her before destroying the rest of the stronghold because she represented the only threat.

Thinking to draw the monster away from the inner compound, she ran to the center of the campfires away from where many had taken refuge. Her heart pounded insider her, and she tried to calm the adrenalin rush. She stood alone, and the dragon towered above her. Her hope hung on a slender thread—Gulth. Perhaps he would see and come to her aid, but no assistance arrived before the dragon expectorated smoke and fire.

She grabbed the left hem of her cloak and threw it up in front of her face to protect her as it had when she carried Marcus, but a piece of the cloak ripped off in her hand. She assumed the magical nature that had protected them had expired, but the cloth in her hand solidified and shaped into a medium sized shield. In an instant a blue aura from the shield deflected the fire. The dragon roared in rage, and the keening wail of the monster penetrated the ears of everyone within the compound. The sweep of the creature's tail caught Annel off guard and knocked her off her feet. Immediately the dragon batted her. She felt talons ripping at the fabric of the clothing she wore, but the cloth became adamant and protected her. She flew twenty paces through the air, and the force of her landing collapsed the high feast table. She remained still amid the debris of the table, trying to determine if she could stand. The dragon lumbered toward the gate of the inner compound.

Her ribs were sore, but Annel pushed herself up, amazed that she still lived. Her right knee had taken the brunt of the fall, and pain shot through her as she took her first few steps. As the dragon moved toward the inner gate, a horse that had escaped from the barn distracted it. When it cornered and killed the horse, it gave Annel time to hobble to the gate. She stood defiant as the dragon approached.

"I am Annel, queen of Dragada, high queen of the Aelfen. I forbid your entrance here."

The dragon snorted and breathed fire. The blast threw her back against the closed gate, but the shield diffused most of the heat and energy. *Use the light.* Marcus' words repeated in her mind. *She had to save these people.* She focused all her thought to pierce the realm of high magic, and as she dodged the wild swipe of the dragon's talons, she sensed a pressure building within her mind. Without any warning, her sight penetrated the dominion of high magic, and the harmonics of the eternal worlds permeated her being. In an instant she sensed intense power and the ability to use light in ways she had never considered.

Raw talent surged, and light coursed through her. She could see in all directions at once as every cell in her body perceived light, and her brain processed and catalogued every detail. Light showered from every conceivable direction and filled her. All the empty feelings generated by her life as a young girl in Eventop and the separation from Widseth were filled to bursting. Light erupted and flowed from her in waves, producing almost giddy energy.

Time slowed at her command, and she examined everything in her vicinity. Nothing moved as she stopped the environment around her. This dragon was a spawn of the material world. Unlike Gulth, it had never been in the world of light. There would be no reasoning with it because its intelligence was little more than that of a dog, more driven by instinct and command than by self will. She pointed her finger and extinguished the grass and structure fires within the outer compound that the dragon had started. She touched her knee and relieved the throbbing pain.

Turning her back to the dragon, she raised her hand. Blue spider webbing sprang from her fingertips and enclosed the gatehouse and turrets of the inner compound. Satisfied that Marcus and the other children would be safe, she turned to face the dragon.

She calmed the exuberant emanations of light that spasmodically jumped from her like mini lightening bolts. She drew her long dagger from its sheath.

"I sorrow that I must kill you, but there's no other way, and honor demands that I release you from the time bondage," Annel shouted at the dragon. She motioned with her hand, and the environment returned to normal speed.

The creature raised its head and roared. A few arrows from the turrets of the inner compound struck the dragon, but only one penetrated the beast's hide. The ruddy yellow scales outlined in green mirrored the torchlight of the compound. The dragon spewed fire at the archers, but the flames crackled as they collided with the magical blue netting. A myriad of sparks showered back to the earth.

Annel took her chance while the dragon concentrated on the archers. She rushed the creature and drove the dagger between two scales in the neck just above the collar bone as the monster extended upward toward the turrets. The creature thrashed violently throwing her to the ground.

The armor protected her somewhat, but she felt a snap in the bones of her shield arm, and the wonderful shield lay on the ground at her feet. As she bent to pick it up, she gritted her teeth and tried to conjure magical protection, but the dragon batted her again like a rag doll. She spit blood and tried to cover herself with the cloak to protect from fire, but the left side of the cloak ripped, and a long sword, sheathed in blue flame, appeared in her hand.

She rose from her knees and met the dragon's headlong rush with sword in hand. She had never trained with a sword, and she felt it was an awkward thrust, but she imbedded the blade to the hilt into the underbelly. The dragon flailed backward, beating at the blue flame of the sword with its talons. It shrieked a high pitched wail that pierced the night. The azure flame engulfed and began to consume the beast. It thrashed for several minutes until only irregular twitches of the tail marked any movement.

Annel sank to her knees and fell forward. As she slipped into exhausted darkness, she heard the horns of Beltor in the distance. For some reason she thought Widseth caressed her cheek.

She heard someone.

A young voice said, "She's over here."

Looking up, she saw a small boy running toward her.

"Marcus, you're safe."

Music with wild and beautiful harmony filled her mind as the eternal symphony of high magic gathered all the vibrations of the night, including the minor chords of darkness created by the dragons, and wove them into the fabric that would define the events of this night in the eternal world. She slipped into unconsciousness.

***

Annel opened her eyes. The dreams had seemed so real. The dragon hovered over her. No, it was a woman, an old woman. Annel winced when she tried to sit up in the bed, but sank back into the pillows.

"M'lady, please don't get up. Yer ribs are still a might tender, I'm sure. You're black and blue on yer whole left side an' that arm and knee will take two months, if a day, to heal."

Annel felt faint, but when she fixed her eyes on the old woman to establish a point of reference, a symbol on the woman's dress drew her attention. It was the same symbol as the clasp that had held her cloak—two opposed dragons entwined around a staff. The bedclothes were unfamiliar. Her clothes hung on hooks on the opposite wall. The beautiful maroon cloak draped over a hanger appeared undamaged, but now she could see without any trouble magical emanations in the outline of a shield on the left side of the cloak. The right side was folded under, but she assumed she would see a sword there within the fabric.

Annel's tongue stuck to the roof of her mouth.

"May I have some water?" she asked.

"Fer sure, m'lady. I'll get it straight out." The woman scurried out of the room.

Annel closed her eyes and tried to take a deep breath, but the excruciating pain almost paralyzed her breathing. She took several short breaths. When she opened her eyes, Gulth stood over her.

"Gulth," she whispered.

"Easy, m'lady. I have tried to assist you, but the healer … ."

"How many days?"

"Two, m'lady, but … ."

"How are the men?"

Gulth looked away and replied, "Before I could get there, the dragon got Hector. He gave the dragon a killing stroke with his sword, but he slipped and the dragon raked him with talons. He died of grievous wounds while defending his cousin, Ferron. Ferron lost a lot of blood, but he should recover. The healers here use good technique." Gulth paused. "I am sorry, m'lady, that I was not able to save him."

Annel swallowed a lump in her throat. She nodded her head.

"There are costs to everything. Sometimes the results of sacrifices are beyond our vision, and all we see is sorrow." She paused. She had trouble speaking, and bowed her head and held her hands over her eyes. Grief filled her.

"There were three dragons, the one you killed, the one Hector killed, and the one that escaped with a rider," Gulth continued.

Annel looked up. "A rider, you say?"

"Yes, m'lady. The rider was Rin. I do not know if he recognized me, but when he tried to control me, I recognized him."

"Control you? How could he think to control you?"

"He has been trained. All three dragons were under his command," Gulth said. "It is as Widseth feared. He confided in me that he thought Deorc would train Rin to become a Dragon Master. The three dragons were spawn of this world, and they were little more than beasts. None of them had ever been to the world of light, but I fear there are dragons of light, like Deorc, who have fallen into darkness, and may serve Rin with vast knowledge and ancient powers. None of the men who rode with the dragons survived. Our men would have saved at least one to question, but Lord Perigreen and some of the Baron's men arrived, and before they could be stopped, they killed the invaders."

"I have to get up. The Baron has to send riders." She tried to sit up again, but pain racked her chest. Gulth restrained her and assisted her to lie back down.

"Riders were sent yesterday to other nobles in the area, and Kreigar arrived this morning with the other patrols."

The old woman entered the room with a water pitcher and cup.

"What are ya doing in here? I told ya to stay out. I don't care if they say ya're a dragon—ya're a nuisance. Get out. Get out," she said to Gulth.

The golden man bent near Annel and slipped something under the covers.

"It is the salve from your saddle bags," he whispered. "I am sure it will help in the healing."

Annel forced a smile, but her thoughts plunged into sorrow for Hector, and the people killed by the dragons, and Rin.

As close as you are to my mother and have been to me, I cannot find words to express my grief. I have never known a day in my life without Hector, and now there shall never be a day that thoughts of him do not enter my mind. When I saw him standing over me, as my blood spilled on the ground, I felt safe. Others told me that after I lost consciousness, he fought like a true dragon slayer and mortally wounded the dark beast. His story will live among the heroic tales of this arena we call life. He will now walk with the children of light protected by dragons of light in the eternal world.

> *Excerpt from a letter by Ferron to Hector's mother*

Chapter 7. Arena

The snap of the whip resounded through the cell. Men awoke to the stench of sweat and straw thinly masking the disgusting odor of open latrines near the rock walls. Widseth stood and surveyed the guards and other slaves.

"Get the body wagon. There's two dead here," a guard said to one of the other sentinels. "You four carry 'em out." He pointed to a group of men near the door who were rolling their straw mats. The men hastened to obey.

Widseth rolled his mat and stowed it in a corner. After a few minutes, the men began to shuffle toward the door and outer compound where they would be served the standard mush and crust of bread for the morning and noon meals. After the meal, work would begin again in the sluice pits a half mile from the prison cells.

"Your name is Widseth, is it not?"

Widseth turned and looked at the speaker. He recognized the thin man. His slight stature set him apart from the others, and his dark eyes shifted nervously. He had arrived at the mines within the previous month. The other slaves had mocked him because he spoke as a well schooled noble, and the guards had treated him like a man infected with the pox.

"Yes, I am Widseth, but I don't think I know your name."

"Of course not. I am no one you would remember, but my name is Almaron third removed heir to the dukedom of Rabala." He bowed with a flourish. "My family claims distant relationship to the duchess of Tabul. I saw you at the Emperor's palace in Tabul when you were judged."

"We can't stop to talk. We need to keep moving to get our food for today," Widseth said. "We'll have a few minutes there to talk before going to the sluice pits."

As the men exited the stone compound into the bright sun, they hurried to the tables where other prisoners dispensed their daily rations. Men from eight other compounds joined in the open area surrounded by a rock fence. The sun's early intensity announced a miserable day ahead. Shrewd prisoners looked around for extra water flasks they could steal to supplement their personal supplies. After they received their rations, a constant procession streamed to fill their water containers in the fresh brook that ran through the compound.

Almaron stayed right behind Widseth. After they filled their water bottles, Widseth spoke.

"I know who you are. You were one of the priests who came to the manor, and you sat with the High Inquisitor at the judgment seat in Tabul."

"So adroitly you have unmasked me. It is as they say; you wield high magic of the Aelfen. Is it true you are an oracle? Can you see events before they happen?"

"I see many things, but there is one thing I can't see. Why are you here, prelate of the Emperor?"

"After Tabul ... I mean after your tribunal, I began to wonder at the feelings I felt as you stood before us. It bothered me for over a year, and I began to investigate any writings about the Aelfen that I could find. At the same time there began to be rumors of the return of the Cult of the Brazen Serpent."

Widseth narrowed his eyes and studied Almaron, as he chewed the handful of pasty grain mush he had been given. He took a swallow of water from the water bladder he had filled in the brook.

"Rumors? What kind of rumors?" Widseth asked.

"Well, holy men came into the city. Many began to follow them. Of course we had them driven out, but 'converts' followed them into the wilderness." Almaron looked away for a minute before continuing. "I followed one of them to learn more about them for the Emperor, rather the High Inquisitor, but I did not experience the sentiment with them that I felt when you were before us. They had power, but it was dark. I recognized it because I had been taught in its rudimentary uses as a priest for the Emperor."

Widseth nodded his head. He looked toward the tables, where some guards intervened in a small fracas between two men.

"We don't have much time for talk. Why are you here? As a priest of the Emperor, you're out of place."

"I had to find the truth. The Brazen Serpent priests offered nothing, and I could find nothing more about the Aelfen in the manuscript halls in Tabul or Dol Ismus, but I found a reference to a great library in Vindry. It took nearly a year. In the time I spent there, I learned as much as anyone knows about the Aelfen and about you."

"And what is it you think you know?" Widseth asked.

"Not nearly enough, but when I returned to Tabul and tried to teach the priests the truth about you, I found unwavering loyalty to error. They sent me here for heresy."

"To every truth in the world, there is a counterfeit," Widseth said. "Some emulate the truth so well they are almost impossible to detect. The architects of these counterfeits carefully drag individuals and societies toward obscurity for their own ends. The shadows in Tabul are nothing compared to the darkness building on the plains in Misdara."

Widseth looked away when one of the guards began to shout directions to the men milling about eating and filling their water containers. He and Almaron moved closer to receive their instructions for the day.

"Ten diggers were killed yesterday in the mines. A tunnel caved in on the fools. I need ten replacements. We'll start w' you, and you, and you. Take this whole lot up to the diggers' camp."

Guards separated out Widseth and nine others, including Almaron.

"Yer gonna die, but nobody'll see in the dark," one of the prisoners yelled at them.

"Nah, the cave creatures'll get 'em first," another said.

"Take a good look; ya'll never see the sun again. In a month's time ya'll be a bunch a skinny white maggots."

"Shut up," a guard bellowed and silenced the jeers with the butt of his spear.

Under heavy guard Widseth and the others started up an unfamiliar path that led upward above the sluice pits toward the digger compound carved into the side of the volcanic mount.

***

Two figures stood atop the battlements on the outer wall in silence looking over the plains. Morning light illuminated the activities of an awakening complex below, and the massive inner gate to the underground city opened, releasing groups of warriors, merchants, clerics, and field slaves. The man-sized dragon turned to Rin.

"It does no good to reprimand you. Our initiative has been lost," Deorc said. "We will make other plans."

His nostrils flared scarce inches from Rin's face. Rin's set jaw appeared chiseled in rock. He knew Deorc was right in every assessment, and that bothered him more than his failure.

"Master Deorc, I had to test the dragons on a real challenge, and we would have prevailed if not for the golden dragon," Rin said. "I know him. His name is Gulth. I tried to control him, but could not find the proper sequence of chords in his melody."

Rin backed away from Deorc and began to pace along the rampart.

"And you may never find them. He is a dragon of light, not one of the simple minded beasts you took with you." Deorc spat the words. Rin sensed the rage just below the dragon's surface veneer, but Deorc sublimated his anger and continued, "They are mere offspring of this world, knowing nothing of the eternal realms. Gulth, quite the contrary, has been trained in the light of the other world. He is young and inexperienced as eternity goes, but his training can be compromised only by one such as he is."

"I don't understand. You never told me."

"Could you not see a difference between me and the lesser creatures that allow you to ride them? I was one of the first to come to this world, but I have chosen another path. And there are others who feed on the darkness. We needed them before we executed our plans."

Rin lowered his head and stared at the pattern of the granite blocks used in the battlement. He wished he had never met Deorc. He preferred clearing water trenches as a slave. At least then he understood his world.

"I'm sorry. I didn't … ." Rin said.

The dragon's next words surprised Rin, not so much with content as with the attitude of near tenderness.

"Rin, my son, let your doubts go. My anger is passed."

Rin looked up and stared into the face of the creature before him. Webs of shifting patterns surrounded the dragon's person like wispy smoke from a smoldering fire, but for the first time Rin sensed a genuine entity hidden by the counterfeits woven into the fabric of Deorc's physical appearance. Often Rin thought of Deorc as a dream, but now he knew reality shaped the dream, and the realization terrified him.

"Why do you need me?" Rin asked. Immediately he perceived a shift in Deorc's conscious effort to mask reality. The brief glimpse of Deorc, as he might have been, submerged beneath waves of magical energy that billowed to obscure his hidden nature.

"Dragons are intermediaries between the eternal world and humankind. It is the nature of the dragons of light to serve humanity, but with several others, I chose to sever my ties to light in favor of the remarkable capacity for control found in shadows of deception. I need a human to focus those powers because even the dragon kind cannot be filled with the aptitude for darkness as completely as a man given absolute control of his world."

"I'm nothing more than a doll to you … a plaything you control." Rin's voice broke. "I thought I was free, and you've put me in chains stronger than fine steel."

"Free? You gave yourself to me as a servant if I would kill the man who killed your father," Deorc reminded Rin.

"But you said, I'd be a master and …."

"And you are a master. I have given you freedom. Who else rides dragons? You are the icon of a new religion. You will be king and high priest wielding powers that emperors will envy. The mystery of magic will exalt you above the commoner, you will control the reins of economic power to give bread or starvation to your subjects, and the ruthless force of your dragons and armies will keep even the most adventurous ruler subjugated. The superficial desire for freedom in mankind is easily overwhelmed by the warm blanket of security. In the end a man will trade everything for a crust of bread, a warm fire, and a happy, if insincere, song."

Rin looked over the wall toward the expanding plain. The excitement created by Deorc's words filled his mind. He felt confidence begin to rise again as he listened to Deorc. He shaded his eyes and looked eastward into the morning sun.

"You spoke of other dragons, more powerful dragons. Where are they? Will they join us, and will I be able to control them?"

"Schadwe, although unseen, has always been here. He brought me the report of your battle before you returned. Lighininge the Blue will join us before the week is out. I anticipate that Blaec or Hwit will rouse from their lairs to aid us."

"Will they obey me?"

"If you learn the keys to their melodies, they will have no choice."

"Good, I want to make Gulth and the caer of that stupid lord pay for humiliating me. They will feel the hammer strike of Rin the Bold."

"And after you make them pay, what will you do then?"

Rin stared at Deorc. "I'm not sure what you mean, Lord Deorc."

"In the arena of Tabul, a man is often pitted against a grey cat, and the cat usually wins. Does the cat have any natural ability to paralyze a man? No. But fear of the cat can and does paralyze men, and they become easy prey. Yet one man controls the cat—the man who feeds it. The cat indeed fears him, or rather, it fears he will withhold food, and thus it becomes a willing captive to the security of food and shelter offered by the keeper."

Rin rubbed his chin and looked over the people below, all involved in their daily tasks.

"After I make them pay, I'll wrap my protective arms around them and offer them the freedom of security. That way I can bind them to my will," Rin said.

"Yes," Deorc responded, "you have learned your lesson well. I will meet with the captains of the army. You need to mend some feelings with Brulon. By defying him and treating him like an inferior, you have lessened his effectiveness with the clerics. His teachings are invaluable. You need him as an ally. Go now. We will make preparations later."

***

Baron Aelan O'Dai sat on the massive wooden throne where his father's fathers had held council and issued edicts since before records were kept in Caer O'Dai. The throne room was neither large nor opulent. Four stone columns along each wall supported beams and a wooden roof. Windows set in the wall between the columns provided illumination during the day, and a massive fireplace on the south wall provided warmth and light at night. The house guard of the Baron stood post at either side of the throne and at the entry way. Krieger, with twenty northern rangers, waited along the northern wall. Other important townsmen and merchants lined the southern wall. Angus and Perigreen entered the hall leading Annel. They stopped ten paces in front of the throne.

The herald called out. "Her highness, Queen Annel of Dragada, presents herself to Baron Aelan O'Dai."

The title startled Annel. She never thought of herself as a queen, and she wondered who had revealed her rank to the Baron. It

117

had been four days since the holiday attack, and although still bruised and sore, most of her wounds had begun to heal properly. Baron Aelan stood, dropped to one knee, and bowed his head. Everyone in the room followed his lead. Annel looked around, stunned and embarrassed by the reception accorded her.

"Please, rise," she said. "There's no need for formality. I'm no different from any of you. Please."

Aelan rose from his knee.

"As the lady wishes." He motioned to everyone gathered in the hall, and all arose. The Baron sat on the throne.

Perigreen and Angus took their places beside the throne, and a page brought a chair for Annel to sit upon. Annel seated herself.

"M'lady, I apologize to you for my behavior when you first presented yourself," Aelan said for all to hear. "I regarded your counsel lightly, and my people have paid the price for my indifference, and yes, my cowardice. I knew very well that dragons, not giant swamp lizards, had attacked farms in my realm, but I didn't have the courage to face the truth. I thought, perhaps, they would take some livestock and be satisfied. But then ... ."

Tears welled in Aelan's eyes. "Then a young boy paid his taxes with a potato, and reminded me of my obligations to him and his family."

Annel felt the anguish in the Baron. She understood his feelings of failure because the same feelings had plagued her all her life.

Aelan continued, "Your Majesty Annel, this boy ... ."

She interrupted, "Please, no titles. I'm Annel. Just Annel."

"As you wish. You rescued this boy from death, and he has no family now. According to the laws of our land, you are entitled to raise him as your own or as a servant. Choose and I will make it so in the records."

"Marcus is precious to me, as are all the children of the land, but I couldn't do anything more than send him to Dragada to be raised there. With the darkness at hand, I've no time to raise a child, and I can't endanger him by taking him with me."

"It would be a shame to send him so far from his home. I've a proposal for you, because by law, you would have to agree before I could offer this. My wife died four years ago giving birth to our first child, a son, my heir. He died ten days after his mother. It would be my honor to take this faithful tax payer into my household and raise him as my son, as an heir to all my titles and holdings."

Annel studied the Baron. His kindness and words demonstrated his desire to correct his inaction to defend his people.

"It's a generous offer, m'lord. I concur," she said.

"So let it be recorded that the boy, Marcus, shall be my heir, Marcus O'Dai."

Murmurs of accord spread around the hall. Annel noted the pleased reaction by the townspeople. One of their own had been chosen as an heir.

"We have other pressing matters to discuss," Aelan said. "I invite all to remain. As long as men sing around the hearth fires of Caer O'Dai, the exploits Lady Annel and the brave rangers of Standel will be remembered with gratitude. We thank you again, and now ask how we may repay our debt to you."

Annel stood and steadied herself holding on to the back of the chair. She knew she could talk directly to the Baron, but fear filled her when she realized he expected her to make her case before the entire room filled with his people. She hesitated to ask women to sacrifice their children and husbands for possible war, but she turned and faced the gathering.

"I am here on behalf of the Lords of Light in the eternal worlds of light."

How foolish that sounded to her, but when she looked out she caught Kreigar's eye. She read in his eyes the fire of hope and the understanding of faith—faith in her—faith in what she was about to say. She looked back at Baron Aelan, and Perigreen, and Angus.

"Speak your thoughts. We will judge from whence they come," the Baron said.

She let loose the back of the chair and stood upright facing the gathering. She tried to muster the bravery she felt when she faced the dragon. When she saw Marcus standing near the front beside a tall house guard, courage bolstered her.

"I am Annel, wife of Widseth the Dragon Master. I know there is a common belief that the Aelfen no longer walk the earth, if they ever did, but they are here, all around. They are no mystical, magical race. They are men and women like you and me, who covenant to live higher laws—men and women who choose to live higher standards—men and women who can wield the powers of light because of the discipline they have chosen to learn."

As she paused, eight men entered the far door away from the throne. She recognized that four of the men wore the livery of Caer O'Dai, but the other four wore insignias from other noble families. The Baron rose and put his hand on Annel's shoulder. She paused for him to speak.

"Welcome, brothers of the plains. I beg you to give heed to the words of the Lady Annel. We will meet afterward to discuss this affair. M'lady, please continue."

Annel nodded to each of the men.

"I also welcome your presence," she said. "During the festival, Angus and I spoke of the kingdoms of the Aelfen. All three great Aelfene kingdoms failed and slipped into the shadows. Misdara, the caverns of crystal wonder, fell first at the end of the Third Age or the Age of Beauty, as it is called in some of the chronicles. Dragada, the crystal palace, was the first of the Aelfene kingdoms in the material world. It is the spot where the dragons of light first came to Aelandra; but Dragada fell into darkness, not long after Misdara, during the dragon wars of the Fourth Age, the Age of Testing. Dragada became a dark and loathsome center for the dragons of darkness until redeemed by … ."

She fell silent. Memories flooded her mind. She stood with eyes closed, lost in the events that brought Widseth and her together. She wished he were here. A man coughed, bringing her back to the present.

"I'm sorry." She looked around and took a deep breath. "My husband, Widseth, called dragons of light back into the material world, and they redeemed Dragada. The Cherubim resumed their stations, and Widseth replanted the tree of life that had been destroyed. Those who are willing to accept the Aelfene way of life gather there now, but they are few in number. The Aelfene kingdom, Taina, lasted long into the Fifth Age, the Age of Betrayal, before they fell into dark paths, but the crystal pyramid still stands, hidden from the world. When Taina fell, remnants of the faithful Aelfen gathered in the hidden city of Meliandra. Most of them have now left this world to join the children of light in the eternal realms. Now is our time to carry the banners of light."

Annel fell silent, unaware of the spell her voice had woven among the people. As she looked at them, she realized they expected more. She smelled bread baking in the castle kitchen down the hall from the assembly room. It reminded her of days at the market when she was a young girl. Mostly she pilfered fresh loaves rather than bought them. She longed to linger in the memory, but returned to her task.

"Darkness grows on the plains. Evil once again inhabits Misdara. An ancient dragon of darkness named Deorc fashions a Dragon Master to perform his will. Evil men follow him, and deceived men are enslaved. Dragons have responded. You may think he will be content with Misdara, but soon he will bind all the caers on the prairie, and from that base attempt to challenge the dragons of light and overwhelm all men."

"I've heard enough o' this tripe. It's all nonsense—Aelfen and dragons. They're stories fer children before bed." The discordant voice came from a man representing one of the noble families. "I rode two days to hear tales that the bards in my caer could sing any night. Baron, this is twaddle, and I'll not soon forget the wasted time."

Annel stepped back, as Aelan stood and addressed the man. "Peace, Lord Paran. Please, hear her out. She stands with honor in our house until time ceases. The people moved the carcasses of the dragons outside the town, or you would have seen them where they died near the outer gate and in the inner compound. I watched the Lady Annel slay one beast, and Lord Perigreen witnessed the northern ranger, Hector, kill the other. Their feats will be sung at our fires as long as fires are lit to warm the night. There are no idle tales in this hall today."

Paran looked around the hall and at the other lords who had ridden from the other three strongholds.

Annel felt relief, when the man nodded to the Baron and said, "I'll listen on yer word. If there's substance, I'll be satisfied, but if not, I leave before the sun sets."

"You'll find substance I am sure. Lady Annel, please continue," the Baron said.

Annel smiled at the Baron. She took comfort from the light streaming in the windows.

"Thank you for your support," she said. "My message is simply this. You must raise an army to defend yourselves. I'll take the fight to Misdara where evil is growing, and I ask no one to risk anything more than what is necessary to defend your homes, but you must prepare because darkness seeks to crush your freedom and enslave you both physically and spiritually."

As her words rang through the hall, sunlight bathed her. She felt the warm glow filling all the empty and cold areas of doubt in her psyche. Conviction in her mind replaced fear. She knew Widseth had not abandoned her as his choice, but that he fulfilled the will of higher powers. For the first time since their separation, she felt united with him in purpose because she knew that she was part of a higher scheme. Looking down at herself, she realized that the light in the room flowed to her. The clothing that she had been given on the Diadem radiated light and filled the room with emanations of high magic.

Holding the clasp on her cloak out away from her neck, she said, "This symbol of the dragons on the staff is an Aelfene symbol. It signifies the healing strength of centering your life on the powers of light. Your healers wear the same symbol. You are descendents of the Aelfen of Misdara. Your fathers fled the disaster of evil, and for centuries you've flourished outside the world of light, but your roots ... your roots are deep and strong. The dragons of darkness want to strike here first because they shrink from the day that you realize who you are ... from the day you reclaim your heritage."

Annel could not gauge the effect of her words, nor did she realize they issued from her mouth with cadence and rhythm, falling on each individual's ears like gentle melodies of the eternal world geared to each personality. At later times, some said her words were as songs of peace, and others said they were battle cries. Still others said they touched their hearts with love and inspiration. No one remained unaffected by the high magic.

When she ceased speaking, everyone remained in stunned silence. She turned to the Baron.

"I have one last thing to show you, if you will follow me, sir."

She stepped down the stairs and walked toward the door. Many, whom she passed, knelt and bowed their heads. Kreigar and rangers of Standel followed her out of the hall. They passed in a procession through the halls and courtyards of the inner castle until they stopped at the open gate into the outer compound where Annel had battled the dragon. A man with golden skin stood in the middle of the field. The area had not been cleared from the time of the holiday celebrations.

"M'lord, Baron Aelan O'Dai, I present to you Gulth, dragon of light. There's no need to view remains of dead dragons as proof of events past, when we can view present reality."

Annel strode over to Gulth and put her hand on his shoulder.

"It's time to show them who you are."

"Yes, m'lady."

Townspeople who had been in the outer compound joined those who had been in the throne room, as they gathered around Annel and the man with the golden skin.

Those who were close enough first noticed, his eyes enlarge and his pupils shape into a vertical slit. He stretched his fingers and sharp talons emerged as his hands lengthened. He leaned forward and put his hands on the ground. He shrugged his shoulders and stretched his neck upward. It elongated in successive movements. The sunlight glistened on his golden scales. In the time it took to take a sip of tea, the man transformed into a long serpent with giant wings folded against his flanks.

"M'lady Annel, what do you wish now? Shall I resume my duties in the air?" The dragon's voice rumbled like a deep baritone chord in a symphony.

"In a moment. Baron, will you and the others, who wish, please come forward?"

The Baron and all the nobles of the caers stepped forward, but Marcus led them all. Gulth lowered his head until his eyes were level with Marcus.

"Young one," Gulth said, "I sorrow at your loss. I pledge myself to end the evil in your land, so that you, your children, and their children may sleep in safety."

With almost imperceptible movement Gulth raised his right hand and extended his talon until it touched Marcus' forehead. It left a curious mark shaped like the sun rising on the horizon with its rays lighting the sky. The image faded in the natural sunlight.

"No dragon will dare harm you now. You wear the mark of my house in the eternal world."

He turned and spoke to the Baron.

"I have guarded your skies for many days. I will continue if it pleases you, or until the Lady Annel commands otherwise."

Baron Aelan could not speak. He licked his lips and nodded approval. Annel reached and stroked Gulth's head.

Perigreen and Angus approached.

"M'lady, where is your husband, Widseth? Couldn't he call the dragons of light and directly challenge this darkness?" Perigreen asked.

Annel lowered her eyes and stared at the ground for a minute.

"He's in the gem mines of Bilbra," she said.

"Bilbra? How can it be that he's there?"

"He allowed himself to be taken. I believe there's something he must do there, just as I have my task here."

Angus pulled at his beard and leaned on his staff. Annel could see the wonder in the older man as he gazed at Gulth. Annel knew his mind wandered through all the tales he had ever sung or heard.

He spoke, "There is the fragment of an ancient tale about Misdara that tells of a marvelous gem called the Eye of Light. One line of the song says the Eye of Light was hidden by the shadows in Bilbra. It's an evil tale of sorrow, but much of it has been lost in the telling through the centuries."

***

When Almaron stumbled over a protruding root in the trail, Widseth steadied him. Widseth sensed the fatigue in the former priest after only two hours of an unbroken climb upward on the path. Windblown scrub vegetation covered volcanic slag. Most of the trees failed to reach the height of a man, but the dense wiry foliage made travel almost impassible anywhere but on the trail. Roots protruded from the rocky soil, spreading in all directions searching for nutrients and water in fierce competition.

"Don't show weakness," Widseth whispered. "The guards will single you out for punishment."

"But I can't keep going like this. My legs are cramping."

"I don't think it will be much further, or we would have stopped for a rest. Even the guards are tiring."

Widseth clutched Almaron's shoulder and imbued pure energy into him.

"What was that?" Almaron asked.

"Quiet. Just keep walking."

"But I felt a burst of warmth along my spine, and it's filling me. The pain … ."

He dared a glance at Widseth, but kept walking.

"The pain is gone! I feel like I just awoke from a good sleep," he whispered.

"I know."

Widseth smiled. It always pleased him when he used the power of healing that had been granted him to help others. As they walked, his mind wandered to Annel and the task before her. He longed to take her place, or at least join her so he could protect her, but an adage from the past entered his mind. *'An obedient heart is the key to unlock the shackles of a world in chaos.'* He knew if he interfered, Annel might rely on him and fail to discover the powers that would open to her. He knew at the proper time he would join her again, and he resolved to heed the directions he had received.

After another ten minutes, the guards signaled for a halt as the trail opened to a flat expanse like a large shelf on the fringe of the mountain. No vegetation grew higher than this area, and the peak towered above, outlined by the grey sky. Steam issued from various cracks in the serrated volcanic slag on the mountainside. A bitter, sulfurous odor pervaded the air, sucking moisture from Widseth's throat, and he knew no amount of water would soothe the malady.

He could see stone structures and the dark jagged mouth of an ominous opening into the mountain. To the left of the cavity, pack animals in a corral brayed in mournful disharmony as a few slaves loaded them with ore and gems destined for a more civilized place. Widseth deduced that the slaves must sleep within the mountain because the sparse buildings to the right of the opening into the mountain appeared to house only the guards and supplies.

"Welcome ta yer hole, ya tunnel rats," a guard bellowed. All the guards laughed. "Keep movin'."

"Are these the replacements?" a man asked.

"Yeah. We got a late start," the guard replied.

"Get 'em over here. We gotta clear a tunnel. Work to do."

A whip cracked, and the line of men moved forward toward the dark entrance where an overseer, holding a torch, met them. The stench of smoke and steam filled the air. A man broke from the line of slaves.

"I'm not goin' in there!" he screamed. He tried to outrun the guards, but tripped and a spear in his back ended his life.

Widseth lowered his head to avoid eye contact with a guard. Tilting his head sideways, he tried to see Almaron, but the former priest stared at the ground with hands trembling like leaves in a wind.

"Get movin'."

The line of haggard men followed the overseer into the hot, dark tunnel. Naked from the waist up except for a leather harness, the digger camp guards followed, holding spears as prods. The torch in the hand of the overseer burned fitfully in the choking atmosphere of the passageway. As they entered the natural cavern, Widseth studied the path that had been leveled and smoothed by hundreds of years of slaves walking to their doom. With his abilities to see in all the dark places of the material world, he felt wonder at the beautiful emanations of the living rock, and at the same time sensed the terror in the other slaves entering this dark place. He knew his mother had walked on these very stones, and comfort entered his heart. Something in this dark place beckoned him, and he knew a task would be revealed.

"I don't like this," Almaron whispered.

"Keep up with the others, or you will like it even less," Widseth replied.

After a few minutes, the overseer turned a corner, and even the sputtering light of the torch blinked out, blanketing the men in blackness until they felt their way around the corner, where the tunnel opened into a large chamber lit by lanterns hung on the walls around the room. Iron doors lined two levels, surrounding a central common area where Widseth assumed slaves could gather for instructions and food. After he and the others entered the chamber, a guard swung an iron gate shut behind them. Widseth heard running water from the far side of the hall opposite the entrance. He knew the diggers diverted water into passages and then back into the underground river to wash gems and ore downstream to be caught in the sluice pits. A bridge spanned the area where Widseth heard the river. Beyond the bridge three black tunnels led deeper into the mountain.

At times, evil exhibits the qualities of a living entity or an attribute embodied within an individual, but as I have studied the scattered histories of Aelandra, I have come to appreciate that an evil foundation, within an individual or society, is built by choices. It seldom materializes after one defining choice, but appears after a myriad of almost insignificant preferences that dispose a person or civilization toward evil. Most of those choices revolve around the acquisition of power, money, popularity, or self-centered activities that titillate the senses and satisfy only the individual, without regard to society at large.

Personal History of Winna—Master Historian of the court of Standel

Chapter 8. Foundation of Evil

When Rin opened the door, a rush of fragrant air greeted him hundreds of feet below the world defined by earth and sky. The smoky aroma of torches that lit the underground city, evaporated in the aromatic gust that exploded from the chamber, like a man exhaling after holding his breath underwater. One by one, beautiful globes, suspended in the air and hung from columns, illuminated the entire hall, like small suns, and revealed the most marvelous scene Rin had ever beheld. From the door leading into the chamber, he scanned the throne room. The passage to this section of the underground city had been cleared within the last couple of weeks, but Deorc had forbidden entrance to anyone.

A chill inched up Rin's spine because Deorc would not be pleased if he knew Rin were here now. Fear crept into his heart, but with his first step into the hall, the terror fled in the full light of the globes. In the distance at the opposite end of the chamber, he could see the dais with two thrones situated in the open mouth of a huge marble dragon's head. Gentle music commenced as he stepped on the marble tile on the floor inside the door. He shrank back and felt his way along the left wall. Throughout the audience chamber, sculpted columns rose to greet a majestic ceiling that appeared to be covered with beautiful mosaics of star-lit skies, mountains, meadows, and the sea. Life-sized relief adorned the walls, depicting men, women, and dragons. The pigment used by the ancient artists to color the statuary looked as if it had been painted yesterday. Even frozen in stone, the men and women reminded Rin of Widseth and Annel. Their bearing and demeanor was stern but kindly.

The dragons were majestic creatures, portrayed in full cooperation with humanity. They appeared in a multitude of colors, shapes, and sizes. Some reminded Rin of Gulth, giant creatures of power and splendor. Others were man-sized, walking upright, like Deorc, and yet others resembled serpent-like birds that perched on a man's arm or shoulder. Wondering who these people and dragons were, Rin spent several minutes walking along the wall to the left of the entrance, absorbed in every figure portrayed on the wall.

He came to the first of two large doors in the wall, but the heavy metal material of the double door would not budge when he tried to push it open. The door was about twenty feet high. After a few minutes of struggling against the elegant silver door, inlaid with brilliant rivers of golden relief, Rin backed away and looked at the pattern. Two stunning dragons coiled around a single pole, until near the top they formed a perfectly mirrored image in polished gold, accented with striking gemstones. Further along the wall, nearer the dais, he spied another door, but a chill gust of air diverted his attention.

When he turned and looked at the opposite wall on the other side of the chamber he could see a massive opening between two pillars. The opening, perhaps thirty feet wide and forty feet high, appeared to be a natural cavern. Light from the globes illuminated the glittering entrance, but darkness swallowed all light within the immensity of the cavern. Rin took a step toward the huge cavity, but froze when he heard a faint voice from the direction of the dais.

He slipped behind a column and hugged the cool marble until he controlled his breathing. He practiced some of the mind and body control exercises that Deorc and Brulon had taught him, and after a few minutes he crept from column to column until he stood at the base of the dais. The voice grew louder, but remained indistinct, originating from somewhere behind the thrones. From the foot of the dais Rin stared at the symbolic base of power inside the marble dragon's head. The stone neck of the creature stretched back behind the thrones, and melded into a beautiful scene, carved and painted, on the back wall.

When he stepped from behind the column, powerful emanations erupted from the mouth, and a web of magical energy ensnared him. Terror gripped his spine, as he began to walk toward the center of the room, against his will. The eyes in the stone dragon's head began to glow like huge yellow gemstones, and the voice from behind the throne rose in volume, quickening the cadence. Rin stood at the foot of the stairs leading to the thrones. He struggled to remain in control of his thoughts, as light from the dragon's eyes peeled away all of his mental defenses and revealed his innermost thoughts and feelings.

He could see himself sitting on one of the thrones, dressed in the black armor Deorc had created. He scrutinized an assembly of people and creatures gathered in the great hall, and he took pleasure as he saw dragons, kings, and peasants bowing before him.

The light from the stone dragon's eyes stripped away the black armor, and Rin felt his vulnerability. He viewed misty visions that seemed to be real, at least as real as a dream. As he sat on the throne looking over the hall, the scene changed and he was in the saddle of a dragon, winging above the plains watching a battle. Ferocious men collided together in a terrible spectacle of noise and chaos. Rin's troops with the aid of dragons swept away the war bands of the plains nobles until a woman raised her sword and stood firm in the path of his armies. A golden dragon and a cadre of warriors without fear followed her. He knew her sword could reach deep into his heart and kill his dream to rule the world, and he feared her because his armor was gone. Once he watched her heal a tree, but now she was the blight infecting his world. He hated her.

Then the light from the dragon stripped all his clothes except a loin cloth, and he sat on the great throne naked and hungry. *That was me when I was weak. I'll never go back to being a slave.* He scanned the hall. It was empty until a man and a woman appeared standing at the foot of the dais bathed in light.

"Da ... Ma ... ."

The boy on the throne cried. Tears rolled down his cheeks and dropped from his chin. He wanted his father to take him in his arms. He wanted feel the touch of his mother's hand on his head. When the sun revealed what the shadows hid, all the power over kings and dragons and armies faded like empty shadows.

"Rashanarth nuanthaa." The harsh words echoed through the chamber.

Rin felt intense pressure as high and low magic collided. The vision on the throne faded. The light from the eyes of the stone dragon faltered and dimmed, and Deorc stepped from behind the dragon's head.

"Rin, you have rushed things a bit, but no harm is done. Come. I will show you your destiny."

Rin shook his head. *How had Deorc gotten here?* Then he remembered the voice behind the throne. *Maybe he had been here all along.* Rin recovered his composure and mounted the stairs. When he reached the top of the stairs, he stretched out his hand to touch the throne.

"Do not touch it," Deorc said. "Your time will come. Impatience will create more problems than you want."

"Master Deorc, what is this place? How could a stone dragon cast a spell on me?"

"When the world was young, Misdara was preeminent among the Aelfene kingdoms. High magic centered itself here among these people. What you felt was a residue—nothing more than ghosts from the past."

"But there's so much power. I mean, I felt it stronger than anything I've sensed before," Rin said.

"Power is relative. Because you have little experience with magic, it appears all powerful to you. My magic easily countered the spell and released you."

Rin nodded his head and looked around the room, as he stood beside the thrones on the dais.

"Master Deorc, will I really rule from here? I mean what if the other Dragon Master, Widseth ... . You know. He has power too, doesn't he? What if he doesn't like you making me a Dragon Master?"

Deorc's hideous chuckle resounded through the empty hall.

"Come, Rin. Let me show you one of the real treasures of Misdara," Deorc said, as he turned and walked toward the wall behind the thrones.

Behind the marble dragon's head, a door led into a small alcove. The entry into the alcove amazed Rin. The intricate patterns cut into the rock doorway were enhanced with beautiful inlaid gems that flashed in the light. At the back of the niche a large stone bowl rested on a marble pillar. The exterior of the bowl appeared to be ordinary rock, but mother of pearl lined the inner surface, and the facade shifted like early morning mist, revealing snatches of scenes. Rin stood transfixed by the subtle movement of the shell of swirling vapor.

"This is the scry basin of Misdara. The Aelfen devised the magic of far sight. This was the first and most powerful basin they designed." Deorc reached his right hand forward and in a tender gesture almost touched the edge of the basin. "A skilled user can turn it to the past and present," Deorc said.

"Can it tell the future? I met a man at festival time in Tabul who could tell your future."

Deorc said, "Some say that by knowing the past and present, the future can be predicted with great accuracy. The king and queen of Misdara used this basin to help them rule their kingdom, but in the end it did not save them. Still, it has its uses."

Deorc began to chant. When Rin looked at the dragon, parts of Deorc phased in and out of sight. Rin disliked when that happened because the ethereal nature of Deorc dismayed him. He always questioned in his mind whether or not the creature was a reality in this world, or some other world. Patterns in the bowl began to swirl until a pinprick of light developed and grew into a picture. Rin could see Widseth sleeping on a stone floor in a dark cell.

"I recognize him. That's Widseth, but where is he?"

Deorc held up the stump of his left fore limb.

"Widseth did this to me. Consequences for him and his gutter snipe wife will fall quickly. He is in the mines of Bilbra, and he does not know it, but the mines are the lair of a special dragon."

Deorc's repugnant laugh filled the alcove before he continued. "He seeks a gem called the Eye of Light. Little does he suspect that my brother, Schadwe, hid the gem after the fall of Misdara in Bilbra and has inhabited the warrens of the mine since that time. The Lords of the eternal world sent Widseth on this quest with no forewarning. He flies like a moth into the flame, and the gaping jaws of my brother will welcome him."

Rin peered again into the basin. Dark red liquid pooled under Widseth's reclining form.

"So, he'll die," Rin said.

"Is that what you see?"

Deorc's eager question puzzled Rin. He noted an anxious timbre to Deorc's voice. *Maybe the dragon hadn't seen Widseth on the stone floor of the cell. Maybe there were things dragons couldn't do.* The thought grew, until Rin gathered courage to ask a question.

"Can't you see what is in the basin, m'lord dragon?"

"You are a perceptive boy. I made a good choice when I decided to assist you. Our bond must be strengthened by trust, so I will explain how this works."

Rin did not feel truth flow from the word 'trust', but he waited for Deorc to finish. He remembered Deorc's first lesson. *Trust is a concept the weak use to control someone stronger.*

Deorc continued, "The ancient Aelfen protected the basin from dragons because they did not trust our kind. I can cast the spells to activate the basin and call forth the images, but only human eyes can view the images until such time that I can break the High magic control the ancients placed on the basin. I assure you, that time will come."

Some of Deorc's explanation made sense, but Rin remembered the pictures on the walls. *Dragons and humans worked well together; in fact it seemed dragons served the humans. No matter. Deorc promised to make him a king. He would be free and everyone would bow to him.*

"I need your assistance on one more count. Please look into the basin one more time, and tell me what you see," Deorc requested.

Rin detected another attempt to mask an anxious request, but he looked into the swirling mist. Brilliant white light almost blinded him. Shielding his eyes, he tried to focus on the source. After several moments his eyes adjusted, and he perceived a beautiful white tree with a scaled, clawed hand at the base. Black shadows oozed from the hand, dimming the radiance around it.

"It's your hand."

"I know. Where is it?" Deorc's excitement broke Rin's concentration. The dragon's attitude startled him.

"It's by the roots of a tree ... a glorious white tree."

Deorc's revolting laugh resounded in the chamber.

"They hid it at a tree of life," Deorc chuckled. "Is there a dragon there?"

"No, m'lord. No dragon that I could see." The images in the basin blanked out.

"Anciently there were only three trees of life planted by the Aelfen. All were guarded by the dragons of light." Deorc laughed again. The sound grated on Rin's ears. "There are dragons guarding the trees in Taina and Dragada. Widseth hid my hand right here in Misdara. The fool had no idea we would build our base here. Anciently, when we destroyed the dragons guarding this tree, the Aelfen moved the tree and hid it. With no dragon guarding the way, it will be ours to find. And when we find it, we will destroy its light and take what is ours. I will indeed make you a king."

Rin smiled and looked at the thrones on the dais outside the alcove. He felt secure in his armor.

***

"You there, come with me," the guard said.

Almaron looked up from the diggings in the lava tube. Earlier in the week, a team of men called burrowers had broken through into a new complex of caverns, carved anciently by super heated rock flowing like a river from the internal furnaces of the volcanic mountain. As the outer edges of the molten rock cooled, the super heated inner mass continued to empty into the open land beyond, leaving a honeycomb of caves often filled with rich veins of precious metals or gems. Wind, weather, and repeated eruptions buried these mazes below the surface. Workers often lost their way in the tunnels and most never returned.

"Did ya hear me, man?" the guard asked. He prodded Almaron with the butt end of his spear. "Get a move on."

Almaron tried to catch Widseth's attention, but Widseth continued to use a chisel and mallet to chip at a promising crystalline outcropping about twenty feet from Almaron. Almaron rose to his feet and followed the guard through the cut in the passage wall into the older tunnels leading to the living areas. After passing several other work crews, Almaron and the guard slowed.

"What is so important to risk me leaving Widseth's side?" Almaron hissed, when they were out of earshot of any of the workers.

"M'lord priest, you've been summoned," the guard replied. "I'll take ya ta the captain's quarters."

Almaron fumed. *Interruptions jeopardized his undertaking. Widseth was too smart. His deft use of High magic provided unseen protection that defied overt penetration. The most subtle craft of Low magic, woven through bonds of trust, would be the only opportunity to strike at him, and he might sense communications like this with the Inquisitor.*

After about a half an hour, Almaron and the guard crossed the stone bridge over the underground river and entered the living compound. They made their way to a structure carved into the wall of the cavern where the captain of the guard met them. He bowed to Almaron.

"M'lord Almaron, we received an urgent message from the Emperor's Inquisitor. I deemed it best to contact you as soon as possible."

Almaron restrained his anger, but replied with an edge to his voice, "You may have jeopardized my position here. Your man pulled me away in full view of the heretic. I told you he sees more than other men. If our plans fail because of an impulsive reaction to a message, you will wish your life had ended yesterday."

The captain of the guard bowed. "Yes, m'lord, but the Inquisitor was insistent."

"Where is my stone?" Almaron demanded

"It's there on the table."

Almaron glanced at the table near the back wall in the room.

"Leave me."

The captain nodded and backed out of the room. Almaron wiped the sweaty grime on his forehead with the back of his hand and walked to the table, where he picked up the smooth ebony stone about the size of a hen's egg. He hated the manual labor in the tunnels and longed to study the dark arts. The stone felt good and familiar in his hand. *He knew why he had been picked for this task. The other priests were fat and lazy. They had no ambition, and the High Inquisitor had begun to show his age.* Almaron knew power was not always acquired by the most able, but often by the most willing to endure unpleasant duties.

Using the stone, he traced a square in the air in front of him.

"Aregna taley nasta," Almaron intoned. Murky vapors swirled within the square. "Purash taley nasta," he continued. The dark mist coalesced into the High Inquisitor's face.

"Ah, Almaron, I've awaited your report. Have you gained the heretic's trust?"

"You place me in jeopardy, m'lord. I feel I've a measure of his trust, but you have no concept of the power of this man. I would not be surprised if he sensed our conversation."

"What power? He's a heretic. The vanquished gods of light disappeared with the Aelfen. Our power rules now."

"Power? Sometimes I wonder if I know what power is," Almaron said. "Just two days ago I saw him, with the mere touch of his hand, heal a man's ankle that had been crushed by a rock fall."

"A mere healer's trick ... nothing more. Have you discovered why he placed himself in a position to be sent to the mines?" the Inquisitor asked.

"I think he's searching for something. The other day he talked about the ancient kingdom of Misdara."

"Misdara? What did he say of Misdara?"

Almaron detected a tone of disquiet in the voice emanating from the vapors.

"What's wrong?" Almaron asked. He studied the High Inquisitor's face. The shifting mist could not conceal veiled excitement.

"A rider from one of the noble families on the plains, south of Marshkata, arrived three days ago at the Emperor's court," the Inquisitor said. "He brought tales of evil in Misdara and begged the emperor to send an army."

"And you think there is some connection to Widseth?"

"I don't know, but now you say he has spoken of Misdara. Trouble begins on the plains. The coincidence strikes me. That's all."

Almaron bit his lip and stoked his thin beard before voicing other concerns. Something unsettled the Inquisitor. *Was the Inquisitor playing him?*

"M'lord Inquisitor, I've seen first hand Widseth's power, but I also perceived a deeper power in this place. At times the darkness gnaws at me, and I know there is an unseen presence that walks the tunnels. Other men have felt it too. I asked Widseth about it once, but he seemed unconcerned."

"What kind of presence?"

A chill crawled up Almaron's spine as he recalled the sinister gloom that entered his mind and examined him from within. He had tried to shield himself, but in the deep recesses of his mind he knew the alien presence knew everything worth knowing about his abilities.

"I've felt it only twice, but it was like a dark shadow that plucked at the fiber of my magic, as if I were an instrument that it longed to play. I fear my magic is child's play compared to the depth of the darkness I experienced. Both times it lasted only a few moments. Then it was gone."

"Did the feelings align themselves with High magic or Low?" the Inquisitor asked.

Almaron thought for a moment before answering. *Maybe he appeared weak to the Inquisitor. He needed to exercise caution to play this situation.*

"I don't know, but it was more powerful than anything I have ever felt." Almaron wanted to change the subject. "Should I broach the subject of Misdara with Widseth, or do you want me to continue to observe his methods? He's gaining a following among the other prisoners. Even guards speak highly of him."

A long silence ensued. Almaron felt increasing discomfort the longer the Inquisitor delayed answering. The vaporous face stared with empty eye sockets. When the first tendrils of dark energy escaped the blank eyes, Almaron knew what would follow, and he waited for the spell's impact. The vacant eyes began to glow with sickly yellow light.

The Inquisitor inspected for thoughts and feelings that Almaron might be hiding, and the first probes into his mind hit him like a lance striking a shield. As he stood before the face in the air, Almaron's fingers began to tremble, and his knees almost buckled. He reached and steadied himself by holding the table. Gritting his teeth, he endured sharp stabs of magical energy that made him want to scream, but the yellow eyes held him transfixed, unable to do anything other than focus on the intense control behind them. He clenched his jaw and endured because he coveted the same power to control others.

Abruptly the probing ceased, and Almaron used the table to stand erect. He did not want the Inquisitor to think him unable to accomplish his task. Taking a deep breath, he used a silent mantra to calm and soothe his mind. The light from the eyes faded, and the Inquisitor resumed the conversation.

"You have learned much by watching the heretic," the High Inquisitor said. "I sense a strength you've developed. Don't get drawn into his web, or you'll be unable to slip the knife in his ribs when the time comes. When he finds the talisman he seeks, your knife must find its home and consign his spirit to damnation. I want the object of his search. It must be an item of power. Don't strike until he finds it. You know the spell to bind him, but you cannot let your intentions waver."

"Yes, m'lord. I won't fail. I've taken the vow, and I renew it upon waking every morning."

"Good. The dark presence left a deep impression on your mind. I sense the tendrils of one of the shadoine of the abyss or perhaps a dragon. The Coven of Power has long known that a sinister influence once traversed the passages of Bilbra. Perhaps the heretic awakened it."

Almaron bit his lower lip. The Inquisitor's intrusion into his mind had been a brutal incursion like a dull knife ripping flesh. By contrast, when the veiled creature in the tunnels touched his mind, seductive chords of almost a musical nature dissected his thoughts with the subtle skill of a master artist. At least he knew and understood the magic of the Inquisitor. Almaron wanted nothing to do with the dark entity that roamed Bilbra, because he could not begin to comprehend the power it wielded.

"I'll not fail you, m'lord. I'll rid the world of this heretic and bring you the talisman he seeks."

"Good. Contact me again in six day's time. Make it at a time of your convenience so as not to alert Widseth."

"Yes, m'lord. As you wish."

***

Annel and the Rangers of Standel had spent nearly two months visiting as many of the nobles in the caers of the plains as possible. Representatives from all the noble families had promised to meet at Caer O'Dai in three weeks time to coordinate efforts to stop the dragons' attacks and assess if Misdara posed a threat. Such a moot had not been held in over two hundred years among the nobles of the plains. Although most of the aristocratic families were related in some way, the caers functioned almost autonomously, and some of the barons seldom exchanged anything more than annual protocol greetings.

Two men, standing at the gate of Caer Amal, doffed their caps to Annel as she nudged her horse's flanks with her heels. Eight rangers from Standel followed her through the gate and onto the prairie.

"She's a firebrand, she is," Ta'un said. "She's the kind what gives flame ta dry grass, and lights men's will ta fight."

"Yes," Me'lik said. He licked his lips and watched riders until they were specks on the grassland.

"Will we be joinin' the O'Dai clan at the moot?" Ta'un asked.

"Well, little brother, I think we'll be missed if we don't, but I'm not gonna be pushed ta follow some woman on a horse into battle. We've a fightin' force the other nobles envy, and I won't have 'em under anyone's orders but ours. Besides, I want ta talk with the man who arrived last night after these northerners bedded down."

"What man?" Ta'un asked.

"Ya were asleep. Didn't want ta wake ya. And he didn't want ta meet this Annel woman. Last night he said somethin' very interestin'."

Me'lik held his finger to the side of his bulbous nose. It was a sign since childhood that told his brother he knew something secret and special.

"Hah. What is it? Is he from the Emperor with a new title fer us?"

"Nah, he's from Misdara. The same Misdara that this woman warned us against. His name's Brulon. He's been waitin' in the common room 'til she left. Seems ta know a lot about us and our family."

Me'lik and his brother Ta'un walked quickly from the gates to the common room in the upper keep. In the common room a man sat alone at the large table, eating a crust of bread. When the brothers entered, he rose and bowed to Me'lik. In his right hand he leaned on a staff. Opposing bronze cast dragons entwined around the staff. He did not look very imposing as he stood in plain brown robes with a hunched posture.

"I am Brulon, Master Prelate of the Order of the Brazen Serpent. Me'lik, I met you last night." Turning to Ta'un, he said. "You must be the other half of the brothers of the plains. The fame of your house reached my ears years ago. Now I have the pleasure of sharing bread at your table." Brulon smiled.

Me'lik liked this man. Brulon was an educated man of words, and last night he spoke of their ancient family line. When Annel had come, she said nothing of his family. She begged like a hungry child for him and his brother to join her in fighting dragons.

"I come to you in behalf of ancient powers. Do you remember what happened when you turned fifteen?" Brulon asked.

The question startled Me'lik. Looking at Ta'un, he could tell the inquiry puzzled his brother also, but Ta'un answered.

"Well, the only thing of any import is the 'manhood' ritual."

"Yes, very good," Brulon said. "And what happens at the rites?"

"There are feats of skill … horsemanship, archery, swordsmanship. Things like that."

"And after the skill tests, what then?"

"The ceremony … the binding oath and remembrance o' the fathers," Ta'un answered.

Brulon stood to his full height and gripped the staff until his knuckles turned white. His eyes focused on the brothers, and his stare seemed to bore into Me'lik like a wood beetle, burrowing into a rotten log. Me'lik wondered if Ta'un felt the same. *This man had power. The woman from the north wielded no strength like this.*

"Do you remember the oaths?" Brulon asked.

Me'lik spoke, "The oaths are learned by memory at a young age, and every year they're renewed on the anniversary of the caer's founding." He looked up at a banner, high on the west wall of the common room, with his family insignia, a black scorpion on a red field. The brothers drew their swords and raised them high in the air, as Me'lik began to speak, and Ta'un joined.

"I bare my sword to enemies in defense of my fathers' land, bestowed in ancient time. As the horizon sheaths the setting sun, so darkness hides my blade as I swear loyalty to power capable of extinguishing life. I will remember who gives, and in return I wear a mask known only to the secret father of my line. I will never reveal to whom fealty is given, nor from whence my strength flows. So be my resolve."

Brulon smiled and nodded his head up and down several times as the brothers finished their recitation. Something about the words filled Me'lik with exhilaration in a manner he had never experienced before. His fingers tingled as he lowered his sword to sheathe it. Out of the corner of his eye, movement startled him, but when he looked, it was gone.

"When you took the oath the first time, did you shed a drop of blood on the ground to seal your oath?" Brulon asked.

"Yes, it's the way, and every year on the anniversary we kill an animal and spread its blood on the ground in token of our own sacrifice," Ta'un answered.

"Good. Do all men of Caer Amal do this?"

"Most do, but some consider it a worthless rite from the dark times," Me'lik answered.

"And you? Is that what you think?" Brulon asked.

"I'm the Baron o' Caer Amal, and my brother Ta'un is my second. We observe the rites and remember those who've sat in the ruling chair."

"Do you know who bestowed this land to your fathers?" Brulon asked. "Do you know who the secret father of your line is?"

The brothers shook their heads, but Me'lik's muscles tensed. He realized a presence other than Brulon paced the room. He could not see it, but it was there, and it engendered fear. He almost panicked when he tried to answer Brulon.

"Family traditions say our land came from the Regent of Misdara. Little is said beyond that," Me'lik's voice trailed off, as he scanned the room for any more movement.

He put his hand on his sword hilt, when the area behind Brulon began to shimmer, and a shape appeared. The shape sucked shadows from every corner of the room to build a horrific image. A creature, a little taller than a man and shaped like a dragon, materialized. The brothers stood fixed in stone.

"Take your ease," Brulon said. "No need for alarm. The Regent of Misdara is here." Brulon turned to the fully formed dragon. "Master Deorc, they know and renew the oath. What is your wish?"

Me'lik shivered inside. He tried to tighten his muscles to arrest the shaking, but his hand trembled as he released his sword hilt and let his hand fall to his side. He tried to attract Ta'un's attention, but his brother stood in shock. All the blood had drained from Ta'un's face, and Me'lik assumed he reflected the same pale and quivering demeanor as his brother.

Deorc spoke, "For centuries your forefathers have repeated the oath that the first Baron of Amal swore to me when I gave him this land after the fall of Misdara. Now I call you to fulfill your oath. Armies rise to oppose me, but your war band is the strongest on the plains."

"A woman leads the other caers. She left this mornin'," Ta'un said.

Brulon cleared his throat. "We know who she is. We did not strike this morning because the men she leads are hardened and skilled in battle, and the golden man who rode with her is a powerful dragon. The time is not yet, but the occasion approaches when we will contest her presumed authority."

"If we satisfy this oath," Me'lik asked, "what do we gain? Meanin' my family line."

Deorc's eyes narrowed to slits. Me'lik stepped back when the dragon began a throaty chant. For the first time he noticed the stump that served as the dragon's left forearm, but the claws on his right hand contorted into a ritualistic motion. A ring appeared in its hand. It was a golden band with scorpions on either side of a large azure stone. Me'lik swallowed hard. He had seen only drawings in some of the ancient tomes in the family records. The family signet ring had been lost for centuries. Songs said the man who wore the ring would be granted magical protection, but more than that he would rule all the clans of the plains.

"I think you recognize this ring," Deorc said. He paused. The air in the room felt ominous and heavy like an approaching thunderstorm. Ta'un stood with his mouth open, as Me'lik carried the conversation.

"Unless I'm deceived, it's the Ring of Amal. Legend tells of marvelous powers, but it was lost centuries ago when a dragon killed my ancestor, Kristan. Or so say the songs."

"Your foolish ancestor refused to heed the oath," Deorc said.

Each word struck Me'lik like arrows hitting the target, but the target was not a bale of straw. He sensed no quarter in this dragon's attitude, and in his mind Me'lik could see the cruel talons raking his chest. He swallowed hard.

"M'lord dragon, what must I do ta fulfill this oath?"

"Join this woman and the other war bands. Give them the confidence that the Amal Clan will be their strongest support, but when the armies clash on the plains, I will send this ring to you. If you join me and fulfill your oath, I will give you not only the ring, but all other caers will pay tribute to you forever. At the appointed time your band will turn on your brother clans and prevent them from retreating while dragons feast on their carcasses. If you chose to stand with the clans, I will not only take the ring from you, but your body will not be fit for the buzzards to eat."

Me'lik knelt before Deorc, and Ta'un followed suit.

Me'lik spoke for himself and his brother, "We take ya as our father, and we pledge ta fulfill our oaths. We'll wear the mask o' friendship 'til the dagger pierces the ribs of our common enemies and destroys 'em. So be it."

As the farmer approached, the blacksmith stood holding a horseshoe in his hand. "Why the sad face?" the farmer asked. The blacksmith turned his attention from the piece of iron in his hand and faced the farmer. "When I made a plow for you," he replied, "I saw you use it to till your fields; and when you completed your task, you oiled it and put it away properly. I was pleased. I found this shoe this morning that a horse had thrown. I recognized it as my work. It saddens me when a rider pays no heed, and cares neither for his animal, nor his equipment. The empty shoe is a token of a man's carelessness. I grieve that my talent and creation is so lightly regarded."

From the Country Tales of the Farmer, the Fisherman, and the Blacksmith

Chapter 9. Empty Shoe

On horseback Annel and Kreigar inspected the multitude of men training on the plains outside Caer O'Dai. Under Perigreen's direction the rangers from Standel ran strict exercises to prepare the Baron's men for battle. Aelan O'Dai had turned most of the military preparations over to Lord Perigreen while he and Annel embarked on the task of gathering an army from all the caers on the plains. Nearly six hundred men from his own land had joined his usual garrison of seventy five. Only two nobles from smaller caers had arrived with their war bands. Together they added an additional one hundred and seventy five men.

Lord Perigreen divided the men into units of ten. Ten units made a company of one hundred. Two rangers from Standel worked to teach every company in hand to hand and unit fighting. Four rangers chose a select few with some experience on horses as mounted cavalry units, but they were few in number. Smithies hammered long into the nights preparing gear for men and horses.

Under the direction of Kreigar who had participated in the great northern war, craftsmen designed carts for transporting stores and small mobile ballistae for fighting the dragons.

"The men are working hard, but they are so few. I hope the other caers respond soon," Annel said.

Kreigar pulled at his beard and ran his fingers through his wild hair in an attempt to smooth it back.

"Aye, m'lady, we're indeed few, but w' trainin', we'll make every man count as three," he responded. His eyes made contact with hers for only a second before he turned his attention to the exercise.

Annel knew his words were empty. Black shadows filled her dreams, and she saw the vision of blood soaking the grass of the prairie. Sometimes at night when she awoke, she imagined that a dark shadow crept into her room and stood over her, laughing at her loneliness and sorrow. Sitting on her horse, she buried her face in her hands.

"I'm leading these people to their deaths," she said. "There's no way they can face the army that Deorc may have amassed, let alone dragons. One dragon could kill them all."

At that moment, a shout rose from one of the companies. The ballista they had fired, hit one of the dragon shaped targets.

"Hah, see there m'lady. Ya may be wrong. It's like shooting a harpoon on rough seas at first. A whelp may miss a few times, but when he hits, he begins ta aim like a man. You'll see; they'll do better. The Standel men fought dragons. They wear armor made from the hides of dragons killed at Falcon Ridge. That's why the breath o' the lizards is like a spring breeze ta them. They take no hurt, and they fear nothin' now because when they had no hope, they saw dragons fall before 'em."

"Brave words, Kreigar, but the Baron's men are farmers."

"Aye, and I was a fisherman, but when it came time ta fight fer m' home and fer somethin' good and right, I put away m' nets and joined m' sword w' other good men," Kreigar answered.

Annel nodded her head. *Good men could accomplish much, but could she ask wives and mothers to sacrifice the love of their lives on her say so? Could she ask men to give their lives?*

"Caer Amal has the only true fighting force, and they're no more than maybe one thousand men," she said. "We don't even know if they'll join us. Other than the brothers of Amal, there are only six or seven more caers that will join us at the moot next week, and there is no guarantee they will choose to serve with us. If they do unite with us they'll add maybe another thousand. Total in the field, we'll put maybe three thousand men at most. I fear we'll be outnumbered five to one from reports the scouts have gathered, and Gulth may not be able to fend off the dragons especially if there are some ancients that Deorc has awoken."

"Would ya have these people sit in their homes and wait ta be devoured?"

"No, but … ."

"Either they die fightin' like the men they are, or they die like the sheep that Deorc thinks they are. Lady Annel, leave yer misgivin's behind ya. Yer dark dreams only cloud yer vision. Ya've given these people hope. Don't let 'em down now."

Annel bit her lip. "You're right. Help Lord Perigreen with the preparation. Have the men train until dark, and then make sure they get a good meal with their units. Let them go home tonight, but after tonight no man goes home. They train, eat, and sleep with their troops. They have to be one. I must find Baron Aelan now. Messengers said three more war bands will join us tomorrow. One of the scouts from the far south returned this morning, and he reported that he observed preparations for an army to move. I fear a decision will have to be made at the moot next week to choose a battlefield that will be to our advantage. I'm sure there are spies here, and they know we're preparing."

Kreigar touched his hand to his brow in salute and nudged his horse toward the command center where Lord Perigreen and four of the rangers of Standel stood discussing the mock battle.

Kreigar and Annel were about one hundred paces apart when, he looked back and shouted, "I almost forgot. Marcus told me ta tell ya he needs ta talk to ya. He had a dream or somethin'."

She acknowledged him with a wave and turned her horse toward Caer O'Dai.

***

Annel walked into Marcus' room. He sat on the bed dressed in clothes that cost more than his family's farm. Angus, the bard, sat on a stool teaching the young boy lessons in language. Marcus' face brightened when Annel entered, and he jumped from the bed.

"Lady Annel, Angus tells me the funniest tales. He says I can't say m' Da no more. He says I gotta be proper and say 'my father.' Dingest thing I ever heard."

Annel smiled. She had no idea what 'dingest' meant, but laughed anyway.

Angus laughed aloud and said, "He is a wearisome student, m'lady, but I told him if he wanted to be able to sing the tales, he needed lessons in proper language."

Annel nodded to Angus and looked at Marcus. "Angus is an excellent teacher. He'll teach you the proper use of language for a young lord."

"Not sure I like bein' a lord when I talk," Marcus said. His innocent face beamed in the sunlight streaming through the window.

Annel knelt in front of Marcus and cupped her hands around his cheeks. She looked up at Angus.

"Master, could I interrupt your lessons for a few minutes?" she asked.

"Certainly, m'lady," he replied.

"Ya shoulda said 'my lady'," Marcus said.

Angus wagged his head and shook his finger at the young boy. "I'll be back and we will continue, you young rascal. M'lady, he can be quite a handful. Be careful, or he will have you talking like a tinker or a blacksmith." He laughed, as he exited the room.

Annel stood, walked over to the stool near the fireplace, and sat down. Marcus sat on the bed.

"You're looking the part of a fine young lord. Are you happy?" she asked.

"The Baron's kind and all, but I miss m' Da and Mum. Never thought I'd say it, but I wish I could milk the cow w' Cristobal one more time. He ... uh. Well ... Angus said I could make a song 'bout 'im."

Annel looked out the window. She could see the wavering lines of the afternoon heat rising from the dust of the plains. Normally people should be planting crops and enjoying the warmth of the summer, but war lingered in the thoughts of everyone in the caer. Within the last month there had been three skirmishes with armed scouting parties to the south. Gulth had engaged two flights of dragons and had killed one of the lesser beasts, which had been spawned in the material world. No ancient dragons from the world of light had been sighted, but Gulth reported that he sensed their presence on four occasions. From what the scouts described, there was no doubt war would come, but most of the Baron's citizens tried to maintain a routine, avoiding the consequences of war. Against the backdrop of uneasy thoughts, an innocent boy sat on the bed in front of her.

"Kreigar told me you wanted to talk with me about a dream," she said.

Marcus stood up and walked over to Annel. He stood in front of her with his hands on his hips. She discerned the care with which he carried out his task.

"Da ya remember the dream 'bout Lord Widseth?" he asked.

"You told me that he said I needed to raise an army. He said the caers had to fight the evil on the plains, but that I should carry the battle to Misdara. You said he reminded me to use the light. I told you Widseth is my husband."

"Yeah, that was a happy dream. But ... ."

"But that wasn't the dream you had last night, was it?"

"No," he said. He bit his lip and looked up at the shield and crossed swords that hung on the stonework above the fireplace. "I dunno what war is, but all th' town's a talkin' 'bout it. I'm afraid like when I was hidin' in the root cellar waitin' fer the dragon to get me. I'm afraid the dragons will get the Baron like they did m' Da."

"I don't know if you'll understand this, but I'll try to help you," Annel said. "Fear isn't the opposite of bravery. Fear is the power of darkness in the world to confuse and destroy. The opposite of fear is faith in the powers of light. Faith is the base of all action. We would do nothing, if we had no faith that action would produce a result. The farmer would never plant a seed. The fisherman would never spread his nets. The hunter would never track the game. When you learn to use the abilities of the eternal worlds, you realize that your faith doesn't produce just action. It gives you power." She knelt in front of him and put her arms around him and drew him close.

"But m' dream was s' dark. I wanted ta hide under th' bed, but I was stuck, watchin'. A black creature came in the room, an' he made me watch the Baron die with all his men. The creature's army killed him. Then the black monster showed me Lord Widseth dead in a cave, an' you wanderin', alone, lost in dark passages, followed by bad things." Marcus' body shook as he began to cry. He hugged Annel and buried his face in her shoulder.

She felt anger building within herself. She wanted this to end. *How dare Deorc continue to try to use children to cast fear in her face?* Her resolve solidified.

"Would it surprise you if I told you that the dark one comes into my room too and puts murky thoughts into my head? Marcus, light is your guide through the maze of evil. It frees you from fear. May I give you a gift?"

Marcus stepped back and wiped his nose.

"Ya gave me a lot already."

Annel remained kneeling in front of him. She reached out her hand and with her forefinger touched a tear as it streaked his young face.

"After I first met Widseth, we went to a marvelous land, the hidden city of Meliandra. I met the Lady of Meliandra there. She became the mother that I lost when I was young, and she taught me so many things. She began to make me whole. I want to help you experience health and freedom, knowing your life is all it can be."

"But ya already saved me from dragons."

"I know, but healing begins in here." She touched him on his chest. She felt the spark of high magic beginning to build within her frame. She knew Marcus could not feel the energy yet, but her fingertips tingled as magical tension increased. The experience of light, flowing into her to be dispensed, always exhilarated her. She took a deep breath as energy pulsed at her beckoning. She studied the light streaming through the windows.

As the magical force filled her, she regretted her earlier depression with Kreigar. The men deserved better from her. Even if she took them from their families and led them to death, she needed to trust that there are some things worth making that sacrifice. As she trembled, filled with magical power to bless Marcus, she realized she had taught principles to him that she did not have faith to live. *No more. Here is the cause of my life.* She remembered a horse on the shores of The Diadem. It told her she could not return until she knew her true self.

"M'lady, Annel, what's happenin'?" Marcus's voice betrayed anxiety, and snapped Annel's attention to him.

Looking down, she realized she radiated. Her hands and clothing winked back and forth from translucent luminescence to solid physical matter like flames jumping from a log. Boisterous uncontrolled melodies ripped through the fabric of the room. Now she understood some of the things she had seen Widseth accomplish. She did not know if Marcus could hear the music, but she focused and joined her voice to calm and control the auditory emanations. Her offering floated through the air, pulling chords into distinct harmonies and soothing melodies. The rhythm of her voice created a distinct imprint until all the wild sounds joined her unique contribution.

She stood, and as she reached her arms upward, light flowed from her fingers creating an intricate tapestry on the walls, ceiling, and floor of the room. When she breached the gap into high magic the night she fought the dragon, unpracticed urges had motivated her. She realized that she drew her abilities that night from random and uncontrolled segments of the magic. Now she created. She had broken the chain of fear and ignorance. She controlled high magic by the application of rules unknown to the material world. The mystery of magic paled in her new knowledge. Faith transcended action and revealed power. Doubt fled before the abilities she had accessed. She realized that, until this time, she had used these hidden abilities as a child of the material world. Now she understood as a child of the eternal world. She lowered her hands and knelt before Marcus again.

"Marcus, I've blocked the paths into this room. The dark one cannot enter here again to deceive you. Now if you will allow, I have a gift."

Marcus stammered. "Yes, m'lady."

She touched the bridge of his nose.

"Such love as I have, I bestow on you to give you courage in the face of doubt and to fill your loneliness."

Torrents of light flooded into the young boy. Annel realized the depth of her reservoir had increased. She removed her finger from Marcus's forehead. The room returned to normal. She could still see the beautiful blue netting that protected the room, but she knew it had faded from normal sight.

Marcus stood in front of her. He sucked in deep breaths like he had been under water too long.

"Never seen or felt nothin' like that b'fore," he said.

"Neither have I," Angus said as he reentered the room. He took a hesitant step as if afraid to break a delicate crystal piece. "Sorry, m'lady, I contained myself poorly. I waited in the hall, but when I glimpsed the light and heard your song, I couldn't resist watching from the doorway."

"Master Angus, wasn't that the dingest?" Marcus said.

"Yes, Marcus, that was the dingest," Angus replied.

Annel smiled.

"Back to your lessons now," she said. "I must find the Baron. I have to prepare for the moot."

Annel rose to her feet, nodded to Marcus, and hurried from the room.

***

As Annel stood in the doorway, she observed Baron Aelan O'Dai sitting at the large round table in the repository of records. Each caer preserved accurate genealogical records in vaults as proof of nobility and lordship. The bards of each keep kept the histories of their lands in songs, but the leather parchments documenting lineage traced families for a thousand years. Many of the older records had fallen to dust, but Aelan prided himself in maintaining and caring for all available records.

"M'Lord Baron, may I enter?" Annel asked.

Aelan looked up from a large parchment spread on the table. Candles in wall sconces lit the chamber, and four large candle sticks around the table added light for work at the table.

"Come in, please. I've found something that may help us. Years ago, when I was a boy, I saw my father studying this map. Since then, I have often thought that perhaps, like me, he harbored dreams of finding a way into the ancient kingdom of Misdara." He shook his head. "Boyhood dreams," he muttered. "Nothing more than dreams."

Annel stood beside the Baron and studied the ancient animal hide. The depiction of a tree of life decorated the upper right corner, and a beautiful stature of a dragon, holding a gem, adorned the upper left corner.

"How old is this map?" she asked.

"I don't know, but I suspect it's among the oldest surviving relics. I'm not sure why it survived so well. Most of the other documents that I found with it have fallen to dust, or they fall to pieces when unrolled, but this map exhibits little evidence of age."

Familiar sensations of magical energy skipped around the beautiful inscriptions on the border, as Annel touched the edge of the map. She recognized the magical signature and the memory surprised her.

"Baron, I've seen something like this once before. For a time I was consigned to the island called The Diadem. While there, I stayed in a cabin for three days. I saw no one, but I feel the same magical energy coming from this map as I felt there. I wrote on some paper with a quill pen to leave a message, but to my surprise, writing appeared and answered me. I wonder if this map is a like item."

"All I see are lines drawn on an animal hide."

With tender reverence, Annel touched the hide, lifting it and feeling both sides. Her hands tingled with energy like when she stroked Gulth in dragon form.

"The creator of this map treasured the information. This is no mere animal hide. It is a dragon scale that has been prepared with great care," Annel said.

"How can you tell? It looks like common cow hide."

She took a deep breath and passed her hand over the map. Some of the lines and writing faded and then reappeared. As she leaned over the table to look closer at the design on the edging, her cloak brushed the surface. A mild electrical charge jumped from the cloak to the parchment, and words formed near the bottom of the map in common tongue.

"What's this?" Annel whispered.

"I don't know m'lady. Nothing like this has ever happened when I've looked at this map."

> **Laena,**
>
> *I hid you with good cause. The darkness begins to close on us. To my knowledge, our daughter escaped. One of the dragons of light resolved to get her to Taina. Our son, Paulus, died in my arms yesterday, a victim of the encroaching evil. He died defending the tree with the great dragon, Nobliskynge. Terrible treachery slew them both. The dragons of light managed to hide the tree from the defiling grasp of the dark ones, but Misdara is doomed. The dark ones have spawned evil creatures from our own people who are filled with hatred. They roam the cavern slaying whom they will. The Eye of Light dims, and I fear the Caverns of Crystal Wonder, the marvel of our age, will sink into ruin. Our only hope lies in this map. It will guide you to the hidden entrance and to the tree. I will meet you there, and we can rekindle the Eye of Light. My only hope is that Oreon will find you, and you can reach Taina with the map.*
>
> **Your loving husband Perrik**
> **King of Misdara**

Annel looked up at the Baron. Aelan O'Dai remained silent with his head bowed. After several minutes he spoke.

"Although no written records have survived, the songs say Oreon built this caer. He's my ancestor. No tale speaks of any quest with this map."

He fell silent again, and reached out touching the map in reverence.

"This explains many things," Annel said.

"And what does it explain?"

"I think King Perrik hid Laena on The Diadem. I think the clothes I wear are hers. The resonance of the magic in the clothing activated the map. It also explains why your healers wear the symbols of the dragons entwined around a staff."

"Always when I thought of the destruction of Misdara, I simply pictured a faceless event in history," he said. "But they were people torn apart by the times in which they lived. They were individuals with hopes and dreams and sorrows."

Annel nodded and studied the map while Aelan continued, "A king lost his beloved wife and son. I wonder if the daughter survived somewhere. How old was she? Would she even remember her heritage? And Oreon. How long did he search for his Queen before he abandoned hope and settled here? I can almost feel his pain. I think he must have spent his early years here, hiding from the evil that overtook Misdara. Why didn't the other Aelfen help? Could he not find Dragada or Taina?"

"Many questions to which there are few answers," Annel said. "King Perrik may have given us immeasurable help, if there is indeed an undiscovered entrance into Misdara."

"We cannot hope to lay siege to Misdara. We've neither the men nor supplies for an extended siege."

"I know, but my path eventually leads there. Do you see where the two rivers join to the northeast of Misdara?" As she touched the spot on the map, the ink responded to her contact. Other areas of the map contracted, and the area of the rivers near Misdara expanded, exposing the terrain.

"What magic can do this?" the Baron asked in astonishment.

"High magic of the Aelfen in Misdara." Annel's voice betrayed her incredulity.

"How could a people with abilities like this succumb and fall to darkness?"

Annel chose not to answer that question because she knew the powers behind the attacks on the caer were the same powers that destroyed the Aelfen of Misdara. *How could she offer the Baron any hope?* She studied the magnified topography of the land between the rivers. She touched the map again in the same spot, and it again shifted until she discerned movement. Minute figures scurried over the face of the hide. She could see traffic on the river as barges crossed the water carrying building material and supplies. She put her hand over her mouth to stifle her surprise and reaction.

"I see it too. They're building bridges. I can see two dragons flying above them and beyond there." He pointed. "There is an army gathering. I had thought to defend the hills between the areas where the rivers converge. Water on two sides would have given us some protection, but they have breached the barrier, and now it is a simple stroll to Caer O'Dai. How is it we can see this? I've never heard of magic like this."

"The map is like a scry basin. The Aelfen delighted in far seeing skills."

Annel let her hand drop to her side, and the map returned to its original configuration. The Baron touched the spot between the rivers, but nothing happened.

"This map responds to Laena," Annel said. "If these are her clothes that I wear, the map is responding to neither you nor me. We're simply recipients of messages sent ages ago."

"And yet, it shows things of our day. We can use it. In a week's time they will have completed the bridges. I fear their march will be swift along the river because there is fertile land and forage there. We defied them once, but the crushing blow will fall here at Caer O'Dai. They know a degree of strength resides here because you and the rangers repelled them. If we ride out at the conclusion of the moot and ambush them from these hills, we'll have a chance for a measure of success. At any rate, I'll order all the women and children to be evacuated north to Marshkata beginning tomorrow."

He pointed to hills on the east side of the river, three day's march south of the caer.

"I'll meet with the captains and the town elders to begin the evacuation," he said.

"A good plan, but I think the map should remain hidden. I fear spies. Most are loyal, but in times such as these, men are tested to the limit, and some may fail. We need to make haste to use the gifts provided or they may cease," she responded. "With your permission, I'll remain here and study the map for a while longer."

"Certainly, m'lady." He paused and rubbed his dark, close-cropped beard. Avoiding eye contact, he nodded his head toward her. "I've never properly thanked you in person for what you've done. I'm sorry for the skeptical reception you received when you first arrived."

He turned and hurried out of the room.

Annel licked her lips and swallowed hard. She felt a little lost. Events continued to erupt around her, and she felt like she participated in a grand puppet show similar to the ones she watched when she was a little girl on the streets of Eventop. *What or who manipulated the strings of expectation? If the lords of light in the eternal world were so powerful, how could they allow so much tragedy?* She immediately repented that thought because she knew the answer. This fleeting existence was no circus or holiday on the streets of Eventop. More like a farmer's field or artisan's workshop, life in the physical world allowed mortals to grow and design lives that either embraced eternal realities or rejected them in favor of temporal shadows that promised security, but failed in the proof. The experience in Marcus' room had demonstrated the available power. The ideology needed no verification. The lords of light tested her willingness to apply and live the principles.

Annel lowered her gaze to the map. One of the islands in the Forbidden Sea pulsed with energy. She looked around the room and found a quill pen at a writing desk on the south wall of the room. Returning to the table, she hesitated, but reached out and touched The Diadem. The map reconfigured until she could see waves gently rolling onto the shore. She followed the path from the shore to the cabin on the hill amid the trees and searched the surrounding area until she found what she sought. The horse stood in the eves of the forest a short distance from the cabin.

"I'm not sure who I am yet, but I know who you are," Annel wrote on the map.

The calligraphy faded into the surface of the leather. The horse reared in surprise. It nervously inspected the open space around the cabin.

As Annel's words on the map faded, new words appeared. "You are the woman on the shore who came to the island and now wears the clothing and mantle of the Aelfen. I have not felt the depth of this magic for ages."

"Reveal yourself, Queen Laena. There is no need for deception between us."

The ink on the map swirled until the horse transformed into the figure of a tall woman, dressed in fine clothing. The artistry on the map depicted her movements as she walked into the clearing in front of the cabin.

"How is it you use Perrik's medium to contact me? I've heard nothing from him in years. I can teleport others away from the island, but my efforts to return to Misdara always fail. It can only mean the Eye of Light has dimmed. Is the war over? Can I return to Misdara?"

Annel paused before she penned the reply.

"Your highness, Misdara fell two and a half thousand years ago. The Diadem distorts time. We are in a struggle with the evil forces from Misdara, and we found this map, intended for you, from King Perrik."

No writing appeared. The ink lines, depicting the slender woman, standing outside the cabin, wavered and faded. Annel scribbled a quick note.

"Queen Laena, you must help us, or your husband and son died for nothing. I assume you received the message sent by your husband on the map. You know the grief he faced. We now face the same terror. Deorc has gathered ... ."

"Deorc? Impossible. He is one of the Cherubim in Dragada— one trusted to guard the trees of life."

"His past honor sinks beneath his present actions. I'm not here to discuss Deorc's fall. I need to know about the hidden entrance to Misdara."

The ink inscriptions on the map faded, but the figure standing outside the cabin remained. Several minutes passed before an answer appeared.

"The entrance my husband spoke of is a tunnel of light, tuned to the fabric of my physical body. I am not sure my clothing that you wear will be sufficient to mask your body so that you may travel on the path, because it is keyed to my corporeal structure."

"I am somewhat familiar with the light travel, but I have yet to conjure paths to teleport my physical body."

"I can construct the path from the information on the map. Do you wish to do so now?"

"No, not yet. I must attend to the affairs here first, and we must draw Deorc and his army away from Misdara," Annel answered.

"What will you do when you gain entrance into Misdara? How will you rekindle the Eye of Light?" Laena asked.

"I don't know. Something I heard makes me think the Eye of Light might not even be in Misdara any longer."

"And where could it possibly be?"

Annel remembered Angus singing the song about Misdara and telling her about the Eye of Light. "I'm not sure, but I think my husband Widseth is searching for it in Bilbra. An ancient song fragment chronicled that shadows hid the Eye in Bilbra."

"Much has changed in the world. Perhaps when this is ended you will return to The Diadem and help me find a way to leave."

"Queen Laena, my faith is weak. I'm not experienced as you are. Perhaps you should use the information and take my place in Misdara."

"My child, I already tried. I tried the instant you first made contact, as soon as I received my husband's message. I'm unable to leave this island until the Eye of Light is of sufficient strength."

"My task lies before me," Annel wrote.

"Even the most powerful mortals cannot alter the tasks placed before them by the Lords of Light. May dragons of light guide your path, young one."

"Thank you. I seek only protection of those I love. May I die in defense of friend and kin, facing my foe."

"Ah, you know the proper response to a blessing. Some good from my era survived. If you will excuse me, I wish to go to the seashore and contemplate my grief."

"Certainly, your highness. I will contact you at the proper time."

The serpent is an unusual beast, both feared and revered. Some cultures have emphasized the death dealing capacity exemplified by poison and fangs, while others have venerated the beauty and capacity to renew and heal by shedding the skin of an old life. I suppose, dear student, that the dual nature of the serpent is symbolic for all life because the image of two serpents, opposed to one another, entwined around a staff represents more than an artistic rendering. It embodies opposites—good and evil, light and darkness, health and sickness—clinging to a staff that represents ultimate freedom—the ability to choose. Without choice, freedom exists only as a lofty concept without any base in reality.

From the Teachings of Leanna, Master Mentor of the Abbey de Testrey—found in the Library of Vindry

Chapter 10. Serpent on a Pole

Widseth strained to pry the large crystalline structure from the side wall of the cavern near the floor of a new digging. Only a week prior, one of the workmen had punched a hole in one of the main tunnel walls, revealing a lava tube, approaching twenty feet in diameter, which almost intersected the man-carved passage.

Often these natural tubes provided rich sources of gems and precious metals. This particular opening, formed by swift flowing lava, ended on the downhill side only three hundred paces from where the workers had broken through. The super heated lava had met resistance and cooled, plugging the natural passageway. On the upward side of the channel, the guards had not found the end of the lava track. Several smaller branches joined the main tube, revealing a honeycomb of warrens.

Danger often lurked in new lava diggings. At times they contained pockets of toxic gas or provided poor ventilation for the torches. Sometimes the route markings made by the sentries as guides, confused both workers and guards, and on occasion men lost their way, wandering for days. More often than not, other work parties discovered their remains weeks or even years later. Widseth learned respect for the unforgiving nature of the mines.

When guards left the workers alone, Widseth provided wizard's light in place of torches. With better light, the workers on the crews with which he labored often found deposits that might have been missed in torchlight. Their increased production assured better food and care, and those factors gave rise to his increasing popularity. Everyone wanted to work with him.

"Can you help me for a moment?" Widseth asked.

Two men hurried to his dig and helped him shift the glazed crystalline formation. Together they lifted it from the lower part of the wall to a cart. The mass weighed forty or fifty pounds. Most would prove to be of trinket value, but when the cutters cut and broke apart the mass, Widseth knew they would find several precious stones of value.

"An excellent piece," one of the men said. "Gems from this wi' grace a king's crown."

"There are some beautiful stones there, to be sure," Widseth said.

He turned back to the indentation in the wall. When he reached down near the depression, he felt the movement of air flowing from the lava tube through a porous layer that had been concealed by the outcropping of crystal material. He touched the wall. It felt warm to his hands. He chipped in several places with the pry bar to make sure he had missed nothing. The soft tapping revealed what he suspected. The hollow sound divulged that another tunnel ran adjacent. As he noticed a faint but straight seam in the rock wall, a sudden chill tickled his spine. He had discerned this same impression of evil several times, but never so strongly. In the past the source had masked the emanations better. Discomfort entered his mind. The low magic signature on this sensation had bound him to a tree in an orchard once before. *Gulth rescued him then.*

A simple noise startled him. A man struck steel to flint to light a torch. The rear lookout threaded his way through the workers.

"Dim yer wizard light. Guards are a comin'," the man whispered.

As the wavering torchlight sputtered to life, Widseth opened his palm and gathered in the small ball of luminescence. A smoky yellow glow replaced the white radiance of his magic.

"Get a move on ya tunnel maggots. Time fer shift change. Any dead up in there?" The voice carried around the bend in the passageway.

Three guards, carrying torches and spears, appeared from the side passage that connected to the old mine tunnels. They pushed aside the workers and approached the cart.

"What's this? Ya tunnel rats done good t'day. I'll put ya in fer extra rations t'night," one of the guards said.

"Thank ya sir," one of the men responded.

"Shut up, or I'll break yer face w' the butt o' me spear. Get movin'."

Four men gathered the picks, shovels, hammers, chisels, and pry bars. Every tool had to be returned to the quartermaster, or a man would die. After the crew leader double counted the tools and loaded them onto one of the carts, the men began the long walk back to the barracks, passing their replacements on the way. The last four men wheeled the two carts filled with the tools and possible gem findings.

Widseth knew that after the workers scoured the new tunnels, they would build diversions for the underground river to wash through the channels and sweep tailings down to the sluice pits. He tried to calculate in his mind how many men had been slaves here in the last thousand years. The number staggered him, but numbers and time meant little in the mines. After almost eight thousand five hundred steps, the crew reached the bridge and crossed to the barracks. The men quickened their pace when they smelled the boiled potatoes and cabbage. After returning the tools to the quartermaster and weighing the crystals, the men scurried to their cells to retrieve bowls and spoons.

In his cell Widseth paused to consider the malevolent sensations he had detected in the lava tube. The slaves openly believed that evil creatures wandered the tunnels. Guards used the stories of phantom beasts to control the workers, but Widseth knew the guards never walked the mines alone.

"It looks as if you had a good day today."

Widseth turned and faced Almaron who stood in the doorway to his cell.

"Hello, Almaron. How's the leg?" Two days previous, a rock fall had bruised Almaron's ankle. He had remained in his cell to recover. The other men on the crew begrudged the former priest's time off because this was not the first time he had contrived a rest from hard labor. They suspected he paid the guards for light labor. Widseth reserved his comments.

"I'm getting around better. Your spell helped, of course. They made me cut potatoes," Almaron said. The tenor of the remark equated cutting potatoes with the hard labor of the mines.

"I'm ready to eat some of the potatoes you cut. Will you join me?" Widseth asked.

"I hoped you would ask. The other men gave me the cold shoulder. They think I'm a slacker, but I do my share."

The remark elicited no response from Widseth. He picked up his bowl and spoon.

"I'm hungry," he said.

The two men walked to the far end of the common area and sat alone at one of the smaller tables. Widseth noted the icy stares from the other men. He knew they disapproved of his association with Almaron. They did not trust a man who engineered so much time off for injuries, and they could not understand why Widseth, who worked harder than any man in the mine, would mix with a man like Almaron. Widseth mulled their oft repeated complaints in his mind.

"You've been in the mines for several months now. Do you know what the men say about you?" Widseth asked in a quiet voice.

"I suppose they say I am a soft piece of flesh who consorts with the guards for favors."

"Not far wrong. They consider you a liability and even a danger. If you persist, you will have the trust of none of the men."

"I do what I do to survive," Almaron said. "Do you think a man like me could endure a place like this without inducements to the powers here? No, I couldn't. You know that."

Widseth paused in silence and stared at the slice of potato and the chopped cabbage leaf in the tepid broth. He sipped the soup. When he looked up, his gaze pierced all of Almaron's facades.

"When I helped you the first day you were here, I knew the Inquisitors had assigned you to assassinate me. You might have even volunteered, but I held out hope for you. I fear no knife in the dark. You must know that by now."

Almaron avoided looking into Widseth's hazel eyes.

"I see I am undone. How long before you dispose of me, Master Aelfe?"

"Dispose of you?" Widseth asked. "I offer you another chance, another life. You can leave the shackles of darkness and bask in the freedom of eternal light, but I can't make that choice for you."

"Freedom? How do you dare say I am in shackles? You are the one consigned to these holes until you die. With a word, I could leave this den of misery."

"And where would you go? Having failed to kill me, could you go back to your masters?"

Almaron sat silent, drumming his fingers on the tabletop before he spoke.

"Why are you here?" Almaron asked. "We all felt your power at the judgment seat in Tabul. Had you walked away, no one could have stopped you."

"Now we're at the heart of your interest. Your masters may have wanted me dead, but you … you've delayed the attempt. I don't think you fear trying to kill me, but more important to you than my death is the reason I'm here."

Almaron licked his lips and looked down. Widseth drained the remaining broth and ate the piece of potato and cabbage.

In a quiet voice he said, "Two hours after lights out, meet me over the bridge near the left tunnel. Come prepared to try to kill me, or to discover what I seek. Your choice."

"How do I get by the guards?"

"The same way you always do," Widseth replied.

As Widseth turned and walked toward his cell, Almaron asked, "And how do you avoid the guards?"

Widseth paid no heed and continued walking.

***

Rin stood at the apex of the new bridge over the river. An ancient dragon sat as a doorpost at the south end of the bridge. Early sunlight glistened from the brilliant blue scales, each tipped with golden edging. The immense creature inspected the surroundings with black eyes that reflected no light. The dragon lazily yawned and stretched its enormous wings. Its maw, filled with sharp dagger-like teeth, looked like the gigantic horned beak of a hideous bird. Thorny protrusions crested the head and continued down the spine of the monster. Rin reveled in the thought that this creature obeyed him. Deorc had called this dragon Lighininge. It had come with Deorc into this world at the dawn of history from the world of light. Rin felt safe because he knew Lighininge could kill the golden serpent that had humiliated him when he first attacked the caer.

The creak of leather harnesses and wooden carts supplanted the morning noises along the river, as men, horses, and carts crossed the bridge in a long procession. The engineers and slaves had struggled for nearly four weeks to bridge the river while the main army made preparations on the south side. A cruel shell of a man had directed the construction. He was one of the shadoine. They had arrived with the magnificent Lighininge. Deorc said that their kind served several of the ancient dragons. They numbered less than one hundred, but their fell appearance caused even the hardened warriors from the north to give them wide berth. Their kind had served the dragon for thousands of years, and because of the secret spells Lighininge cast upon them they straddled the world between the living and the dead. No one had observed them sleeping or taking any kind of sustenance.

Rin shivered as one of the shadoine passed. They served as captains in many of the companies of men. Rin knew the human soldiers thought they were spies for Deorc, but no one questioned a dragon. All the shadoine dressed similarly with archaic brass armor and black plumed helmets that covered their faces. A white skull adorned the upper left breast of their black cloaks. They carried a long sword and evil looking daggers. They struck fear whenever they appeared. As a group, they charged the atmosphere with dread, darker than the worst nightmare. Rin wondered if he really commanded them. They never spoke, but seemed to obey his instructions without hesitation.

A man in black livery, riding a horse with a dragon crest embroidered on the barding passed Lighininge and made his way toward Rin at the crest of the bridge.

"What news?" Rin asked as the man approached. "How much longer will it take to get the army across?"

"Lord Rin, things are moving well. In an hour's time most of the strike force will be on the north side of the river. The supply train and support units will follow. By noon, all will be in place. I suggest we spread the first units that crossed this morning as pickets and set camp. This afternoon we can plan the order of march, and in the morning … ."

A thrill of excitement shot through Rin.

"Captain, in the morning begins the end of the old world and the beginning of a new age."

"If I may ask, sir, where are Deorc and Brulon?"

"Two other ancient dragons may join us, but I haven't learned the proper chords that will control them. Deorc will try to persuade them. Brulon is with the first units that crossed."

The man nodded and said, "I'll return to the supply units and make sure they are ready to move."

"Well enough," Rin said. He turned and looked up river. As he examined the river, he walked toward the north shore. Work barges still lined the shores on both sides. The southern shore had developed into a small town filled with smithies, piers, and other industrial enterprises to build the bridge and supply the army. As Rin walked across the bridge toward the northern shore, he began to sing a harsh tune filled with discordant harmonies. His favorite mount lifted into the air from a hillock on the plains and descended in a circular pattern on the north side of the river. Rin met the lesser dragon and mounted. He touched the guides to the beast's neck, and the creature beat its wings and ascended.

Nothing pleased Rin more than the wind in his face. He remembered his terror the first time he saw a dragon. In four years, so much had changed. Now he delighted in the dragons because he mastered them. He knew their songs. He knew the special chords that controlled them. He had conquered dragons. Every one responded to a different melody, but if he discovered the proper refrain, the creature sublimated its will to his. Now he anticipated putting the world of men under his feet. He remembered Annel's lesson that she taught him in the orchard about freedom, but her words rang hollow. He relished his self made freedom.

Rin scanned the rolling grassland along the river. The line of the army looked like a dark snake slithering through the grass. He liked that thought. *His army ... his own personal army, ready to deliver a poisonous blow to anything that approached. That troublesome woman, Annel, and the stupid Baron of that caer would be the mice hunted by his snake.*

***

The last work crew had returned from the upper mines. Four hours remained before the next group of men would leave the common area for the diggings. Widseth stood in the deep shadows near the left tunnel, listening to the river rushing beneath the stone bridge. Occasionally men's voices carried from the common area.

He saw Almaron before he heard the soft foot steps. The former priest had enveloped himself with a low magic shroud of darkness. It compared unfavorably with an invisibility spell, but in the low torchlight, it sufficiently shielded Almaron from other eyes. To Widseth's superior abilities, Almaron stuck out like a blaze in a dark forest.

When Almaron neared, Widseth stepped out of the shadows and whispered, "Over here."

Startled, Almaron jumped. Holding his hand to his mouth, he took several deep breaths.

"You shocked me. How is it that I cannot see you in the dark as you see me?" Almaron asked.

Widseth ignored his question, and asked, "Have you come to kill me, or has your curiosity overcome you? Either way … into the tunnel. We haven't much time."

"No," Almaron said. "We put things in the open now, before we take a step. As you guessed, you live at my pleasure, but there is a power here that I can't explain. I assume you seek the same source of power that I've discerned. I've no love for you, heretic. Your sacrilege threatens my world, but before I kill you, I need to know what you awoke here in Bilbra."

"It's a dragon."

"Dragon? How would you know? Why not one of the shadoine, or one of the other foul creatures that inhabits the depths of the mines?"

Widseth faced Almaron at close range and put his hand on the priest's shoulder.

"I'm the Dragon Master of this age," Widseth said. "It's my lot in life to know these things. You had best try to plant the knife now because when we find the beast, it'll either align with me or attempt to destroy me. If it destroys me, you'll stand no chance of escape. Either way you'll not have the pleasure of letting my blood."

Almaron bit his lip. The dim torchlight cast fitful shadows around the entrance to the tunnel. He pushed Widseth's hand off his shoulder.

"I'm not your friend, heretic, but something compels me to let you live a little longer. I wish to know more of this creature."

Widseth noted uncertainty in the threat. He nodded. "Follow me." Turning his back on Almaron, he walked into the tunnel. Only a few strides into the tunnel and the familiar sound of dripping water replaced the underground river noise. Mentally Widseth prepared for a struggle if an attack came from behind, but he relaxed when he heard the footsteps of the priest following him. He held his fist in front of him and opened his hand. Soft light gathered into a ball and rose into the air. It floated three or four paces in front of him just below the ceiling.

Widseth set a quick pace, and even with the wizard light, shadows nipped at their footsteps. The history of misery compounded over a thousand years multiplied the gloom. The horrible specter of men, lost to society, haunted their steps, and the empty corridors amplified the futile thoughts of men digging to find freedom from the overseer's lash. Widseth's mind numbed as he remembered his mother struggled to survive in these very pits. She had walked these halls. He wondered how many times the lash had sliced her back. Had Almaron known it, the time to strike presented itself. Widseth's depressing thoughts consumed him until he remembered his mother after her trials, bathed in light, standing in Dragada. Purpose returned to him, and Almaron's window of opportunity passed unnoticed.

Every ten minutes or so Widseth stopped and inspected the markings that the guards had scratched on the walls. In a short time they entered the new lava tube where his crew had worked earlier. Widseth patted the wall of the lava tube.

"I think the path to the lair is on the other side of this wall," he said.

"You feel no fear as you approach an unknown like this?" Almaron asked.

"I have faith that the lords of light would not send me on an errand that had no possibility of success. If I allowed it, fear would destroy that faith."

Almaron shook his head. "Your words are hollow. Your quest is a vain imagination, concocted by fantasy. I don't deny there're powers of light and dark, but they're elements of this world. There's no world of light. Reality proclaims birth, life, and death ... nothing more. You're a dead man, and this mountain will be your tomb."

Widseth studied the curved wall of the ancient lava channel. He ran his finger along the line of a natural crack in the surface.

"Why did you come with me?" he asked. "I don't think you thought it would be easier to kill me tonight than at any other time. Did you perhaps think to win the argument with yourself?"

"What argument?" Almaron snapped.

"Which is more powerful, high or low magic," Widseth answered.

He lowered his hand and stepped toward Almaron. Staring into the priest's eyes, he continued, "Power attracts you like lodestones placed next to each other. You want to see a contest of wills. You've sensed the darkness in these mines, and you know my abilities. But there are things you don't know."

"I should kill you now. A simple command word to paralyze you, and I could take my time to put the knife through your ribs."

"But you won't because you want to see which is stronger. You want to see which choice you will make when the time comes."

Almaron held his hand up. The priest closed his eyes, and Widseth could see the man's lip trembling.

"Do you feel it?" Almaron asked.

"Of course I feel it," Widseth replied. "I felt it a thousand steps back. It's the aura left by a dragon, and the door is here. You have this opportunity to turn back before I open the door."

Widseth turned his attention to the wall and traced the outline of a wide entry on the concave surface. Silver ribbons of light defined a door wide enough for five men abreast on horseback to enter. Holding his hand in front of him, he flicked his fingers one at a time toward the entrance. Diminutive bolts of electrical energy jumped from his fingers and danced on the silver trimming. The rock wall responded and the entire section outlined in silver vanished, revealing a dark opening. Widseth expected an adjacent lava tube, but glowing light from the far wall exposed an immense natural cavern. The warmth of the room hit him in the face. He looked at Almaron.

"Life is a series of choices. You can still turn back."

After Widseth stepped through the opening, he looked back and studied Almaron. The slender priest clenched and unclenched his hands several times. Licking his lips, he looked into the gaping chamber. His dark eyes exposed his fear, but he stepped into the cavern. The orange glow from the far end of the cavity provided sufficient light, and Widseth doused the wizard light.

"Stay close," Widseth whispered, as he began to explore along the wall to the right of the doorway.

After a dozen steps into the room, the opening from the lava tube closed behind them. The glow cast eerie shadows from boulders and broken slabs of volcanic slag, but traveled paths wound between the stone debris.

"What's making that light?" Almaron asked.

"It's an open lava flow. Can you feel the heat? It would cook our hides, but I think the hot gasses rise and vent to the outside. The rising vapor sucks in fresh air from lower vents. Can you smell it?"

"That means there's a way out of here."

"I'm sure the dragon doesn't enter through the mines. This area might not even be its lair," Widseth whispered.

"You said you're the Dragon Master. Can you control this thing if we come upon it?"

Widseth cocked his head. He considered his response because terror bubbled just below Almaron's thin veneer.

"I don't know yet," Widseth replied. "I thought that's what you're here to see. I think your masters want you to try to understand my abilities before you kill me so they can use them." He paused. "That's not it, is it? You want to learn my abilities so you can gain mastery over your superiors." Widseth shook his head.

"And what concern would that be of yours, heretic?"

"Well, it's my life, or have you forgotten? The power entrusted to me is based on principles of the eternal worlds. If delegated to you, and you tried to gratify your pride or ambition, it would be useless to you. Low magic is based on this world, but it's only a counterfeit of a higher reality."

"I perceive the reprimand and reject it. You stand talking philosophy in the den of a dragon. You're more of a fool than I thought."

Widseth smiled. "You followed me in here, ignoring your fears and pursuing your avaricious desire for power."

A rock fell from the wall, interrupting the conversation. Widseth quickly scanned the surrounding area.

"We're being followed," he whispered.

"What? Is it the dragon?"

"No. Keep walking."

"But, I ... ."

Widseth signaled for silence, and motioned Almaron to hide in the shadows. Both men crouched behind one of the boulders near the wall about twenty paces from the door where they had entered. Two tall figures walked from the center of the chasm toward the door on one of the trails between piles of slag. Widseth risked a glance around the corner of the boulder as they passed. He noted that they wore helmets with black plumes. As the personages moved, he heard the creak and jangle of armor, but a dark cloak with a skull emblazoned on the left breast covered most of their bodies.

"Who could open the gate without the master's leave?" one of them asked.

"Only one with power like unto the master," the other responded.

The flat tone of their voices echoed as if they spoke in a long tunnel. Widseth felt Almaron trembling as the priest pasted himself as close to the boulder as possible. With a slight gesture of his hand, Widseth conjured an area that masked all sound and light. Secure in the enclosure of silence and invisibility, he hummed one of the peace songs his mother had taught him when he was a child. The melody calmed and focused his mind. Looking at his companion, he realized the man could not even recognize their safe position because terror crippled him beyond the ability to think calmly.

Widseth examined the two men, standing in front of the gate. One of them knelt and sniffed the rock floor.

"Two came this way, but the scent has faded. One of the scents was familiar."

"If they are still here, the master will find them," the other voice replied.

"Do you think it could be him? In over two thousand years no one has breached the master's realm."

The second voice ignored the question. "We need to report. The master will handle this."

When the dark figures passed by the boulder, one of them paused and looked at the void Widseth had created.

"What's the matter?" the other asked.

"Nothing. For some reason I thought of a tune my mother sang when I was a child."

"Your mother's been dead for over twenty five hundred years as the world counts. Come. The master will want our report."

The shadowy entities continued toward the center of the cavern. Widseth cancelled the spell and looked around the boulder.

"They were shadoine," Almaron said.

"Tell me of the shadoine."

"The tales say that they're not dead and not alive. They're held to the will of their master by magic from before the beginning of time, known only to … ." Almaron paused.

"You can say it … known only to dragons."

"Yes … known only to dragons. Widseth, this is madness to confront a dragon. It'll know we're here. We could leave. Open the gate again."

"The beast already knows we're here."

"I'll go to my superiors. I'll tell them there is nothing to fear from you. I can get you released."

"Almaron, I obey the lords of light. My choice is to confront the dragon."

"You've no weapons to kill a dragon."

"Almaron, you misunderstand. I am the weapon."

Widseth stood and stepped from behind the boulder. He followed the same trail the shadoine had used. With his sight, he could see faint emanations of their footprints on the rock route. After a few moments he heard Almaron's soft footsteps behind him. As the glow of the far wall drew closer, he could hear the hissing crackle of superheated rock. Sulfurous gasses filled the air and the heat increased. Sweat trickled down his back and off his forehead.

Near the embankment holding the lava, the trail turned toward a huge fissure. Grotesque outcroppings of rock spilled over the embankment where in ages past the lava had overflowed its channel. The trail climbed upward beside the river of molten rock, toward the split in the wall. When Widseth reached the crevice, he saw it opened into a large hollow space. Precious stones and gold filled the floor of the room. For ages, the dragon had scattered the plunder of many cities and civilizations in this room. A monstrous creature lifted its head and stared at him.

"What human dares to enter my presence?"

Widseth ignored the immense dragon.

"Show yourself, Schadwe. You know who I am, and I know you are here."

The huge dragon's shape, among the plunder of ages, dissolved as the illusion dissipated, and a hideous creature from behind an outcropping of rock reared up on its hind legs until it was twice the height of a man. Schadwe's bellow echoed through the cavern. A crown of horned spikes adorned the dragon's head, and scores of sharp teeth flanked dagger-like fangs that protruded outside its jaw. The dark scales of the beast reflected the orange glow of the lava and broke the light into a myriad of colors that melded into a murky cloud-like appearance around the monster. Widseth realized that gems encrusted the scales of Schadwe. Scanning the spectrum, he determined the gems were held in place by a dark aura of mystical power. Schadwe manipulated shadow and light in confusing patterns designed to deceive and camouflage. In the sunlight, the effect would have been stunning, but in the underground, the unnatural combination magnified the dragon's evil appearance.

"Yes, I know you, Dragon Master, and I relish the thought of consuming your essence."

Schadwe clicked his talons together and cast a spell, but Widseth pitched his voice to a note, and light sprang from his fingers. The energy collided in a thunderous impact. A large outcropping above the lava crashed into the liquid, and the concussion dislodged a myriad of smaller rocks and pebbles that trickled to the floor. The last rock found its resting place and silence filled the cavern. Widseth and Schadwe stood opposite one another. The dragon dropped to its belly and began to undulate, moving toward Widseth like a serpent enclosed in a malevolent cloud of light and shadow.

Widseth backed to the apex of the trail and readied himself to dodge if the serpent struck.

In a quick sensation, Widseth felt the knife pierce his back and slide between his ribs. He fell forward on the rock floor.

"Die, heretic." Almaron stood over Widseth's fallen form. "Master dragon, I come to learn what you can teach me. I seek the roots of low magic. I present you this heretic as a gift." He pointed to Widseth, and walked down the trail toward the dragon. Ten feet from Schadwe, Almaron knelt and bowed his head.

Widseth concentrated to stop his head from spinning. He felt a sticky substance running down his side. He reached back and tried to pull the knife out, but the exertion spent his strength.

Widseth murmured, "Almaron, you failed the test. I can't protect you from your choice."

The next events blurred in Widseth's mind, but he heard Schadwe's voice directed at Almaron.

"Who are you? I needed him alive, you fool," the dragon growled.

Then Almaron screamed. Ignoring stinging sweat, Widseth forced his eyes open. Schadwe moved quicker than a falcon. He batted Almaron like a gray cat plays with a lamb. The priest stumbled toward the lava, but the dragon grabbed him lifted him above its head. Almaron shrieked in agony as bones cracked. Sorrow filled Widseth as he watched, but the screeches ceased when Schadwe waded into the lava and plunged Almaron beneath the surface. The walls of the cavern shook as the dragon roared its frustration and displeasure.

Widseth nearly swooned when strong arms lifted him and carried him away from the grizzly scene.

"Through here. Take him to the hidden room. He's our only hope. Quickly while the dragon rages."

Widseth strained to maintain consciousness, as his mysterious rescuers bore him away. It hurt to breathe, but he configured a healing melody in his mind. Despite his efforts, darkness overtook him.

***

"He stirs," a voice said. To Widseth the voice sounded distant and muffled. He struggled to open his eyes, but to no avail.

"His wound heals itself. He's healing himself from within," another said.

"He must be the one."

The clarity and volume of the voices increased. Memories flooded Widseth's mind. Someone had placed him facedown on a coarse blanket covering a stone slab, and had removed the dagger from his back. In his mind he heard Almaron's screams again and saw the hideous horned head of Schadwe. He lapsed back into troubled sleep.

***

Widseth sat up and scanned the small cubicle. He conjured a small globe to illuminate the room. The pain where the dagger had entered tingled, but he knew without doubt that it had healed properly. *Where was he? How much time had been lost?* Against one of the walls, he detected the silver outline of a small door in the rock similar to the one from the lava tube into the dragon's chamber, only much smaller. Opposite at the foot of the other wall, rocks had been piled to cover a grave. Armor and a shield had been placed at one end of the grave with a helmet and sword at the other end. The workmanship displayed an ancient craft, long lost to the world.

Widseth approached the mound of stones and knelt near what he assumed to be the head of the grave, where the sword and helmet had been placed. He lifted the helmet and inspected the beautiful workmanship. The gold and silver inlays had suffered no tarnish. The crest had been cast in the shape of a dragon with wings spread. Rubies served for the dragon's eyes. Ancient glyphs and designs graced the nose and cheek guards. The leather interior padding and throat strap appeared supple and strong. Widseth detected high magic dweomer shielding all the items from the ravages of age.

"Who are you?" a voice asked.

Surprised, Widseth stood and faced two shadoine who had silently entered through the stone door. Dark cloaks and closed helmets covered their bodies and faces. The figure that had spoken lifted the visor on his helm, revealing a cadaverous face. Cankered patches of skin with wisps of hair and beard clung to the skull. Empty eye sockets stared at Widseth.

"He handles the king's helm with no harm. He *is* the one," the other figure said.

"At last m'lord, you have come. Can you tell us if the armies of Taina and Dragada have reclaimed Misdara?" the first individual asked.

"How long have you been here?" Widseth asked.

"We are the king's guard. We rode with him to recover the Eye of Light that Schadwe stole from the Hall of Radiance in Misdara."

"Misdara fell twenty five hundred years ago. In the next age, Dragada fell. Taina nearly fell, but now lies hidden from the world. Most of the remnants of her people have joined the children of light," Widseth said.

"There is no hope. The dragon holds us in his service by dark spells," one of the shadoine said.

The other asked, "If Dragada fell and Taina is no more, how is it you can handle the king's armor? Who are you?"

"I am Widseth, the Dragon Master, high king of the Aelfen in Dragada. With power rendered from Taina and the lords of light, I cleansed Dragada, and recalled the dragons of light to the world. I've been sent to redeem Misdara."

"It is as King Perrik said. He fought Schadwe in fierce combat, but succumbed to the beast. Many of our brothers in the High Guard gave their lives to buy time for us to aid Perrik. Before he died, we secreted his body here, but then we were captured and enslaved by the dragon. Before the King died, he told us the lords of light would send one to contend with Schadwe."

Widseth paused and examined the former high guards of the king. The spells the evil dragon had cast held them between life and death.

"The Eye of Light must be the gem that the Unnamed One sent me here to find. Do you know where Schadwe has hidden it?" Widseth asked.

"Schadwe is the master of illusion and shadow. He wears it as a trophy in the midst of the horned crown on his head. The jewel's light has dimmed, but Schadwe also masks it in shadow."

"I ask leave to use your king's armor and sword to right the wrong of his death," Widseth said.

"As you will."

Widseth continued, "You saved my life. If you wish, I will release you to join your king in the company of the children of light."

The two robed men bowed.

"We are pleased if you would render that service for us."

As Widseth place his hands on their shoulders, he dispelled the dark enchantment that held them captive in the material world. The cloaks collapsed and the helmets rattled to the stone floor. Two images of light in the shape of tall men briefly appeared and then dissipated.

Widseth began to examine King Perrik's armor.

*The most daring mariners tell stories of lands beyond
the realms of Aelandra, but to reach them treacherous
uncharted oceans must be crossed. Most of the
currents in the known seas are charted, and although
often perilous, foreknowledge can prevent disaster.
Only mariners of exceptional skill can prevent
disaster if the charts are not heeded. A simple riptide
at a beach can suck innocents into dangerous water
beyond their skill.*

Manolo--Royal Cartographer of Marhome

Chapter 11. Riptide

Baron Aelan O'Dai pounded his fist on the massive table.
"We have to unite our forces. An army has crossed the river.
Scouts bring reports daily of the pillage of dragons. Units of men
march under the black banners," he said.

Annel stood against the wall behind the Baron's chair where
she observed each of the caer leaders. Two days had been spent
with protocol issues. Now the Baron hammered on the key issue of
commitment. Two of the caer lords still refused to believe a problem
existed.

It gratified Annel that the brothers from Caer Amal readily
threw their support behind the Caer O'Dai on the first day. They
demanded to lead their own units, but in the end acquiesced to accept
Baron Aelan's overall management for the campaign. Mostly Annel
listened to the troop strength that each caer could add. Three of
the nobles of the smaller caers had arrived with their entire fighting
forces. They bolstered the ranks by a thousand men. Me'lik and
Ta'un had arrived from Amal with an additional nine hundred men.
Immediately they joined in the daily exercises with the other troops
under Perigreen and Kreigar's direction. Daily, men had been
arriving from outlying districts, and the troop strength now stood at
nearly three thousand men, but a third were untrained farmers and
fishermen from the river towns. She tried to assess the speed with

which the other three clans at the moot might be able to respond, or if they would respond at all.

"Friend Aelan, you say a dragon supports the scouting efforts, but I've seen no dragon. My men will arrive on the morrow, but it would be good to know that if dragons, indeed, walk the earth, that one of them is with us," Lord Balfot from Caer Antrey said.

"Seven days ago, fifteen of the rangers from the north ..." Aelan began

"You should call them what they are," another voice said. A deep scar on the man's left cheek deformed his face. Lord Pulon from the eastern most caer had expressed his distrust for Annel and the rangers several times. "They serve the upstart king of Standel. His name is held for ill in my land. I've heard no good about these vagabonds who roam our lands as if they own them. If I decide to support you, Baron Aelan, I have one hundred men camping not two hours from this spot, but I'll not join them to any army with men or women from Standel." He looked at Annel with a scowl on his face.

"Your words are noted," Aelan replied, "but we hold these men in high regard in O'Dai. They've spilt blood defending us. Fifteen of them left with the dragon named Gulth to do what they can to impede the advance of the Misdaran army. We've heard nothing since they left."

Annel appreciated Aelan's adroit words. No news had come from the men, but using Perrik's map, she had monitored Gulth and the rangers. She knew they had harassed the supply lines of Deorc's army several times, forcing the advancing foe to waste time chasing ghosts. She guessed the enemy had been delayed at least four days.

Baron Aelan continued, "The rangers and the dragon have interrupted the march of the army to give us time." The Baron pointed to a large map spread on the table. "Two days hard march south of here, there's a hilly region near the river. If we can secure that area, I think we have a good chance of inflicting heavy damage on the invaders. I sent two hundred workers and supply wagons a week ago to begin fortifying the area. Unless the dragon and the rangers can buy us more time, the Misdaran army will pass that area in four days. If we can pin them between the hills and the river, we have a chance."

"Why could we not just man the caers and fight from behind walls?" Lord Balfot asked.

"No caer on the plains could withstand a determined siege. No. Our best course is to ambush this army that marches so confidently to burn our homes," Baron Aelan said.

In the distance the noon bell rang.

"We'll break for the noon meal, but this afternoon, I need your firm intentions. In the morning, my men and I march."

***

Two men crept along the ridgeline at dusk.

"There's one of them there. See ... by the fire," the man whispered. He pointed to a tall figure with a black helm and dark cloak. Rin's army had bivouacked for the night. Cooking fires had been lit with no regard for secrecy.

"Do you think we can rescue the dragon?" the other man asked.

"No. Gulth's gone. I watched that huge blue beast and another smaller dark one trap and subdue him. I don't think they killed him right off, but he was helpless. That was right before the three men in black attacked us. We gotta get back and let Lady Annel know."

"I still can't believe three of those men killed eight of us, and Gulth's gone."

"They're not men. I don't know what they are, but they're not men. I saw one of 'em take four arrows in the chest. He just pulled 'em out and kept fightin'. I think we're blessed that some of us got away."

"Let's get the others and get out of here. The lady needs to be warned."

"She'll take the dragon's loss hard."

"I know. Gulth gave all of us hope."

***

Annel's finger trembled as she touched different areas of the map in the hall of records. Something had happened. Only seven rangers remained. She searched the entire area for Gulth, but she found only the fallen figures of eight men in a hollow near the encamped army. She ran her fingers through her hair and wiped her brow. Her panic gave way to anger, but after a minute she calmed herself with a peace song. She considered contacting Queen Laena, but after thinking about it, decided that course would serve no purpose.

She buried her face in her hands and focused on Widseth. She thought perhaps the map could convey a message to him, but when she touched the area near the mines of Bilbra, the map failed to respond. Instead a message in beautiful silver script appeared.

"Widseth is masked by dark power. He holds his fate in choices that he will make. No light can reveal the outcome, until his feet are firmly planted beyond the evil shadows that seek to destroy him."

Annel grabbed pen and ink, and scribbled hurried words.

"And Gulth ... I suppose you'll deny me knowledge of his fate also?"

She waited for a reply, but the map remained blank for several minutes before the beautiful characters reappeared.

"Choice is the root system that feeds the core of your being. It is the nourishment for the fruit that your life will produce, but choices for you cannot be made by another. Widseth knows this. Gulth knows this. This is your time to choose, and you cannot relegate that responsibility to outside influences or to others. There can be no blame or excuses beyond your abilities and willingness to exercise this right afforded you. We will always be here to support and strengthen you, but Widseth, Gulth, nor I can take your responsibility to make choices from you. It is sufficient for you to understand that Gulth cannot help you, but he is not slain. You must become the light to guide the events on the horizon."

Annel bowed her head as the writing faded. She took the pen in hand and asked one last question.

"Who are you?"

Instead of words, the silver lines formed into the exquisite depiction of a dragon wrapped around a column outside the gates of Dragada. Annel leaned forward and kissed the illustration of Veramag, the Cherubim of Dragada. Quiet confidence filled her. She knew the dragons of light watched her. Carefully she rolled the map, tied leather thongs around it, and slipped it into the travel pack she had prepared.

The bell rang, signaling the conclusion of the noon meal. Annel gathered her things and started up the stairs toward the conference hall.

***

In terse whispers, Annel conveyed what she had seen on the map to the Baron.

"We cannot delay a single day. Something terrible has happened to our men and to Gulth. I urge you to say nothing of this to the other nobles, but I cannot find Gulth's presence on the map," she said.

"Are you saying the dragon will not be there to help us? How can I ask men to face this evil without the assistance your beast would have given?"

"Baron, I don't know all things, but the powers of light will provide assistance if we trust them. If something prevents Gulth from assisting us, other powers will arise to give us what we need. We cannot abandon hope."

Her urgent tone emerged from the core of her beliefs. Vocalizing the words galvanized her spirit and determination, but she could not be sure of the effect they had on the Baron. He turned from her and addressed the gathering nobles.

"Friends and brothers," he paused and looked back at Annel. "I trust you enjoyed your meal. It is the last meal I shall enjoy until I drive the invaders from our land. Word has arrived that our diversions will no longer delay the army marching toward us. I march today before the daylight burns any longer. If you choose to join us, our caer will hold your names in high regard as long as the wind blows on the plains. If you choose otherwise, I cannot hope you will rise above the darkness of our day."

Baron Aelan O'Dai motioned for his men to follow him, and he walked out of the conference room.

Annel watched the stunned nobles as the room erupted.

"It is our lot to stand together. This threat is real. Farms have been burned in my land."

"You're all fools. The O'Dai clan has always considered themselves better than the rest of us. This entire escapade is a ruse to gain control of our fighting men."

Similar comments continued for several minutes. Words almost led to physical blows, but at the last moment, a calm voice rose above the din.

"Well, I stand with Baron Aelan," Me'lik of Amal said. He and his brother, Ta'un hurried out of the room.

When they left, several other clan leaders followed. In the end, only Lord Pulon refused to join with the other caers. He stood alone near the large table. When he noticed Annel, he spat in her direction.

"You're the witch that brings so much trouble to the plains. Where is the emperor? Why has he not been informed?"

"Lord Pulon ..." she began.

"Shut your mouth, woman. Just because I asked questions, I didn't give you leave to speak."

Annel assessed his haughty mannerisms. Something beneath the surface tore at the man. She pitched her voice to tap high magic resonance.

"Lord Pulon, I believe your anger began long before the moot. I can help you put your resentment to rest if you will allow it. I can loosen the shackles that chafe your mind." The fluid sound penetrated Lord Pulon and calmed him.

"What would a witch from the north, like you, know about me?"

"You would join the other lords of the plains, if it were not for me and the rangers from Standel," she said.

"In the great war, my son and I fought under the banners of the dragon against your precious Standel." Lord Pulon's face clouded. "My son died at the hands of rangers like those who ride at your side. Why should I now think they are here to help us? It is more like that their presence will lead to more destruction."

Annel bowed her head before speaking.

"I can't replace your son, but I can assure you that these men and I are here to help preserve the freedom you cherish. In the great war, as in all wars, much was lost that cannot be restored. I can't promise there won't be further loss."

"Your honey coated words will not return my son and heir to me."

"Lord Pulon, ride with us. The evil that assaults us has no regard for any nation. It's driven to destroy sources of freedom and light. It's the same evil that fought against Standel in the great war, but it's reborn here in the south, and as you can see, its architects have no regard for former allies."

He looked down at the table and tapped his finger before speaking. "Your words are like arrows that pierce my breast. None can doubt their accuracy, but they also deliver undeniable pain."

"The pain of my words will seem as nothing, if you ride back to your caer and ignore the malevolence now. It will come for you," Annel said. "No one wishes to be sucked into a conflict such as this, but our time to fight against the current is now. Will you join us?"

He bit his lip and ran his fingers through his beard. "I want my life to stand for something, but I still don't trust the rangers from Standel. I do this for my caer and my son."

"So be it."

***

The new moon shed no light, but the night was clear, and the stars seemed to be jewels in the sky. Although most of the supplies had been sent ahead, several supply wagons trailed the Baron's army. The last cart caught up to the main encampment of the Baron's force long after dark. Aelan had insisted on no fires. He hoped the army could slip into the hills and the makeshift fortifications without detection by dragons.

A man wrapped in a dark cloak approached one of the night sentries.

"Where can I find Me'lik of Amal?" the man asked.

"And who be you?" the sentry asked.

"I am Brulon from Caer Amal. I bring word to the lord of the caer that another two hundred men will arrive two days from now in the hills."

"Good tidings, to be sure. You can find the Amal clan on the left of the line. Me'lik and his brother Ta'un will be there. Off in that direction." The picket pointed the direction.

"Thank you. I am weary from a hard ride."

The man wrapped his cloak about him and walked in the direction the guard had pointed. He met two more guards before he reached the camp where the men from Caer Amal had bedded down. He found the brothers eating jerky as they prepared for bed. Ta'un's hand went to his sword when Brulon stepped into view.

"Easy man," Brulon said softly. "I bring a gift."

He held his hand out toward Me'lik. The azure stone pulsed with soft light in the darkness, illuminating the scorpions and the golden band. Me'lik's hand trembled as he reached for the heirloom.

"Since you accept the ring, I assume our bargain is sealed," Brulon said.

"Yes, the bargain is arranged, and we will fulfill our end," Me'lik replied. He put the ring on his left forefinger.

"The ring is yours. Lord Deorc will be the judge of your deeds now. Fight aside this petty baron until you hear the trumpet sound four times in succession. Then you must turn on him and drive a wedge to split his force. Show no quarter. No man is to be spared."

"It shall be done as you say, Master Brulon."

"Deorc thanks you for the information you have been sending. By the time they reach their puny fortifications, this doomed band of heroes will be surrounded, and their ambush will turn to disaster. Until we meet on the field of battle," Brulon said. He turned and walked from the dark camp toward the outer picket lines.

***

At first light Annel awoke. Already the morning air hinted at the coming heat of the day. A hard march remained to arrive at the hills above the road by the river before nightfall. Last night under veiled wizard light she searched the map for Gulth again, but to no avail. She had noted the ponderous movement of Rin's army along the river road. The enemy was more than two days from the hills where Aelan hoped to ambush them. The seven rangers had already arrived in the hills. She hoped they had said nothing about the missing dragon to the men who labored there to build some earthen barriers.

She thought about the brave men who had served her so faithfully. They served King Fyan, but they said Widseth had sent a plea for Fyan to guard her. Although Annel had been at Fyan's coronation, she had never met the young king. She knew Widseth and he had been companions for a short time, and that the great dragon Veramag had a special bond with Fyan. She marveled at how the rangers served and loved him. Most of them had been with him at the battle of Falcon Ridge when he slew two ancient dragons with the legendary sword, the Talon of Light.

Four of the rangers had returned to Standel on various errands to report to Fyan. Eight of the fifteen men with Gulth had died. Only seven would return to rejoin their remaining eleven comrades. Annel was never alone on the plains. At least four stayed with her at all times. The others worked tirelessly to train and lead the Baron's raw troops. Kreigar acted as their commander and interfaced with Lord Perigreen and Baron Aelan.

After eating some cold grain mush, she unrolled King Perrik's map to search one more time for Gulth. She stared in silence. Where she expected to see Rin's army only scattered supply wagons struggled along. His army had marched through the night and a large cadre had broken from the main army and turned onto the prairie. Baron Aelan's left flank in the hills would be completely exposed. The well laid trap might become a mass tomb for the lords of the plains. Annel swallowed hard. Two dragons circled in the sky to the south of the hills. If they realized the men digging the fortifications were helpless, a horrible slaughter would ensue. She rolled the map and stuffed it into her saddle bag.

"To horse," she shouted to the men near her. "Get every man on a horse who can ride. Saddle my mount. I have to find the Baron."

She ran from the supply wagon camp to the encampment where the Baron had bedded down. Men looked up from breakfast as she ran past them, but paid little attention. Hunger and sore feet concerned them more. She spotted Aelan talking with Perigreen and Kreigar near several mules used to haul the two ballistae.

"Lord Aelan, we have to raise the camp and move now," Annel shouted. She stopped for a minute and took several deep breaths.

"What's wrong?"

Annel lowered her voice. Only Perigreen, Kreigar, and the Baron could hear.

"We've been spotted, or there's a traitor. Deorc and Rin's army marched through the night. It split in half in a maneuver designed to surround the hills by the river. I saw it on the map. They are stopped right now, but I surmise they will move again soon and try to gain the high ground."

The Baron pursed his lips and ran his fingers through his thinning dark hair.

"I'll send for the captains. We'll march until we drop … ."

"M'lord," Annel said. "I'll take a unit of horsemen and secure the hill until you arrive."

"I'll take the horsemen," he said.

"No. It'll take your presence to keep these men moving. If they sense panic, they'll flee."

"Perhaps we should retreat to the caers as Lord Balfot suggested."

"That would consign several hundred workers to a horrible death," she said.

Aelan rubbed his eyes. He avoided Annel's stare, and clenched his hands together in front of him.

"I can't allow you to endanger yourself by going with the riders," he said. "Perigreen will go."

"M'lord, there will be dragons there this afternoon. Without Gulth, I am your only hope to counter the dragons."

He nodded his head. "Kreigar and Perigreen, go with Annel. A month ago, while in the hall of records, I read the account of a battle. A large armed force split to attempt to surround an army half its size. The commander of the smaller force drove a wedge between the split army and threw all his might and destroyed one flank. Then he turned and attacked the other flank, destroying it."

He knelt down and drew in the sand. "We need a smaller but trained unit to keep the left flank occupied while we drive the enemies on our right flank into the river. If we can keep the enemy from rejoining, I think we have a chance to cleanse the plains of this rabble."

"A clever plan, m'lord," Perigreen said. "Allow me to lead the men on the left to keep the enemy from joining."

"No," Aelan said. "Go with Annel. We must secure the hills. That will be our refuge and point of attack for both flanks. I'll send one of the brothers of Amal and half of their men. They should be able to keep the left in check while we throw our whole weight at the right."

"I think that is the best plan we can make for now," Annel said. "We leave in ten minutes with as many riders as we can muster. If anyone asks, it is a scouting party. Baron, you have to make the hills by late afternoon."

She held his gaze with her eyes.

"Your time is now," she said. "Seldom do men have such clear defining moments. Men will die in the next few days, but those who live will sing you into legend."

Aelan bowed. He reached over and kissed the hem of her cloak.

"You are a queen. I should have recognized that the first day we met."

He stood tall and surveyed his awakening army.

"Perigreen, Kreigar ... before you leave with the Lady Annel, have your captains get the men moving. Bring any mounted men you can muster with you. May the light guide you."

"There is an ancient Aelfene covenant process. If I may ..."
She paused. "By sun and sword, I seek no man's life, but I stand with
you, my brothers until I take my last breath. May I die in defense of
friend and kin, facing my enemies. M'lords, may dragons of light
guide your paths."

***

Annel and nearly fifty horsemen pushed their mounts after
watering them at the river. After about ten minutes, the company
split from the river road and followed a winding track through a
ravine up into some small mounds rising from the plains. Workmen
had cleared the makeshift road as it led upward. Annel, her personal
escort of rangers, Kreigar, and Perigreen led the troop toward the
summit of the hills. About halfway up the gentle incline, a man
stepped from behind a large boulder.

"Lady Annel. It's good to see you. Lords, welcome to our
humble abode."

"Lambert ... good ... where are the others?" she asked.

"Up above. It's not much, but these men have done the best
they could. Where's the army?"

Annel could see where the men had augmented many of the
natural features to construct obstructions and barriers to impede a
force climbing the hill.

"The main body is probably five hours behind us. I think all
the supply wagons can be here by mid evening," Annel said.

"Good. The enemy's moving quickly. We arrived here
yesterday, but we've been tracking their progress. They marched
through the night, and a segment split off. As I see it, they'll try to
surround us."

"As I thought," Annel said.

"M'lady, the dragon ... ."

Annel interrupted him. "Not now. We'll talk further."

After a few minutes, riders arrived at the flattened summit
of the hill, and Annel surveyed the landscape. The three hillocks
were no more than a hundred feet of gentle elevation. The original
plan had been to conceal the army in the ravines between the hills,

and ambush Rin's army pinning it against the river. Now the hills would have to become bastions for defense. In addition to building earthwork barriers, the laborers had gathered mounds of rocks and debris. The blacksmiths had designed small catapults to rain stones on the enemy. The workers had brought two of the catapults and two ballistae.

The sight of the equipment pleased Annel because she knew Aelan might have to leave the ballistae with some of the supplies behind to make better time. In her mind she placed all the units. A ridge connected the three knolls. Young runners and the workers could convey supplies from the northern hill. Except for the ridge connecting it to the other hills, it had the steepest terrain and afforded the most protection.

Perigreen and Kreigar placed mounted patrols on the road. Other horsemen rode circuit around the hills. Lambert and the surviving six rangers stayed with Annel on the crest of the south hill near the battery of catapults and ballistae.

"Now, while the others are busy, tell me about Gulth," she said. "I know he is gone, and you suffered grievous loss. What happened?"

"We had good success disrupting the enemy's progress, but a few days ago, a creeping dread touched all of us," Lambert said.

"What do you mean?"

"Just a feeling, kind of like someone or something always watched us. For several days some of us were able to infiltrate the enemy camps. We saw the shadoine for the first time. Maybe they watched us, or maybe it was the dragons."

"Shadoine?"

"That's what men call 'em. I call 'em scum from the depths of evil."

"What are they?" Annel asked.

"I don't know. They're some sort of servants of the dragons. Three of 'em killed eight of our men. They're not alive, but not dead either. They can't be killed in battle. They ... well, we had to run."

Annel looked out over the plains. Dust rose in the south where Rin marched his army along the river road. To the east beyond the edge of sight, more units of the foe kicked up a cloud of powdery sand.

"Not a word to any of the others, but what of Gulth?" Annel asked.

"Somehow they caught him off guard. It was the huge blue dragon and that little black one."

Annel closed her eyes. "Please continue," she said.

"We'd seen both dragons before and there are three other dragons we've seen. The boy you call Rin rides one of 'em. I think the other two are what I've heard you call spawn of this world. Two of those have flown close here today. What's the difference in the dragons, m'lady?"

"The ancient dragons originally came from the world of light, but the blue one and the little dark one have fallen from light to darkness. They wield powerful dragon magic drawn from the empty realm of shadows. The spawn of this world have never experienced the eternal realms. They are monstrous beasts, with no special intelligence."

"We tried to help Gulth, but that's when the shadoine attacked us." Lambert lowered his head. He knelt before Annel.

"Lambert, please, rise. No long faces. The Baron's men will need every fiber of your courage and experience."

"But to be unable to help Gulth or our brothers in arms has tortured us."

"I've knowledge that they did not slay Gulth, but at present he is beyond our help." She scrutinized each of the rangers standing around her. "You men have paid a great price to defend me, more than any man should. If you wish to return to your homes in the north, do so now."

"M'lady, begging your pardon, but if the evil is not stopped here, it will be at the doors of our homes next year or the year after. We stay," Lambert said.

Annel nodded to each of them in turn. "I could expect no less from the greatest heroes of our age. Thank you. We have no dragon; the shadoine are an unknown issue; we are outnumbered probably four or five to one; and our ambush is laid plain in the enemy's eyes."

Lambert forced a smile. "We've stepped in a bog. That's for sure," he said.

"We've the seven of you here. Find Kreigar and tell him to bring the other four rangers. That'll give us twelve men. Tell Perigreen to have the others continue preparing for the arrival of the Baron."

"Yes, m'lady, but … ."

"We've several hours before the Baron arrives. You said two dragons approached earlier. Let's help even the odds before we have to deal with men and shadoine and dragons at the same time. Let's go dragon hunting."

The men grinned.

"Yes, m'lady," said Lambert.

***

Within ten minutes ride from the fortification on the hills, Annel and the men found dragon spoor. Two different sets of tracks were evident. The beasts had approached the hills several times, but one set of tracks always led toward the river road and the other set to the open plains.

"Which beast should we take first?" Kreigar asked.

"It makes no difference. If one is attacked the other will respond. We have to prepare for that. My guess is that the one laired near the river road will be closer to the hills. We haven't much time to take at least one of them out. I think we'll find the creature sunning itself in one of the depressions."

"What are your orders, m'lady?"

"You all wear armor made of dragon scales. It will provide you some protection. I will provide a shield when we approach the dragon to give an added measure. Let me see your swords and quivers of arrows."

Annel touched each of the weapons and imbued high magical energy into them.

"The spell won't last long, but the dragons will know your swords and arrows bite with harsh teeth. Kreigar, take two men as a rear guard toward the plains. Unless I've missed something, the second dragon will come from there."

"Aye, m'lady."

"Lambert, Pelton, Carston."

"Yes, m'lady?"

"Spread out and track the animal on foot. We'll be two hundred paces behind you. As soon as you flush the creature, try to put a couple of arrows into it and flee back toward us. We'll hit the beast on a full gallop. Your horses will be with us."

The men indicated agreement. Kreigar and the two others heeled their horses and turned toward the open prairie. Lambert, Pelton, and Carston dismounted, readied their bows, and fanned out following the tracks toward the river. Annel and the other men waited until the three were at a good distance.

"When the dragon shows itself," Annel said, "Spread out and hit it from every angle. The first choice is swords on horseback, but if it takes flight, we'll use bows."

Annel nudged her horse forward, and the others followed in a spread formation. In about fifteen minutes, the three men on foot slowed and crouched. One of them dropped to his belly and inched toward a small rise. He hand signaled the others to approach cautiously. They drew bows and let a volley of arrows fly over the rise and into the hollow. An angry bellow resounded in the air, and the silhouette of a horrific creature rose out of the small basin. The huge head with horned snout snapped at the men. The three rangers scattered in different directions.

The neck of the monstrous beast rose at least twenty feet into the air. It extended its wings to their full span and beat them with a force that created a dust storm.

"Now," Annel yelled. She reached for the image of the sword in her cloak. The blade broke free of the cloak and emitted blue flame. The horsemen dug their heels into the flanks of their horses, and their steeds bolted forward toward the ugly winged fiend. Lambert, Pelton, and Carston ran on separate courses toward Annel and their horses. Annel, with her golden hair flying, raced toward one of the running men that the dragon had picked as its first target.

The creature took a swipe at the running man and knocked him from his feet, but Annel arrived and threw up a protective netting of blue fire over the man. At almost the same time, the other six horsemen hit the dragon from different angles, inflicting sword damage. Their weapons, edged with the magical energy created by Annel, bit deep into the flesh and sinews of the beast.

Soon the brown diamond patterns on the creature ran with blood from arrows and swords. The roars of the dragon sounded across the plain. Lashing out with spiked tail and talons, it knocked one of the men from his horse. The horse screamed in agony when the jaws of the dragon closed around its haunches, but the unhorsed ranger ran at the dragon and buried his sword deep into its breast. The dragon wrenched the imbedded sword from the man's hand, and knocked him across the sand.

The creature staggered, but in a last effort, it batted its wings and lifted into the air. Instead of attacking, it tried to flee.

"No. You'll warn no one," Annel muttered.

She lifted her sword skyward. It glistened in the sunlight. To the amazement of the men closest to her, she began to vocalize a single musical note that built in power and intensity until she raised her other hand and pointed it toward the dragon struggling to flee. A thunderclap deafened the area. The concussive explosion of sound knocked the dragon backward, and it crashed to the ground. It rose once and then fell forward.

"Lambert ... Carston ... get over there and behead it. Take care. It may only be stunned. I want no surprises from this one when the other one gets here." She pointed to a black dot in the sky. "I hope it overruns Kreigar and sets down between us. Spread out two by two. This one will come in hot with breath of fire and all the anger we'll ever want to see."

Annel dismounted. She handed the reins to the man who had been unhorsed.

"Take my horse. I can protect myself better on foot. Get over there with Lambert and Carston. I think you have a sword in the belly of that beast that you'll need."

"Yes, m'lady."

The men scattered in several directions, preparing to charge the next dragon. At first none of them realized that Annel had not joined any of the companionships. She stood calm in the center of the coming vortex. As she watched the approaching horror, she sifted through memories of peaceful times. She remembered sitting with the Lady of Meliandra near a waterfall. That was so long ago. *How could the world continue in chaos and ignore the simple path to peace?* It amazed her how nations continued to choose the chains of war rather than the freedom of peace. Tomorrow she would face Rin, a boy she once loved and longed to care for. Now he sought to kill her and all she held dear. *How could this be?*

She could almost make out the shape of the dragon flying toward her.

She said aloud, "By sun and sword, I do not seek your death, foul creature, but by my choice, I stand between you and friends. I choose to die in defense of my friends, if that be the will of the lords of light. One of us shall die before the sun sets today."

As soon as the flying horror approached, Annel threw up a display of brilliant fire to attract its attention. The dragon altered its course by a slight amount and dove toward her. She conjured a protective shield and pulled the shape of the shield from her cloak. Standing under an umbrella of energy with shield and sword, she faced the plummeting dragon. The two men closest turned and galloped toward her when they realized she was alone in the open, offering herself as bait, but scorching fire descended from the sky as the dragon careened downward.

The fiery breath ignited the dry grass, but Annel stood impervious in a cone of blue fire. She raised her shield arm and blasted the winged beast with a shaft of energy. The violent impact ripped a huge gash in one of the creature's wings, forcing it to the ground. Through smoke and fire, the rangers charged. Annel sank to her knees exhausted by the expenditure of magical energy, but she took a deep breath and began to sing an entrancing melody to amplify her power. Through the dust and smoke, she watched the lightning attacks by the rangers, who mortally wounded the monstrosity, but not without loss.

In a violent counter, the dragon swept two men from their mounts. The screams of the injured horses intruded on Annel's song, but she maintained focus and flung another bolt of energy at the creature, striking it in the belly as it reared up to attack the men on foot. Carston struggled to stand, but Annel could see his leg was broken. Lambert placed himself between the creature and Carston, but he was not quick enough to avoid the raking talons. He stumbled and fell to the ground. Blasted by Annel's energy bolt, the dragon beat at its breast. Pelton and two others slashed gaping wounds in the creature. Exhausted, the beast finally fell forward, and Pelton chopped at the neck of the monster until his sword sliced the last of the tissue holding the head to the body.

Annel ran to the fallen men. Carston sat in the sand holding Lambert's limp body in his arms. At that moment Kreigar and his men rode into the charred area. Annel looked up at him. She wiped the sweat and dust from her eyes.

"Send a couple of the men to get two carts from the hills. Lambert's dead. Carston's injured. I want to leave the dragon remains here as a warning to Rin's army, but we take the heads as tokens of hope for the Baron."

"Yes, m'lady. Hurry men … get the carts."

As I have tried to record some of the personal accounts of battles through the ages, I have come to appreciate that sometimes the size of the battle, in terms of numbers involved, does not always correspond with the historic significance. We think of momentous struggles between masses of men, but often the fate of history rests on the shoulders of a very few individuals caught within those struggles, and sometimes the greatest armies are defeated by small events completely unrelated to the battle like a chance rain storm or freak accident.

Personal History of Winna—Master Historian of the court of Standel

Chapter 12. Gulth's Tribulation

The ritual burial drew to a close.

"Who will speak for this man, whose body we place in the earth?" Annel asked.

"I was his friend and comrade in arms," Carston said. Although hobbled with a broken bone in his leg, he insisted on being with his friend and had been carried on a litter. "Lambert saved my life more than once."

"I was with him when we faced the shadoine. He was the first to battle and the last to leave the clash," another said.

"I saw his generosity with children. He always gave a hungry child food, even if he had little to spare," Pelton said.

Annel bowed her head to each man as he spoke. Behind the group of rangers, she noticed Perigreen and other men from Caer O'Dai gathering. Then she spotted the Baron. His army had begun to arrive, but the Baron's retinue watched in silent reverence.

After each man who knew Lambert had his say, Annel asked, "Who will take Lambert's sword and deliver it to his family after the events that face us?"

Kreigar stepped forward.

"Lambert was a man o' the sea, same as me. I claim the honor t' find his family, an' tell 'em the tales o' how he wielded the sword in defense o' others."

Annel handed Lambert's sword to Kreigar. Kreigar stepped back and bowed to the mound of stones covering Lambert's grave.

"Men, we have to return to the business at hand. Return to your posts. The Baron has arrived. In the events ahead, show yourselves well and hold your heads high."

"Aye, m'lady," Kreigar responded.

Two men lifted the litter with Carston and carried him back toward the supply hill where a physician's area had been set up.

Annel paused and looked at the grave. After a moment of silence, she turned and walked toward the Baron.

"We secured the hill, m'lord," she said. The flat tone of her voice revealed the emptiness she felt inside.

"The men told me you've done more than that," the Baron said. "You killed two dragons."

"Yes," she paused. "We killed two dragons. We lost Lambert, but we killed two dragons."

A constant procession of men and equipment began to fill the hills. As the men passed near the area where the workers had placed the ballistae and catapults, they stopped to stare at the dragons' heads, placed as trophies.

"I think we have a good position, even if the enemy knows we're here," the Baron said.

Annel pointed to the dust rising to the south. "We know they marched through the night. I think they'll stop short of here to let their men rest. And out to the east there, I think they'll drive their men as far as possible tonight in an attempt to cut our escape."

"Then my plan has a chance of working?" the Baron asked.

"We saw only the two dragons. I think they were scouts for Rin. Perhaps he's hampered now. I sent scouts to the south to keep us appraised."

"Good," the Baron said. "I sent Lord Me'lik and about five hundred men from Caer Amal into the prairie with instructions to prevent that group out to the east from rejoining the enemy's main army. With two of the dragons gone, I hope we can deal with the two flanks of our foes separately."

"It's a good plan," Annel said. "I suggest we make this hillock the bastion of our primary defense. On the hill to the east we can place the reserve, and there to the north where it is most protected we can position the supply wagons. I think that will be the best area for healers to treat the wounded. The workers who have been here and the boys with the wagons can be runners with supplies where they are needed after the battle starts."

The Baron acquiesced. "I think I'll put Lord Ta'un on the reserve hill. That way he can either support us here from the ridge or reinforce his brother on the plains."

Annel licked her lips. "We killed two dragons, but we know there are at least three more, and two of them are ancients. If I'm to face them, I need rest. If you'll excuse me, please?"

"Certainly, m'lady. We'll handle everything. You've done more than your share today." The Baron bowed to her and walked to where Perigreen stood talking with Kreigar.

Annel looked at Lambert's grave one more time and walked toward the north hill where workers organized the supply wagons. As she walked she reviewed the faces of all the men who had fallen so far from their homes. Then her thoughts turned to Widseth. She wondered if he knew Gulth had been captured. She could not abide the thought of Deorc's foul talons rending Gulth's beautiful golden scales. She shuddered. Four rangers followed her in silence.

***

Annel awoke to the sound of a trumpet. She had slept wrapped in her cloak with a saddle for a pillow. Rubbing her eyes she stood up and looked around. The sun had just risen above the horizon and early morning shadows lingered in the ravines.

"M'lady, I'm sorry the trumpets disturbed you. We wanted to let you sleep a bit longer," the ranger named Wallace said.

"It's time for me to rise. I slept deeper than I have in months, and I've recovered sufficiently. Have you seen Carston? Is he well?"

"He's in the healer's area. Your skill helped him, and the Baron's healers and nurses are very good, but I fear he will not be able to walk for some time."

Annel nodded her concurrence.

"Here's a ration of bread," Wallace said. He handed her a pouch and a small water flask.

"Thank you," she said. "Please take a message to the Baron for me. I'll visit Carston for a few minutes, but I suggest we meet with all the commanders and make sure everyone has a clear understanding of our order of battle."

"Yes, m'lady," he hurried to the ridge connecting the hills.

Annel munched a piece of the bread and took some water as she walked to the healer's area. The wagon drivers had put all the supply wagons in a tight circle around the area where wounded men could be brought. Fifty warriors from Caer Balfot guarded the area and supervised the runners assigned to carry extra arrows, spears, and swords to where they might be needed when the fighting began. Annel immediately spotted Carston on a blanket near a cart and approached him.

"How are you this morning, knight of Beltor?"

"I'm spoilin' for a fight. I told the healer they could put me on a horse and I could fight on horseback."

Annel smiled at his words. "None the less you will stay here under the watchful eye of the Baron's healers. If something happens here, you'll be here to defend them."

"I understand m'lady. I can't see from here; did the enemy arrive on the field last night?"

"I don't think so, but I haven't been up the other hill yet. I'm going there now, but I wanted to check on you."

"That's kind of you, m'lady."

"I also wanted to thank you. We took some risks yesterday and paid a heavy penalty, but you and the other men may have given us the advantage we need to survive today." She bit her lip and turned away to wipe a tear. She walked quickly from the healers.

"You be careful, m'lady," Carston shouted after her.

She held her hand up and kept walking. After a few minutes, she spotted the Baron with all of the other clan lords, standing under the clan standards, near the ballistae placements. She quickened her pace. As she approached, the Baron stopped speaking and motioned her forward.

"Lady Annel, please join us," he said.

As she approached, several of the lords dropped to one knee and bowed their heads as she passed. The Baron bowed before her.

"I've told all the captains of your bravery and the courage of the rangers of Standel in killing these dragons." He pointed to the two heads rotting in the sunlight. "We've been discussing the order of battle. The scouts informed us early that the enemy did not rest long. You can see the dust rising there in the distance. We estimate they'll reach the bend in the river road in about three hours."

Annel noticed that all of the smaller caer lords, including Pulon, looked to her to measure her reaction to the plan.

"Baron Aelan, as we spoke yesterday, with the foe's force split, we have an opportunity. I will face any dragons if they arrive," Annel said.

Balfot asked, "What of the dragon that you told us would fight for us?"

"He won't be here," she replied.

"What's this?"

The Baron interceded, "The Lady Annel with fifteen men defeated two dragons yesterday. Powers of light are manifested in her. I choose to place my trust in her."

The others look at each other.

Balfot finally spoke, "We've come this far. There's no honorable road back to my home other than the path we now tread. I stand here with you."

"Good," the Baron said. "In the next half an hour we need to position our men. I need at least fifty of your best archers with little or no armor. I want them hiding singly or by twos wherever they can. As soon as the enemy comes in range they need to loose every arrow they have, aiming for the horsemen and leaders if they can manage it. Kreigar, I need you to lead these men."

"Aye, m'lord. That I can do."

"Won't there be a great risk for them to be killed when the enemy closes?" Pulon asked.

"As our opponent mounts an attack, the skirmishers will flee. No heroics, Kreigar. You flee. I want two lines of lightly armed men with bow, sword, and shield two hundred paces behind the skirmish lines. We need four hundred men there. The skirmishers will flee behind those lines and replenish their arrows. Perigreen."

"Yes, m'lord?"

"You will command these men, but I want the same action. Fire arrows and flee around the outcropping of the hill."

"I begin to see it m'lord," Perigreen said. "It's ingenious."

"I will be there with twelve hundred fully armed men with spear, sword, and shield. The skirmishers will take to the hill and fire into the advancing foe. Perigreen your line will form behind and to the flanks. Until the enemy actually closes with us, you will continue to unleash arrows. Then with sword and spear, we'll drive these barbarians into the river."

The lords looked from one to another. Annel read the fire in their eyes. The Baron had kindled hope.

"Ta'un."

"Yes, m'lord, where is my place?"

"You are in reserve. The men of Caer Amal must be ready to support us or your brother out on the plains wherever the need arises."

"I understand," Ta'un said.

"Lord Pulon, I need you here with the men who have trained with the ballistae and catapults. I believe the catapults can reach the road, and you'll need the best men on the ballistae in case dragons arrive. I'll leave the balance of our men here to continue to prepare our defenses. The workers who have been here will act as runners from the supply camp."

"Yes, Baron Aelan. I can manage that."

"Good. Lady Annel, can you stay on the high ground with Lord Pulon and watch for the dragons?"

"As you wish m'lord."

Annel looked to the east. The dust marking the path of the army to the east appeared much closer. She hoped Me'lik would be able to hold that wing of Rin's army in check until the Baron could execute his plan. She stared at the horizon and wondered if Rin's army had split again because she noticed another cloud of dust on the horizon further to the north. The Baron's plan had to work; otherwise they would be hemmed in with no avenue of retreat.

"May the powers of light bless your lives this day," Annel said.

The captains separated, and they began to move their men into position.

***

"Can you see them?"

"Where am I?" Gulth asked.

The swirling dark mist foiled his eyes. He felt no ground beneath him, but he was not flying. The sensation resembled when he floated underwater in a lake or in the sea. Before he answered the call of the Dragon Master, the lords of light permitted him to soar through currents of pure energy and light where he perceived everything around him through every cell. The thought tantalized his mind, and for a moment he thought he had returned home to the world of light, but the sinister mist left him sightless, and he realized he stood at the edge of the abyss where entities wander until they lose all memory of who they were.

"I rule this world," a voice said. "I can give you power here."

"I want no power from the darkness," Gulth replied.

Hollow laughter filled Gulth's head, and the vapors churned more rapidly.

"Do you not even wish to see your friends?"

"What have you done to them?"

"Ask and I'll show them to you. I've many powers to share. In time you'll enjoy them as others have."

Gulth tried to move, but realized any movement hastened his fall into the abyss. He shuddered as he stood on the boundary dividing the worlds of light and darkness.

"One more step Gulth, and you'll be mine forever. It is a simple step ... an easy step."

Gulth heard something other than the voice. He heard a clear high note. The note multiplied into a chord, and then to a melody. It was the song he heard when he answered the Dragon Master's call and entered the physical world.

"Ignore it," the voice said. "I will show you the racket's composer." The words hit Gulth like darts.

The mist cleared, and the still form of Widseth, stricken on a rock floor, emerged. Schadwe loomed in the background with slavering jaws. The scene shifted. Annel fell to the ground, blood oozing from her forehead. Men in dark cloaks surrounded her. Then he saw the Baron and his men fighting for their lives as their battle lines collapsed. The inconstant fog covered the scenes.

"Where are your friends? Why are your father and mother not here to protect you?"

"Your arguments are compelling," Gulth said.

"Yes, and it's so simple. Just step off the path and allow the darkness to fill you with power ... my power. You need never look back."

"Oh, but I will look back," Gulth said. "The music of the Dragon Master will always guide me. The love of his wife strengthens me. My sire's words sustain me. He told me to 'Hold to the Light'. My friends may die. My family may fail me. The world may fall to pieces, but I reject your chains of darkness. I am and always remain a servant of the lords of light."

"Then I will cast you into the abyss."

"If you succeed, I will bring light to the empty souls that wander there."

The mist cleared, and Gulth looked into the vast gulf of emptiness. He heard the moans and vacant voices of beings lost in the shadows.

***

"Let loose the catapults. Put your backs into it. Come on men. Load and release," Lord Pulon shouted.

Annel studied the battlefield. The Baron's plan had worked to perfection. Rin had approached on dragon only once during the battle, but Annel drove him off with bolts of energy. She worried about the ancient dragons. *Why had Deorc and the blue one not appeared?* Now arrows and rocks rained on Rin's army, as it rounded the corner of the outcropping. The skirmishers and the first line of men had given the impression of a retreat after inflicting as much damage as possible with arrows.

As the enemy rounded the outcropping, the Baron's heavily armed line charged with a vengeance. Shouts and screams of men filled the air. The enemy's more numerous force turned to flee, but ran into their own reinforcements. Men were hewn like weeds in a field. Annel turned away from the horror and closed her eyes. When she opened them, she looked to the east.

"Lord Pulon, look," she said. "Why is Me'lik retreating? The enemy's on his hindquarter. Why won't he turn and fight?"

"I don't know, but he's got to keep a wedge between the enemy's two halves, or Baron Aelan will be overwhelmed. There's another dust cloud even further to the north. Either the wind's howlin', or they're comin' mighty fast."

Annel stared at the plains. She could see two scouts with the Balfot Clan symbols riding hard, but horsemen from the Amal Clan intercepted them and cut them down.

"What's this?"

"Treachery," Pulon said. He drew his sword.

Annel mounted a horse.

"Stay here," she said. "Prepare to defend this hill." She knew the five hundred men here stood little chance, but this was their best possibility to survive.

"Where are you going?"

A trumpet sounded four times. Ta'un's men began to move toward the Baron's rear.

"I've got to warn the Baron and slow Ta'un," she said. "Every man with a horse, come with me," she shouted.

She knew Pulon would organize the defense as well as it could be. The horse jumped when she dug her heels into its flanks. Four rangers galloped after her ahead of another twenty five men. With blonde hair streaming behind her, she dashed along the ridge until she came within range of the first of Ta'un's men.

"Turn back, you traitorous dogs," she screamed.

The first ranks of footmen stopped and looked at her. She felt their murderous intentions. Blood lust seethed from their eyes until the first flash of light knocked them from their feet. Annel's stallion reared as she threw protective blue netting around the horsemen, gathering at her sides. Her clothing appeared as brilliant gold and silver armor. Bathed in the sunlight, her hair radiated. None who saw her that day could ever forget the magnificent image of the Lady of Light.

"Wallace!"

"Yes, m'lady."

"Get to the Baron. Tell him to get here with all his men, or we're lost."

Four times Ta'un's men tried to amount a charge, but Annel and her men drove them back with blasts of luminosity and lightning charges with the horses. Fortunately Annel's men blocked a ravine that prevented Ta'un from surrounding them, but the arduous task of maintaining the shield wore on her. Gaps began to develop, but forty more horsemen from the Baron's company arrived with Lord Perigreen. Annel looked back. The Baron's force began an orderly retreat, using another ravine to mount the hill. As Perigreen arrived, Ta'un and his foot soldiers retreated back to the east hill to avoid the horsemen.

"What's happened?" Perigreen asked.

"Cowards. Caer Amal has joined the enemy. They've been the spies in our midst. Treacherous cowards," Annel said.

"Come, m'lady. We'll secure this ridge. They'll not find it easy to surround us."

"Lord Perigreen, go to the Baron. He'll need your help. I'll begin to move the carts and the wounded before the enemy thinks of cutting our supplies. Get all the men on the hill."

"Yes, m'lady. We prepared the trap and fell into it, didn't we?" He looked at Annel and straightened to his full height. On his steed he looked like one of the heroic warriors in the frescos on the walls of Dragada.

"I'm sorry," Annel said.

"It wasn't your doing. The consequences would have come to us whether you brought the message to us or not. I know that. The Baron knows, and our people know it. Make haste. I suspect we'll see the dragons next."

Perigreen and the other riders started for the top of the hill where the Baron's men from the battle gathered.

Annel and the four rangers started toward the physician's area.

"Wallace, if we survive this, I'll tell King Fyan to give you and the others castles."

"M'lady, if we survive this, I want to live in Dragada with you and the other Aelfen."

She smiled. "You've earned that."

"If we survive," he said.

Annel's smile faded as they neared the supply wagons. Carston lay motionless on the grass with a bloody sword in his hand. Eight men with the scorpion on their tunics surrounded him. Ta'un's men had attacked the north hill even before trying to attack the Baron from behind. The soldiers from Caer Balfot had been overwhelmed. The boys who were supply runners and the workers had been slaughtered. Annel dismounted and walked around in a daze. One of the healers struggled to breath, but died as Annel held her head in her arms.

"These were boys and healers and a few wounded men. The workers had no battle skills. How could these *animals* do this?" Annel asked.

"Lady Annel, over here," Wallace yelled. "One's alive, hiding under a blanket." He threw back the covering. "Marcus, what are you doing here?"

***

Brulon approached Rin, as he sat in the dragon saddle.

"Lord Rin, the battle proceeds according to plan."

"Does it? I hadn't noticed. We fell into a trap this morning on the road because my scout dragons are dead." Rin spat on the ground. "That woman knocked me from the sky. Me ... . The tree healer dared to oppose me!"

"She will die with the others," Brulon said. "I urge you to attack now while the enemy is still trying to organize their defense."

Rin considered his options. Deorc and Lighininge were busy with the gold dragon. Schadwe had not arrived yet. Two other ancient dragons, Blaec and Hwit, had refused to join. He would make them pay when this war ended. He clenched his teeth, and reached to pat the neck of the dragon he rode.

"Kill all except the woman. Deorc needs her alive for a special purpose," Rin said. "When she's found, use the shadoine. They know the spells to trap her."

"Master Rin, with the men of Caer Amal, we have almost circled the hill. After two or three attacks, those mounds will become the table, and our enemy will be the feast for vultures."

"Good. How many men oppose us?"

"Lord Me'lik of Amal said they number not more than twenty-five hundred. We have ten thousand men in the field, and the reinforcements continue to arrive."

Rin wiped his brow and looked over the battle field. Then he threw his head back and bellowed a throaty snarl. The discordant tones melded into the afternoon air. He trusted the numbers Brulon gave him, but he wanted no mistakes. Lighininge would respond to his call. Besides, the ancient dragon needed to feed.

"Brulon, begin the attack. Lighininge will be here soon. I want this over quickly. Send the shadoine to find the woman. Bring her back alive."

***

When Perigreen approached, Baron Aelan stood in heated discussion with all the caer lords and Kreigar. Perigreen dismounted and joined the group.

"Good. You're here. Are all the men on the hill?"

"Yes, m'lord. Annel and a few rangers are at the supply wagons. She figured it'd be best to move the supplies here. With the workers and runners we can draw a tighter defensive circle."

The Baron nodded. He ran his fingers through his hair. "I put the least experienced men on the back side of the hill, but I fear the enemy will eventually surround us. It's going to be a hot afternoon. Make them pay."

"We're in a storm. That's sure," Kreigar said. "When the night's dark, an' the swells are crashing on the bow, it's hard ta see makin' it 'til the morn, but more often than not if ya hold the rudder tight an' keep the ship into the wind ya make it."

Perigreen, who had never seen the sea, loved the quips Kreigar used. Perigreen looked around the hill. The enemy with the traitors from Amal surrounded them on all sides except the ridge to the supply wagons and the small ravine down to the river road.

"What are they waiting for?" Lord Balfot asked.

Just as he finished his question, the sound of drums echoed across the plains. Trumpets answered from the right and the left.

"It begins. Captains, tell your men to sling rocks until they can be effective with arrows. Save the spears for close combat. Keep a good reserve back from the line so you can see where you need to reinforce. Use the earthworks and the terrain. Let's send this scum back to the caves they crawled out of. To your posts."

Perigreen mounted and hurried to the section of the line under his command. His responsibility included a full third of the line around the hill. Kreigar, to his left, faced forces consisting mostly of the men from Caer Amal. The Baron defended the right, and Pulon commanded the men at the catapults and ballistae.

All of Perigreen's men looked at him as he rode up. Excited anticipation filled the atmosphere. The drums boomed in the distance.

"I want every other man of you to form another line here, behind me."

The men hurried to respond.

Perigreen shouted his orders to the men. "The enemy will come in waves. We are the rocks upon which they will crash. Behind me is the reserve. In the lull between attacks, the front line and reserve will trade positions. Under no circumstance is the reserve to advance unless I command it. There are piles of rocks the workers gathered. Use them as if you were hunting game at home, until the enemy closes."

The rhythm of the constant drum beat increased in tempo. The first line of the enemy advanced in unison. Guttural chants in time with the drums filled the air.

"Steady, men!" Perigreen shouted. "Hold until they're closer."

Then Perigreen noticed the dragon on the ground behind the enemy line. The lanky figure in black armor had removed his helmet. His red hair surprised Perigreen. The boy gave orders to several runners. Perigreen smiled. *He fears to take his dragon into the air. He's seen the carcasses Annel left on the plains, and he remembers that she nearly blasted him from the sky this morning.* The whirr of slings pulled him back from his musings. A constant hail of stones pelted the enemy, but fallen men became objects to be trampled underfoot by the dark crush of men. When the advancing line approached within twenty five paces, the buzz of arrows obscured the sound of the drums, and the encroaching track of men faltered and almost broke, but the press of warriors struggled on until the clash of steel rang along the earthworks.

Vicious swordplay ensued. The oncoming enemy breached the line several times, but on each occasion Perigreen and the reserve drove them back and sealed the rift. Blood stained the sand and brown summer grass. A vast sense of sorrow for the fallen men invaded Perigreen. Broken and pierced bodies became monuments to the chaotic evil. His men were farmers and artisans. None of them had seen war before. Now the shouts and screams coupled with the stench of spilt blood defined every moment.

"Fill that gap." Perigreen pointed with his sword, and five men from the reserve leaped into the breach. Perigreen presented a striking image riding behind his men, shouting instructions and encouragement.

A trumpet sounded, and Rin recalled his men. It had been a brief feint to test the lines and explore weaknesses.

"Hold your ground. Arrows and stones only," Perigreen shouted, as the men of the caers cheered, thinking they had won. They soon realized that their opponents had reformed, and were preparing another assault.

"Front line, pull the wounded back, and take your place as the reserve. Reserves take the forward positions."

Perigreen looked around the hill for healers, but none were present. Then the flash of light on the north hill caught his eye. Annel.

"I need a messenger," he called. A young man from one of the smaller caer's hurried to him. "Take some men. Get over to the supply hill. Lady Annel's in trouble."

"Beggin' yer pardon sir, there're no men ta take ta her. The devils are comin' again." He pointed down the hill. The drums began again, and braying horns sounded like a wild cacophony of marsh geese.

Perigreen looked to the Baron on his right flank. The enemy had hit the right flank hard. Aelan spread his line thinner to keep a presence so he couldn't be flanked, but the overextended line revealed sizable gaps. To his left Kreigar strutted like a captain on his ship. He carried a sword in each hand, and both were dark with blood. His men had held against the traitors from Caer Amal.

Perigreen turned to his reserve. He pointed to a man. "From this man to the end of the line, double time over to the Baron. Tell the Baron that the Lady Annel is cut off," he bellowed. Over one hundred men took off on a run.

The tall lord turned to the messenger.

"You're right, son. There're no men to send to the Lady Annel. What's your name?"

"Tom, sir."

"Well, Tom, stay close."

As Perigreen looked at the advancing foe, a stray arrow caught him in the shoulder in the crease of his breastplate and his left arm pauldaron. He slumped on his horse, but gripped the saddle horn. Gritting his teeth, he yanked on the arrow, but it broke off leaving at least three inches of shaft exposed and the tip imbedded. He cut off a piece of his cloak with his dagger and stuffed it into the wound to staunch the blood flow. He pulled his cloak over his shoulder so the men could not see the blood. Looking out over the plains with the afternoon sun at his back, he realized the enemy's reinforcements had arrived. The cloud of distant dust from the northeast had transformed into a line of horsemen perhaps two miles in the distance. A vanguard of nearly fifty horsemen began to gallop toward the hills. It appeared to Perigreen that over a thousand riders followed them.

"Lord Perigreen," another messenger shouted. "Lord Perigreen, can you send some men?"

The excited young man panted as he bent over with his hands on his knees.

"I've no one to send," Perigreen said. He looked beyond the men advancing up the hill. An immense dragon with blue scales edged with golden trim landed. Its roar could be heard above the drums. Chaotic thoughts settled into Perigreen's mind, and it took a minute to calm feelings of despair.

"But, sir," the youngster pleaded, "there's an army coming from around the hills on the north road. They'll start up the ravine in not more than twenty minutes. We can't hold 'em."

The pain in Perigreen's shoulder throbbed.

"Tom, ride to Kreigar, and tell him to send one of his rangers to command here. Tell him I've gone to secure the back of the hill. Go now."

"Yes, sir."

"Come on, boy. Let's go see this army that threatens the rear." The boy took off on the run, and Perigreen followed. He saw another flash from the north hill.

"M'lady Annel, I'm so sorry, but with your skills, you'll probably survive longer than any of us," he whispered.

***

"How'd you get here?" Annel asked. Marcus stood, shaking like a leaf in the wind.

"M'lady, I just came w' the other boys ta help run supplies. I wanted ta do m' part in the war, so I hid in a wagon. Didn't know it'd be like this."

Annel thought better of reprimanding Marcus. He deserved to fight for his freedom, rather than hiding in the caer waiting for destruction.

"Very well, young master Marcus ... ."

"M'lady, look there," one of the rangers shouted from across the open area. He pointed to a group of more than a hundred men from Caer Amal approaching, including Lord Me'lik.

"Marcus, stay behind me," Annel said. She sprinted to the center of the open space enclosed by the circle of supply wagons. She donned her shield and held her sword in front of her. Two rangers stood on either side. Marcus remained behind her. She sang a soft canticle, and within a circle of energy, enclosing the group, the grass began to fade from sight. Visibility pulsed with the cadence of the song. She fell silent for a moment as the invisibility spell masked their position.

"I've blocked their ability to see or hear us," she said. "Mark in you minds where we stand. When I signal, close your eyes to avoid the flash that will temporarily blind them. In your minds you'll hear my voice commanding you to attack. Then I'll tell you when to retreat into the shell of invisibility. There's no clemency for these traitors. Do you understand?"

"Yes, m'lady."

"Marcus, under no circumstances are you to leave my side." She looked down at him. He nodded up and down.

Annel could hear the drums and screams of men from the other hill where the Baron and the war bands of the caers stood against the onslaught of Rin's army. Voices floated across the still area corralled by the wagons. Me'lik entered the enclosure with his men.

"M'lord, I saw some of the rangers here," a man said.

"Well, I see no one now," Me'lik said. He looked around and pointed to Carston. "I want this man's armor. Strip him and take it back."

Tension mounted inside the shell of invisibility. Annel refused to see her friend dishonored.

"Close your eyes," she said.

She unleashed a command word, and a brilliant silver flash of energy struck the men around Carston. Me'lik's men staggered in dazed confusion, blinded by the light.

"Now," Annel said.

The four rangers at her side dashed from the protective defense. Three of them slew fifteen of the traitors while the fourth carried Carston back to Annel. Lord Me'lik's life ended in dazed confusion as Pelton ran him through with a sword.

"Return," Annel commanded. Her men slipped back into the invisible shielding. Two more times the rangers struck with devastating results.

The men from Amal scrambled to flee the area. One of their captains tried to mount a defense, and men began to sling rocks and fire arrows in random directions on the chance they would hit their invisible attackers. A stray rock hit Annel in the forehead. She stumbled and fell to the ground. Blood dripped on the loose sandy earth, but she maintained consciousness and sustained the void of invisibility. Crying, Marcus wiped the blood from her head. The rangers hovered around her with shields up for protection, but the men from Amal left the enclosure and hurried back to Ta'un. Me'lik's body lay in the hot sun.

As Annel struggled to her feet, she looked after the retreating men from Amal. Horror gripped her. Twenty men in black cloaks, with embroidered white skulls on the left breast, entered the compound and walked directly toward her. Their black plumed helms dully reflected the afternoon sun. When the shadoine were about fifty feet away, she heard one of them say, "The one Deorc wants is there. The others matter not."

"They can see us," Annel said to the rangers.

She began to sing another of the melodies of the eternal world, but the knock on her head from the rock cause her thoughts to spin. Dizzy, she staggered and fell to her knees. The last thing she remembered, the shadoine drew swords, and Pelton gave an order to the other rangers to defend her to their deaths. Marcus stood close to her holding her up. She leaned heavily on him.

Sometimes, to gain a desired attribute, a fearful price must be paid. The obvious warrior skills are physical in nature and demand constant cultivation. There is no substitute for the practice arena. The physical strength of the warrior is built by breaking down limitations and barriers within his own abilities, and then building them to a higher level. The arduous activity of pushing limits can drain men of their will, but if they persist and sacrifice more than the next man, their skill will eventually surpass others and their chances for survival in battle will increase. The process is no different to develop the vital mental and spiritual skills required by all men and women, if they wish to improve themselves.

From the Manual of Discipline found in the library of Vindry—author unknown

Chapter 13. Silver Lining

Widseth opened a pouch he found beside King Perrik's breastplate. He discovered a small round of cheese, a biscuit, and a small water flask within the pouch. The cheese looked fresh, and the biscuit, although hard, appeared palatable. He opened the flask and sniffed the water. He took a tentative swallow. The pure liquid tasted like high mountain spring water, and exhilarated him, as he drained the small water container and ate the biscuit with cheese. He put the flask in the empty pouch. As he drew the leather string, weight returned to the bag. Opening it again, he found another small round of cheese and a biscuit with a full container of water.

"Let's see what other wonders are here," he whispered. The stone walls absorbed the sound of his voice.

He lifted the breastplate. The golden material gleamed in the wizard light's soft glow. With his finger he traced the engraved symbol of two opposed dragons entwined around a column inlaid in silver on the upper left breast. He removed the slave rope belt and tunic, and dressed in Perrik's outer garments that had been folded beside the armor.

He slipped his head and right arm between the cuirass and back piece. As he cinched the leather straps, he noticed the supple feel to the fastening and the metal protection. The leg armor covered his lower thighs and upper shins down to the calf high boots. When he donned the boots, energy gushed through him. As he twisted and stretched, the remarkable protective covering adjusted in response to his movements. He fastened the right shoulder spaulder and the metal bracers for his forearm. The left spaulder supported no bracer, but a small buckler two feet in diameter covered from his elbow to his hand. He clasped the King's burgundy cloak to attachments on both shoulders, and hooked the pouch to a beautiful leather belt around his waist.

Widseth walked to the head of Perrik's grave. He slipped the baldric containing Perrik's sword over his head and adjusted the strap. Widseth held the King's helm under his arm and knelt. He pulled the sword from its sheath, and raised it above his head.

"King Perrik, I raise this sword to our enemies. Their blood shall testify they sought their death at my hand. By sun and sword, I seek no creature's life. I seek only protection for those I love. May I die in defense of friend and kin, facing my foe!"

White fire burst from the sword in response to Widseth's oath. He lowered the sword and sheathed it. Still on his knees, spoke to the King.

"I thank you for the use of your armor and weapons. If I am successful, I will return, and your remains shall be placed in hallowed ground within Misdara. That, I promise you, King Perrik."

Widseth stood. He placed the open faced helm on his head and fastened the chinstrap. He readied his buckler and drew the sword. With gentle pressure, he opened the stone door and reentered Schadwe's world. Knowing the dragon would be searching for him, he stepped forward into a lava tunnel. In the downhill direction, he detected a source of light. Approaching the jagged end of the tunnel, he realized the passageway to the King's burial chamber was one among many tributaries of lava tubes that emptied into Schadwe's cavernous lair.

His armor made no noise. It was almost as if it had bonded to his skin as living scales for his protection. He crouched behind the jagged boulder at the opening into the vast chamber and surveyed the cavern.

***

The shadoine encircled Annel, Marcus, and the four men guarding her. The black cloaked shapes took a step forward. The rangers readied their weapons for the task they knew to be impossible. Annel began again to hum a simple healing melody to help her focus her mind and energy. Through the chaotic noise of war, her simple tune carried beyond the curtain of invisibility and silence. She knew the shadoine could see her little group, so she ended the invisibility enchantment, and focused her energy to construct a protective web.

"Sheathe your swords," one of the shadoine said. The others complied immediately. The figure who spoke knelt on one knee. The rangers remained at the ready.

"Queen Laena, you've returned. We could never draw swords against you."

Annel stood and walked between Pelton and Wallace. They attempted to hold her back, but she waved them off. She touched the shadoine's shoulder.

"Please rise," she said.

The tall personage rose to his full height.

"After Paulus died and King Perrik left Misdara on his quest to regain the Eye of Light, we defended the city for several years looking to your return," he said.

Annel paused and considered her words, "I'm not Queen Laena."

The shadoine's hand gripped the hilt of his sword. "Her image is in your face, and you wear her clothes. What have you done to her?"

Annel stood tall and stared at the closed helmet of the shadoine.

"I am Annel, queen of Dragada. My husband is the Dragon Master. He has recalled the dragons of light into the world."

"It is no surprise that the dark lizard, Deorc, desires your capture, but that does not answer the question. What have you done with my Queen?"

"King Perrik hid her on The Diadem. She has been trapped there these many years. You can best serve her by helping me now."

"What proofs have you that this tale is true?" The shadoine lord asked. Abruptly all the shadoine cringed and held their gauntleted hands to their helmets.

Annel detected a whine, and with her sensory training, she recognized the sound.

"The dragons call, and we must answer," the shadoine said.

He put his hand on his sword hilt. The rangers responded and surrounded Annel, but she stood calm and began to sing, melding her voice with the subtle discordant drone of the dragon call. It amazed her how easily she combined her voice with the incomplete chords and blended them into a pleasant melody. The shadoine relaxed.

"We've only a few minutes," she said. She pulled the folded leather map from her travel pouch under her cloak and spread it on the ground. She touched The Diadem until Queen Laena appeared standing near the cabin in the trees.

Touching the map where she had written messages before, she wrote on the map with light emanating from her fingertip.

"Queen Laena, I need your assistance."

Writing appeared. "I stand ready to aid you, as I am able."

Annel began to write again, but the shadoine lord said, "It is easier to speak." He touched a curious glyph on the edge of the map.

"Queen Laena," he said, "it is I, Nedron, of the Royal High Guard. We have waited long for your return to release us from the terrible chains that bind us to the dragons' power. Will you liberate us from this awful slavery?"

The queen stood in silence. Then a beautiful voice filled the air. Annel could not understand the words, but when it ceased, the dark shapes had collapsed. Only the helms and cloaks remained. Annel scanned the area, and the rangers hurried to examine the empty cloaks.

"Annel, if the High Guard fell to the dragons, I have little hope for you," the voice said.

"I have no choice," Annel's voice softened. "I must attempt to use the hidden entrance your husband spoke of. This evil can only be confronted in Misdara at the tree of life."

"Unless I am mistaken," Laena said, "there is a glyph of the tree somewhere on the map. I am not sure you can use it because Perrik would have attuned the passage to my structure, but I can think of no other door because I do not know where the ancient dragons of light hid the tree before they were killed or fled the physical world."

"There is a tree in the upper corner," Annel said.

"You are a daughter of light. I saw that when you were here on The Diadem. Draw strength from the source of your being. Take no one with you who is unwilling to face and reject darkness."

Annel circled her hand over Laena's ink figure on the map. "Queen Laena, as High Queen of the Aelfen from Dragada, I release you from this world and allow you to join your husband and the faithful Aelfen of Misdara in the world of light." Laena began to fade.

"Thank you child … chi … ." The image faded.

Annel looked at the rangers inspecting the cloaks of the shadoine. She knew they would be angry, but focusing her mind on an image of the tree of life, she touched the glyph on the map. A door of light opened. She rolled the map and stuffed it into her travel pack. Swallowing hard, she closed her eyes, and stepped through the door. She heard Wallace yelling. The door snapped shut, but not before Marcus scurried through the door behind her.

***

Baron Aelan O'Dai studied the army advancing up the hill. The incessant drums pounded in his ears. Perigreen's men arrived and he dispersed them to fill the gaps in his line. Grim thoughts entered his mind when informed that Annel had been cut off. When the flashes of light on the north hill ceased, his despair increased. He watched the blue dragon land behind the advancing enemy. He wiped the sweat from his brow, as he watched the horsemen from the open plains, galloping to reinforce Rin's army.

"Lord Pulon," he shouted. "We need to bring that beast down. Ready the ballistae. Wait until you can smell what it ate for dinner last night. Target the catapults anywhere the foe gathers."

The shouts and din of the battle increased as the enemy advanced within bow and sling range. Aelan noticed a prairie hen alight near an outcropping of rock. He marveled that the bird had no idea of the horror engulfing the hill. The hen's only irritation was with the men who were too close to her nest.

"Baron! Look there!" Pulon shouted. Aelan's attention focused back on the earthworks as swords clashed along the line. Groans and screams of men pierced the air. The caer men's line began to give way as the throng of the enemy pushed forward. Confusion mounted, and panic stood at the door, but the Baron ordered all the reserve forward at a quick march.

Pulon rode up. "Didn't you hear me? We've been betrayed by that witch. She led us here to our deaths."

"What are you talking about? Annel's cut off on the north hill."

"Look. Can't you see? Look there where the vanguard of the horsemen has halted." He pointed to the unfurled banners of the horsemen. "She betrayed us. Those standards are from Dimron, and Vindry, and Standel itself. That black bear on the red field is the house of Halbairn, and the galloping white horse is the royal standard of Rildain."

Aelan stood shocked. Nothing made sense to him. In his mind he processed what he saw, but it had no meaning. *The line with reserves held, but for how long. Did it really matter?* He looked at dead men staring at the sky. He could smell warm blood soaking the sand. He wanted to shut out the screams and the drums. He looked to his left for Perigreen, but all he saw was one of Annel's rangers. Maybe Perigreen was dead or had fled. Kreigar strutted behind the lines beyond that. How long before Kreigar and the remaining rangers turned on him? Aelan blinked his eyes. All the individuals on the hill blurred into a mass of moving color.

Dazed he looked at Pulon. "What do I do?" Aelan asked.

"We die. There's no escape now."

The Baron wiped the back of his hand across his mouth.

"It's a hot day to die," he said.

A rider reined his horse to a halt just in front of the Baron.

"Lord Perigreen says you have to hold for a few more minutes. Can you do that?" the messenger asked.

"Where is my friend Perigreen?" Aelan's voice tailed off. He had no hope of seeing any friend again. He stared toward the back side of the hill away from the battle.

Standards rose above the crest of the hill just before Lord Perigreen crested the backside. A cadre of rangers rode at his side. One of them bore a beautiful green standard with a white tree superimposed on a golden pyramid. Beyond them rank upon rank of men dressed in greens and browns followed on foot. The commander next to Perigreen gave the order to quick march.

The Baron stood dazed and watched as men ran past him to strengthen the defense line. Battle hardened men with long swords joined the mêlée. Confused by the sudden strength to the lines, the enemy wavered and retreated down the hill.

"Baron, have all your men retreat. Bring the wounded. My men will hold the earthworks for you," the commander said. "Have them put wounded here. We've some men with healing skills."

"Yes, but who ...?" Aelan asked.

"I'm Will Willowman, loyal subject to Lord Widseth and Lady Annel. I serve as their ambassador to Standel, but there's no time now. There's still a dragon and a sizable army down there. We've seen this dragon before. He's a nasty creature, and the army with him may be confused now, but it's like an animal in a trap, very dangerous."

Perigreen slumped in the saddle and began to fall from his horse. Three men rushed to his side and eased him to the ground. They laid him back and stretched him out.

Will and the Baron knelt beside him. Will used his dagger to cut the leather strapping on Perigreen's armor. The Baron peeled back the metal spaulder and the studded leather breastplate, revealing a nasty wound with the shaft of the arrow protruding from his shoulder above his left breast. Lord Willowman cut away the under tunic, and the Baron put the corner of his cloak in Perigreen's mouth.

"Bite hard on this," the Baron said.

Will gripped the short arrow shaft and pulled. As he did so he used the tip of his dagger to ease the arrowhead out of the wound. Perigreen's groans broke into a jagged sob. With a final jerk, the barb broke free, and Will applied pressure to the wound. Reaching into a pouch he retrieved some salve in a small container. He smeared the unguent in the wound while another man pressed clean linen into the gash and bound it. Perigreen lapsed into unconsciousness, but his breathing returned to normal.

Aelan looked at the men scattered on the ground who had been carried from the front line. Most had grievous injuries. He knew many would never recover, but the healers with Willowman practiced competent medicine.

"I feel your sorrow, Lord Aelan, but there's a battle to be won here before we can mourn properly. Our horsemen approach. Soon the King will contest the dragon's position. Either the dragon will flee the field, or the King will kill him."

A man approached. "Lord Will, shall we use the original plan?"

"Yes, I'll lead the strike force. Leave at least half of our men and all the healers here under the Baron's command."

"As you direct," the man said. He hurried and gave instructions to the assembled captains.

Another messenger arrived as the men from Standel prepared to descend the hill.

"M'lord Will, when we reached the crest of the north hill, we found a terrible slaughter. Wallace, Pelton, and two others survived, but the Lady Annel is gone."

"Gone?" Will asked.

"Pelton said she and a young boy walked through a doorway of light. She's gone."

"She can't just be gone," the Baron said. "Who was the boy?"

The messenger remained silent.

At length Lord Willowman spoke.

"We must finish this business here. The Lady Annel's quest is beyond our help now. She brought us all to this point, and we need to accomplish the tasks before us."

"But she can't ... ." The Baron's voice trailed off, as he looked out over the prairie. Companies of horseman had begun to harass the enemy retreating from the slopes Kreigar defended. The ever impetuous Kreigar had not waited for orders. When the reinforcements from Standel arrived, he ordered the advance down the hillside, pursuing the traitors from Caer Amal. Ta'un had been caught between the anvil and hammer. The soldiers from Caer Amal fled, and most died, singly or in small groups, caught between the horsemen and Kreigar's men.

"Swords at the ready!" Will shouted. "Hie to the King."

"To the King!" his men shouted in response. Ordered companies descended the hill under the proud banners of the caers and the cities of the north.

The rumble of their voices exhilarated Aelan. He looked along his lines of defense that were now better manned than when the battle began. The blue dragon captured his attention as it began to move toward the vanguard of Standel's cavalry. In practiced routine, the fifty horsemen fanned into a single line, flanking one man, wearing a red tunic, who prodded his horse forward toward the dragon. He held aloft a sword that gleamed in the late afternoon sun.

"Who's that man?" Aelan asked of one of the lieutenants who Will Willowman left to help command the defenses.

"That's King Fyan of Standel," the lieutenant said.

The Baron noted the hint of pride in the man's voice.

Standing near, Lord Pulon added, "He's called the dragon slayer."

"You know of him?" the lieutenant asked.

"I fought against Standel in the great war. I lost my son."

"For that, sir, I sorrow. War's a savage beast that feeds on innocence. I hope our arrival today will help assuage your loss."

"Your words are kind. Baron, I ... ."

Aelan held his hand up for silence. The scene on the battlefield below fascinated him. Only three hundred paces separated King

Fyan and the blue dragon. The King spurred his horse, and it leaped forward. Aelan marveled at the King's courage. No hesitation slowed either the King or the dragon. The other horsemen with the king spread their formation further and formed a semi circle around the ancient dragon. A second dragon with the rider in black armor lifted into the air and poised to dive on the king. With wings spread and extended to its full height, Lighininge remained on the ground, towering above the attacking King. The horsemen in the semi circle charged the dragon.

A hideous wail erupted from the azure creature as it expelled a violent bolt of energy from its mouth. Aelan could not believe what he witnessed. The sword that the King brandished attracted the forked bolt of light from the dragon, shielding the King and his charging men. When the shaft hit the sword, wreaths of flame surrounded King Fyan, and he pointed the sword at the dragon that bore Rin above the battlefield. The sword expelled the captured energy in a single pulse that blasted Rin's flying mount. With a badly damaged wing it spiraled downward toward the earth until, at the last moment, it controlled its descent and veered southward, carrying Rin away from the battle.

"Bring me my horse," the Baron shouted, amid the cheers for Fyan from the men on the hill.

When his squire brought the mount, Baron Aelan swung into the saddle, and slapped the flank of the horse with the flat of his sword. The horse responded and dashed down the hill toward King Fyan. Aelan expected fear to strike him as he careened down the slope, but a surge of adrenalin coursed through him, as he focused on Fyan making his first pass at the dragon at full speed. He swung his sword and wounded the beast on the left fore limb. All around, small battles raged, as pockets of the enemy reformed and stood against Will Willowman and Kreigar and the men from Standel, but Aelan paid no attention. His entire awareness centered on Fyan and the dragon.

A terrible cacophony of strident sounds rang across the plains, as the grating clang of steel on steel melded with the moans of dying men and the screams of wounded horses to the background of drums and discordant horns. Above all, the ferocious bellow of the dragon unnerved friend and foe alike, but Aelan pressed forward through the clusters of men waging war on one another. The Baron realized many of his men from the caers had followed the men from Standel into battle. Aelan slipped through a gap between the battling companies of men and continued toward the dragon.

Aelan reached the outer area where the horsemen had first set their line around the dragon. He slowed to a stop. The beast swatted at the riders like gnats. The swords and spears of the riders often failed to pierce the tough hide, but every time Fyan charged, his sword bit Lighininge somewhere. The creature extended to its full height and beat its wings. The force of the air knocked men from their shrieking horses. Dust and rocks stirred by the wind pelted Aelan. He thought he had entered one of the violent prairie dust storms. He could see only a few men still on horseback. When the dust settled, he searched for the King, but failed to spot him. As men tried to remount, the monstrous barbed tail knocked them from their feet. Snapping jaws and wicked talons did not discriminate between man and horse. The shrieks of good men stung his ears.

Aelan spurred his reluctant horse forward. Brandishing his sword, he hurtled toward the dragon. The creature ignored him. A single man in red, holding a bright sword, demanded all its attention. Lighininge snapped at Fyan, but the lithe leader sidestepped and slashed at the neck of the beast. As Aelan approached at a gallop, his heart sank as the dragon knocked Fyan from his feet. The beast poised for a death blow, when Aelan plunged his sword into deep into the dragon's side. His ancient sword handed down from generation to generation for over a thousand years split the blue scales. As Lighininge jerked in pain, he wrenched the sword from Aelan's hand and knocked him from his horse.

The keening wail of pain stilled the surrounding battle as men paused to stare at the badly wounded dragon. Aelan stumbled and fell before the creature, but his distraction released Fyan, and the King rose and sliced the head of the dragon, blinding one eye. Mad with pain and rage, the creature struck out wildly, but as Aelan watched, Fyan stalked his prey to deliver the killing stroke.

The Baron struggled to stand. He wanted to retrieve his sword to help Fyan, but the young King moved with the speed of a falcon.

A well placed blow behind the horny head of Lighininge severed the spinal chord and the dragon fell to the ground. The head came to rest not far from Aelan. The creature blinked its undamaged eye twice. Aelan stood dazed, not fifteen feet from the dragon. He felt he had witnessed the death of an entity that might have been in the world since the beginning of time. He stared around the battlefield. With the dragon down, the enemy took full flight. A company of horsemen arrived, and Aelan could see Will Willowman and Kreigar in the distance.

"I owe my life to you. I pledge a bond of protection to you and your house, if you will give me your name."

Aelan turned to the speaker. King Fyan stood before him. The King walked over to Lighininge and pulled Aelan's sword from the massive beast's side. He presented it to the Baron. Aelan gripped the hilt.

"Thank you," Aelan said. "Your debt is paid a thousand times over. If you hadn't arrived, we'd all be dead now."

The afternoon heat had begun to abate. A cooler breeze from the river kicked up, announcing the beginning of the late afternoon, early evening.

"I'm Baron Aelan O'Dai of Caer O'Dai, and you are King Fyan. Your rangers have acquitted themselves well. I've never seen such bravery."

Fyan put his hand on Aelan's shoulder and said, "I see true courage when men defend their homes and families even when there is little or no hope." He squeezed Aelan's shoulder. "I have to find my commanders. We need to gather the wounded. I would have us try to save as many of these men as possible so they can return to their families."

The Baron assented. He looked at the dragon's carcass, and then turned his gaze to the sorrow of the fallen men on the battlefield.

***

Annel stepped onto the polished rock floor. Marcus stumbled into the back of her, nearly causing her to trip and fall.

"Marcus, what are you doing? Why are you here?" she scolded.

"Ya tol' me ta stay right behind ya. An' I did."

Annel shook her head and bit her lip. She brushed back the hair from her forehead and tucked it behind her ear.

"You should have stayed with Wallace and the others."

"But ya tol' me."

"I know what I told you, but what am I going to do with you now?"

"I'll stay right behind ya."

Exasperated, Annel looked up and studied the darkened ceiling.

"You do that ... right behind me."

"Where are we?" he asked.

"If the light path led us where I think it did, we are in a cavern deep below the surface of the plains. People once filled these halls. They built a great city here."

"Where are they now?"

"Many years ago the evil dragons destroyed them. I think they fell because of their pride. Only a few writings exist from that time, but the people were powerful, maybe too powerful for their own good. They thought nothing could harm them, but some of the dragons chose to follow a dark path. In the end the Aelfen who lived here lost their homes ... everything."

"Why does that happen?"

"What do you mean?"

"Why do good people have ta die because o' bad people? Carston died. Before I hid, I saw those bad men with th' scorpions on their shirts kill 'im. They killed lots a good people like ol' Nan the healer. She never hurt anyone. An' m' Da, why'd a dragon have ta eat 'im?"

Annel bent down and looked into Marcus' face. She pulled him close to her, and tried to calm the trembling she felt building within him. She closed her eyes and steeled her resolve to see this through even if she never saw Widseth again, even if the Baron and all his men were killed. She would finish her task for Marcus, or she would perish in the attempt.

"I don't know all the reasons why bad things happen to good people, but I've learned some things. When I was young, I thought I was a good person, but I was beaten and forced to do terrible things … things that still give me nightmares. But I found that if I didn't give up, and if I tried my hardest, I became stronger and stronger until I was like a caer on a hill where I could always feel safe. Then I met Widseth."

"He's the man who came ta me the night ya saved me at the farm."

"Yes," she said. "He and I learned many things together. I learned that this life is only the beginning. Some times bad things happen, and they help us stretch and become stronger than we every thought we could be. Beyond this world is the world of light after we die, and there all things are made right."

"Is that where Widseth let Da and Ma and Elena and Cristobal go? The first night he came to me, they were there."

"Yes, that's where they went."

"He was worried 'bout ya. He tol' me ta tell ya to go to a place called Misdara. He said ta take the battle there, but ya couldn't take an army, only a few."

"I remember," she said. "And now I'm in Misdara. This is the ancient kingdom of Misdara."

"Here? This place? It doesn't look like much of a kingdom." Marcus looked around the dark room.

"It's a lot bigger than this room. I have to find out what I'm supposed to do here," Annel said.

"You're lookin' for somethin' aren't ya?"

"Yes, and I think it is there." She pointed to the opposite wall.

The only light in the room originated from an alcove straight ahead of Annel and Marcus at the far wall. A soft glow spread through the chamber outside the recessed room. Annel concentrated on her cloak. The outline of the shield and sword appeared. She withdrew each item from the cloth and poised herself in the event of trouble.

"Follow me."

She walked confidently toward the alcove's entry, and Marcus tagged along behind her. The silence in the room permeated her being. After the discordant noise of the battle, the still hush of this room rang in her ears. Her impressions magnified the sounds of their feet on the stone floor. She slowed and veered to the left as she approached the arch leading into the alcove, and peered into the room from the left side of the archway.

Sickly yellow light emanated from the tree, and black tendrils like ivy wound around the slender trunk and branches. A black object rested at the base. Annel recognized Deorc's clawed hand that Widseth had severed from the dragon at the gates of Dragada. She swallowed hard.

She remembered the summer day on the steps of the manor on the Fendry estates outside Tabul, when she and Widseth had traveled a path of light to hide the dark hand. She thought it must have been the tree at Taina. She had not guessed that he had taken her here to Misdara. Widseth had said something about using the clawed hand as a bargaining chip with Deorc if necessary. Grim thoughts entered her mind. *What could induce her to use a bargaining chip with Deorc?*

She examined the interior of the alcove around the tree. She tried to scan the spectrum of light to determine if the room harbored evil. Only the dragon's paw with blood encrusted talons and the black veins strangling the tree emitted auras of evil. Upon closer inspection, the paw and the blackened vines around the trunk did not appear to be related. Although the light of the tree had begun to falter, Annel felt the room would be a safe place to rest. She replaced the sword and shield within the cloak.

"It's been a long day. We'll try to get some sleep here," she said.

"Do you have any food?" Marcus asked.

"I have a little in my travel pack."

She slipped the small bag from its sling under her cloak. She pulled the Baron's map out. It tempted her, but she needed sleep. She did not want to know the outcome at the ill fated hills. She handed one of the three hard biscuits and a small packet of dried meat to Marcus. After they each ate a biscuit and shared the dried meat, Annel sat in the corner of the alcove next to the tree, facing the doorway. She put her arm around Marcus, covering him with her cloak, and within minutes, he fell asleep.

Annel leaned back and closed her eyes. *Misdara. She found the tree. Now what?* She fell asleep under the light of the dying tree.

***

Men sat around hundreds of crackling fires. Some of them tended wounded comrades. The night was warm, but some men sat at the fires warming their hands, trying to erase the chill that had grown within them as they buried the dead from the battle. Warmth eluded them. Baron Aelan made sure every man had food who wanted it. Aelan, King Fyan, and all the captains spent several hours wandering to every campsite. They talked with the men, not as nobles and servant or captains and soldiers, but as brothers who had shared in the terrible losses.

Satisfied the outriders and pickets were sufficient, Baron Aelan returned to the central fire near the ballistae and catapults. He found Kreigar kneeling beside Lord Perigreen conversing softly. Fyan and Will Willowman spoke with Lord Pulon and several other caer lords. Several of the other captains and rangers stood or sat in groups talking in low tones.

Aelan stood outside the firelight and listened to the night noises of the plains. In the distance he could hear the howls of predators. The men had buried as many of the fallen as possible, but Aelan knew the scavengers would feed tonight. He pushed the thought from his mind and listened to the chirping crickets before he entered the light of the fire.

"Baron, you drive yourself too hard. The captains who have the night duty will take care of everything. Please, come and join us before we retire for the night," King Fyan said.

"Yes, your highness," Aelan said.

"No *'your highness'* talk here tonight. I'm Fyan. This is Will. We'll leave the titles and protocol for the palace and caers. Tonight we're brothers and we speak as brothers."

"Yes, tonight we're brothers. I like that," Aelan said. "But my heart is heavy. Lady Annel ... ."

Fyan interrupted. "Wallace reported what they saw. My best guess is that she's in Misdara. It seems Misdara is the key to all of this." He gestured indicating the battlefield.

"That makes sense, but what do we do now?" Aelan asked.

"Well, the army we defeated today is scattered, but still dangerous because the dragon Deorc, or so I've been told, leads it. I've a score to settle with him."

"Actually, a human named Rin is the commander. Annel said he's being trained to be a Dragon Master," Aelan said.

"The boy, riding the dragon ... he's Deorc's puppet. No doubt, his powers are governed by the dark dragon," Fyan said.

"I'm sure you're right, but this is much for one day. We'll discuss our plans in the morning."

"Well stated," Fyan said. "Sleep will soften the terrible events of the day. Good night all."

"Before I sleep tonight, I must know one thing," Aelan said. "How is it that you and your army travel through the land of the Emperor with impunity? Do you not fear your actions will lead to war with the Empire?"

In the firelight, Aelan detected a smile on Fyan's face. The king motioned to Will.

"Find Xeran. He can explain our presence to Aelan."

"Certainly," Will said.

After several minutes a fussy balding man accompanied Will back to the campfire where Fyan and Aelan sat.

"Your highness requires my presence?" the bald man asked.

"Baron Aelan is concerned the emperor might not understand our presence here on the plains. Can you explain it to him?" Fyan asked.

Xeran looked like he had just awoken, but he straightened his shoulders and rubbed his hands together.

"My name is Xeran. I am the Magistrate of Records of Tabul. I am the emperor's man."

"Make this a quick version, Xeran. The Baron is tired tonight." Fyan said.

"Yes, m'lord. Well, Baron O'Dai, I invited the king because I became aware of the events here on the plains, and I feared the emperor's interests would be jeopardized if a measured response to the evil was ignored," Xeran said. He straightened his robes and stood as tall as his physique allowed.

"And this met the emperor pleasure?" the baron asked.

"I wrote him a letter, detailing the excursion by King Fyan, but there has been no time."

"No time for an answer?"

"Well, not exactly. I am sure you know how slow the emperor's court works," Xeran said. "We did not have time to send it to him. As soon as this business is completed, and King Fyan is well on the road back to Standel, I will make sure the emperor receives a full account."

The baron smiled and nodded his head. "Thank you Master Xeran. Indeed, you're the emperor's man, and you've saved his land."

"Thank you Xeran," the king said. "It's time to sleep. I bid you good night, Aelan. My men will take care of the watches and changing the pickets. Good night, all."

The gathered men dispersed into the night until only Aelan stood by the fire.

"She was right," a voice said. The Baron turned to the source.

Wrapped in a blanket, Perigreen sat propped against a saddle.

"What do you mean?" the Baron asked.

"She said powers of light would rise to our defense. The men did well today, didn't they?"

Aelan sat down and leaned back on a saddle. He stared up at the sky. The stars glittered.

"Yes, they did well," he said. He closed his eyes.

***

Rin burst into the throne room deep in the underground of Misdara.

"Deorc, where are you? Deorc!"

"I am here." Deorc's voice came from the dais. He sat upon one of the two thrones.

Rin approached the bottom stair of the dais.

"M'lord, I think they killed Lighininge and almost blasted me from the sky. Where were you? With you we could've won. Now the army's fleeing here like a whipped slave."

"Where is Brulon?"

"He's with the army, tryin' to maintain order. The shadoine are gone," Rin said.

"I know, but the plans are progressing."

"What do you mean? We lost!" Rin shouted.

"I mean that the woman is here. As her presence entered Misdara, I detected her vibration in the medium of light. Schadwe will dispose of Widseth. I will dispose of the woman and claim what is mine. Plans are progressing despite the loss on the battlefield."

"What do you want me to do?" Rin asked.

"I care not. Leave me," the dragon snapped.

Rin hung his head and walked away from the dais.

***

Annel walked on a meandering path toward a summit along a sharp ridge. To her right the full luminosity of the sun filled the landscape. To the left, murky shadows churned, masking everything. She had no trouble holding to the path as long as she kept her eyes on the sunlit land. When she glanced to the left, the swirling mists snatched at her mind inviting her to fall.

Ahead in the path, a golden dragon dug its talons into the soil and struggled to pull itself into the light. Hordes of black insect-like creatures nipped at the beast's hindquarters and tried to pull it into the chasm of empty nothingness to the left of the path. Annel hurried to aid the creature when she recognized him. Gulth. She shouted, but no sound escaped her lips. He could not hear her. She pled with him to persevere, but he began to slip into the gulf. She ran until she reached him, but he slipped beyond her grasp. She could still see him clawing his way back to the light, but he began to lose form.

Further along the path she spied a tree. Fruit and leaves fell to the ground. The dying tree emitted sickly yellow light. As she approached it, she picked up a piece of rotting fruit that had fallen in the path. The fruit was shaped like the golden dragon. If she saved the tree, she could rescue the dragon.

Annel woke from her dream. As she opened her eyes, she saw the dying tree in the alcove. She had to save the tree.

Balance. The key to a defensive posture is balance. The key to an offensive strike is balance. A warrior knows that if he can unbalance his opponent, he has won the battle. In the realm of general living, deviation from principles unbalances a man, and he is easily defeated because he can neither counter nor overcome forces that test and try him. He is blown like chaff in the wind.

From the Manual of Discipline found in the library of Vindry—author unknown

Chapter 14. Knife's Edge

"*Schadwe is the master of illusion and shadow.*" The shadoine's words repeated in Widseth's mind. From behind the jagged rock in the entrance to the tunnel, Widseth considered his course of action. He searched his memories for things he might have read about Schadwe in any of the annals about dragons. Though mentioned, the scribes never explained any of Schadwe's attributes other than he avoided the affairs of men and Aelfen. He remembered one notation that expressed an opinion that Schadwe was the first of the dragons of light to fall into darkness.

As Widseth looked into the cavern, he concluded that this passage opened nearer to the active lava flow than the door into the gem mines. He judged the door to be to his left. If he followed the lava flow, it would lead him back to the sham lair where Schadwe had first tried to deceive and confront him. The dragon could be hiding in any number of passages or fissures in the rock wall of the chamber. The live lava flow had carved hundreds of tunnels and warrens. Widseth judged that there would be no warning this time when the dragon attacked. He knew he could make no miscalculation.

He gripped the hilt of Perrik's sword in his hand. As he stood up, he adjusted his vision to scan the chamber through every nuance of the spectrum. The sword gleamed with soft white light as he drew it from the sheath. Stepping from behind the rough boulder in the entrance of the tunnel, he hummed a low tune and called upon the power of high magic. For a moment the glow from the lava river wavered, and the view of the cavern distorted, but Widseth's vision adjusted and returned to normal.

Masked by his conjured enchantment, he edged along the wall in the direction of the lava flow. The ground was uneven and jagged, but King Perrik's boots served him well. Only the sound of occasional rock slides competed with the ever present hiss of the super heated rock in the distance. Widseth could feel the tunic begin to cling to him as the heat grew, but he continued toward the open lava. He wiped sweat from his eyes.

About a hundred paces from the lava, the ground began to slope toward the hot river. Widseth stopped and surveyed the flowing magma when it began to flow downward until it submerged beneath the floor of the cavern, carving a future lava tube. He looked toward the upward flow of the molten rock, in the direction of the lair where he first confronted Schadwe. A trail of sorts wound along the ridge where the ground sloped to the lava. Sharp edged boulders, spewed from the mouth of the flowing rock in ages past, haphazardly decorated the landscape with weird shadows and shapes.

Nothing moved. Only the sizzle and crack of distressed rocks made any noise. He kept the magma to his right and walked toward the lair, four to five hundred paces in the distance. He scanned the trail ahead looking for any light emanations that might suggest recent passage of the dragon, but nothing indicated Schadwe had been in the area for some time. Widseth knew the dragon would not leave his den with a threat still here.

He continued toward the lair, but stopped where the path wound away from the ridge around a huge boulder. Something bothered him. The rock formation did not look quite right. Then he realized the shadow it cast was not consistent with its shape. He used the tip of the sword to touch the boulder, and the huge stone vibrated and dissolved into fine mist. The trail led directly through the boulder. Had he stepped on the trail to go around the boulder, he would have stepped into a deep crack in the cavern floor. *Schadwe is the master of illusion and shadow.*

Widseth wondered if by dispelling the deception he had in some way alerted the dragon. Then he glimpsed movement ahead to the left of the path. The beast slithered low to the ground between the strewn boulders, pulling itself with all four appendages and its wings folded along its back. The thorny horned head and spine resembled the jagged outcroppings of rock. Widseth froze because he saw another image of Schadwe, standing upright, beside a large rock formation near the trail two hundred paces in the distance. The beast spread its wings. Another simulacrum crawled out of the lava about a hundred paces ahead. *Clever lizard.*

Using all the ability he controlled, Widseth tried to separate the light patterns to expose which were illusions, but Schadwe's skilled use of low magic had been practiced for millennia. The illusions defied detection. Widseth reasoned that an illusion could distract, but not cause any damage. He would have to test them individually until Schadwe attacked.

Widseth adjusted the buckler and gripped King Perrik's sword. He wiped the sweat from around his eyes and stepped toward the first dragon. He tried to keep his vision focused to spot the slightest inconsistency or clue to reality about what he saw. The dragon continued to snake its way toward him, occasionally lifting its head and sniffing the stifling air. Within ten feet the creature rose on its hind legs, extended its wings and bellowed. The vile wail echoed off the walls and ended in a threatening hiss, but the beast held its ground. The roar dislodged showers of loose rock along the sides of the cavern. Although wary, Widseth ignored the creature.

He weighed his choices. To reach the nearer dragon, basking in the heat of the magma, he would have to traverse unstable footing and approach the molten lava. He thought better of that. If he ignored that beast and approached the third image, it would follow him if it were Schadwe and ignore him if not. Widseth resolved to investigate the furthest dragon, and attempt to draw the creature near the lava up onto the trail. He ignored the first and second dragons, and strode toward the third by the outcropping of rock.

He swallowed hard when he realized all three dragons reacted and moved with him, keeping him in the center of a triangle. The third dragon backed away from the rock and began to beat its wings. The oppressive heat of the air swirled around Widseth. Each of the creatures bellowed and roared, as they moved closer tightening the triangle. Widseth brandished his sword and charged the third dragon. An illusion beating its wings should not produce any movement of hot air.

The dragon hissed, "Foolish Dragon Master, you die today. That blade did not kill me before, and it will not touch me now." Snarling and hissing, it backed further from the outcropping. It inhaled and exhaled in rapid succession, preparing to discharge a deadly conflagration.

Widseth directed all his attention to the dragon in front of him and backed toward the possible protection of the huge jagged boulder, but behind him the immense rock changed shape. The horrific shape of the horned monster loomed behind Widseth. All the other dragon shapes faded

"Die, Dragon Master." Schadwe raked his claws across Widseth's back and snapped his jaws onto his torso, but the claws and bite found empty air.

In an instant Widseth dispelled the image he had constructed of himself and dropped his shield of invisibility. He struck Schadwe's hind quarters. The sword bit deep into the dragon's haunches. Black blood sizzled as it hit the rocks. Screaming in pain the creature swung its head around, but Widseth had prepared himself, and his sword sliced at the beast's thorny head. The blade rang out as if it had hit a metal shield, but the edge severed several protective horns. Schadwe shrieked and lifted into the air. Widseth cast a bolt of light that slammed into one of the dragon's wings. The dragon's wild keen resounded through the air, as Schadwe retreated to a hidden den.

"Shadows can create illusions, but so can light," Widseth said. He wiped his brow.

He started to follow the creature, but a glint of radiance at his feet caught his attention. One of the severed horns, as long as a man's forearm, had fallen near a small crevice in the rock floor. The horn partially covered a faceted object the size of a hen's egg, wedged in the fractured rock. He knelt and pulled the gemstone out of the crack. The Eye of Light glittered in his hand. He sheathed his sword and conjured a doorway of light.

***

Annel brushed a dark brown lock of Marcus' hair back from his eyes. The boy stirred, but his soft even breathing continued. Annel gently shook his shoulder.

"Wake up," she said.

The boy cracked his eyes open, but then he closed them tight and gripped her arm.

"I thought it was just a bad dream."

"Coming here?" Annel asked. "No, it's no dream. You followed me here through the door of light."

"I know," he said. "But I mean the dream I tol' ya about where ya got lost in dark tunnels and bad things were chasin' ya."

"I kind of thought this might be that place. I'm not afraid," she said.

Marcus smiled. "What do we do now?" he asked.

"First, you eat this biscuit. Then we need to find a way to save this tree." She gave him the remaining hard biscuit and a swallow of water from her flask.

Marcus munched on the biscuit and then asked, "Why do ya have ta save the tree?"

"I don't know all the answers yet, but somehow this tree is connected to Gulth. He needs us to save this tree. The trees of life are guide posts for men. Maybe they are for dragons, too. I don't know."

Marcus examined the tree.

"It looks like it's dyin'," he said. "How ya gonna save it down here in this room w' no light or good dirt?"

"Unless something damages them, trees of life create light, but eventually they need nourishment and some outside source of light to help replenish their reservoir. Usually the dragon that guards them provides this for them, but this is an ancient tree that has been untended for a long time. I think the branches have overgrown the roots. See all the thin straight branches with no leaves. They're called whips. They suck strength from the roots but provide no nourishment. We'll start by pruning them. Then we'll have to dig around the roots and loosen the root ball if we can. After that we'll search for something to fertilize the soil."

"How do ya know all this stuff?"

"Remember how I told you about Widseth saving me from Eventop?" she asked. "Well, after that, I worked for a gardener for a while. He taught me."

She approached the tree and picked up Deorc's severed paw.

"What's that?"

"It's a dragon's paw."

"Musta been a little dragon," Marcus said. "The claws o' the dragon at m' farm were lots bigger."

"This dragon is small, but his heart is black. He caused the war. His name is Deorc, and he's more evil than any of the other dragons. Widseth cut his hand off, and now he tries to destroy the good we try to do."

"Why's the paw here?"

"We hid it here."

"You been here b'fore?"

"It's too long to explain, but yes, we were here, but I didn't know we were here."

"Oh."

"Don't worry about it now. Let's see if we can help this tree." She stuffed Deorc's appendage into her travel pack.

Annel gave Marcus her short dagger, and she used her longer fighting knife to trim the whips from the tree. The tree rose out of the planter only ten feet. By standing on the lip of the planter, Marcus had no trouble reaching the low branches. Annel climbed into the tree and methodically pruned the trunk and branches.

"Marcus, be careful and start with the low branches. Use the knife to cut only the branches that have no leaves," she said.

"Sure, I can do it."

After about fifteen minutes, Annel and Marcus gathered all the clippings and piled them in a corner. Annel knelt at the base of the planter and began to dig the soil with her dagger to loosen the hardened dirt. Marcus followed her example. After an hour of arduous labor, she wiped her brow. The soil was broken and she had been able to sever and remove some or the root ball.

"Hard work isn't it, but you've done a good job," she said.

Marcus beamed in the pale yellow light of the tree. "Diggin' taters is harder," he said. "I used ta like helpin' m' Da, but it was hard."

Annel smiled and nodded.

"Now let's give this tree some water." She took her flask and squeezed every drop into the planter at the base of the tree. The meager amount of water barely moistened the soil.

"I dunno if that'll help much," Marcus said.

"Me either, but maybe this will."

Annel placed both hands on the trunk and opened all the channels within her to conduct light. She tapped all the resources of happy moments and memories. Events and people and experiences sped through her mind. A memory opened. She could see herself, reclined on the mossy floor of a forest. A dragon's head snaked toward her from a doorway of light. The dragon ministered to her, giving her a gift that she could decipher now. It bestowed a connection to the eternal world. Torrents of light coursed through her body and gushed from her fingertips into the tree. It seemed to her that every moment in her life had prepared her for this instant in time.

As her light began to fill the tree, she felt the flow of energy pulsing through her. Her cloak flared as if caught in a stiff breeze, and her golden hair stood on end, energized, as every cell in her body emitted radiance. After several minutes, she tamed the wild rush of power and attacked the vines of darkness that beset the tree. Her energy force mitigated the strangle hold of death that gripped the tree, but Annel could tell it was not enough.

She remembered the experience with the tree of life in Dragada. She had been told that a tree of life is nurtured by sacrifices made by those who are pure of heart. This tree needed more than her light to sustain it. She had to find a way to nourish it. She squeezed the flow of power and controlled the wild rush. The tree radiated, lighting the room with brilliant white illumination, but a few dark streaks remained on the trunk.

"M'lady, that was the dingest! How'd ya do that? I could see right through ya. An' look at the tree! We did good!"

"But we're not finished," she said. "We have to find something to nourish the tree or it will slip back to the way it was."

"How we gonna do that?"

"I have to go into those tunnels where bad things may chase me. You have to stay here with the tree." Annel deemed Marcus would be safer in this room. She assumed Deorc could not approach the tree.

"No. I'm comin' w' ya. I'm not stayin' here alone."

Annel paused for a few minutes and considered options and scenarios.

"Maybe it would be best to stay together." She did not want to face the possibility of bargaining for Marcus with Deorc's severed claw.

"That's good," Marcus said. "How do we get outta here anyway? I didn't see a door."

"A long time ago, good dragons hid the tree here to protect it. They used a door, but it's probably well hidden," she answered. "We'll have to find it."

Marcus walked out of the alcove and began to search along the nearest wall. His unfailing purpose amazed Annel. She followed him. In a short time they completed the circuit of the room with no success. Marcus began again, but Annel stopped him.

"Maybe there's an easier way," she said.

She pulled King Perrik's map from her travel pack, and spread it on the floor. She touched Misdara and concentrated on the tree. The ink contours contorted and reconfigured until she saw a rough estimation of the room and the alcove with the tree. She could see Marcus and herself. On the far wall she distinguished a large opening into a wide tunnel. She looked up from the map and concentrated on the wall. The silver outline of a wide opening appeared and gleamed in the light of the tree. She rolled the map and put it in her pack.

"Follow me, and stay close. No talking," she said.

Marcus nodded. He gripped her short dagger. Annel pulled the shield and sword from her cloak. The shield glowed with a delicate white light. It provided ample light in the darkness. She wondered how to activate the door, but when she touched it, it began to open inward. She and Marcus slipped into the tunnel that ran left and right. The door clicked shut behind them. Annel wondered how they would find the door again, when Marcus tore off a piece of his tunic and stuffed it into a crevice of the rock wall.

"We can find it again with this," he whispered. He pointed to the right. "Do you hear the water?"

She nodded, but pointed to the left. She put her finger to her lips to signal silence. Marcus trailed behind her. The passage branched several times and other hallways intersected it. At each junction, Marcus wedged a small piece of cloth in the chinks of the wall. All the passages were wide with high ceilings, but Annel followed the widest hall at every crossroads. They moved with caution, but heard nothing other than the sound of flowing water growing more and more distant.

The path grew broader until it emptied into a huge cavern. Annel and Marcus froze. The pale light of the shield revealed ghostly shapes in the room. The walls glittered under the subtle illumination, but the glow extended only partially into the cavern. Shadows concealed the far walls. Annel knelt.

"What's the matter, m'lady?" Marcus whispered.

"This is hallowed ground. There is where the tree used to be."

She pointed to a raised platform. The relief carvings matched the sculpted container that held the tree now, but immense skeletal remains, stretching into the darkness, drew Annel's attention. Bones and broken weapons littered the floor.

"I think the last defense of the tree took place here. The dragon, there," she said, pointing to the remains, "was the last defender of the tree. They must have hid the tree just before the battle. This is the largest dragon I have ever seen."

She rose from her knees, took Marcus by the hand, and walked toward the skeleton. When she reached and touched one of the ancient ribs of the dragon, a vision unveiled before her. Her natural eyesight expanded to almost three hundred sixty degrees. Every corner of the cavern blazed into sight. She could distinguish the hues and shades of all the elements. Shadows hid nothing from her.

Again she saw the dragon's head emerging from the doorway of light in the forest, but this time she recognized the creature. It was this dragon, guardian of the tree. The gift it bestowed extended beyond a connection to the eternal world. It bequeathed knowledge and power. She watched a vision as the tree burst into radiant glory when she and Marcus put splintered shards of some of the bones into the receptacle around the tree's roots. A sacrifice made thousands of years ago nurtured the rebirth of the tree. Then she saw herself as a child and her mother as a child, and so on until she saw a kingly man, kissing his young daughter as he put her on the back of a small dragon. She saw the tears in his eyes and heard his pleading voice, begging the dragon to keep her safe. The shock of her ancestry jarred her back to the glittering cavern.

"Marcus, gather some of the shards of bone that are scattered about. I don't think we need much, but this will help the tree."

"Look how big that foot is," Marcus said.

Annel looked at the remains of one of the huge hind feet. The sharp talons on the toes measured close to three feet in length, but someone had cut and removed one of the talons.

"We'll come back and investigate further, but help me gather some bone fragments about this size." Annel held up a sharp sliver about a foot in length. "I want to take them back to see if the tree responds."

Marcus began to collect the bone splinters. Annel paused. She heard footsteps of someone or something running toward the cavern from one of the many entrances.

***

Widseth stepped onto a polished marble floor of a wide hallway. He held the Eye of Light aloft. The fading glow of the light channel he had traveled caught the crystal, and the Eye burst into brilliant azure flame. Globes of light suspended from the ceiling and columns responded, and gleaming luster erupted along the passageway. One extremity led into a spacious chamber. A metal double door about twenty feet high closed the hall in the other direction. Two golden dragons, inlaid in the silver door, coiled around a pole. Beautiful gemstones heightened the luster of the polished gold and silver.

Widseth heard voices on the other side of the door.

"Where is Brulon?"

"He's with the army, tryin' to maintain order. The shadoine are gone."

"I know, but the plans are progressing."

"What do you mean? We lost!"

"I mean that the woman is here. As her presence entered Misdara, I detected her vibration in the medium of light. Schadwe will dispose of Widseth. I will dispose of the woman and claim what is mine. Plans are progressing despite the loss on the battlefield."

"What do you want me to do?"

"I care not. Leave me."

Widseth gritted his teeth. He slipped the Eye of Light into the pouch at his hip and drew King Perrik's sword. The long sword vibrated in Widseth's hand, as if by some arcane power it knew it had returned to the halls where masters had forged it. Widseth licked his lips and approached the doors. With a gentle push, the doors swung wide, opening into the magnificent throne room. The dazzling light from the hall back lit Widseth.

Rin halted and stared. As Widseth approached, the young man backed away toward the opening to the glittering cavern on the side of the hall opposite the silver doors. Widseth turned his attention to Deorc.

"King Perrik?" The dragon scrutinized Widseth.

"No," Widseth responded.

Deorc's eyes gleamed. "You filthy ragtag pretender. How did you escape the mines? One such as you, from such a dishonored ancestry could never overcome my brother, Schadwe. Did you crawl out on your belly hiding behind the clothes of a dead king? You are not fit for your imagined title, *Dragon Master*." Deorc spat the words with acidic distaste.

"Nonetheless," Widseth said, "I am here to end the sorrow you have brought to the world."

Deorc began to conjure an invisibility spell, as he walked down the stairs of the dais toward Rin.

Widseth reached into the pouch and held the Eye of Light above his head. All the lamps in the throne room tripled their intensity.

"Your spell will avail you nothing. You cannot hide from my eyes," Widseth said.

Deorc snarled when he saw the Eye. "How did you ... ?" His howl filled the room. "Schadwe ... ." Venomous words spilled from his throat. "I cannot hide from you, but he will never see his death approach." Deorc faded from normal sight and started for Rin.

"Run, Rin!" Widseth shouted. He sprinted toward Rin.

The confused boy looked around, but he did not see the invisible talon that raked his face.

"I release you from your service to me. You have been a foolish but useful tool."

Deorc fled into the large cavern and into one of the many passages that led to other areas of the vast complex. Widseth knelt beside Rin, but the open welt on the boy's cheek already burned to the bone. Widseth rose to follow Deorc.

"Master Widseth, please help me." The boy coughed and began to shake. The poison traumatized his body. Widseth knelt and cradled the boy's head.

"Rin, listen to me," Widseth said.

"I'm sorry. I shoulda listened ta Lady Annel, but I thought I could be free," Rin gasped.

Widseth remembered the night he first saw Rin in chains in the stocks. The stocks were of no account compared to the fetters that now bound the boy. Widseth considered the consequences if he healed him. Certainly he would be held accountable before the plains people and put to death for the evil he had promulgated.

"Let him come to us. Please."

Widseth looked up. Two figures of light, a man and a woman, stood at Rin's feet. The boy's spirit rose and stood beside them. The woman wiped tears from his cheeks.

"He has done much evil, but we love him," the man said.

Widseth nodded in acquiescence.

"Thank you." The man paused as if listening. "We are instructed to tell you to place the Eye of Light in its proper receptacle."

"I have to follow Deorc," he said.

"No, you must place the Eye first."

Widseth looked into the cavern with its many exits. Deorc could escape again.

"I don't think this to be wise, but I'll trust your words," Widseth said.

He lifted Rin's physical body and carried it to the foot of the dais. After taking a final look toward the cavern where Deorc had escaped, Widseth entered the hall behind the silver doors.

***

Annel gripped the sword and adjusted her shield. The sound of footsteps ceased. She could see nothing, but she recognized the evil presence. She knew Deorc had entered the room. Once before she had felt the evil disruption he created in the fabric of the material world.

"Deorc, I know you are here! Show yourself."

The air shimmered and Deorc appeared, not twenty paces from Annel.

"As you command, m'lady. How grand you appear in the ancient garments of a dead queen." The dragon's forked tongue darted from his mouth, as if it tested the air.

"Your army is destroyed. Your plans for the plains are thwarted," Annel said.

Deorc's hideous laughter filled the grotto of bones.

"Your husband has failed his task. He holds death in his arms. Gulth slips into the gulf where he will lose all knowledge of who he is."

"The tree of life burns brightly. It will guide Gulth to safety, and if Widseth is to die, it will stand as a testament to his good works," Annel said.

"You speak so casually of what you do not understand. Give me what I seek, and I will spare your husband, the dragon, and your life." Deorc stepped toward Annel.

"You shall have Queen Laena's sword separate your foul head from its body."

Annel crouched and prepared for the dragon's strike. Deorc began to weave spells of shadow and darkness. Wispy smoke wreathed him, and he began to fade in and out of the visible world. Annel closed the ground and struck, but the blade found no home. With a power word, the dragon created a blast of force that knocked her from her feet. She struggled to stand, as the beast approached to deliver a killing stroke, but a young boy ran and stood between Deorc and his prey.

"Leave her alone!" Marcus stood defiant.

"I killed one whelp earlier. I will eat your heart, boy."

"I was afraid before, and hid in the bones, but I'm not afraid o' ya," Marcus said.

Annel struggled to her feet, but the dragon moved quicker and spun Marcus around, holding him with the stump of his left arm against his scaled belly. One of Deorc's talons rested on Marcus' cheek.

"Give me what I want," the dragon said, "or he dies now."

Annel knew Deorc would kill Marcus no matter what she did, but she was not prepared for the boy's pure love and desire to defend her. Marcus stabbed backwards with one of the splintered bone shards. He buried the bone deep into Deorc's upper thigh. The dragon screamed in pain, as the splinter burst into white hot flame. Marcus held onto the shard, and he began to glow until white light blazed from him. Annel shielded her eyes. Marcus became a translucent conduit for pure energy. It flowed through him and into Deorc through the splinter.

Annel ran toward Marcus and pulled him away from Deorc. They backed away as the dragon shrieked and flailed.

"Stay here!" Annel pointed to the floor. She need not have worried. Marcus collapsed on the marble floor, but he continued to stare at Deorc. Annel turned, gripped her sword, and strode toward the creature.

The dragon hissed at her, as she approached. The chilling sound sent waves of fear through her, but she stood her ground and slashed at the beast. He dodged her strike and rose from the floor.

Deorc jeered. "You gutter snipe, crawl back into your sewer. You have no right to wield the sword of a mighty queen. I will heal myself, and drink your blood." He reached to pull the bone fragment from his thigh. The second he took his attention from her, Annel knew he underestimated her courage.

"Start with a drink of steel." She leaped forward and drove the sword deep into the beast. She pulled the weapon from the creature's chest and Deorc staggered, falling forward on all four limbs. Before he looked up, Annel chopped down. The sword severed the dragon's head from its body. Deorc twitched and fell forward. Annel pulled his withered paw from her travel pack and dropped it on the floor beside the carcass.

"I think this is what you sought. Gutter snipe indeed ... no more... Queen Laena, I claim this sword and my heritage," Annel stated. "I know who I am. I am the descendent of a good King and a beautiful Queen. By sun and sword, I dedicate my life to your memory. Widseth and I will rebuild your dreams. We will defend and restore those who have lost so much to the darkness."

Annel knelt on one knee and bowed her head. She felt Marcus' hand on her shoulder.

"I'd like ta help ya," he said.

Annel stood and looked down at him.

"Thank you, Master Marcus. I'm counting on you."

Lights in the chambers and halls began to glow. They burst into brilliant illumination. Gemstones imbedded in the ceiling and walls glittered like stars.

"Something's happened," Marcus said.

Annel smiled. "A great evil is gone from the world. I think we need to take these bone fragments to the tree," she said.

*The King and a few of the High Guard left the city
to retrieve the Eye of Light. The Queen is hidden;
her son is dead; and her young daughter is lost to
our ken. Darkness encroaches. Our last hope, the
great dragon, fell in dreadful conflict defending the
Prince. The faithful dragons hid the tree, but without
the light of the universe, our halls and passages have
grown dark. Murder and death haunt the city. One
of the dragons prophesied that light will not return
until one faithful child stands as a willing sacrifice
for one he loves. We yearn for such a child.*

> *The last entry on a scroll—found in the Hall
> of Records in Misdara*

Chapter 15. One Faithful Child

Widseth entered the jeweled chamber. Soft white light
illuminated the room. The light emanated from simple
globes suspended from the walls and high ceiling. On the right wall
he recognized the golden pyramid of Taina captured in a beautiful
fresco. On the left wall, familiar scenes of Castle Dragada graced the
statuary and relief carvings. Beautiful murals depicted the crystal
caverns of Misdara on the far wall. Embedded in the depiction of
each Aelfene kingdom, dragons guarded trees of life.

In the center of the room, statuary rose majestically as two
massive metallic dragons wrapped around a beautiful column that
ascended toward the apex of the cavernous ceiling. Each dragon
extended a front appendage, and together they held a beautiful
golden sphere high into the air.

The walls and floor glittered with inlaid metals and gems,
accenting geometric designs. Widseth scanned each wall and object
in the room until his gaze came to rest on an unadorned carving,
resting on a stone base in the corner of the room to his right. At
first he did not recognize the object, but when he approached it,
he realized it was a wooden statuette of a toddler with one hand

outstretched as if taking its first step. It had been knocked over. Widseth righted the figure on the marble column.

The inscription on stone pilaster intrigued Widseth. *You can change the future, but only by understanding the past.* Widseth wondered why this unremarkable figure graced such a beautiful hall, but then his thoughts turned to Rin. Rin was a common slave, but he desired to see the world through the eyes of freedom as much as the greatest artisan. Deorc deceived the boy, and Rin followed the path to counterfeit freedom. Then Widseth pondered the common men and women who had chosen to live by the laws of the Aelfene world. They had become multifaceted gems filled with beauty.

Thoughts of Annel filled his mind. Fours years had slipped into the past while they were apart. He missed her laugh and gentle touch. *How much longer would he have to wait to caress her cheek and her golden strands of hair? How long before they could return to Dragada and rest from the trials of the world?* He smiled. *Rest from the trials of the world? Indeed. If they rested from the trials of the world, they might as well not be in the world. That's what she would say.*

He stilled his thoughts and examined the outstretched hand of the wooden statue. He noticed an indentation in the palm. Knowing what he should do, he placed the Eye of Light in the palm. A deep thrumming sound commenced behind him. He turned and looked at the central pillar. The eyes of both metal dragons, entwined around the column, began to glow and a stream of illumination emerged, filling the golden globe they held. Sparks of energy jumped from the orb as if seeking destinations elsewhere. Every time charges of energy lurched from the ball, they covered a greater distance until four constant streams of light reached the walls depicting Misdara, Dragada, Taina, and the palm of the child holding the Eye of Light.

In wonder he approached each of the walls. Tiny figures walked the streets of Dragada. Veramag surveyed the valley atop her column. When he touched the great hall it opened and he could see the tree behind the thrones. The dragon, Agrar, guarded that tree. Widseth walked quickly to the back wall and examined Misdara. Men walked on the battlements and in the upper levels. Then a burgeoning light caught his attention. The light generated from the room in which he stood began to fill the passages and rooms. As the globes in the rooms and halls burst into brilliant illumination, shadows fled. Further away another light burst into flame. The tree blossomed, showering radiance on a woman and a child.

"It is time to rejoin her."

The soft voice from behind him startled Widseth. He turned. An image shimmered, and the man, who Widseth knew as the boatman, solidified. Widseth bowed.

"I've longed to hear those words for four years," Widseth said.

"You have accomplished your task, and Annel has completed hers. There is work yet to do, but that can be realized as you work together. Come. Follow me. I love to walk the halls of Misdara."

Widseth followed the boatman into the audience chamber.

"Master boatman, before we leave this room, there is something I must do."

"Certainly."

Widseth ascended the steps to the throne and placed King Perrik's sword on it. He removed the dragon helmet and breastplate with cloak and laid them on the throne.

"I assume I have no further need for these here," Widseth stated.

The boatman smiled. "You are correct. You are right to honor Perrik, but they are yours at need."

"I understand," Widseth replied.

***

Annel and Marcus followed the trail Marcus had marked with scraps of cloth. As they walked, rivers of light began to fill slender filigrees in the ceilings and walls. Previously, the muted glow barely held shadows in the corridors at bay, but now rich luminosity banished the gloomy atmosphere of the passages. Annel felt like she had emerged from a dark pit into a world of peace and joy. Her thoughts turned to the day she and Widseth joined their lives together at the base of the tree in Dragada. She longed to hear his voice. After she finished this business in Misdara, she vowed to travel to the mines and find him.

After ten minutes, Annel and Marcus arrived at the last marker. She touched the outline of the door and it swung open. The room glittered.

"The light fills the room, Marcus, but the tree is fading. I pray these pieces of bone will serve as sacrifice enough to rescue this tree."

She and Marcus hurried to the planter and began to mix the smaller chips into the soil. They drove the slender splinter into the soil around the edges and next to the trunk. After a few minutes the dark lines disappeared and the leaves and flowers on the tree pulsed with light.

"Look, it's doin' good," Marcus said. His face beamed in the light.

Annel bit her upper lip.

"Yes, it is," she replied. She stood with her hand on his shoulder. "That was a brave thing to do with the dragon."

"Not so brave," he said. "I almost ran and hid, but I knew he'd find me. An' I was pretty sure he'd kill you. You was always savin' me. I jus' thought it'd be good if I saved you once. I was more scared than brave."

"Most men are," she said, "but one of the rangers told me, Ferron I think, that men who are called brave are just men who decide there is something of more value than saving themselves, so they choose not to run. Marcus, you're one of those men now. Angus will sing songs about your courage."

He smiled.

"Annel."

Annel and Marcus spun around when they heard the voice. She hesitated and licked her lips, as she put both hands in front of her eyes and wiped tears from her cheeks. She ran and flung her arms around Widseth's neck and buried her face in his shoulder. She sobbed uncontrollably.

Marcus stood beside her. He rubbed his hands together and clenched them. When Annel looked down at him, she felt his sorrow and nervousness.

"Widseth, I present to you Master Marcus, heir to Caer O'Dai. He helped heal the tree of life, and he wounded Deorc, saving my life," she said.

"Marcus and I have met before," Widseth said. He knelt and pulled the boy close to hug him.

"Master Boatman, I did not see you. I am sorry." Annel bowed to the boatman.

"Tend to one another's needs. I will always be there when you need me," the boatman said. "You have much to do. I leave you to your tasks." He turned to walk back into the corridor.

"Wait," Marcus said. "Who are ya? Ya look so familiar..." He hesitated for several moments as he studied the man who appeared neither old nor young. "I know... I remember. I saw ya in a dream like Widseth. The dark shadow came for me, and ya wouldn't let 'im take me. I was scared. I remember. What's yer name?"

The man smiled. "Master Marcus, I love your spirit. Yes, we have met, and we will meet again, but I think it best that I remain unnamed for now. Widseth and Annel call me the boatman. That will do." A doorway of light formed in the corridor. After he walked through it, the door winked from sight.

Annel squeezed Widseth's hand, and she looked around the room.

"What more is there to do?" she asked. "I did the best I could."

"Of course you did," Widseth said. "You did everything the Lords of Light asked, but we have to return the tree to its proper location, and a guardian must be placed. Then Misdara can be cleansed."

"How can we move the tree?" Marcus asked. "It's too heavy."

"Very little is too heavy for a dragon, let alone four," Widseth said.

The Dragon Master began to sing and to call dragons to his service. As he sang, he pointed to the four corners of the room. Cracks opened like tears in fabric, indistinct objects floated through the rifts. Each entity gained definition and a shadowy mist dissipated. Gulth, in man form, stood nearest the tree of life. He shook his head.

Annel laughed with delight as she watched three grizzled men in ancient armor join Gulth. Gulth took one corner of the planter and the three brother dragons, Anfelt, Anafalz, and Braes, lifted the other corners. Annel, Widseth, and Marcus followed the procession to the hall of the tree. Not a sound broke the silent reverence as the dragons in man form carried the treasure and placed the planter containing the tree on its pedestal.

When the tree was in place, Widseth spoke. "Gulth you have been chosen to be the guardian of this tree. You must leave your human shape forever and dedicate your days to defending the tree. Will you accept that charge?"

"I am unworthy of such an honor. This is the greatest honor afforded the dragon kind. I approached darkness and failed to defend Lady Annel."

Annel spoke. "Gulth, forever you will be known as the dragon that faced darkness and clung with every fiber of your being to the paths of light. No dragon has ever surpassed your endurance."

Gulth knelt. "I accept this great honor." He hunched his back, and twisted his neck. His neck and torso elongated and wings burst through the hide of his back. When he completed the transformation, Annel wiped away a tear. Gulth was magnificent.

"Anfelt, Anafalz, and Braes, I want you to transport the bones of the great dragon to the room where the dragons hid the tree anciently," Widseth said. "We'll also lay King Perrik's remains to rest there after we retrieve them from Schadwe's lair. Braes, go to the throne room. Deorc killed the young slave, Rin, there. It is my wish that his body be place there with the dragon and the king."

"Yes, m'lord Dragon Master. It shall be as you say," Braes answered.

Annel scanned the room. Frantic emotions filled her. The mention of Rin broke her heart. Sorrow overwhelmed her as she thought of the potential Deorc once had, and the death of a misguided boy. Tragic sentiments flooded her with incessant waves.

"Where are Deorc's remains?" she asked. "I killed him right over there." She pointed to a section of the floor.

"No unclean thing could contaminate the hallowed place," Widseth said. "When the boatman and I came through here, we made sure that not a single particle of the dragon's physical body remained in the material world. He is gone."

Annel breathed easier. "There are other dragons of darkness still in the world, aren't there."

Yes," Widseth answered. "Several remain."

"I am sorry to interrupt," Anfelt said, "but what do you want us to do after we finish?"

"I distracted Widseth. It is I who sorrows. I'm sure he has further instructions." Annel said.

"When finished," Widseth said, "assume your true forms. The upper levels are filled with Deorc's followers and parts of Rin's army. We need to clear the entire area. Some of them are evil men and may choose to fight. Others are simply deceived. Give them the opportunity to leave. In three or four day's time, I want Misdara empty."

"Yes, m'lord."

The dragons hurried to their tasks. Gulth curled his body around the planter that held the tree. Annel thought he appeared quite regal, like the dragons in the carvings on the walls. She approached him and kissed him on his snout.

"I'm glad we didn't lose you," she said.

"Yes, m'lady ..." He paused. "At the end, just when I thought I could endure no longer, I saw light rekindle the vision of a tree. I knew it was your light. I held to your beacon."

Annel felt the tears well within her eyes.

"Since Widseth called you to the world, you've always been our loyal companion. You served beyond all expectations."

Braes returned from the throne room carrying Rin's body. Anafalz and Anfelt began to carry the skeletal remains of the great dragon to the room that would serve as an honored crypt.

Widseth whispered, "Let's leave them to their task." The reverent demeanor of his voice reflected the hallowed duty the dragons performed. "Come with me. I want to show you the Eye of Light. The room is astounding."

"I'm hungry," Marcus said as soon as they trio left the cavern and entered a tunnel that led to the throne room.

"We need to find food," Annel said.

Widseth smiled. "Well, I found this pouch. I eat my fill from it, but every time I open it, it is full again. How are bread and cheese?"

"It's alright, I guess. Do ya think I could wish for a boiled potata, and maybe it would come in the pouch?" Marcus asked.

Widseth and Annel laughed. "I don't know, but you can try," Widseth said.

***

"This is curious," Baron Aelan O'Dai said. "It appears completely deserted."

Baron Aelan, King Fyan, Will Willowman, and Kreigar, followed by a cadre of rangers and caer men, surveyed the outer gates and wall of Misdara from a safe distance.

Fyan shaded his eyes from the noonday sun and peered at the battlements. "We've seen no resistance since the skirmish at the bridge three days ago. Scouts have seen individuals and small parties fleeing the area, but where are the dark lizard and the leaders of his army?"

"I suggest we proceed with caution. It could be a trap," Aelan said.

"I agree," Fyan replied. "But we'll have a better idea when the forward scouts return." As he said that, four men rounded a bend in the road through the debris outside the outer wall. They approached swiftly and reined to a halt.

"M'lords, the outer gate is open, and all the defenses are abandoned," one of the men said. "We entered and searched the above ground complex. There were what appeared to be dragon stables and barracks, but they're empty. The gate into the hillside to the underground city is closed. We could find no way to open it. The enemy abandoned stores of weapons and supplies." He smiled. "We'll eat well tonight."

"Thank you. Rejoin your units." Fyan saluted the scouts. "What do you think, Aelan? Shall we enter and assume Deorc and his army have not barricaded themselves inside the underground?"

"It's been a hard march. I think we owe it to the men to rest behind walls and in comfortable barracks after filling their bellies with something more substantial than hard biscuits," Aelan responded.

Fyan nodded. "Will and Kreigar, enter the compound with the vanguard. Post your men in the towers and on the walls. Set a strong guard at the underground gate. We'll move the rest of the army and supply train in after you have secured the ramparts."

"Yes, m'lord. As you say."

Baron Aelan relaxed and sat back in his saddle as he watched ranks of men enter Misdara. Within three hours, the entire army had entered Misdara. Baron Aelan and King Fyan entered last, escorted by their personal guard. The workmanship and architecture of the outer portcullis and outer parapet contrasted sharply with the gate into the hillside. Aelan guessed that the exterior compound had been constructed atop an older base. The new construction reflected inferior workmanship, whereas the old foundation and gate into the underground revealed meticulous detail to beauty anchored in precise stone craftsmanship and metalwork.

Aelan and Fyan dismounted and approached the inner gate into the hillside. Intricate carvings decorated the massive stone doors. On the right side of the door, an immense pillar hinged the door to the hillside. Carved into the pillar, a stone dragon overlooked the entrance. Absorbed in the beautiful monuments, Aelan did not hear a subtle sound from inside the hillside.

"M'lords," a man shouted, "the gates are opening."

A cordon of men surrounded Aelan and Fyan, as they backed away from the gate. The eyes of the stone dragon flared to life, and white light engulfed the knot of men poised for battle. The giant stone door swung inward. Aelan expected to see a dank opening to a cave lit with flaming torches, but to his surprise majestic light illuminated a bright thoroughfare into the hillside.

A young boy stood in the middle of the passageway, flanked by Annel dressed in the clothing she wore at the battle, but the apparel dazzled his eyesight. On the other side of the boy a man stood, attired in beautiful golden armor. His breastplate gleamed, and the beautiful helm resembled a crown with a dragon, wings spread, adorning the crest. Three burly men stood behind them in the thoroughfare. They were a head taller than any man Aelan had ever seen, and their appearance was so similar that telling them apart defied the baron.

One of the men stepped forward.

"Hail, Widseth, the Dragon Master, and his Queen, the Lady Annel."

Aelan realized Will Willowman had dropped to one knee. King Fyan ignored formalities and ran toward Widseth. It amazed Aelan when Fyan threw his arms around the young Dragon Master. Will rose and ran with Kreigar to join the king, but Aelan stood rooted to the ground until he felt a tug at his tunic.

"Baron, it's me, Marcus."

Aelan looked down. "Marcus, how is it that you are here?"

Marcus smiled. "Angus won't believe this tale, but he's gonna have ta make a long song for this adventure."

Annel's clear voice rose above the reunion.

"Baron Aelan, welcome to Misdara, the caverns of crystal wonder. Enter into the home of your ancestors, and find joy in the new caer for the people of the plains who have fought the darkness."

Baron Aelan O'Dai nodded to Annel. He looked back at the circle of caer men who had gathered. Lord Perigreen smiled at him. Aelan held Marcus' hand and took his first steps into his heritage.

About the Author

R. Dennis Baird grew up as a military brat. He has lived in Georgia, Alabama, Texas, Germany, Washington DC, Ohio, Utah, Washington state, and Oregon.

As a youngster in Europe nothing delighted him more than crawling around ruins of castles on the Rhine River or exploring Roman ruins in Germany, Italy, and Spain. Fondness for ancient societies gave rise to his love of language and culture. He has studied Spanish, German, and Russian along with English literature. He has enjoyed time in Mayan ruins in Yucatan, and studied ancient civilizations and the lessons they have taught us.

He spent years spinning yarns around campfires with the Boy Scouts, and has combined his storytelling with a multilayered world reflective of great civilizations.

Visit the author's website at www.brazenserpentchronicles.com

Other Books Included in
The Brazen Serpent Chronicles

Talon of Light

CPSIA information can be obtained at www.ICGtesting.com
Printed in the USA
266479BV00002B/1/P